AND I'LL
TAKE OUT
YOUR EYES

AND I'LL TAKE OUT YOUR EYES

A NOVEL

A. M. SOSA

ALGONQUIN BOOKS OF CHAPEL HILL
LITTLE, BROWN AND COMPANY

The characters and events in this book are fictitious. Any similarity to real persons, living or dead, is coincidental and not intended by the author.

Copyright © 2025 by A. M. Sosa

Hachette Book Group supports the right to free expression and the value of copyright. The purpose of copyright is to encourage writers and artists to produce the creative works that enrich our culture.

The scanning, uploading, and distribution of this book without permission is a theft of the author's intellectual property. If you would like permission to use material from the book (other than for review purposes), please contact permissions@hbgusa.com. Thank you for your support of the author's rights.

Algonquin Books of Chapel Hill / Little, Brown and Company
Hachette Book Group
1290 Avenue of the Americas, New York, NY 10104
algonquinbooks.com

First Edition: October 2025

Algonquin Books of Chapel Hill is an imprint of Little, Brown and Company, a division of Hachette Book Group, Inc. The Algonquin Books name and logo are trademarks of Hachette Book Group, Inc.

The publisher is not responsible for websites (or their content) that are not owned by the publisher.

The Hachette Speakers Bureau provides a wide range of authors for speaking events. To find out more, go to hachettespeakersbureau.com or email hachettespeakers@hbgusa.com.

Little, Brown and Company books may be purchased in bulk for business, educational, or promotional use. For information, please contact your local bookseller or the Hachette Book Group Special Markets Department at special.markets@hbgusa.com.

Design by Steve Godwin

Some of the stories in this book originally appeared in the following publications: *Zyzzyva* ("Cannon"), *Santa Monica Review* ("Invisible").

ISBN 978-1-64375-691-2 (Hardcover) / ISBN 978-1-64375-693-6 (Ebook)

LCCN 2025941033

Printing 1, 2025

LSC-C

Printed in the United States of America

Para mi familia

Fuck you, I won't do what you tell me
Motherfucker

> —Rage Against the Machine,
> "Killing in the Name"

CONTENTS

I

Cursed 3

Bedtime Story 27

The Desecrationists 33

Plant Mother 38

Deditos 48

Brother 54

II

Cannon 61

Mírame 73

Cría Cuervos 75

Hotboxing 98

III

Invisible 121

Kalopsia 124

A Losing Game 157

A Family on Fire 199

IV

Past, Present, Continuous 221

Acknowledgments 291

CURSED

You'll be seven, crying, with a knife in your hand, when your father finds you in the kitchen. His voice will reach into your dreams, tell you, drop it, éste siempre con sus pinches pendejadas. He'll shake you lucid, slap you around like some shitty TV. Crazy-eyed, half naked, he'll ask, what the fuck is wrong with you? You'll say you don't know what he's talking about. He'll say you're doing it for attention. Ma will ask you questions but you won't hear them, you'll be too busy keeping an eye on your father, wondering whether he'll start to beat you with something or just keep using his hands. And though you're also half naked, ma will spin you around, checking you like there's a bomb hidden away somewhere. Brother will keep his distance, looking on horrified at the rest of you, at the spectacle. Events he wishes didn't concern him.

The next night you'll sleepwalk again. The night after too. For two weeks this will continue. They'll put the knives on the highest shelves, complain about the pain in the ass that you are, but still, you'll be found with a fork, a spoon, a butter knife, and always crying.

A few days before this all began—all these pendejadas, as your father calls them—your aunt had shown up on the porch, big rectangular glasses in thick frames, just like your father's. First thing, she scowled at you, her broad back all up like a wildebeest's getting ready to charge. You could almost hear it, a feral drumbeat, the kind they play on Animal Planet. Your cousin clung to her side like an ornament. A bunch of neighborhood kids huddled behind them. And the way she held you with her eyes, pure unadulterated scorn. Your body tingling with the possibility of meeting the devil. And every part of you shrank, shrinking down to nothing. Annihilation. That's what she wanted and she demanded you be punished there, in front of her. Your cousin peeking out, wet cheeked, from behind her legs.

You could easily guess what he told her, what he left out: you all staring at naked bodies in magazines. You looking at everything, until he called you a faggot. You hadn't known what to say except, no, no I'm not. But it wasn't enough to make him stop. Brother had to tell him, shut it, Jamón. Everyone laughed, repeated the gibe—Jamón, like it was his name. Then Jamón got encircled, pushed around with jeers of Chuleta and Queso de Puerco. They had said, let me slice some off yo back, come on, puto. Squeal. When Jamón ran away, you thought that was the end of it, his tears, everyone's taunts pelting his back, and a chorus of *Jamón el mamón*. Jamón el mamón. Jamón el mamón.

You left the back of the apartment complex feeling pure. Came home, sat down on the couch, and flipped through channels until you were watching Private Pyle fuck it all up for everyone, him getting tied and beaten in consequence, then seething and blowing his own brains out. Then the doorbell rang. Immediately followed by a loud constant knocking, then back to jabbing the doorbell. No one was closer, so you got up and opened the door and there she was, your aunt, staring down at you.

Ma came down and your cousin and the neighborhood kids stood there listening as ma denied everything. She said you wouldn't have made your cousin cry—though you would've if you could talk shit like brother. Ma said she wouldn't punish you, not until your father heard. He'll be the one to decide, she said, what his son deserves. That made you feel worse than any stare could.

Your aunt spewed more shit about respect, about the old ways, this being another land, but our children, mine, at least, she said as she looked you dead in the eyes again, will know our customs.

And all the kids' eyes darting back and forth between you, ma, and her, everyone looking on with that same intensity that you had all shared as you pored over the magazines, cutting and pairing different pages, different bodies, making a collage there, on the dirt. Ma then asked, ¿y qué costumbre es éste? Pointing with a head nod at all the neighborhood kids behind my aunt and cousin. Ma took a step back, grabbed the doorknob, and slowly closed the door on your aunt's face.

A week after, lying with ma on your parents' bed, being the little spoon, you'll listen as she tells you, remembering as she goes, how your aunt's mother was suspected in their village of being a witch. Everyone there believed she killed her husband. The proof: He went missing in a village where no one ever had before. His body never found. That and your aunt and her mother and sisters were known for going out in the middle of the night in all white and bathing in the river. It didn't matter the season or if there was moonlight or not, whatever timeline they followed, it was their own. How else, ma will tell you, could anyone explain how the witch's daughter, your aunt, married your uncle? He had left her, had started seeing someone else, a nice girl from the next town over, beautiful and so personable, not like that ugly beast, but then that girl also went missing. The girl's family spent all their money, lost their business, searching for her.

And so, nasty and plain as your aunt was—*is*—your uncle was somehow brought back, ensnared, and married her. Whatever he sees in her, ma, your other aunts, all know, brujería is involved. No other explanation.

And then ma will ask, like she's coming out of a trance, mi niño, how exactly did she look at you? You'll tell her about the goose bumps, the cold pang in your stomach, that feeling, like in nightmares, of the devil sniffing at the nape of your neck. And ma will say to herself more than to you, esa desgraciada. Would she really be capaz? ¿Hacerle mal de ojo a un niño?

Mi niño, were you sleepwalking before or only after tu tía vino?

You'll start biting your nails. Nightmares beginning to form as you remember the way she looked at you. Only after, you'll say.

She'll get up, go over to the window, peeking through the blinds at the porch, have you seen? La ruda se secó.

Ma's told you how ruda is used to dispel evil energy, placed near the entrance of a home. But the yerba buena also wilted, died, she'll observe, too much negative energy for la ruda to absorb. And so, you'll suppose the rest of that dark fetid energy is roiling in you. Eating away at your insides.

You won't tell her how you feel your stomach, your knees, starting to wilt too. Ay, qué malas vibras, she'll say as she rubs her arm, trying to shake off the chills.

When your father and brother come home from baseball practice and the batting cages after that, brother will be talking a mile a minute, did you see how I was hitting them? I can hit anything. Swinging an invisible bat as your father smirks triumphantly, we'll see, we'll see this weekend. Ma will whisper into your ear, mi niño, todo va estar bien. Your father, seeing you on his bed, will say, ¿y tú qué haces ahí? You won't answer. Ma will fill him in. At first, he'll act like his usual self, saying it's all fucking bullshit and, ay, por qué le dices esas chingaderas, tú sabes cómo se pone. But ma will remind him about your aunt's history and you'll see it in his eyes, how he can't dismiss it like with fantasmas or even nahuales. Brujería is different.

And seeing him like that, staring at the floor, not saying shit, it'll start to hit you.

You're going to die. For something you didn't even do.

You'll bury your head under the pillow, going fetal as you think of your death, the pain. Will it happen when you're alone? How many days do you have left? And all the things you'll never do. Ride a bike, catch a lizard, set off fireworks.

Te dije, your father will say.

Ma will pry the pillow off your head, mi niño, vas a estar bien.

Algo malo me va a pasar, you'll whisper.

She'll say you're wrong, explaining that there's good magic too, and that her aunt taught her to perform limpias. Everyone and everything carries intentions, and that shapes the energy around us, energy that can be shaped like fire, for both the good, like warmth and cooking, or to burn everything down. We'll have to do three limpias, but after each one, you'll see, you'll get better. You'll try to believe her even though, ultimately, it's your father's face you'll keep seeing.

Ma will tell you to get up and take off your clothes. She'll send brother and father for: an egg, a bowl, a glass of water almost full. Your father will complain, he'll say she should've told you about good magic first. And before he stomps out, he'll slap your brother's head and say, don't stand there como pinche inútil. Brother will trail after him and you'll wish it were brother that had been cursed, because if he had, you know your father would've been over there already, at your aunt's house, slapping the shit out of her instead. Ma will go to wash her hands. You'll imagine punching brother in his stupid mouth, making the gap between his front teeth even wider. But seeing yourself in the mirror, trembling in your underwear, you'll lose all nerve, waiting and anxious, while they gather the supplies.

Your father will come back with the water, setting it down, carefully, on the doily on the dresser. He'll see you trembling, crying a little. He'll brush against your shoulder and yell, though not so harsh as other times, ¡ay, no llores! Be a man, be a man.

You'll try, but the more you do, the harder you'll cry, breathing spastically, your father saying it harsher and harsher until he's saying it just as harsh as he always has. He'll reach back for a belt hanging from a hook on his closet door, and only then will you choke it back down, swallowing the crying like a dried-up dead little worm. The scrape of the shell on your scalp reminds you of tires rubbing pavement. And you'll remember the day you wandered the apartments and saw El Mudo on his bike, the vicious grinding whirr of the wheels on asphalt and the chop of a ghetto bird overhead. And down the street you saw her, Selena. The day before, you'd been playing house together, undressing, taking turns being husband, wife, avalanche, falling all over each other. Then she was there, standing, screaming, not getting out of the way as El Mudo pedaled toward her, staring her down like she was the reason he couldn't talk. Ten feet away and she was frozen. You wanted to close your eyes but instead curled your hands so tight they went numb. Then all that noise, instantly replaced by the dull thud of the bike crashing into her body, flinging her like a dead bird, another small thud, her body scraping to a halt before he drove right over her, up between her legs, as if to split her in half. He never looked down as the tire ran over her chest. Though he couldn't keep the bike steady and swerved left, tore off her ear, blood flew but El Mudo, he just kept pedaling, getting smaller and smaller as he drove out of Gateway. You didn't help after, as she lay limp and bleeding from the side of her head. When her sister, Kari, came out and saw her, you ran; ran and ran, as far as you could, hoping Kari hadn't seen you.

Ma said to think good thoughts, but this is what you'll fixate on. Your father, seeing your frown, will yell again, asking if you're doing what ma said. You'll say sí and try to smile as she rubs the egg on your armpits, chest, back, and though you'll know it won't work, you'll keep smiling. She'll move on to your thighs, shins, the soles of your feet—in the background, you'll hear your father saying, goddammit, why the fuck is he crying now? He'll throw his arms up, like he does to say you're useless, and ma will kneel down, lightly squeezing your hand as she asks you what's wrong. You'll tell her you're fine, you're already feeling better. She'll nod. It's the bad spirit coming out, she'll tell your father. It goddamn better be, he'll reply. Yeah right, your brother will scoff. Your father will stare him down and he won't say anything else.

When ma cracks the egg, the yolk will sink to the bottom of the glass. Stalagmites of egg white forming and spiraling up toward the rim. While the yolk, a gold you've never seen, gets brighter and brighter, almost glowing. She'll explain to your father in a hushed but excited tone that the more there are, the higher they reach, and the brighter the yolk, the more evil the curse. Pero nada te va a pasar, she'll say, tickling the back of your neck. Vas a ver. You'll try your best to believe her as she tells you to flush it and to keep thinking good thoughts. As you leave, you'll hear her tell him you'll get better now, the glass is just showing all the bad that's been pulled out and transferred onto the egg. How will we know? he'll ask. We'll just have to wait. Puras pinches malas vibras con ese—his voice carrying into the bathroom as you contemplate the still water in the toilet bowl.

You'll flush the egg like you're told.

When you're back in the room, you'll want to go next to ma, but with brother and father there, you won't. The four of you will stand there, staring at each other, father will let out a long exasperated sigh, ma will smile at you, and then brother will say, can you make him sleep on the couch? NOOOOOOO, your father will yell. He'll grab his belt and you'll both run away.

Later, in your room, brother will tell you not to touch him, I don't want to get whatever you have. And you'll lie on your bunk tired but too scared to sleep. Your cousin, Jamón el Mamón, having shown you a few weeks ago that movie with Freddy Krueger. You'll wonder if it was your aunt who suggested it. Because somehow the curse seems connected to Freddy: your fear of being eaten by him, living on in his stomach—in perpetual agony—with a million other souls. He's already appeared to you in a dream, a silhouette cloaked in steam, washed in vermilion light, a high scratching noise as he approached, and screams, and hands pressing in through walls made of latex. You escaped only by forcing yourself awake. And ever since, you've been pissing the bed, fighting sleep.

When you hear brother snoring, you'll want to go to ma, to sleep beside her—a thing your father never allows. The last time he found you asleep on the floor beside their bed, he dragged you out by your hair, slapping you until you were crying, and saying, nothing's going to happen to you, so just quit your fucking acting and go to sleep, pinche niñita.

You'll fight sleep until you can't, praying that the limpia has taken out whatever evil had taken hold inside. But what if you've been double cursed? Hasn't she had it out for you? Ever since you refused to say you loved God more than your family. And the way she laughs, arching her back, her cackling cracking the sky open, isn't that exactly the way Freddy laughs as well? Then you'll be waking up again in the kitchen, a pair of scissors in your hand. Everyone around you, and your father angry, staring you down. He'll say he has to shower, no point going back to sleep now. Again, you won't know what happened. You'll want to apologize but instead you'll say, I feel better, I swear. Brother will tell you to swear to God and though you don't believe, never have, you'll look at ma and the way she looks back, all you'll muster is, but I do. Then she'll say it too, swear to God, Christian.

That night, during dinner, for a long time, no one will talk. Only the sound of the news will punctuate the clinking of spoons against dishes, the hiss of steam escaping the tortillero. You'll grab a tortilla and listen to the TV in the living room: something about the death of Prop 187 two years ago and what they're trying to do now, raids starting up again. You don't like tortillas, but your father always makes you eat at least one. He's afraid of what you might become. One of those Mexicans you see on TV, against immigration when that's how their parents got here or, worse, that's how they did themselves. You won't know what this means until much later. You'll grab another tortilla, hoping that if you take a second, he won't make you eat salsa.

But he will, he'll slam his fist down on the table, telling you to be a man, eat some pinche salsa.

You'll do as you're told, hating how it burns and lingers in your mouth, your stomach becoming unsettled and everyone else showing no signs of distress. Like being the only one born here does make you different.

Ma will prod brother into sharing his own news. Citizen of the Month at school. For outstanding behavior, he'll say, and upholding the school's values. Your father will keep eating, paying more attention to the TV news. Ma will keep prodding, reminding him that that's not why she had to pick him up from school. Brother will then take a deep gulp of air and add how he got in trouble for going into the girls' bathroom and didn't get to walk at the assembly.

¿Qué? your father will say. And brother will repeat himself. Your father will smile then, saying, éste sí es varón. Hombrezote. And brother will stick out his chest and they'll laugh together. Ma will sigh, then go back to finishing her meal. And when your father isn't looking, you'll scrape some salsa off your tortilla.

After dinner, you and brother will meet up with Moco, Selena's little brother. His face covered in grime, a wet spot near his crotch. It'll dry, he'll say when brother points. You'll both follow him around the complex as he finds and swallows gum, paint chips, and bottle caps. Everyone just thinking he's fucking gross. No one knowing it has a name, his thing. And even after he's diagnosed, most won't believe it. Not his sisters or dad, and definitely not his mother, who says she's seen enough puercos in her own village to believe some fucking doctor that writes prescriptions like we're all rich. Besides, it's just Moco being Moco, and no one in her village ever died for acting like swine. When your father found out, he said: That idiot just wants attention, it'll serve him right when he's in the hospital. You better not do something so fucking stupid. No tengo para tus pendejadas. ¿Entiendes? He waited for you to assent before shutting the door on you. When he locked it, you knew it'd be a while before they left their room.

Following Moco around the commons, you'll hear gunshots, sirens, beer bottles exploding on asphalt like cheap fireworks. Another day in Stockton. You'll find a grocery cart lying on its side, Moco playing with the wheel, tugging on it like it's candy that won't budge. You'll all see the homeless Walking Man go by and you'll take it as a sign. Good luck. Brother will nudge you, say in a hushed voice, that means he's going to eat more stuff. You'll both grin and Moco will catch the glint of a red plastic leg of an action figure sticking out of the dirt. He'll swallow it, make a satisfied noise, like he's just downed the coldest glass of Sunny D. Then he'll stretch, his little weird brown stomach glowing in the light, looking slightly bloated but also warm, inviting. You'll want to press your cheek against it. You'll take a step toward him, but brother will pull you back. Don't get too close to the animal, he'll say. Moco will smile knowingly and brother will laugh. You'll all laugh.

The three of you will look up and pretend that the ghetto bird is after you. You'll run and hide between bushes, under trucks, until you're all by Anna's porch, Selena's best friend, hearing her blast "Suavemente" for the thousandth time. You'll take out a stink bomb and squeeze it to life. As it expands, you'll throw it up into her porch, waiting for her screams to start before you all run away, laughing again. You'll keep laughing as brother and Moco throw more bombs at other porches, rows and rows of townhomes getting the same treatment.

After the sun has started to set and all the stink bombs are gone, the three of you head back by Anna's, wondering if it'll still stink. You'll see a fire truck parked out front. Its lights flashing, turning everything red. You'll all see the firemen entering her apartment and no one will stop you as you follow them in. The lights will be off, the smell of cigarettes in the carpet and sofas, and the walls too. You'll hear voices coming from one of the rooms, and they'll get clearer. You'll all see Anna—her eyes wide, unblinking, and a thin black pole sticking through her neck—in the arms of one of the firemen. He'll whisper to her at a volume too low for anyone else to overhear.

You'll wonder then if this is your doing, if you've spread it, this disease of yours. You'll all move out of the fireman's way as he carries Anna past. And with her, you'll share a glance. She'll know it was you.

Something in her eyes, the way you feel looking into them: mix of pain, tenderness, surprise, as when, expecting laughter, a hug, you're smacked instead.

She knows. She knows.

Outside, you'll all watch as the firemen work on her. With bolt cutters, they snap off the metal pole's ends. They'll tell her she's going to be fine. They'll say it again and again, like an incantation. Protection against your curse.

Brother will ask if she's going to die.

The firemen will say, don't worry, your sister will be all right.

She's not our sister, brother will say, and they'll tell you all to leave then.

Moco will ask for a piece of the pole and they'll change their tone. Get the fuck outta here, you stupid little spics.

You and brother will go straight home holding your throats. You'll tell yourself it was an accident; Anna had an accident, that's all. Meanwhile, Moco will crouch behind some bushes, waiting for a piece of that pole.

You'll almost be home and still holding your throat, trying to believe curses aren't contagious, when Jamón rounds the corner. He'll cough, fiddle with his pockets before offering you a piece of candy, a Lifesaver. Take it, brother will tell you. You'll think of your aunt, of Anna, and without meaning to, you'll swallow, the Lifesaver lodging in your throat. You'll dry heave and lurch on all fours, grasping for anything to hold, to take away that pain, of not being able to breathe, and making the kind of noises you first heard when, flipping through channels, brother landed on a scene where a man pretended he'd entered the wrong house, a woman shouting, wanting him to leave, before getting slapped and undressed and forced to crawl around the kitchen, then taking his dick in her mouth, and the man pushing into her over and over. The whole time, her making those sounds.

You'll be making them yourself, like you've got a dick in your mouth, as you scratch and dig into your throat, writhing on the grass, turning blue, before brother yanks you up and does the Heimlich, over and over, until the Lifesaver flies out.

And you'll all have that same stupid surprised look that the woman did, at the end. Brother will grab you by the neck, tell you it's time to get back.

We're not talking to stupid fatass anymore, all right? And chew before you swallow, fucking moron.

Yeah, okay, you'll say.

I mean it. Crazy bitch echándote el ojo, what we ever do to her?

I didn't do nothing.

And I did? Come on, before a Ouija board appears or something.

Back home you'll wonder if this will ever end, if ma just told you all that stuff to make you feel better. Brother will tell her what happened, and she'll perform another limpia. She'll remind you, you need three, okay? And this time your father won't be home and you'll have better thoughts.

The Saturday after the second limpia, you won't piss your bed or sleepwalk or wake up screaming, and you'll begin to believe it's working, you aren't going to die. Your father will be in a good mood and you'll think it's because you slept well the night before. The curse, finally lifting. He'll decide to take ma, brother, and you to the flea market on El Dorado.

In the car—your father's Cadillac, red suede interior pocked with grease stains—you and brother play your favorite car game: seeing who can squish and collect more ants before the ride ends. Father will put cumbias on, one of the same songs you've heard at every family function and have learned to tune out. Ma will look back at you both and smile, asking, who's going to win today? You'll be at it for five minutes straight, thinking you have a real shot at winning this time, only to lose focus when, instead of showing ma your progress, you'll fixate on her arm stretched against the dashboard, bracing, and you'll remember last year driving home from a cousin's wedding, having left early because ma, drunk, had cried in front of everyone. Your father didn't love her. He was seeing someone else, una sucia, gran puta. In the car, bound for home, going forty on

El Dorado, she'd undone her seat belt and opened the passenger door. Your father slammed the brakes and she braced against the dashboard. Grabbing her bracing arm, he convinced her to close the door. The rest of the drive, silent.

In the parking lot of the flea market, brother will be all grins as he opens his shirt, showing you his collection. Assume the position, he'll say. You'll close your eyes, stick out your chin, he'll fling dead ants onto your face. You'll claw them off, each rigid like tiny paper clips, spitting the strays that stuck to your lips.

The two of you will be left to wander the aisles, churro sugar coating your hands and mouths as you bob and weave through stalls of airsoft guns, used video games, old movies, shitty plastic toys. Brother will use his last dollar on a snow cone, tiger blood, you'll use yours on some Pop Pop snappers, marking your path with them, throwing them down and listening for the crack, and wishing, always, you had more money.

Before leaving, ma will want an elote, the longest line in the flea market. She'll make the rest of you stand in the hot sun for ten minutes, groaning and shuffling. Just as the vendor's passing it to her over the cart, you'll hear people screaming, panicking. Your body will freeze the same as when your father reaches for the belt. Three wild-eyed and bald sureños chasing a norteño through the parting crowd. They'll manage to grab hold of his red button-down just a few feet from ma. She'll stand, frozen, as they rip his shirt off, the one with brass knuckles will bust his mouth. He'll answer by elbowing one in the jaw, hard, and they'll punch him until he's covering himself and they're slamming him down, head bouncing off ma's shin before hitting the ground—white crumbs of cotija from her elote falling, disappearing into the wrinkles of his wifebeater. You'll see the knife then, its glint, and then it, too, will disappear into the norteño's abdomen. The sureños will take off, everyone screaming even louder and getting out of their way.

Blood will ooze through the norteño's wifebeater. Like a rose, you'll think, blooming. He'll try to contain it, face contorting as his Cortezes kick and scrape against the pavement. He'll spit, hyperventilate, grip his wound. The blood staining his fingers, painting his nails. And his eyes will have that same look, surprise is the thing that brings death. Your eyes will meet, his as wide as yours feel. A curse—somehow, your first thought will be that you're responsible for this too.

You'll only then notice your father's hands holding on to the back of you and your brother's shirts. He'll drag you over to ma. You'll hear sirens, screaming, tires screeching as cars peel out around you. The four of you will make your way back to the car.

Buckling your belt, you'll think about the blood seeping through the norteño's fingers.

Your father will glower at you in the rearview. Hijo de la chingada, los vas a matar a todos. Looking longer than he should, he'll swerve. Once, twice. Y tú, he'll say to ma, why'd you just stand there? He'll reach out roughly to thumb away the speck of blood from her temple.

No sé, she'll say. No sé. She'll flip through radio stations in search of something cheerful. She'll settle on a salsa, turning up the volume. No sé.

I thought this was supposed to work, your father will say, turning it back down right away, shaking his head. He'll punch the wheel, drowning out ma's music with his horn.

You'll focus on the ants crawling on his seatback.

Todavía le falta una limpia, ma will say. The last one is the most important.

He won't say anything for a while. Turning the radio off, he'll laugh softly to himself. You'll get the same feeling you had when your aunt stared you down. You'll try counting all the ants you can see but you'll lose your place when he says, why don't you do another already?

I can't do 'em all at once. Así siempre lo hacían.

Necesita un pinche curandero de a deveras, he'll say.

Pay for one, then.

No me hables así en frente de ellos. He'll grip her bicep and you'll know by the way she arches her back that he's trying to crush it.

Brother will keep his eyes locked on the passing buildings, seeing all and none of them. Ants will crawl over you. You'll let them pass, unharmed, over your dirty churro-sugared hands.

That evening your father will side-eye you all through dinner. You won't want to eat, but knowing what'll happen if you don't, you'll take small, slow bites. When ma asks what's wrong, you'll ask, am I gonna die?

Bet you will, brother will say. Before slurping up a spoonful of lentil soup.

¿Y qué crees, que no sé? ma will lash back. Si él no lo hizo llorar, ¿qué piensas, que no sé quién es capaz? sounding like the rapid venomous hiss of a snake.

Your father will slam his fist against the table, staring her into silence.

After a while, brother will say, I didn't know he'd get cursed. When no one else says anything, your death will feel definitive. A memory will occur to you then, a scalding night with all the neighborhood kids getting together for freeze tag; it was someone's birthday, past midnight, and no one yelled at any of you to get inside. You'd all spotted him at the same time, this cholo reclining behind one of the dumpsters, all of you ambling over to where he lay, under the sick orange glow of a lamppost. Blood from the crown of his head matted his hair, strands of it looping across his forehead.

You all stared into the red jeweled mess of his torn-up mouth, disgusting as it was beautiful.

His breathing was labored and the green forty glowed and fizzed as he swigged from it. Brother, always the leader, asked what happened, and he stared at you all like a cornered animal. When he finally spoke, his voice was strained but no fear in it, only fury. Those fuckers jumped me, what you fucking think, foo? Brother moved closer. Everyone else did too. Someone asked if it hurt. Nah, he said. He took another swig then lowered his arm, the forty clinking hard against the pavement. I'ma get those fuckers. I'll kill 'em. Be at them funerals. Watch.

Maybe, brother said.

Fuck you—the cholo stared him dead. Brother moved closer, close enough to touch him, and then you all closed in. First, I'ma sleep, then watch, watch what happens, the cholo said. Leva motherfuckers, I'll get 'em, he said, I'll get 'em, I'll get 'em, over and over, like a prayer.

Yeah, but first, brother replied, we gone get you.

And leaning down over him, you all laid your hands on the crown of his head, his shoulders, your palms slick and gleaming. His eyes like .45s. But the longer you touched him, the more they seemed to dim, like you were taking the glow from him. Absorbing it into your bodies: that hot bright sick animal fury, with its alcoholic stink. Reducing him into a bleeding, listless, aching body. He closed his eyes then and only the outline of a body remained. You all went running, screaming, singing, we win, we win we win we win we win.

Still, that cholo had known what it took to win. You thought his words a prayer, I'll get 'em, I'll get 'em, I'll get 'em. His anger pointed, decisive as a gun, something you've never possessed. You curse or you get cursed. You beat or get beat. And since that day, you still haven't known what it's like to have that rage.

And taking another bite of your soup, you won't be smelling it then but tasting it instead, his fury, and your aunt's too, sizzling on your tongue, rising up from within, like reflux. No one will look at you, your father focused on his food, ma and brother too. It'll be like you're already dead, already a ghost. Somehow your fear will keep you from crying. Dinner will end without another word.

The same night, brother will complain from the top bunk that the ceiling's looking bare, too many plastic stars and planet stickers fallen. Soon, he'll say, new ones will have to be stuck. You'll want to tell him to plan on doing it himself; you won't be here much longer. Instead, you'll shut your eyes, you'll say nothing. Brother will ask you to tell a story. You're better at it than me, he'll say—the same way he's always tricked you into talking him to sleep, leaving you alone with your thoughts. Though this never stopped you. You like making things happen to them, Ángel and Misterio, your characters; sometimes going on the run, from cops, SWAT, the whole nine, robbing banks, exploring deep space, the only constant, they're always together. But on this night you won't be able to think of them. Or brother. Even hasta mañana will be beyond you. Instead, you'll turn in your bed and cover your mouth as you whisper, don't cry, don't cry, like your own shitty prayer.

You'll be sleepwalking when your family finds you in the kitchen cutting off your fingers. Everyone screaming, running in circles, like chickens with their heads cut off. By the time you're lucid enough to realize this isn't a nightmare, they'll have closed in. Only then will you feel the pain of exposed bone, your two smallest fingers only just hanging on to your hand. You'll flail all over the kitchen while brother looks on in disgust.

Your father will shout for him to hold you down. Brother will pin your hand against the table while ma presses the fingers back together, your father wrapping them in gauze, saying, éste no va a parar. All their hands covered in your blood. Your eyes will dart from the blood blooming through the gauze to the knife and back again. You'll whimper. And your father, who hates that sound above all, will say, ya, ya, cálmate ya. You'll close your eyes as ma rubs your back, telling you to breathe. You'll be hyperventilating as you tell her you want another limpia. Though really, you'll know you should be telling them all to stay away. Because they might catch it. Your curse.

The next Sunday you'll all wait silently outside the curandero's house on Eighth Street, one of many families waiting to be seen. When your number's finally called, your parents will tell the curandero everything. He'll be dressed in all beige, everything loose and flowing, like a curtain. There'll be candles throughout the hall, and as he leads you all toward the living room, you'll note the walls plain and white, though everything is seemingly touched by sunlight, it's somehow brighter inside his house than out. When your parents are finally done relaying the events, they'll ask the cost, and he'll shake his head, touching his chest as he says, esto es un don, he can't charge for his gift. They should pay whatever seems fair.

The curandero will ask you questions and you'll answer as best you can. He'll ask for your hand, thumbing your palm before placing his own hand, rough and swollen like a catcher's mitt, on your forehead. He'll tell his daughter, dressed in the same linen clothes but in a light blue, to inform those still waiting that this boy will have to be the last for the day. He'll tell your family that you need to be cleansed. A grimness stretching over his face as he says it'll require una sobada que pueda aniquilar. The evil needing to be extracted from your entire body.

    The curandero's daughter will lead you to the bathroom. Laying a towel on the floor, she'll tell you to take everything off, including your underwear, and to lie down on the towel. She'll press on your stomach like she's kneading it, searching for something, and once she's found it, she'll take her knuckle and corkscrew it into your body, working it slow and deep into your abdomen. You'll wince only slightly, holding in your discomfort as you're made to feel like a molcajete, grinding down an herb into powder. She'll move across to your other side, letting you relax for a moment before beginning the process again. After, she'll tell you you're ready, to roll onto your side and hug your knees. You'll do as you're told, waiting while from a drawer she retrieves: a rubber pouch, adobe red, with a dull hollow nib. She'll go to the sink, filling the pouch through the nib, saying something you won't quite understand; it'll sound ancient, like a forgotten language produced by wind. When the pouch is full, she'll tell you to breathe—long, slow breaths—and to keep hugging your knees. You'll shiver as she runs a finger down your spine, explaining that the red pouch will make you clean, driving out some of the poison inside, so her father can do his work. Your whole body will tense and you'll want to get up and run as far as you can. Instead, you'll follow her command, exhaling like she says as she sticks the nib inside you. When you feel the water going in, you'll squeeze, pushing it back out. She'll say she has to do this and that you need to relax. Think of your father and brother, she'll say. Do it for them. For your mother. If we don't get this curse out, who knows what might happen to them. You love them, right? You'll turn your head enough to face her, her breath like cigarettes and chrysanthemum. She'll see in your eyes that you won't push back. As she goes back in, a sharp rasping pain, you'll whimper. You'll keep reminding yourself, this is for them. Respira, she'll say. You'll breathe in and out, in and out, waiting for it to end.

After, she'll let you put on your underwear. It won't be long before you'll feel the need. To go. You'll assume she's done and will leave. But no. You can sit on the toilet, she'll say, but she's going to have to wait there with you, because you can't go. Not yet. You'll turn away and pull down your underwear. You'll sit on the toilet, your legs dangling off the ground, and she'll remind you again, not yet, you have to wait, or none of this will work. You'll nod back. A minute will pass and then another, you'll ask how much longer, and she'll just repeat, wait. You'll clutch your stomach and wonder why she let you sit on the toilet in the first place if she isn't going to let you go. Even after you stop asking, she'll keep saying it, wait. Wait. Espérate. And as the minutes keep passing, she'll tell you this is what it takes to draw out all the poison. You'll be wincing then and saying, please, please, can I go now? You'll grab your sides, wincing and folding in on yourself from the pain, and just straining to hold it all in for another minute because you need this to work. You don't want to be cursed. Don't want to die. Don't want anyone in your family to die. Chills and sweat all over your body. She'll tell you to breathe but you won't be able to any longer, the pain, like your stomach's collapsing; then it'll come out of you. For a second, relief, but almost immediately, you'll picture ma sleepwalking, falling out the window, your vision will blur and you'll say sorry, I'm sorry. Ma. The panic halting your voice, and as more comes out of you, you'll resolve to do it again. It's okay, she'll say. No one's ever held it that long. You won't understand. She'll say you just had to hold it as long as you could, to give yourself the best odds. Then she'll pick up the rest of your clothes and leave. More and more will come out of you. Your stomach caving in on itself, like her knuckles are still kneading it, and you'll think, this is how it feels to be empty. A void in you. And you'll know, emptiness itself is a kind of curse.

After, you'll clean yourself, washing your hands the way surgeons do on TV, soap up to your elbows. Your bandaged fingers getting soaked and heavy, and the dried, crusted-up blood all around the gauze making you feel like you're still dirty. You'll press your bandaged hand into a towel, wincing and whimpering and knowing you have to stop crying. You have to be different. You'll repeat, no one will die, no one will die.

Your family will have been sitting on chairs against the wall of the curandero's living room, ma praying and holding on to your clothes, brother staring at the floor, and your father staring you down. A large rug with another towel at its center, and you'll know it's there for you. The curandero will tell you to lie on your chest. He'll circle you, speaking in that same language made of wind. He'll do five laps then reverse course and do another five. He'll close his eyes and kneel beside you, rubbing his hands slowly, methodically, his breath matching them, and both gaining momentum like a steam engine.

His palms on your back like hot coals, you'll lurch and he'll tell you to relax as he lifts them off and goes back to rubbing them. His breath louder now than any breath you've ever heard. He'll press his hot palms onto your shoulder blades, your spine, hamstrings, nape, and calves. Your whole body growing hotter, brighter, and you'll even smile as he says, todo va a estar bien. He'll begin with your legs. He'll say this is how he'll pull all the bad energy, all your pain, out. It was his grandfather who taught him. He'll say, all bodies are conduits, and to free one of brujería, the energy needs to be redirected out. This is what he's doing, he'll explain as he massages your upper thigh, squeezing it out. He'll move down your leg to your knee before starting from your upper thigh again. He'll do this over and over, from thigh to knee, then knee to ankle, from your ankle to each toe, one by one, and at the end of each toe he'll exhale, opening his hands like he's throwing something out. He'll move in on your torso, beginning at the bottom of your back first and moving all the energy up and out your arms; you'll feel yourself getting lighter and lighter as he finishes each limb. And as he moves his hands, finally, up over your scalp toward the crown of your head, you'll feel like you could finally sleep with no fear. Slowly, gently, he'll pull the energy out of your hair and throw it away. You'll think this is the end, but he'll only say, almost. He has to make sure first that none of the curse is left in your body or it'll come back worse. He'll call your family over but only brother and your father will come, crouching near you with the curandero's daughter. They'll each grab a limb as the curandero props another folded towel under your forehead. His daughter will slip her hand under your chest, telling her father you're ready, and before you can ask—he'll slam, hammer his fist into your back, your shoulder blade, knocking the wind out of you. You'll try to get up, but each of them will hold you down. Cálmate, his daughter will say as you look around frantically for ma, and brother not looking you in the eye, and your father not saying a thing as the daughter insists, tranquilo, you have to be limber—you'll remember the cholo, everyone's hands on him. The curandero will strike you again. And you'll breathe strong enough to knock a tree down, while you're looking to your father. Nothing in his face at all. For this to work, the daughter will say, you need to relax, breathe, slow and even. She'll shake your arm like rope.

And then your father will say, be strong, ya casi, ya casi, but he won't sound sure, and he'll keep his hands on you and when brother lets go, your father will shout at him and tell him to keep his pinche hands on you. More than anything, you'll want ma but when she's finally there, in front of you, crying, you'll only wonder why she isn't stopping them. She'll run her trembling hand through your hair and tell you, you're almost done, ya casi, ya casi. The curse almost out of you, this is the last thing left to do, and yet with every subsequent blow, you feel it, death, approaching. Looking at them all holding you down, brother and father, the daughter, and even ma now too, another strike will land, and you'll feel like you're nothing.

You'll grit your teeth, breathing methodically as the tears stream down your cheeks. Another blow will land and ma will run her hand through your hair again but you'll shake and twist, wanting her fucking hand off you, the daughter will repeat, relax, relax. Another half dozen blows will land. When ma finally says, you're done, mi niño, you're done, you'll look her dead in the eyes and in the faintest whisper, you'll tell her, over and over, I curse you, I curse you.

BEDTIME STORY

For Ángel and Misterio, it'd been years since they'd been outside the archipelago that harbored their lighthouse. The lighthouse hadn't worked in years. Still, it was home. Creaky, dilapidated, and wooden as it was, with no insulation, and so cold. Always so cold. In the sporadic hours of the night, a drunken, somnambulant wind would gust, buffet against the derelict door. Its demand always the same: LET ME IN. LET ME IN. That old, battered door barely holding on. The patina gone from its hinges, just rust and a screeching rattling noise, which the brothers could never ignore. Inside their sleeping bags, eyes closed, nothing to quiet their fear but hope, desperate foolish hope that the front door could withstand the onslaught just a little longer than the wind. That drunken tornado of rage, harbinger of disaster, their waking nightmare. Without shelter, the outside world would come rushing in. And it was only a matter of time. The front door would break down and then the ceiling and all the walls too, all of it getting blown away. Leaving them to feel it all, raw, exposed, nothing but their sleeping bags to weather that biting cold atop the cliffside while underneath the crashing waves called out to them: Join me. This is where you belong. Let me be your new home. I'll drown you, you dirty little sacks of shit.

And every morning when the golden amber light crested like a giant yolk over the blue horizon—a temporary refuge. Though escape but a liminal fantasy. And even then, what the days brought forth was the quiet loneliness of waiting. A dance of hope and anticipation. Each brother holding on to a separate dream as the hours ticked by, the night edging closer while each, for different reasons, still hoped that that day would be one of those when their mother returned.

This is how they lived: nights of terror, days of solitude. Until one day, coming back from her trips outside the archipelago, their mother brought back a book. *The Keepers*. An old damaged book, waterlogged and mildewed. Though in the middle, a story remained intact. At first, she read it to them every night. Each finding a different comfort in the ending. She read it as distraction from the wind but somehow the story itself held another power, as soon as the story commenced, the wind would quiet, then diffuse. For a time, the wind altogether disappeared. For a while they knew peace. The lighthouse remained broken but still, they had food, shelter, and she didn't have to leave. They lived days and nights of quiet joy. But all too soon the wind returned, diminished as it was, it returned. And their food supply dwindled, and their mother again had to venture outside the archipelago. Their joy and peace shifted. Always she'd return, but they never knew when, and that time of reading had changed. She then only ever read to them on the nights before she'd leave. Gone before they could wake.

She's been gone for about a week. Longest she's ever been away. If she doesn't come home tomorrow, Ángel will have to look for food himself. He knows he needs to rest, prepare himself for the world outside the archipelago. But the wind, the crashing waves, the brine that corrodes everything—gutters, windowpanes, doors, foundation—remind him that it'll all be swept away. Devoured.

With sleep heavy on his mind, he first takes out a notepad, a pen, thankful for that book, its images: trees, plants, root systems, the moon, and the dark itself, all of which he draws. Last year she brought back a tattoo gun and vials of ink, called it Christmas though it wasn't December. He practiced on himself first. Tattooing a system of roots from his waist all the way down to his feet. Just yesterday, he tattooed branches and cherry blossom petals over Misterio's torso, his throat. A present for their mother. Tomorrow's her birthday. He looks out the foggy window, at the moon, a brilliant pearl shining over the sea. Sometimes Ángel doesn't know if he actually wants her to return. He draws a series of moons, their return to the sky, the heartache displaced, and finally, he sleeps.

The next morning, Misterio sits by the window, reading, looking out now and then onto the dirt path. The sun directly overhead when she appears at the edge of the path. Empty-handed. Misterio runs out into the yard, unbuttons his shirt, and lies supine like a present on the grass. The tattooed petals on his body glowing in the afternoon sun. She inspects him there with his eyes closed, notices the wrinkles at the edges of his eyes, like flowers. His thin frail body, like a sick blade of grass. It hurt so much, Misterio says. She runs her finger along each petal brimming pink. Ay, mijo, they're...beautiful, she says. In his excitement, he forgets to say happy birthday. He gets up off the grass, hugs her, burying his tears into her waist.

Ángel sees it all through the upstairs window. Hands in his pockets, ink hidden. He knows he'll be blamed, punished. Though it wasn't his idea. Only after Misterio begged, for days and days, did Ángel finally relent. Descending the stairs, he walks out toward them, smiles. He faces his mother, and each pretends not to know what the other is thinking: She holds his cheek in the palm of her hand, cariño, she says. He gently peels her hand away. She smiles, they hug. Happy birthday, he says into her shoulder.

Inside, she lies on the red suede couch. She shivers. Her hands cold. She sweats, smiles, what did *you* get me? Ángel stares at her arm. Get the hot plate, she snaps. Rolls her sleeve down with a force that says, don't you fucking stare. Ángel brings in the last two cans of beans, opens them. He puts the hot plate down on the floor by the couch and turns it on. The electric buzz, wind, and point break, the only carousel of sound while they wait, hungry and tired, for the first can to heat. Her arm all Ángel can think about. A galaxy of cuts, punctures, and bruises. No erasing that image. Her eyes are closed and Misterio watches her with wonderment. Ángel goes for his notebook, flips through to his favorite drawing. In it, a tree glows, all its roots exposed, with the moon at its core. He carefully rips it out. Writes his name in the corner, underlines it twice. Presents it to her. And before he can say happy birthday, she asks, is this finished? It's not even colored in. Her eyes close as the drawing slips from her hand onto the floor. She laughs, high and distant as if in her mind already being carried out past the sea. It is, Ángel whispers. Finished.

Food's ready, Misterio says. You both eat, not hungry, she answers. With her eyes still closed, she turns away on the couch. Ángel staring at his drawing on the floor before picking it up, bringing it to his chest. I'll get the—he stops himself, holds in his tears. He gets up and brings back two spoons. They eat. She sleeps.

After dinner they lie in the silence of the lighthouse. Misterio reading while Ángel gazes out the window onto the dirt path. Misterio watches over the top of the book as Ángel begins to gather pens, pencils, charcoal, notebook. He puts it all in a shoebox with the tattoo gun and ink, stares at it for a while before shutting the lid. As the sun sets, Ángel takes the box outside. Misterio looks from the window as his brother digs a hole with a shovel. The hole, deep, as deep as a grave. He watches as Ángel puts the box in, crouches, becomes hidden from view before rising then climbing out of the hole. Everything in Misterio wanting to run out, tell him to stop, but as soon as Ángel shovels that first clod of dirt into the hole, he loses all will. He slinks down from the window, turns away, hugging the book and crying. Outside, for Ángel, the rasp of dirt hitting the box signaling the end, all childish things left behind. He gives a half-pained smile, he can finally let go.

That night she asks for the book. They knew when she came back empty that she would have to leave again. They don't fight it. Instead, they nestle on opposite sides of her as she opens the book and reads to them. Annihilation. Pitch-black darkness. The world of night hemmed in absence of the moon. Nights of silent terror. Emptiness. Everything forgot. All was the same until a family rose from the deep. The Keepers. Clad in antediluvian scarlet robes, chanting an ancient language, making their way through the darkness toward the lone cherry blossom tree rooted near the edge of a cliff. A dark wind slashing through them, trying to steer them off course. Somehow, they know the way. Though darkness is not their kin. Arriving, they press their palms against the trunk, chanting louder and louder, a rising guttural resonance, digging to the core, and roots, then climbing up the trunk, branches, the petals themselves, all of it beginning to glow. Brighter and brighter, a radiance that shakes the earth. A howling wind comes and carries the pink neon petals out across the sea. Beacons for the missing, the lost, the forgotten ones.

A voice in the glowing petals. You thought that you were not. All that has been forgot. But there are other ways to be. Not abandoned, just lies you've come to believe, now follow and set yourself free. In the pink flickering light of the petals, out from the darkness, the silhouetted shadows begin to emerge. Each petal gliding in the gentle breeze, bringing each one toward home. A distant chorus of voices, getting closer, and as music begins to emerge, closer still. A beckoning. The forgot standing outside, showered in the radiance of light.

All possible only so long as the Keepers, creators of the moon, keep their promise, for the light borrowed, given to the tree. They promise safe passage; once a month, the moon can travel across the sky. Become more than dream signal. Keeper of its own light.

Some of the forgot will go inside where the light, the music, will surround them. They'll realize they've always been remembered. Others, seeing their old homes, will look up toward the night sky, a black sheet without end, they'll recede, choosing to go back toward the dark. Though more and more will choose the light, the return, each passing day. But The Keepers themselves will be forgotten, and already they're losing strength. Soon, sooner than they know, they will falter. They won't be able to speak the ancient language anymore. The tree's glow will dim into pulses, the time between pulses growing until the light ceases altogether. The moon trapped down in its trunk and the missing left alone in the dark.

On the nights that follow, with their mother gone, Ángel will pretend he's asleep while Misterio reads the story to himself. She'll return for a while. But before long she'll fade into the night. Each brother will look out the window and see a different kind of moon. Misterio will dream, hoping for a return. On the nights when Ángel leaves, Misterio will stand atop the lighthouse, he'll take his shirt off—he'll glow.

THE DESECRATIONISTS

We're seven, a few months after the incident. Meeting by the tree and shrilling the only songs we know, faggot and retard and fuck you, fuck you, fuck you. Pecking at each other's skulls—we'd hollow them out if we could. Hear only ourselves. Summer. It lands like it always does over Gateway, a dilapidated rat-infested complex made of row after row of diseased brown townhomes. That raw stench of school replaced with a smell more industrial but also more feral: half-open barrels of tar, plum trees, dumpsters overflowing with diapers that smear the oil-slick pavement. Piss soaking everything: alleyways, fence posts, trees, tires, whatever can't move or get out of the way.

We slap each other's backs, lurching then sunning our black wings as we perch atop fences and the hoods of cars, brooding, hatching a plan for the day. Same as yesterday. Same as tomorrow. Same as will always be: fuck shit up, whatever's whole or living, to the ground, fuck it all until it doesn't move or hold together anymore. Shrill. Shrill we call, and shrill our laughter. Gateway apartments, kingdom of ours, an inheritance of bipolar schisms, ballistic-induced dreams, beatdowns, beatdowns, beatdowns, kingdom of pit bulls, Rottweilers, chains, ice cream trucks, elotes, raspados, stink bombs, kites, cops and robbers, and which of those you think we think we are?

Covet. Covetous are their eyes, the men who call us over to their cars, wishing they had what would lure us, catch us. More alluring is the chime, the rolling clinking sound of empty 40s going into each other, we chase after and sing: cocksucker, puto, chúpamela 'cause your mother already has. We gnash, cyclone of fists and beaks and claws. Tearing, plucking, pulling at him, and him, and him, and me. Genius. Stupid ghetto geniuses. We snatch at grass, old paper, an older brother's lighter, rolling then smoking, until the smoke ripping from our chests makes our lungs collapse. High with thrush, we shake and cough, phlegm staining our teeth, battling tears, until we're moshing. A conniption verging on religious until exorcism, exorcism, exorcism. Lightning strikes. That's how we fall, tail spinning out of trees, gates, roofs. Fun. Everything. Everything. Everything. We do it all, over and over, smoking, slapping, pushing, screaming, falling forever, dive bombs, somersaults, corkscrews, getting closer and closer to Gateway heaven.

Summer vacation, brief and wondrous, won't last, and neither will this day. But we'll try the impossible, squint to see the sun as anything other than fuse and bomb, tick, tick, ticking away the days till school. We hear a pattering like rain, an older kid firing his paintball gun at the sky. We ask what he's doing. Killing crows, he says, can't you little maricas see? Pointing behind him with his gun. And everywhere past him, a marvel. We crouch, crawl, crab-walk through the open installation: orange dye shrapnel, every surface bleeding, cars, walls, metallic beams splattered and glowing in the shadows cast by roofs. We look at the sun and back at the paint, its afterimage burning into our retinas, the paint glowing brighter, a festival of color, glued into the scattered plumes of crow feathers. Trail. We follow until we find it. Dead, its beak broken and painted orange, feather gun made safe. Ants—marching—taking what they can. They vanish in the feathers, reappearing on the "black hole suns" of its eyes, and in the small flutter going in and out of its tongue. We piss on the crow, drowning the ants in our runoff: tacos, Pulparindos, and pizza; howling at the sight, our cackles bursting into echoes and chanting the last vocabulary word unforgotten: desecration, desecration, desecration.

Our taste for blood whetted, we aim with our hands searching for our next target, the kid, the commons, or the sky? We give each other boosts, climb trees, fences, roofs, trying to snatch a piece of sky, yelling—puto, selfish fuck—as we fall, hands empty, hungry, curse thickening our mouths. With a stolen magnifying glass, we lie, bellies to the ground, examining the crow, sponge of orange, urine, blood, and ants. With the magnifying glass, we sic the sun's death-ray laser on the ants and they evaporate, one by one. Carapace of steam.

We quiet, hoping to hear their bodies crackle, instead a dog yelps and we get up, motor oil and crow blood staining our hands. We wipe them off on each other's clothes, laughing and passing the stolen round glass between us. With it, we burn each other's arms, tattoo, tattoo, tattoo. We squirm, scream, cry, until we've all felt the stinging kiss of the sun. We walk, hands covering our wounds. Until a crunch of a snail and the syrupy mucus trailing from a shoe. With nothing better to do we scatter, only to regroup, bearing more snails, in bowls, in pockets, pinched between our fingers. We place them around the crushed one, taking fistfuls of salt and pouring it over them. A parade. Curdling. Vibration. Life over life.

And as the sky runs gold into lavender, we meet behind the apartments, arms pregnant with: fireworks, jars of spiders, lizards, and beetles. Emptying our arms, we bend to our works. Dumping lit fireworks into glass bottles, hurling them like grenades, fuse and spark zipping across the sky, before crash-landing, bursting, sonic waves rapping our chests. Spectacle of disaster, again and again. Glass shrapnel strewn in a crystalline sheen on the pavement. With all jars done, we remember where there are snakes. We'll get 'em, we scream, and we do. A little green one. With the longest fuse we have we tie a firecracker to its back. Passing it around like a bomb, in harried whispers counting down, and with the night air thick, we rapture. Whispers becoming insults, shoving and backslapping until we're cackling, looking on at the fuse then we're all running away, sharp blinding light, and the explosion, shock wave on our backs. Glad in the wonder, the blood, the resiliency of snakes. A pale moon shining on our parade: tails, abdomens, split carcasses, and the coiled snake still whole, streaming with blood. Meaning do over, do over, do over, until scales give to bone, and it's limp like a dead rubber band in the grip of our hands.

Then we're ripping it open, unspooling it. A sacrament. We hold the snake to the moon and howl the names of everything we hate. Belts, boots, grown-ups, school, any kind of rule.

Still, day's end. The first of us goes home, then a second, a third, fourth, and fifth, until you're the only one there, in the quiet. In Gateway. Alone.

It's like you've been holding your breath all day and only now noticing it. Your breath, the air against your skin, the stillness of cars, trees, lampposts, the steadiness of light, soft and orange. You have to go home but can't yet. It's the weekend, parents off somewhere, dancing, an older cousin babysitting, too busy with the stolen cable box to notice you're not where you're supposed to be or when. You find a branch glowing with orange paint and, with it, take the long route back, scraping it against chain-link fences, brick, rosebushes; a slug gleams in the moonlight. You fidget with an unlit firework, remembering what your father sometimes says before smacking you, cría cuervos y te sacarán los ojos. Raise crows and they'll take out your eyes. Cursed by your own unforgiving, your anger. By pride, by memory. Your father—barely there, if ever—knows this. Staring down at your shoes after he smacked you, heat pulsing across your cheek, you tried not to cry. You saw your shoes untied. Wanted to tie them, strangle one lace with the other, set at least that right. About to crouch when another smack came, and another, so hard, the last one, it slammed you into the wall. You let yourself fall. When you looked again, he was gone. Only stupid fucking bitches cry, was that the lesson? Your father knows. You will betray him. Better, he thinks, to start punishing you now. If he can make you a man, he reasons, the curse might lift. You toss the firework, letting it hover, a little closer to the stars, before it feathers back down into your palm. You toss it as you walk, until you're back, staring at the porch.

You don't know why but you want everyone inside awake. In fear. Brother, cousin, your parents too, if they've come home. Want to burst through the door, stomp up the stairs, and wake them all up. You want them to sit, watching, while *you* sleep. So afraid they dare not ask any questions. Silence them with your power, make them listen, make them see. You take the lighter from your pocket and play with it, grinding the spurs against your thumb until the pad is raw, smooth, not yours anymore. You light the firework's fuse. Take aim at the door. But just before you throw it—an opening.

Brother. His look is one you know well. Pain, shock, all joy driven out by your own menace. And though he isn't crying yet, you know he will. The truth in his face frightens you, disarms you, and in your panic, you hesitate. Hold it too long. It explodes. ¿Qué hiciste, qué hiciste? is all you hear, clutching your arm. A darkening crimson. On your knees, sucking in air. Brother looking for your fingers. The same two you've had in bandages for the last couple of months.

Brother searches, not crying but croaking. Hurried, scrambling, he'll find one.

You won't really be there anymore.

Like a premonition, you'll hear the voice of your father, an anger, a power: ¿Qué hiciste pendejo, qué estabas haciendo? ¿Qué hiciste, pendejo? ¿Qué estabas haciendo? ¿No piensas?

One day, you'll love.

PLANT MOTHER

We're in a heat wave, though ma doesn't know. She's upstairs in the bedroom she never leaves. Two weeks straight over 100 degrees, 115 it'll get today, hottest day ever. While ma lies in bed and dreams, caught in moon time, forgetting there are plants that need water, sunlight. Homesick, our father's explanation. Tired of arguing with him, mine.

We're downstairs and everything's off, out, down: TV, clock, blinds, kitchen, and bathroom. Everything dark. Plants hanging like dead chandeliers from the ceiling, off coffee tables. On any shelf where there are photographs of us, dead plants are there too, watching us, reminding us to be quiet, not to wake her. When she's awake, she cries. When we play a game, we forget. But then we hear her again and are paralyzed. Brother says it's dad's fault. I think it's mostly mine. Her crying, it isn't fair.

Our father is slowly disappearing like a bad ghost. Somewhere else with someone else. One of his sucias. Just like tío and tío and tío and cousin and cousin. Ma says we'll be the same, it's in our blood. Men leave, and ella, por pendeja se queda. I'll be different, I want to say. Want to run over and hug her, make her take it all back. But instead, I say nothing.

She's upstairs, weeping.

As the heat rockets to 115, brother slaps me, out of boredom, and I slap back. We're laughing. Then he pulls my ear, hard, and I stop my laughing, use my knuckles. Our lips glow vermilion in the dark of the house.

But I'm sweating, huffing, and puffing and he's not. He yawns, checks his wrist like he owns a watch. When he sees me looking, he smirks.

I want him dead. I hammer-fist his back, want him to crumble. I scream, say sorry, say sorry! But he just laughs, turns around and pushes me away, makes a stupid face and says, pinche mosquita muerta. I scream louder, start slapping my own face. Fucking chill, stupid, vas a despertar a ma. I hate you, I say; don't care, didn't ask; I scream as loud as I can.

Her door opens, we stop. Every step down the stairs rattles my birdcage chest. She's all headaches and dirty clothes. Her hair a crow's nest, lard thick, dangerous, it could hide the sun. She looks at us and all I can think of is yesterday, her recounting the story of how her own ma died, in Mexico. A spell of anger had twisted her fingers, curled her lips, left eye stuck and half her face drooping, melting off. She couldn't talk, her teeth and her whole body clenched, all she could do was let out exasperated puffs of air, animal groans, as tears streamed down her face. Ma was brother's age.

If we can make her laugh, everything will be okay. With our bleeding mouths we call her plant mother, pointing to all the starving, bleeding pots (plant mother, plant mother, plant mother). We suck in our cheeks, pretend we're dying, wilting, call ourselves her plant children. Her face twists until she's screaming through clenched teeth, SON HER-MA-NOS. ¿NO ENTIENDEN? She grabs our wrists and yanks, drags us to the kitchen.

She opens the drawer and takes out the biggest sharpest knives we've got. Puts one in each of our hands, closing our fists for us. We want to drop them, but she tightens her grip over our hands. Grinds the handles, hard and unforgiving, into the bones in our palms; we try not to wince. With her twig-like arms she pulls us around until we're facing, knife to knife. ¿QUIEREN PELEAR? THIS WHAT YOU WANT? She tells us to kill each other.

She lets go of our clasped hands and stalks us in circles like we're prey. Her stare drills down into the crowns of our heads, MÁTENSE. MÁTENSE. Shriller and shriller. MÁTENSE. We stare at each other's shoes. We hold the knives as far from our bodies as possible. She keeps yelling it, MÁTENSE, over and over. Her voice breaking in the middle of the word, MÁ-TENSE. She looks like, any second, she might fall.

We don't know what to do. We keep standing, waiting. She paces the kitchen area, bites her lip, hugs herself while stealing furtive glances at us like we might actually do it. But we can't. We won't. Entonces, she says. But her voice is back to normal. Slow and steady we bring the knives down, let them clatter to the floor. Ma starts to cry.

If this were our father, we would escape into the heat, throw ourselves like birds into fire. But it's ma. And this whole thing is our fault. We close our eyes and listen to her strained, jagged cries. I'll be your ruda, let it all out, I want to say. But when I picture myself, I'm already wilted. Cold. Alone.

Ma wipes her face, plucks the knives from the floor, drops them back in the drawer. She stares at one of her withered plants. Brother tugs at my shirt, pulls me toward him until we're touching. Ma drifts up the stairs like a wisp.

The door shuts behind her and brother asks, softly, wanna go outside? I shake my head. Wanna watch TV? I shake it again. Wanna take out the army men?

* * *

We look at the slanted light filtering through a bent blind, it gets skinnier and skinnier and after it disappears, I ask, how do you say sorry without saying sorry? He walks over to the old grandfather clock, before it was broken it would make a deep clanging noise, I never liked it, reminded me of Freddy visiting me in one of my dreams. Brother taps on the glass, then leans back and falls over the couch, he reaches for the remote, then stops, sighs. I don't know, he says, they both hate it so much when we say sorry. For different reasons, I want to say, but I don't.

Cautiously, we ascend the stairs after ma and stare at her always-closed door, try to see through the slit beneath it. Watch for shadow movements, though we're too far. We inch our way toward her door, eyes adjusting to the dark, staring at the doorknob in case it starts to turn. In my mind, I can still see her the way she was before, her round cheeks rippling as brother and I pinched and hugged her before she'd haw and raspberry our bellies. We hold our breath and count down, brother taps me three times, I tap him twice back—but then—just as we're about to turn the knob, we hear a key enter the door downstairs and we sprint downstairs like we're escaping murder.

Our father looks at us the way he always does, like we're in a staring contest or playing chicken—games we never win. He spins the key ring on his finger, all his keys jangling. Casually, he sits down on the sofa and turns on the TV. We want to tell him ma's asleep, but instead we take off his boots and grab a bottle from the fridge. He sees us searching through the drawer, the knives we just held, there, we carefully move past them, he whistles us to attention, grins, says, don't need an opener for a twist-off. He puts his hand out, signals us for the beer like he's a martial artist. Drunken master, maybe. He smirks, opens it, and shakes his head, no saben nada.

* * *

We're on our way to our room when he asks where we're going. He says, why don't you stay down here, make less noise for your ma? He asks what ma made for dinner. We tell him there is no dinner, he lets out one of his long-drawn-out sighs. Well, he says, why don't you give her a break and make something? Tanto que la quieren, a ver, ayúdenla. He flips to the news. We go into the kitchen. He turns his head now and then to check on our progress.

We don't want him to laugh at us for needing a chair, so we only use what's in our reach. There are big pots under the oven, no pans. We look at each other and know exactly what's for dinner. Something he doesn't really like, something that ma makes for us, caldo de pollo.

We try to remember what she puts in it: chicken, onion, water, tortillas, salt, and lime. That has to be everything. Brother grabs the pot strongman style and places it on the stove. Mira que sí pueden, y yo pensando, he says, his eyes back on the TV screen, que su mamá los hace inútiles. I dig through the fridge, take out what's necessary.

Our father's watching something else now—screams, metal crashing against metal. In a cabinet I find the canasta, where ma keeps the garlic and onion. Brother slides out the cutting board. I grab a knife but he takes it away, cuts the onion himself. I call him a niñita for tearing up. He puts his pinky in my face, says, I still have mine. Apúrale, he complains.

I tear tortillas apart, remember what ma always says, like paper with nothing but bad news. I let the tortillas fall like confetti over the cutting board, and brother whispers, I'm using *this*, stupid. But I keep them coming and we laugh under the noise of thundering horses, piercing sounds, metal going into flesh and screams cracking the sky open.

* * *

Ma, are you sleeping? The noise doesn't wake her.

Brother cuts the chicken out of the bag, places it whole in the pot. Tosses both halves of the onion in, then my tortilla shreds, burying the chicken under my bad news. He adds water, almost to the brim. He turns the dial on the stove, the burner clicking like a strangled bird. No flame. Our father yells from the couch, keep turning it!

Brother turns it as far as it'll go. We get so close to the blue flame our eyes water. We take out more tortillas and hold them near the flame, pretend we're camping. The water roars, a bone broth foam rises from the pot. We look from it to each other and back again. Brother tries pushing it down with a wooden spoon, but soon the water's spilling over, a hot crashing sound as it pools under the pot.

Our father, never taking his eyes off the screen, shouts, ¡bájale! We do but not before the smoke detector's going off, the sound needling into our ears. The water extinguishes the flame and as the alarm keeps blaring, we start to clean up. He does another of his trademark sighs, gets off the couch, shakes the batteries out of the alarm, and slams them onto the counter. Open the windows, he orders. You think AC is cheap? He grabs another beer, sits down, and we set the kitchen table, sit at the table, chins on the place mats as we wait for the food to cook.

We get up and check if it's ready, stab the chicken and cut off chunks. It's tough and firm but still, we put it into bowls, onto the place mats, one for ma too. We sit down. Should I go tell her? I ask. No, he says, rising from the couch, I put my hands on her bowl, unsure of what to do, he sighs, ya déjalo.

The caldo is a porridge now, with most of the tortillas dissolved. He asks for water, con hielos, he says. We grab our spoons and wait for him to take the first bite. He does. As he chews, he looks for the salt, the lime. He douses his bowl in both, takes another bite, swallows, and puts his spoon down. Grips the table like he might flip it, but then he just gets up, orders us to finish our food, and his and ma's, and the dishes too. He turns the TV off, puts on his work boots. When he's at the door we panic, we want McDonald's, we say, surprising even ourselves. He looks at us pit bull–like, but leaves without saying anything back.

We throw everything out, everything down the garbage disposal. With the disposal on, I say the sound reminds me of pa's voice. Smells like it too, brother says.

We look at the same withered plant ma had been studying before she wisped away upstairs. Do you think if we water them they'll come alive again? I ask. We put the dishes to soak. I don't know, maybe it's too late, brother says. If we could surprise ma with new plants, alive ones, maybe she wouldn't be in her room so much. What if we give them all the water in the world? I ask. He flicks the light on, off, on, off, what's more important? he asks. Water or light? For our father the answer would be simple—light, when the curtains are open, the light bill goes up.

We put our ears to her door. No change. No sound, no light; a stillness and a kind of pressure. We take deep breaths, like we're going underwater. Then we turn the knob, step inside.

We're in darkness, calling out to her in the same hushed voices, like falling leaves, ma, ma, ma—she doesn't answer. Blinded by the dark, we bump into the bed, trace our hands over its soft rim; this is ma's planet, her maceta, that's what brother called it the last time she was like this. Blankets pooled like a rim around the edge of her bed, the fitted sheet damp and gritty like soil.

*   *   *

We call the bed ours, claim it for ourselves, sowing our bodies, like seeds, into her linens, one on either side. She's a big coniferous tree, we're saplings. Still, she doesn't wake. Brother says, let's be her roots, and we shut our eyes, hard. And the wind, I say. And the grass, he replies, and the sun too, each word softer than the last.

When she finally wakes, her voice is that same rustling, ay, ¿y ustedes, qué hacen? She turns to one side, the other, cradles our faces in her palms. ¿Ya no pelean? No, we say. Entonces, ¿qué hacen? We want to be trees, like you. Like me? she says. Yeah, so together we can be a gang, says brother. A forest that beats up the other trees, grow taller than all of them, taller than the clouds. Light, whenever we want. Moonlight too, I say. Her soft laughter like branches, her body shaking gently in the wind of our words.

Ven acá, she says. She rakes us into her, places our hands over her mouth, her voice vibrating into our bodies; immediately we know, this is how the rings of trees are made. Her voice will be in us forever. Los quiero tanto, she says, nunca se les olvide, más que mi vida.

But her voice cracks, and in the dim light her eyes drift away from us. We're useless. We want to hug her but can't. It wouldn't be right. Instead we try poking her, her arms and then her cheeks. She shakes her head until we stop. We tangle our legs with hers, and just the same, she shakes, uncoils us from her. I reach for her hand, wanting to say ma, I love you, but before I can she kisses us both, her heavy eyes closing. She whispers good night, and she returns to sleep, her arms snaking back to cradle her own body. We both say it back, good night.

In the dark, our father wakes us. Stench of chicken and alcohol. He tells us to go to our room. We pretend not to hear. He turns the light on, we shut our eyes harder. Get out, he says. We shelter under the canopy of her arms as he says it again, váyanse. We stay in place. We hear the cold crisp snap of his belt, ready in his hand. Brother says we're trees, we're trees, we're trees. We cling to her as he pulls at our legs. DÉJALOS, ma says, her voice like falling trees.

I wait for more yelling. Hear the bird thrashing in the hollow of her trunk, harder and harder. I hug her tight. The leather twisting in my father's fist.

I just want to fucking sleep, he says. Como tú.
 Ahí está el piso, she lashes back.
 He sighs, one even longer than ususal. Ya quítalos. Me tengo que despertar temprano.
 ¿Pa qué? She laughs a wry dead kind of laughter. ¿Ahora ella te va a pagar también? Qué trabajador me saliste.
 Don't do this. Not in front of them.
 Tengo pinches fotos esta vez. No cambias.
 He drops the belt; it makes a soft thud on the carpet. Esas fotos, he says, lo que hice, it was a mistake.
 Las fotos, ese fue tu pinche mistake.
 He doesn't say anything back.
 Vete si eso es lo que quieres hacer. Pero nosotros, estoy cansada. Nadie los quiere aquí. Ya nos vamos.
 For what? There's nothing back there.
 Familia.
 There's no future there. Míralos, he says, nodding toward us. You know why we're here.
 Y qué tan rápido se te olvidó.
 You know that's not true.
 Entonces, ¿cómo fue? A ver díselos, aquí, a tus hijos.

He stands there awhile, I can't talk to you like this.
¿Cuándo has podido?

I see the air go out of him, hesitation in his eyes. He can't look at ma, or even at us. He takes his keys from his pocket, holds them like they're heavy. He says, I'm not going where you think. But I'm tired, I can't miss tomorrow. He leaves. We listen to his footsteps: down the stairs, the closet opening, he's grabbing his tools, the front door opens, there's a pause, then it closes, we hear the dead bolt lock, he's left.

I feel ma's heart beat softer and softer until it's like a lullaby. No le crean, ma says. Mírenme. Por favor. Cuando me muera, todavía van a tener uno al otro. Nunca se les olvide. Nunca.

Ma, we know, we swear, brother says, shakes her lightly like he wants her to know he means it, we mean it.

She doesn't make any sound, but with my hand, I feel her tears.
We're sorry, ma, we're sorry. We put her hands over our mouths and say, te queremos mucho, we're sorry. She looks down at us and says everything we cannot: ¿De qué, mis niños, de qué? Los quiero más. Más que mi vida. Más que mi vida.

Still, she keeps crying and we hug her, saying, sorry, we're sorry, ma; we say it until we don't know what for anymore: fighting? teasing? our own powerlessness? knowing she loves us better than we can ever love her?

Or is it the knowledge that without us, us boys, she wouldn't be stuck here. She could finally go home.

DEDITOS

Deditos, that word, what your extended family has been calling you at parties for the last six months, that's what you heard, what awoke you. Deditos. That single word ringing out from a dream, a chattering of laughter, and beer bottles clinking. You're sweating. Eight years old now. A little over a year since the incident that took your pinky and half your ring finger. The morning progressing as usual: waking up at five, getting dressed, ma kissing you both goodbye, and then you and brother walking over to Selena's to sleep a little longer before you all catch the bus to school.

Getting off the bus, brother quickly disappears, going into the hallway toward Mrs. Vasquez's class. You're left to walk over the blacktop, toward your own class, the last in a row of portables. That's when it happens. Some older kids laughing. Leering at you with their toothy grins, saying it, Deditos. Hey, Deditos. Immediately you know this is Jamón's doing. A kid in a Big Dogs T-shirt and jean shorts asks, is that your *strong* hand? He hides his two bottom fingers, puckers his lips, and makes as if he's going to pinch you with his claw hand.

How's that freaky little thing feel? his friend in a neon orange beanie asks.

You keep walking but they keep pace and then the kid with the slicked-back hair and gold chain asks, you ever play with yourself with that ugly thing? You close your eyes, pretend it's some retarded girl?

Nah, nah, Big Dog chimes in, he pretends it's a crab.

They're howling.

Leave him alone, it's Lizette, one of brother's friends. You've heard them call her Long Legs. She's in shorts, hoop earrings, her hair teased, dark, and shining. That's Julio's little brother, she says.

They stop. For a second they stare, Gold Chain squints, *Julio* Julio or SoggyPussyPanocha Julio? The bell rings. Your cue, you make a break, run toward class.

During class no one says a thing. Mrs. Herrera asks you to solve the fraction on the board and you do. It's a lesson you've already learned, after finishing your work you go around the room and help others. Everyone smiles. Like usual.

During free time you stare at your hand, mangled, scarred, a smooth little nub where your pinky used to be. You press your finger against the top of it, it feels like an eraser. Does that make it strong, stronger than regular? Nobody in class says a thing, nobody has, not since the first day you came to class, and then only to ask what had happened.

During recess you run around the jungle gym, hanging from the monkey bars until tired, thirsty, and separate from your friends. You go and get a drink from the fountain. After, some older kids approach, a classmate's older brother, with shoulder-length blond hair and JNCO jeans and his friend with bloodshot eyes and a green beanie that hangs just above them, and two others at their side. They wall you off, surround you against the fountain. Green Beanie picks up your hand, and the way he grins it's like he thinks it's a sandwich. Check this shit out. He yanks your hand like it's something that could come off. You stumble, and the two hangers-on laugh.

What do they call you? JNCO asks. Some fucking beaner name, ain't it?

You try to pull away, but Green Beanie holds the back of your elbow, just like fucking science class, he says. We can get a head start on what we'll be doing next year. He pinches what's left of your pinky.

You squirm. Look at this crab boy. You try pulling away again. Try to wiggle and loosen his grip but instead he just pushes you against the wall, rough and cold like little jagged teeth pressing into you.

You ever probe someone with that thing? Green Beanie asks.

Nah, man, JNCO says, that's how he lost 'em. Ain't it? His teeth straight, white, perfect. Probing accident. The two hangers-on start cackling. Maybe we should give him a taste of his own medicine? They all bare their teeth like they're getting ready to eat you. You press your back, your whole body against the wall, want to sink into it. To be taken whole. JNCO takes a step toward you, you try to shout but your voice cracks, breaks into a pathetic whimper, they inch closer, closer, surround you with their shark grins, and you slide down, plant your ass on the ground, and cover your head. You close your eyes.

Leave him the fuck alone. It's Lizette again. The fuck is your problem? She's snapping gum, her shadow covering JNCO's face.

What? JNCO says. This your fucking cousin or something? Yeah, you're all fucking related.

Look at your nose, is your mom or dad the pig? Green Beanie laughs. JNCO pushes him and then everything's quiet.

Hey! a yard duty yells, and Green Beanie freaks out, starts walking away. Hey! the yard duty yells again, and then they all start running. Then it's just you and Lizette. She looks down at you. Her eyes soften, shoulders relax, she looks over at the yard duty, I have to go, she says. Tell Julio...I'm looking for him. You want to thank her, ask her to stay, but before you can, she turns away, hard, fast, disappears around a corner. The yard duty blows her whistle, but they're already gone.

During lunch you stay in the cafeteria. Your friends all leave. Your whole class leaves, is outside playing. You stare at the nubs of your fingers, wish they were as dark as the rest of you, instead of wet little toes soaked in water all day. You wrap a napkin around them. Make a fist. They'd understand you better if you wore a mask, one that covered most of your face, left you with one gleaming eye, and scars peeking at the edges of the mask. If you had a shawl, went around skulking in the dark. Warts over your skin. A hump on your back getting bigger and bigger with each passing day. Had a career goal of stooge, or henchman. Maybe then they'd be scared, maybe then they'd leave you alone.

There's only a few stragglers left by the time the lunch bell rings. You put your hands in your pockets and make your way across the blacktop as quick as you can. You make it to class without a problem.

When the school day ends, you take your time packing up your things. Reshuffle everything in and out of your desk's compartment. When you finally leave the classroom, brother is outside, waiting. His eyes narrow, like his face is a fist and is asking, why? Why did you let it happen? Can you quit being such a fucking bitch? Lizette is with him. Is it true? he asks. You look at her. She gives you a once-over and then she just stares at brother. He looks at her from the corners of his eyes, we gotta go, he says.

She looks like she's getting ready to cry. Can I... she says.

Come on, he tells you. And though you don't want to, you do.

Keep the fuck up, he says. He's walking, but you're having to jog a little to keep up. You want to say sorry, but the way his eyes dart back and forth, you can't. He's not there, he wouldn't listen. Just a smaller version of your father.

He stops. You're both a few yards away from JNCO. Brother puts his hands in his pockets, he's making a fist. You hear the breath coming out of his nose. JNCO smirks when he finally notices you. He looks for your hand, and then his own, is getting ready to say something, but brother doesn't wait, starts walking toward him, doesn't say a word, nothing. He takes his hands out of his pockets and slugs him right across his jaw. JNCO stumbles back and the look on his face, it's like he's looking at Freddy Krueger. He leaves himself open and brother hits him three, four more times. When JNCO is on the ground, brother tries to kick him in the mouth but misses. A yard duty grabs him then. Brother doesn't scream or cry like he does other times he's mad, just has that same look you've seen on your father, like nothing will ever get in; to kill, to destroy, the only objective. The yard duty tries to drag him away, but he sidesteps her, looks JNCO dead in the eyes, says, make fun of my brother again. Come on, bitch boy, do it. Do it. By the time the principal rushes over and drags brother off to the office, there's another yard duty helping JNCO back up. JNCO buries his face into her body, cries. He gets dragged away too. Then everyone's eyes are on you. For a second, you hold your breath, scared they're going to laugh. But instead another bell rings, buses getting ready to leave, people start walking away, you exhale and make your way toward the principal's office.

When ma comes home, she already knows. You half expect her to scream, to be angry with you, with brother. To start game-planning on how you'll tell your father about what happened. Instead, she tells you to go to your room. She needs to talk to brother.

You creak the door open, try to listen, nothing. Doesn't matter, whatever happens will be your fault. You can already imagine father coming home. The screaming match. Father's belt coming off. Ma looking on as brother runs, is caught. The whip of the belt as it finds brother's ass. And then his loud clunking steps coming up the stairs, opening the door, the belt still in his hand. You'll deserve it.

You move away from the door, you get in bed and wait under the covers for the inevitable.

Nothing happens. Father comes home and not even the TV gets

loud. No one mentions a thing during dinner. You wonder if they're waiting for you to ask, if that's what'll set everything off. You don't risk it. Dinner ends.

Hours pass. Ma and your father are in their room, sleeping. And you're still downstairs, watching TV with brother. It's ten, brother turns down the volume. He's sitting on the other end of the couch. He flips through the channels until he gets to the movie channels. *Next Friday* is about to start. You both watch it.

After, brother mutes the sound. You want to ask him about what they talked about when you had to go to your room. Hey, you whisper.

Shhhhh, he replies. Let me watch this. Something hard at the edge of his voice. There's that look, the one you expected earlier, how he usually gets when he's mad. His eyes, gleaming and impenetrable. He's trying not to cry, hard as he can. And without taking his eyes off the screen, he points at you with the remote, then points, like he's aiming a gun, toward the TV. It's porn. This late at night, it's always porn. Hardcore fucking.

BROTHER

It's two summers later and your brother is twelve years old and drowning. You'd been at the edge of the pool, arms and head resting over the lip, looking out into space. You're ten years old, one among a half dozen who've jumped the fence in a whirlwind of screaming, diving headfirst into the black, summer night air cradling heat. You'll remember everything, even what you didn't see: your brother doing backflips, trying for your attention while you're ignoring him, eyes just over the water like a crocodile eyeing a girl taller than you, standing over everything like a lighthouse, her body a midnight glare that invites you while your back faces your brother, and moon and water glimmering on all of you like twilight desert neon body flares, clandestine angels. Tomorrow will be his birthday. Under your bed you've been hiding his present, a car track set with a double loop and crash intersection. Aged seven and up, the only reason he won't ask for it, doesn't want to seem like a pussy. So you saved up all your allowances and bought it anyway because you know how happy it'll make him. You've been fighting and it's your peace offering, you know he'll cry because that's what he does and you'll just smile, hug him. The first time you'll be able to. You've been waiting for an excuse to say sorry, tell him you love him. You haven't been talking and you think the present will fix it, fix everything, make it so it's the last time it ever happens. But just now, you're not thinking of him, you're looking up at the tall girl's body, while behind you, water fills his lungs, giving him chills, the sensation running up his spine, catalyzing a memory: the weekend after your father's promotion, you and brother playing on the beach. Spending all afternoon building a sandcastle before watching the tide rip it away.

Neither talking nor blaming the other, just the crashing of waves, and his arm across your shoulders. It hadn't mattered that it was all gone, because he was there, and you were as well. And even though that's what he remembers, you can't know that and every time you'll think about him at the bottom of the pool, you'll wonder if he still thought you hated him—and as he gasps, a small crop of bubbles rise to the surface, bursting quiet and invisible as he passes out. Later you'll imagine everything you didn't see. His body: curling into itself, fetal in the pool. Thinking of everything that curls: seashells, fists, tornadoes, flowers waiting for the sun. He's all of it and he's coiling like a time-lapse montage in reverse: He's alive, breathing, expressing himself in transition before lungs fill with water, before remembering the sandcastle buried by sea and mind fading in a chill, muscles contracting, turning him inward—coiling. Caught in a negative bloom. You'll be the last from the group to notice. Your back still to the pool, taking occasional furtive glances at the tall girl. And your brother at the deep end and still everything normal. Midnight. Summer heat. Warm breeze kissing your chlorine-charged lips. Hearing water lapping, the omnipresent debris slushing along its surface. The filter echoing a dense and hungry splash like the pool is drinking itself. When water sloshes into the drain, everything else going quiet. That noise, reminding you of the ocean, of swimming alone, of the quiet you get when you place a seashell next to your ear, hear its ocean story told in ancient seashell breath. So, as you hear the water *glug glug glug*, the yells and cannonballs of other kids, the electric night breeze raising bumps on your cool skin, the tall girl will start to circle and poke your shoulder with her long toes, the water from her midnight black hair dripping onto your face. You'll want to kiss her and tell her your secrets, listen to hers. Wanting so much more but you won't know what—not sex, sex you know about—but something else, the sensation you get from all that teen girl TV you watch in secret, and from women's magazines, the ones ma always dog-ears and stacks in the bathroom. Your mind going wild as the tall girl smiles in a way you've only ever seen on TV, beads of water dappling her face, lips—the dark strands of her wet hair clinging to her face and throat, eyes wide, delicate, and sincere. A sightseer, beholding, taking you in. And you're just trying to appreciate it because you don't know when this will ever happen again. More. More, that's all you can think of, as you smile back at her, starting to rise, to pull yourself up out of the pool. And then her eyes shift off you. Everything goes quiet. Panic setting in. You look around for brother. You catch sight of him facedown in the middle of the pool, a crimson glow haloing the crown of his head. He isn't moving. You call his name, swim toward him, wading chlorine and a piss breeze slashing at your pendulum arms. You pull him, drag him along, looking back only long enough to see his face bloated, a blue lavender shock in the moonlight, his body limp and so heavy in your arms, he isn't helping at all. The other kids aren't either, they're frozen, watching you struggle, frantic now, to lay him at the edge of the pool and roll him over. At first you won't want to give him mouth-to-mouth, still thinking he's about to wake up, about to spit up all that water and you don't want any of that on you, you don't want someone else to say that you've kissed a boy even though you've kissed two and just one girl, you remember all the times you've heard brother throw around faggot cocksucker pussy and always let yourself go numb, ignored his aimless hate because you never felt alone around him. You don't want him to look at you and think that you saved him with your faggot lips. You know he'll come around but don't want him to feel he owes you that. You turn him on his side and his skull makes a wet slapping thud against the pavement. You hit his back, slamming it with your palm, your fist, hammering into him, harder and harder. You say his name and cry bleach-evaporating tears, everyone around and their feet pointing toward you both and you cry help and they say do something do something and before giving him mouth-to-mouth you blow the boogers out of your nose. You fumble trying not to make it look like a kiss, you blow and he sounds hollow and ancient, his lips swollen and lukewarm and you keep blowing, willing him to cough up all that water you all peed in. You put your arms around him like a fucking bitch and you keep begging him, wake up wake up wake up and you hear, oh shit shit shit what the fuck are we gonna do, and you want to tell them to shut the fuck up and help and you see the tall girl, clothes in her hand running away, jumping the fence—and how will you explain this? Ma will retreat into her room and will never see the sun again and your father will wake up and finally finish the job, better to snuff you out than have to live with such a fucking disappointment. The sirens will send the other kids running as the firemen arrive. You'll stay with him, your brother, his body translucent, steaming—evaporating. Hugging him won't stop it. You'll whisper in his ear, you're pretending, right? He's just pretending. And I'm sorry, I'm sorry about everything, please get up, please please get up get up get up and then you're not talking to him but to the firemen, save him save him save him. They try to move you out of the way, but you won't budge. All the way to the hospital you hold on to him, his hand, his foot, a string of his hair as it hangs from the gurney they wheel him out on. The sirens sounding muffled and forlorn from inside the fire truck like you're hearing them through water. And everything they say and do to brother's body, it's like they're also underwater. At the ER, ghosts in white coats will wheel him away. When your parents arrive, they won't scream or hug you either. Your brother will sleep, he'll sleep for three days before waking. And when you finally see him, you don't tell him how you've missed him, don't hug him either. You remember how you kissed his cheek in front of everyone, and you're too worried, afraid of what he might think if he knew. On the car ride home, neither of you says a word. Ants crawl over you both with abandon and when you look over at your brother his eyes staring straight ahead it'll feel like the pool is still there, between you. You'll never give it to him. His present. It'll stay crammed, hidden under your bed.

And for you, the next twelve years will pass without the kiss of another person. And all that time, you'll carry that guilt, that hollow feeling stemming from the knowledge of knowing the kind of burden you are, you'll haunt bars house parties motels—midnight fog—drinking yourself senseless, lying down in strange beds, rising again at dawn, walking alone in the quiet. And not remembering waking up, it'll be like you never did. Sleepwalking, you'll dream all different things. Of him, your brother, drowning. How much easier would it have all been to solve, you'll wonder, when you were boys? But you'll be men. As a man, you'll be alone, walking in the early morning when someone says it. Again. Because still, people think they can hurt you with a word like faggot. But for you there is a word that has always hurt more. Brother.

CANNON

2009, Stockton's deadliest year, a few months before tenth grade. Our summer school English teacher is telling us we're going to earn the highest murder rate in the nation. Whoop-de-fucking-do. She says she doesn't drive past Harding no more. Where she think we live? Now she's talking about Shakespeare. I'm sure Shakespeare and his boys were hard. *I bite my thumb at thee.* I piss and shit on thee, how about that? I need to get out of here. *We* (me and Bighead) need to get out of here. We do. We ditch, blaze in the car, and drive on the good side of Harding until we see a cannon, alone in the empty lot of an abandoned store. The lot looks fucking chill too.

It's an old beat-up cannon, about as tall as I am. The rust gives it a glamour like it belongs in a museum. One of the wheels is busted, makes it lean to one side. Some would call that character. It could be faultless with the right stupid eyes. Not mine. It's heavy as shit too. It doesn't budge when we try to tip it over. How'd it get here, in front of the store, standing guard?

It looks at us with a dead, uncompromising stare. Respect.

Me and Bighead are on the ground, getting our hands dirty, examining the old iron fucker for value. You never know with old shit, old can be tricky like that; most of the time, though, rust just means old and useless as shit. Guess that's why it's out here, they tried to sell it, but Stockton wasn't buying. Still, I have to check, do my due diligence: rusted, old, heavy, and out of place. But maybe it isn't. It could have belonged here in a different era, no concrete, no empty stores or abandoned lots; instead: tall grass, crickets, a creak, and some enemy to point the fucking thing at. But here, the enemy is everywhere, and in everything. What the fuck could this thing do, even if it were in working order? On the underside of the barrel there are grooves, ridges, and dents—rust has made the metal brittle. Any value this has revolves around a reverence for a particular past, and a hallucination that nothing of equal value can exist now. White people would go crazy for this. They should've tried to sell this on Miracle Mile or at Lincoln Center.

If I did have a cannonball, how long would it take to load, aim, and fire? How much longer would a war have to last? Screams, dismembered limbs, cannonballs, dirt exploding like fireworks, grown men hugging their knees crying mommy, mommy, mommy. How many letters would carry the messages of ghosts by the time they got delivered? Goddamn, this is good smoke.

What would we hit with it? Bighead asks from the other side of the cannon.

I don't know, that billboard there. I point across the street, a lawyer with big fake white teeth grins his *American Psycho* grin: YOU GET INJURED, I GET PAID. None of this said aloud, the conversation happening telepathically, with our eyes, our nods, our laughter.

Bighead points at the cannon as if to say, you think this thing would really fire?

Even if it did, my eyes going big, you think it'd be easy to hit that fucking thing?

In the arch of my eyebrows, there's a reason why it's rusted over, it isn't just 'cause it's old. Though there is that too.

I can't believe we haven't learned about this thing, look at it, goddamn useless. Bighead runs his hand over it like it's a cat.

Oh, we will, I knock on it, there'll be chapters dedicated to it, just watch.

Me and Bighead stay laughing on the ground, our ribs hurting so much we can't stop kicking and turning, making dirty concrete angels on the sidewalk.

I hear shoes shuffling and don't even bother to turn. The fuck you guys doing down there? Whiteboy asks between mouthfuls of Hot Cheetos. Paisa and Cuco also there on his left.

Looking for your MOM, Bighead says.

Shit ain't even funny no more, Whiteboy says, staring at the Cheeto dust staining his fingers.

They laughing.

They laughing at you. Both of you, he says as he plays with the Swisher tucked behind his ear. Y'all need to get off the ground, shit is embarrassing.

Y'all hear who got shot? Cuco asks, taking the Hot Cheetos from Whiteboy.

Yeah, Bighead says, that's why I don't be out by Victory.

It ain't like that's the only place people getting clapped.

Cuco keeps munching Cheetos. *BANG BANG BANG.* We look around. An old shitty truck drives by. Cuco grabs another Cheeto, says, I thought y'all had summer school anyway.

Apparently they said fuck it too.

We sit in front of the cannon, keep two blunts in rotation along with the chips, the Gatorades. Cars pass by. Across the street I see the homeless Walking Man who always posts up in front of the 7-Eleven, when he isn't walking across town anyway. He makes eye contact with me, mimes a blow job, smiles. Crazy fuck. He's lucky he's been around since my parents got here, they gave him a dollar once, and after, they won fifty on a scratcher. It'd kill my high to yell at him, might then have to do something more. Gross-ass motherfucker.

Was that billboard always blue?

Cuco waterfalls a red Gatorade—beautiful in the sunlight—then passes it to Whiteboy. Paisa turns toward the cannon and asks, what the fuck is this shit even? He kicks it. The sound the barrel of the cannon makes is dry, metallic, like an old church bell going off. A warning rattling up my spine. I'm a newborn being shook and I'm shaking all the way up, teeth chattering as I stand and try to move toward the cannon.

Look at this fucker's eyes. Cuco waves his hand in front of me, how many fingers I got up?

I slap away his dirty Cheetos hand before slumping onto the cannon.

Ay, is this fucker trying to sleep?

I think he's trying to fuck it.

Cuco plays the Stockton version of David Attenborough—I hear him whispering as I hold the cannon tighter and tighter:

What we have here is the savage Mexican. If you take a look at its shoes, you'll see that they ain't got no creases, their lack meant to denote sexual prowess to the hood rat, though with this specimen the trick has been snuffed, as this one's never gotten any bitches.

They snicker and bump into each other like they're ready to slap each other in the back or howl or pick lice off each other. *Socialized grooming.* I hear David Attenborough in my head, haunting me with those words. The homies are socializing. Grooming each other. The fuck is going on? They encircle me and I grow dizzy, lightheaded. I try batting them away but it's no use, they're too far away. They spin and laugh and I let them. I have to keep holding on to the cannon or I'll fall. If I fall, I might keep falling. Back into the past, where I'll be stuck, trying to get the cannon to work, to load and light it in the dark, under the canopy, surrounded by the enemy. The fucking enemy! Time is making its move on me. What can I do? How can I defend myself?

I shut my eyes tight but I still hear the fuckers shuffling around. Someone pokes me with a stick as they talk in hushed voices. Cuco going on with his act:

If we move to the front of the beast, we see that the Mexican creature (of the fuck boy variety) prefers to get lined up to signal to the other males of his species he's one of them, and their tricks to steal away his hood rats won't work so easily. Though perhaps with his shit fade that should've been cleaned up a week ago, that's exactly what happened.

I feel the stick scratching the outline of my hair. Fuck off, I whisper.

The lined-up Mexican (of the fuck boy variety) is more prone to ask to borrow money, in order to sustain his fuck boy predilections. They are also likely candidates for dropping out of high school. Ahh-ahh, don't get too close now, Whiteboy. See those canines? They can and have ripped a man's elote clean off.

I'm too high to get up off the cannon. They talk, howl, and all I hear is Paisa's shuffling feet taunting me. His lazy-ass way of walking, mirroring their laughter. Like his stupid-ass shoes are laughing at me too. That scraping laughing noise scratches and scratches its way into my ear, Paisa shuffles by, I scream, FUCK YOU, SHOES! I know what the fucker is doing, following Cuco around, playing the cameraman, moving in and around (scrape, scrape, scrape), crouching (scrape), angling to get the best shots of Cuco, of me, of all of us (scrape scrape), fucking side-eyeing creep.

Now, this homeboy prefers the clean-cut look—again someone is at it with the fucking stick, poking me with it—but make no mistake, the slicked-back Mexican and the lined-up Mexican are one and the same. Hide your sisters from these types, they are known for attracting the sluttiest hood rats in the vicinity. They are dogs, yes sir, the Mexican is a dog; and like a dog, it'll find any hole to stick it in. It is believed half of all high school pregnancies within the next decade will be caused by the Mexican dog. Oh yeah. Even this one's elote, I can assure you, will get most dirty.

If only I were less high I could slap them away. Instead, they're just laughing while the sun cooks my fucking neck. And the cannon's so cold on my chest it's starting to burn. Still, I have to keep holding on to it. It's keeping me from falling. And I can't fall. If I do, I know I won't ever recover. I let them go on with their stupid fucking game. I hug the cannon harder and keep my eyes closed.

WHO THE FUCK DID THAT?! WHO THE FUCK JUST SLAPPED ME?! I rub my head and pace the lot. They're laughing like fucking hyenas. Where the fuck are my keys? Fuck all y'all.

Chill, dude, chill, no one fucking slapped you, bruh bruh.

The fuck you mean no one slapped me? I felt it.

Bighead just slapped the cannon to wake your ass up, that's it.

HE-HE-HE, I hear Bighead laughing.

You fucking traitor, I say.

Open your eyes, dude, Bighead's over there. Everyone just keeps laughing.

Yeah, over here, he says, his shit-eating grin coming into view, slowly, from behind a cloud of smoke.

I spit on the ground, stretch, slap my face a couple times while pacing the lot, fucking pieces of shit.

We're peering into the barrel as Bighead asks, how much WD-40 and OxiClean would it take to fix this shit? It's too dark to see all the way down, but we try. A draft hits us. I put my ear as close to the opening as I can, the ocean, that's what's down in the pit of the cannon, roaring and never ending.

Paisa then has a turn, nah, man, that's my mom in there, she's vacuuming. Always fucking vacuuming.

We spark up again.

You know, there's something about this cannon—the color, the size, the way it doesn't belong, like not just in this place but this time—makes me want to take it with me. Really, I think I just want to give it to someone, someone who'll know how to use it.

Look at it, can y'all hear it? I still hear it.

Roaring and never ending. The sound coming from all the way down the barrel, all the way down its mouth. Maybe it isn't the ocean I'm hearing. Maybe that's what it sounds like when it's loaded with a cannonball. A metal ball rolling and rolling all the way down the chamber, preparing itself to be shot. Probably sounds something like that. That's the rolling sound I hear, a metal whirl descending and descending until—

Did y'all hear that? That clunk?

The cannon's loaded. Time will slow and there'll be a silence right before. The whole universe knows what's about to happen. Everything about to be divided: before, and then after the cannon is shot. The whole city will hear the cannon firing and no one will know if it's pointed at them.

I wanna take it; I can fix it. I'll find some way to shoot it. I wanna know how this fucker sounds. Want this whole city to hear it. That everlasting boom across the sky. The first sound a newborn baby hears. Educated. Without ever having read Shakespeare. Bulletproof.

We cross the street to the hardware store, Orchards, for some rope. They're having a fire sale, which only makes it easier for Paisa and Cuco to keep lookout while we shove a bunch of rope down Big-head's pants. He shuffles out the automatic doors and back across the street. I move the car into position, the trunk facing the cannon's mouth.

I check the rearview. They're moving like monkeys back and forth from the car to the cannon. Throwing different ends of the rope to each other, tying parts of it to the cannon and others to the back of my car. While they do all of this they're howling, scratching their heads, waterfalling Gatorade. It's a jungle out there. The language of animals. I can't understand. BANG BANG BANG one of them slaps the hood of my car. I fucking launch it. I get a good ten feet, then suddenly I feel a tug, like a tooth being pulled. My stomach drops. I park it. I take the keys out of the ignition and throw them onto the passenger seat. I'm sweating. I check my mouth, my teeth are still there.

The same can't be said about the back end of my car. The cannon hasn't moved a fucking inch. I kick the fucker, stupid useless old fucking thing.

Now are we sure? Cuco asks, he's not talking about his car.

Look at the bumper. Paisa carries it with both his arms extended, lays it at the foot of the cannon like it's an offering.

I knew it was heavy but this hadn't been part of the equation. I agreed to let them tie it to the car 'cause I imagined the cannon getting dragged along, a huge shower of sparks all down Hammer, turning onto West Lane and trying for downtown. Maybe even the cops giving chase while I did doughnuts, using the cannon like a flail to keep them at bay. Channel 3 News, aerial shots, an errant spark lighting the cannon, and it going off, a miracle. I was ready for that. Instead, my shit car is falling apart. The cannon remains. Rusted but intact. I peer down the barrel, scream as hard as I can. The noise bounces around, shoots out and back into me, knocks my ass down.

What you think we should do with the thing?

I don't know, not try to move it.

It's probably not even that accurate. Like if you did shoot it. A gun works way better, you know?

Yeah, but there's still artillery, they still use shit like this.

Except better, can reach further, do more damage and all that.

The thing is, Bighead wags his finger at the cannon, it's obsolete. But worse than that, it's fucking boring. He hawks a loogie down the barrel, it splatters, echoes. I do the same. Whiteboy kicks it, spits on it, calls it dumbfuck, useless, and mother. Paisa unzips his pants, pisses on it. Cuco's next but we'll all do it. We piss our Gatorade and Hot Cheetos piss all over it. The whole thing smelling like a Mickey's tall can or Wilson Way with its constant stench from everyone there selling their ass.

It's seven and still bright as fuck but that'll start to turn. Fewer cars driving by. Across the street I see the homeless Walking Man on the ground. He's grimacing, trying to say something, we're too far to hear. He grabs his chest. One of us says, oh shit, think he's having a heart attack. He kicks slowly and turns onto his side.

I can see it already, the chalk outline forming around him. I saw them do it once, draw an outline. Not with chalk but with these little red flags. I was hiding in some bushes. I was six. The legs never moved. And now, looking at my clothes, the cracks in the ground, the five of us sitting here in this empty lot, it's all a kind of fucking outline. It's like a bad trip, I can feel myself spiraling even if I can't help it none, that dude was fine and now he's—

Hey, Bighead says, you guys ever see that cartoon where this dude's heart comes out of his body? In a rage, the heart starts beating the shit out of him. Paramedics come and take him away. Now, that, that was a fucking heart attack.

We keep watching as the Walking Man kicks, grimaces. Two people walk by, one with green hair, leather jacket, the other with facial piercings, they look at him for a second. They then continue into the 7-Eleven.

What did the heart do after that? Whiteboy asks as he hands Bighead the blunt.

I don't remember, I think it just runs down the street, disappears. In a rage. Probably went to beat the shit out of someone else.

I feels it, Cuco says.

A few more people walk by, they all go into the store. Then an old lady comes by, crouches over and talks to him. Her cell phone's out.

I try passing the blunt to Paisa, but he isn't there anymore. He's behind the cannon, aiming down the sights, his nose wrinkled in concentration. I jump back a little. I'm staring but he's not registering me at all. I'm not the target. It's the Walking Man. The cannon's old and fucking useless, but the way Paisa stares, there has to be a chance. I push Whiteboy out the way, myself too. I wait. Paisa inhales and this faint heat in my hand grows. The longer I stare, the more intense it grows. Like Paisa's focus, I can feel it sharpening. His eyes narrow and it's like a hot blade pierces my hand. I flinch, look down, see the roach sizzling my fingers, and let go. Paisa whispers, *bang*.

The sun is finally setting as the paramedics arrive. We're out of blunts, Cheetos, and Gatorade.

You know, when we were over there? Cuco says, pointing to the 7-Eleven, that dude was straight geesing on them. Fucking saying Paisa was his wife, that he needed to go back to the barn where he keeps all his other cows, wives.

What'd you say back? I ask.

Nothing, he just took it, Whiteboy says.

Yeah, you did too. Paisa claps and wipes his hands. He pretends to aim a camera at the scene, they roll him into the ambulance. What was I supposed to do anyway?

Not nothing, Cuco says.

The ambulance slowly merges into traffic. No sirens.

Y'all ever hear about his cows? The ambulance gets smaller and smaller. Paisa continues, sometimes when people fucked with him or played along with his crazy-ass stories, he'd throw in some aliens. That, or the person he'd be talking to would end up as one of his cows or sheep or whatever the fuck. His name's John. That's what the cashier called him anyway. I'll kick your motherfucking ass out, *John*. I don't play those games, *John*. Shit like that. Anyway, sometimes he'd say he lived out on some field, sometimes alone or with his wives, and he was always whipping them.

He was always smiling too, I say. He wasn't usually a creep, just a fucking weirdo. This one time I was with ma, we were driving to Food 4 Less and I saw the dude bite it. Just fell over on the sidewalk. No one was around and my mom was like, OH MY GOD, so I pulled over and helped him up. He was bleeding a little bit from his hands, you know, from stopping the fall. It was the first time I saw him look scared. I remember my mom talking to him, making sure he was all right, asking him if there was anywhere we could take him.

All I could think about were how his hands, how his arms felt when I helped him up. All leathery and loose. Not like mine. I never met my grandparents, I mean I met one of them once, but that was weird. Anyway, I didn't know if that was just what old skin felt like, but helping him up, there was something sturdy there too. It made me think cow, like a cow's hide. I almost started laughing. The look he gave me, it was like he knew what I was thinking, 'cause then he started to moo. *MOO, MOO, MOO.* He told ma he was fine. He started up again, mooing as he walked past us. We just got back in the car and left. His name's John. His name was John?

Huh?

Hmmm?

What the fuck are you muttering over there? Paisa asks. You fucking psycho.

Really? Me? I ask. Didn't you get caught playing piss 'n' slide in sixth grade?

Bighead stands up, points at all our trash, looks down at his own empty hands, yeah, it's getting late anyway.

Yeah, yeah. I'm hearing crickets.

You know what would be cool right now, though? Whiteboy says.

What?

If we turned into cannons.

I hold my breath. No one makes a move. Just our eyes, shifting. Whiteboy, Bighead, Paisa, Cuco, the way the moon hits them, I can't tell if they're turning. Am I? Something, though, is becoming possible. Blunts, cows, broken forgotten cannons: ghetto magic's in the air. What would turn first? Legs or head? Would we scream? Would we cannon? Who would be more afraid? The ones who turn or the ones who don't? Which would I rather be? Do I really want to be a cannon? The Walking Man, John, he was a cannon. Look at this fucking thing: old, abandoned, useless, reeking of our piss. Fuck that, I say. Paisa and Bighead say it too. We counter that ghetto magic with our own. We want to be guns. Guns that work and no one fucks with. Paisa stands tall, picks up his feet—there'll be no more scraping. We start heading back past Harding, the sidewalks will narrow and then completely disappear. With each step, our magic will grow. Growing colder, harder, more steel than flesh. Everything a target. Our eyes nothing more than iron sights, aiming and claiming everything around us. Our chests out, our fists clenched, bodies cocked and ready to go. Fuck whoever doubts it, we'll make it home. We'll make it home.

MÍRAME

I open the door, it's dark, no one's home. Blood still leaking, not a lot, but I hear the drip, a tapping against my shoe. No more adrenaline. Chest on fire. Knuckles like they've been through a grinder. Should've stayed in the car. My whole body's been through a grinder. Need glasses. Head fucking ringing. I turn the bathroom light on, hair matted, a rat's nest. Hunchback meets the Elephant Man. I wet a towel. Cold and heavy, it soothes my aching fingers. I strain but manage to reach the top of my head, place the towel slow, gentle against my skull. Feel like I ran a marathon. *They* ran a marathon, all fucking over me. My eyes water. I throw the towel on the ground, grab another. Strain. Just as bloody and useless as the last one. Where the fuck are all the towels?

The front door opens. I hold my breath. The keys drop into the bowl. He doesn't keep them in his pocket anymore. The heavy thud of steel-toe boots. I exhale. The steps get closer. Lights are being switched on. I hear his coat laid over the sofa. The bathroom door opens. My father smiles. His eyes are glassy, he doesn't say a thing, just puts his finger up, looks around like he's had an idea. He leaves. Comes back with more towels, a first aid kit. A ver, agáchate, he says. After the third towel, a splash of peroxide, a balm, I'm clean. Clean but bruised, swollen. Looking in the mirror, I start to feel a pressure. Something wrong with my face. Something unrecognizable. I'm broken, not just my body, I'm diseased. Alone. The light flickers. He rinses the towel, wrings it out, takes his time laying it on my head, like he's playing Jenga. He takes my hand, I wince, makes me hold the towel in place as he digs through the first aid kit.

I knew they weren't gonna pay, and still, what the fuck is wrong with me? Why the fuck did I get out of the car? He takes out some gauze, scissors, tape, the light flickers again. Gonna have to replace that, he says. Or else, who will? Why couldn't I just leave after they saw me? Instead, became a provider of hood therapy. Now there's all this bruising on my left side, can only see out the one eye. And the longer I look at myself, the more wrong I feel, haven't felt like this since the mushrooms. Brother said, just don't look at yourself in the mirror, trust me. Never doing mushrooms again.

Our eyes meet in the mirror, he smiles, takes the towel off and says, deja ver si tienes piojos. He laughs, stinks up the bathroom with his alcoholic breath. Through the mirror I see him look at the scars. Must see the old ones too. Maybe it looks like the moon up there. He traces the scars, one by one. Not playing Jenga anymore. His smile fades. I lean forward, steady myself, my eyes fixed on his. Quédate quieto, he says. I want his eyes to meet mine. Want to say, remember? Remember. He does it quick, covering the top of my head in gauze, taping it all down under my chin, then cutting it with the scissors. He lets out one of his long-drawn-out sighs, stumbles, lays his hand against the wall, his knuckles stained with my blood. He starts to put it all back into the first aid kit, then the light flickers, and he sets everything down. Esa pinche luz, he says. He turns, gets ready to leave, and with one foot out the door, hands me a towel and says, a ver si no te dejas. I didn't. He leaves. I won't. Never again. I close the door with my foot. In the mirror, I meet my own eyes. The light keeps flickering, and the water from the towel drips into the sink. Fuck shrooms. The bulb finally dies. In the dark, I make out my own outline. I'm still here. I'm still here.

CRÍA CUERVOS

You'll want to call the police, but you'll settle for CPS. You'll wait until no one else is home, searching the number online, then stretching, taking deep breaths, and pacing across the living room like you're preparing to jump from a burning building. When you punch in the numbers and get closer to getting rid of him, your chest will tighten, on hold you'll have a coughing fit, and when you finally get through, you'll answer everything in a falsetto whisper. And between every answer, your mind will slingshot: What the fuck were you thinking? and Hang up, just hang up, hang up right now. But you won't, and instead, you'll keep answering. Then waiting. You'll wait an hour, a day, a night, a week. Regretting the whole thing. Waking at all hours of the night and thinking that someone's knocking on the windows, the doors, you'll picture someone holding a clipboard and you'll have to get up off the bed in order not to vomit. And then, one afternoon, there'll be a knock at the front door and you'll know, your stomach twisting into knots. You'll want to run. Stop this somehow. Instead, you'll creak the bedroom door open and stare out at the back of your father's tank top as he blurs across the living room, from the old-ass TV to the sofa covered in multicolored sheets. He'll answer the door, ¿Qué, qué quieren? Sí... pero ¿por qué?... No, no entiendo. It'll feel like someone's taking an aluminum bat to your stomach. You'll keep listening as sweat forms on the bridge of your nose.

The woman's voice will be stiff, sir, that's why they are here. You must let us in. Solo estamos aquí para ayudar. Tenemos derecho de entrar. I can provide documentation. Her tongue will break Spanish, turning every *s* into *th* until you're wincing, not understanding how you thought someone like her could be part of the solution.

Your father will answer in his own busted-up English, yes, sure.

The woman's tone will change once she's inside, sounding like it's her home when she smiles and asks your father about his wife. ¿Tu esposa?

Brother will go out into the living room too and you'll try to suppress your nausea, cotton mouth, throat closing 'cause you're a fucking bitch for not being out there as well, instead hiding behind the bedroom door. Isn't this your home? Your family? You'll be relieved to hear brother answer, she's at Delta. She takes night classes.

A rush of footsteps overtakes the hardwood floor. The invaders: a woman and two men. Your father stands tall, responding to everything in one-word answers. While your brother leans against the sofa, eyes drifting toward the window, and then to you. You'll backpedal, only to go back to the cracked door and try to close it. When you finally manage, you'll hear them walking toward the kitchen on the other side of the living room. And in all that noise, you'll wonder, when was the last time this many people were in the house? You'll remember last year's Christmas party—uncle's hand, your knee, his calluses felt through your jeans as he squeezed, making you kick the air involuntarily, while six of your cousins huddled around the computer, on some chat room, tried to think of the nastiest shit to say back to hornyforyou209 even though it was probably just a guy—until you hear the woman using your name, asking for you.

As quiet as you can, you'll go to your bed. You'll pick up the book you've been reading, trying to look busy, expecting the door to open—it won't. Not yet. You'll read the same page over and over, twenty times, and still, you won't know what's going on. Had Ender failed? Killed someone again? You'll read and reread, then ask those inane questions, over and over.

At your door, a knock then a muffled voice, the woman asking if she can come in—asking like that, like you have a choice. You'll grow angry. She really thinks people fucking knock in this house? You'll place the book under your pillow before answering, yes, sure.

You'll judge her based on how she looks: hair big, blond, curly, straight out of the eighties, and her dark purple lipstick making her look like the kind of prostitute you'd find on Wilson Way or, worse, like some vocalist for a hair metal band that never made it. She'll have thick-ass glasses, just like your father's, and this is what you'll hate most about her appearance.

Hell-o, my name's Camille, but everyone calls me Cammie. She'll stick out her hand, her bracelets will jingle and you'll pretend not to notice, instead keeping your eyes on the frayed edges of your jeans. And, well, I'm here because of a call we received. She'll pull back her hand and lean in. There're some questions I need to ask. She'll pause. For one, were you the one that called?

This will be your lifeline and you'll cling to it as such, answering quick and harsh, no.

It's okay, nothing wrong with calling. That's why my helpers are out there. No one's gonna hurt you for making a call.

Fuck does she fucking know? But I didn't, you'll say.

Chree-stee-an—she'll pronounce it like those robocalls you get from school announcing all the periods you missed—can you look me in the eyes and tell me?

You'll grit your teeth, I didn't call.

Okay. Okay. She'll put her hands up. Sometimes these things happen. Well, since I'm here... She'll smile and you'll fucking hate her for it.

She'll ask a series of questions about brother and ma, all with that same smile and soft tone. You won't know why she keeps pretending as if this isn't just a job. You'll turn away from her, and answer every question asked with, don't know.

She'll walk around to the foot of the bed, trying to force eye contact, she'll hunch over, that's a funny shirt, she'll say. Pointing at the nuns holding guns on your bootleg Rage T-shirt.

Yeah, guess so. You'll shrug your shoulders and quickly swipe at the sweat on your nose.

She'll look around your room. There won't be much. Bare walls, a CRT TV with a jammed-in Power button on a dresser and a lawn chair leaning in the corner. She'll peek through the blinds then wipe her fingers on her magenta pantsuit. This is a nice room, bigger than mine growing up. She'll chuckle. Do you like it here?

Yeah.

More of the quiet type, huh. That's okay. She'll soften her voice even more, do you have friends, at school?

Yeah.

Is there a reason you've missed at least a day of school every week this year? And it seems your sophomore year you did that too.

Sweat will form on the back of your neck, across your hairline, everywhere under your shirt.

It's okay. Okay. There're no wrong answers. She'll eye the lawn chair in the corner of the room, will claw at it with her long purple nails, laying it out in front of you and sitting her nasty ass on it like you're friends. Your brother tells me that your mom takes English classes at Delta. That's really wonderful. You must be so proud of her.

This is when you'll be certain, no stupid fat white fucking bitch is ever going to help. Love isn't contingent on their fucking education.

She'll ask another question.

It's as if you didn't know about Steven, the way everyone knows his dad puts cigarettes out on him, and yet Steven's in a group home. His mom and brother still living with the dad. And Sarah, always with that dead far-off stare when anyone asks about her foster parents. What the fuck were you ever even expecting? Besides, he fucking pays for everything.

So I'm just gonna say it, okay? Does your dad, has he ever inappropriately—

You're sixteen but you know, as you stand, looking down on her, they'd try you as an adult for the way you'd beat her within an inch of her miserable fucking life. Leave.

She'll have a flash of shock across her makeup-caked face, then will hide it almost as quick as it showed, this will shame you; she'll carefully, slowly, stand up. She'll back out, and will close the door behind her.

A silent dinner. No one looking at each other.

You'll wash the dishes with brother. He'll go to his girlfriend's house after, and for the first time in your life you'll wish for more dishes. You won't say anything. No dishes left. Your father will thank brother for washing the dishes. You'll go to your room, waiting on your bed. You'll listen as brother drives away. Rereading those same fucking pages, over and over.

Your door will open and your father will demand with eyes bulging, ¿qué dijiste?

I didn't say anything, you'll say.

Pinche mariquita. No sabes valorar. Hijo de tu puta—

Man, I didn't do anything.

Tenías que ser, 'eda. Trabajo todo el pinche día. With almost half a smile he'll say, cría cuervos y te sacarán los ojos. He'll take off his belt.

I didn't do anything. You'll get up off the bed, fists clenched inside your pockets.

¡Quítate la pinche playera! he'll yell.

You'll take off your shirt. Then wait. He'll close your door. You'll wait.

The next day he'll wake you up before leaving for work. He'll tell you that he better not hear that you didn't go to all your classes. He'll throw your blanket on the floor and slam your door behind him. His truck will back out, the hum of the engine will trail off. Fucking asshole, you'll mutter.

By the time lunch rolls around, you'll think about getting in your car and fucking off. Instead, you'll head to where your dumbass friends post up. The three of them will be leaning against the shit-brown portables, kicking the walls of a classroom, some teacher yelling hard enough to rattle the window. Your friends will all laugh, and inside, the students will too. Gold particulates will gleam in the sunlight with the thrumming of the wall. Asbestos probably. You'll think about those class action lawsuit commercials, the ones asking, whether you or a loved one... and as you walk up on them, you'll know every one of you is in the process of contracting mesothelioma. *Cha-ching.*

Ernesto will be the first to notice you and greet you with a head nod. He'll be wearing a long-ass white tee and looking like a prettier version of Rob Zombie but with way tanner skin. At this thought of yours, you'll cringe. He'll ask, what's gucci? Where you been?

Chilling, what's up? you'll say.

Foo, you missed it, Kari's little sister got—

Which one?

Whiteboy will come in with a handshake, saying, Selena foo, the hot one. She got into a fight and her titties popped out and everything, they were just bouncing like this, and dude I swear the way the clouds parted and the light was hitting them, it was like God approved.

Cool, you'll say as you put one foot up against the wall and look out into the lunch crowd, everyone looking so happy it'll start to annoy you.

Pinche puto, Roberto with the fat rolls on the back of his head will say, don't you wanna know what they look like?

How they look? you'll say.

They were big, Ernesto will say, round, even had nipples in the middle of 'em.

Fucking bitch asses be playing too much, Roberto will say.

Whiteboy will say Berto's eyes got cartoon big, and they agreed, God is real. But also, we should all thank the other chick for making fun of her ear.

Wait, you'll say. Wasn't she wearing a bra?

Nah, man, Roberto will give you a stupid-ass look and start shaking his head. Pinche marica. What a bitch, for real, though.

Dude, Whiteboy will say, she's a feminist. Feminists like their tits to hit their knees by the time they're thirty. Free the nipple? Shit's gonna look like two sad pizza slices, one lone pepperoni hanging off each tip. He'll be looking toward the sky, enjoy 'em while she got 'em. He'll nod the same way he does when he's high, as if he just figured out the secret to the universe.

Then he'll start pointing toward his crotch, miming like he's unzipping his pants, every feminist could free 'em right here, I'd put my dick between 'em and fuck the shit out of all of 'em. You'll start to wonder what it would be like to hang with Whiteboy alone, whether he's capable of talking about anything besides dicks and pussies. You'll smile at the thought until you notice Ernesto side-eyeing you.

Bruh, Roberto will say, what the fuck this dude talking about? He won't be able to stop laughing and you won't either. He'll point at Whiteboy like a stranger, he weird as fuck.

Man, don't act like you haven't seen that shit on the hub. You know you'd all fuck 'em. Y'all just hating.

Man, shut the fuck up, Ernesto will say. Them titties too big for your little-ass dick.

Bunch of hating-ass motherfuckers... I'ma get some Cheetos.

You'll notice two random fucks holding hands, jogging toward the cafeteria. Pizza day. You'll remember doing the same for the first few days of middle school until you told brother and he said to stop, unless you liked being a virgin and getting your ass beat. You'll feel the need to point them out to the rest of the dumb fuck crowd, look at these fucking idiots. You'll all bare your teeth to the gums, like Mexican hyenas still needing braces.

But before becoming their self-appointed teacher, you'll just wonder, how is it that these two dumb fucks think they can do this, frolic at school like some faggot-ass *Mary Poppins*–type shit? Their clothes saying it all, one rocking cargo shorts down to his ankles like baggy capris, the other, the ugly one, a T-shirt tucked into faded black jeans, no belt, all pale and bloated, like a Steve Jobs that drowned and wasn't pulled from the Delta for a month. Basically, signaling to the world they're people to fuck with, the opposite of the Wu-Tang Clan. You'll spit onto the dirt.

After the fifth faggot joke, Roberto will stick out his arm in front of Whiteboy's chest, he'll say, fuck your Cheetos, get slushies.

You'll interrupt, saying you'll go instead. Everyone will pitch in a dollar and call it the limosna.

In line, you'll clock Selena, almost as tall as you, and her bronze skin, radiant in the sun. Her face will be flawless, no scratches or black eye, just that scar she's always had where her ear was reattached.

No reason to ask who won. You'll cut and she'll say, what's up? Give you a side hug. You'll stomach the pain from her pressing on your shoulder, arm, saying instead, heard you got hands.

Pfft, always, dummy.

Not better than me, though.

Right, that's why I had to save your ass from Anna back then. She'll hip-bump you and giggle, you'll note she's wearing a bra today, and still, her chest will bounce. Jiggling the way you see in those late-night commercials, college chicks with their tongues out, jumping up and down for the camera. For the money too, you figure. You'll remember telling Whiteboy that there's no way she won't have back problems, and all he said, almost annoyed was, who cares?

Where were you yesterday? Selena asks. Art class fucking blew.

Right. You missed me, and I missed class 'cause I was making you something.

You should, who's more important than me? Like, hello, I let you copy off me—you'll stop paying attention around there. Instead, focusing on those two smiling fucks, hugging it out. Still not understanding how they could run, all faggy, holding hands. Couldn't wait for their square pizza. Where they from? Brookside? Nerds. Just academically submissive, all that is. No fucking self-respect, listening to their teachers, to all the adults in their lives. Probably got nothing from the underground on their MP3, no David Lynch collection, don't know who Rufus and Bling-Bling are. Just dick suckers for an after-school special.

Like, oh my God, hello, yes or no?

Uh, yeah, man, of course.

AHHHHHH, OKAY. She'll hug you hard, and you'll wince while being wafted with the smell of her cocoa butter.

She'll leave, running, won't even order anything. Well, fuck, you'll keep thinking, as you massage your ribs.

You'll get two slushies and walk up to them. Asking if they know David Lynch. Dude with the tucked-in shirt will give a smile like he does. You won't believe him. Instead asking what his favorite movie is. He'll get out *Eraserhead* before you slam the first slushy down on his faggot head. You'll focus on their paralysis. It will affirm everything you thought about them. Pussies. The green slushy will sluice down over drowned Steve Jobs's clothes, and you'll think, this is the Stockton version of a Jackson Pollock. When it's clear neither of them will take a swing, you'll chug the other slushy right in front of them, then flick the cup at Steve. You'll walk away.

Back with the dumb fuck crew, they'll all be laughing. Ernesto shaking his head, foo, you got more of that shit on you. Should've let Whiteboy done that shit.

After school, they'll all go to Ernesto's for a kick-back. Some hoes coming over, supposedly. You won't have the energy for that shit. You'll go home.

Ma will be in the kitchen, cutting vegetables. You'll sneak into your room and change your shirt before going to the kitchen. When she sees you, she'll say, mi niño, ¿cómo te fue?

Bien, you'll say, like always. You'll take a seat next to her backpack and talk to her in Spanish. She'll have a paper due that day for her English class. She'll try to practice her English, but you'll tell her to stop. It unnerves you, makes her sound like a stranger and there's enough of those in your life. Besides, it's confidence not fluency she lacks. Either way, she can always ask you or brother anyway.

You'll get hungry, grab a cucumber and lime out of the fridge, Tajín and bowl from the high cupboard. As you reach, your sleeve will slide back, exposing purpled skin. She'll see only the smallest portion but will fuss anyway, what happened? she'll ask, her eyes narrowing around your arm as she tastes the soup for flavor.

No sé. You'll roll your eyes.

¿Adónde te andas metiendo? She'll start waving her hands all over the place. Wooden spoon flicking caldo everywhere around the kitchen. You'll shrug, yawn, smile as she continues, mmhm don't know. Right. I'll take you to un pinche doctor. Look at you. Spine and belly button touching. You're skeletal.

You'll let out a long-drawn-out sigh, trying to focus on the snack. You'll cut the lime, the cucumber, douse it in Tajín before saying, estoy comiendo.

Can you try something with less salt? She'll mean-mug your food intake.

You'll grab your head, trying to understand how you can help her by letting her talk to you in English. But the difference in her voice, never hearing it growing up, it's like she's sticking her hand out on your chest when all you're wanting is a hug. You'll feel her eyes on you, and will go back to your snack, trying not to wince as you lift the fork and take a bite. And feeling her still staring, and not wanting to think about last night, her not being there, all of what that means, you'll ask, ¿Y cómo te va?

Better than you. She'll add more thyme, rosemary, oregano, and when she thinks you're not looking, another bouillon cube.

D's get degrees.

You used to care so much about your grades. You cried when you got an S on your report card, do you remember?

Ay, no me hables en inglés. You'll raise your voice higher than you mean.

Pues, tú empezaste. She'll walk over, sit across from you. Legs crossed and hand on her chin, staring.

And the way she sits, knowing you have her undivided attention, you'll want to tell her everything—but where to begin? The bruises, the way you flinch when you hear his car, and punch the fucking wall when the smallest thing doesn't go your way. And that usually means every time brother goes to visit his girlfriend or when she goes to class, and you're left with no place to go. The reason why your knuckles haven't stopped aching in...forever. You'll put your head down. Pressing your forehead against the table, bringing the bowl to your knees, you'll take another bite of your snack.

She'll put her hand on your shoulder. ¿Qué tienes?

Nada, you'll say. You'll shuck her off, I just don't like when you talk to me in English. We're not fucking strangers. You'll take another bite, and stare at your shoes while the cucumber turns to mush that you refuse to swallow.

Cuando ya no esté, a ver qué piensas de cómo tratabas a tu mamá.

¿Como ayer?

Igual que *él*. Igualito. She'll get up. Will go back to the stove.

A minute will pass. You'll ignore the impulse to go to your room, turn on Rage, and punch a wall. Instead, I'm sorry, you'll say. I'm sorry. You'll get up and hug her, I'm sorry.

Está bien, está bien. She'll hug you back, hard. Eres el único que me abraza, ¿sabes?

You won't know what to say. You guess you've noticed that too, how he and brother don't hug her but they also don't yell at her, brother not at all and even him not as often as you do. You'll wonder, for her, which is the better trade.

Eres tan inteligente, ¿sabes? You'll try to squirm away and she'll only hug you tighter, she'll laugh, and even with the pain, you'll be able to laugh as well. Mi niño, eres tan inteligente.

And because she's still pestering you, you'll ask, what time's your class?

Oh shit. She'll let you go. Ay, le apagas a la estufa en quince, okay? You'll hand her her backpack, kiss her on the cheek as she leaves, saying, y come algo que no sea chingadera, okay?

As you watch her back out, you'll say, yeah, love you too.

At Ernesto's house, they'll all be in the garage, in a circle. Selena will gesture to the seat beside her. She'll hand you a beer. You'll complain it's already open, she'll laugh, tell you to stop being such a fucking square. Too Short's "Blow Job Betty" will be bumping from someone's shitty-ass phone and you'll wonder how long until someone's drunk enough to pour one out for a homie. Or maybe even for John. Your thoughts will wander, the kick-back going on in the background. Selena will whisper in your ear and you'll try to listen, but her slurry voice will make you think of ghosts, you'll imagine fucking up La Llorona with a haymaker and you'll laugh like a psycho to yourself. Only when Selena calls you a weirdo will you remember you're around other people, you'll sober.

And since being sober isn't really your thing, you'll chug another Mickey's tall can. Selena will hand you another. Whiteboy will start talking about his girlfriend sucking his dick, how he wouldn't let her kiss him until she had brushed her teeth, that this made her cry. You'll all start howling, Roberto will even shed a few tears, slapping his knee. In response, one of the hood rat chicks will swivel her neck side to side like a cobra and start saying, see, that's why I don't do that shit. They'll all tell her to shut the fuck up, and eventually, she will.

After the fourth beer, Selena will ask if you got some trees. Everyone always assumes you do, looking eternally stoned, even though you don't smoke as much as Whiteboy and Ernesto. You'll hypothesize it's the bags under your eyes. You'll tell her you don't even though you do, in your car. Ernesto will overhear, throw an arm over you and say, what the fuck are you doing? Just use my room, foo. His sweet hot breath tickling your ear. Your face will throb, and feeling his arm across your shoulder, you'll want him to spoon you. So instead, you'll slink out and reach for another beer, trying to replace the taste of salt heavy in your mouth. You'll feel his eyes still on you. You'll imagine telling him how you grew up, what you've done with other boys, it'll sound like a good idea—shit, you're drunk, could play it off later if you have to. You'll want to slap yourself. You'll wipe your palms on your jeans, tell him you're straight, you have the car. He'll reply, all right, just don't get fuckin' caught, foo. You'll nod like you know what's up, and you'll lead her out by the hand.

In the car—still without a rear bumper—Cheetos wrappers will cover her shoes. Selena will tell you about her brother, how he's about to come home. Another good reminder that whatever happens, whatever you do, don't end up in a group home. Her lilting voice will distract you, not harsh or high like all the chain-smoking hood rats you know. There will be a pause like she's waiting for an answer, you won't know whether she was still talking about her brother. After a while you'll put your seat belt on for comfort, she'll laugh and ask, where we going?

To the moon, you'll say, pulling out a dub sack from the glove compartment.

Why'd you lie back there, then?

I didn't, but I can't smoke out your brother when he's back if I smoke everyone else out. You'll slightly stick out your tongue, tap your temple.

She'll look at you funny, likes she's trying to see through your bullshit. How's your brother, by the way? Kari was asking about him, thought she saw him over on Wilson.

You'll stare straight ahead, a dude in a red hoodie will take his time crossing the street. His girl lives out there, so, probably.

He still painting people's backpacks? You think he could do my brother's?

I don't know, actually, maybe. Could give you his number?

Why'd you have to give me his number? Why don't I have it? Can't you just ask him, it's for me, for my brother, hello?

Yeah, yeah, anyway, you'll take out the rolling paper, the weed out the baggie. You'll roll it. You've had some, right?

Pssh, more than your square ass. But before you can light it, she'll snatch the lighter and will put it in her bra, she'll smile. What kind is this anyway?

You'll try not to stare at her. At the lighter. Caught between her breasts.

It's a hybrid. You'll try to sound friendly, adding all these extra hand movements, your mind will be sharp, your body resonant...I, I like that resonant feeling, you know? Like when your whole body goes all sensitive.

She'll smile and you'll notice with tenderness the little tooth beside her canine, smaller than the rest in her square, white rows.

She'll put her hand on your knee, fingers spidering. The muscles in your face will tense as you realize how sore you are—you'll try not to flinch.

Out the front window, a police car will race by, no sirens, you'll tell her you want to hit the blunt first. You'll take one and then another, and another, blowing it into her mouth when she asks. Then you'll close your eyes and think simple thoughts, your skull against the headrest like a...pillow. Pillows. Fucking pillows. Who the fuck was that genius? Thought of pillows while everyone else was thinking of ways to kill and fuck each other. Goddamn iconoclast. The headrest—heaven, like the best pillow in Stockton, right here in your car. What comfort: in pillows, feathers, crows, the color orange. Orange coming through your eyelids, reminding you, you're not alone. When you open your eyes...she'll be staring at you with that uneven smile of hers.

You'll hope she can't hear it, your pounding heart, as she climbs on top. Her hands pressing against your chest, you'll cringe and she'll look hurt, you'll try to keep it together, telling yourself it's okay, nothing has happened, and the next second she'll be back to smiling, staring, waiting for you to make a move. Though, still, you'll doubt if that's actually what she wants. Nothing good about you. And trying to take your time, to suss her out, you'll recline the seat not accounting for her weight and her head, her body, will crash down on yours. She'll immediately massage your face, the tenderness in her touch, the word cariño, will finally make sense. This will be the closest you've been to crying in years. Then she'll lean, press her chest against yours, until you grimace. This time her smile will twist, it'll be too late, she'll feel rejected, and in her hurt, you'll fear she's getting ready to lash out. To put it all on you. Why wouldn't you want her? The only answer: You're a faggot.

You'll remember sixth grade, how she spent the whole year cupcaking with this dude who, after summer, came into middle school rocking tight little shirts with flowers on them, his stomach showing, pink ribbons in his hair. You'll remember, too, the ridicule he'd endured during every lunch period and how she turned away from him, in disgust, in shame. This time, she'll have to be more proactive, let everyone know, and try to gain greater distance.

You won't try to stop her from getting out of the car. She'll dismount, open the passenger door, and get out. Without looking back, she'll slam the door, fish the lighter from between her tits, and throw it back through the window before walking off down the street. Your thoughts will loop, on what she'll say, and when. You'll force yourself to remember: You're high, fucking paranoid, just like her brother. No reason to run after her, in fact, that'd be the wrong move. Right? Worry about her tomorrow. Your eyes will go to the dashboard, the glove compartment, you'll grab the blunt, will smoke more. You'll massage your chest.

It won't have felt like you were out there long, and still, when you go back in, everyone will be gone. Ernesto will say he thought you bounced. Then he'll ask about Selena. You'll say she got picked up by her brother. He'll tell you, foo, you should've taken her home... Hey, how come I've never seen you with a girl?

What the fuck you talking 'bout? I was just with Selena.

You tryna tell me you got some out there? You get your dick sucked at least?

Dude, you want my dick? Why the fuck you care so much?

I'm just saying—he'll be picking up cans, smiling as he says—I've seen you with more books than bitches.

Books over bitches, that's me. You'll take a seat and smoke some more.

After a while he'll ask, what you tryna do?

Watch a movie?

Yeah, fuck it—you good to drive, though, right?

You'll say you're straight, nothing to fucking worry about. He'll tell you to hold on, he'll go inside his house, come out with some paisa-ass shit, a baggie with cut limes in it and the smallest bottle of Tapatío, for the movie, he'll explain.

The trick to driving while cross-faded: Don't trust yourself. You'll think you couldn't possibly go any faster, but the speedometer will tell you you're going thirty-five. It won't matter that you think you're flooring it. Thirty-five on the freeway is too slow. You'll tell your foot, harder, pressing down on your knee until the speedometer responds. Jesus, Ernesto will say, you're going to fucking kill us. And meanwhile, you'll be repeating your mantra, *I'm cross-faded, I'm cross-faded, I'm just cross-faded*, and it'll work, you'll be fine. You'll exit on El Dorado next to St. Mary's Church. Foo, Ernesto will say, put your fucking blinker on before you get pulled over. You'll park off Miner. As you open the door, the shit-infested smell of the waterfront will singe off your nose hairs. *Go Stockton.* You'll get your tickets, smuggling in Ernesto's shit. You'll go halves on a bag of popcorn and sit the fuck down. For a moment, you'll think you're still driving. You'll laugh.

Then—he'll move, putting a seat between him and you.

You'll think of going to the movies with brother, always sitting next to each other and that never being weird. Yet Ernesto got up and put a seat between you. You won't find comfort in knowing you're the only two in the theater. The trailers won't start for another fifteen, but his eyes won't leave the screen. His bag crinkling as he empties it into his lap. Reeking of lime, butter, and Tapatío. You'll want to vomit, pretending not to know why he isn't looking at you. You'll keep checking your phone, ten more minutes before the trailers start. You'll be annoyed that the lights aren't down. Your leg shaking as you wait. The cold theater growing hotter and hotter until you're sweating all over, drenched and angry by the time the trailers start, and your whole body glowing green. You'll want to leave Ernesto stranded as he laughs at the fucking movie, punish him for forcing you to pretend the last thirty minutes haven't been fucking weird. But you'll know this would be a mistake, that the best thing to do is to pretend, ignore his putting that fucking seat between you. You'll try not to think about that lady from last night, the things you couldn't tell her. Throat tightening, like it's full of your own teeth, vision blurring as, for ninety minutes, you sweat in your seat.

When it's all over, you'll drive him home. Radio on, no words.

Once you've dropped him, you'll feel defeated. You'll roll the window down, turning the fucking music off, and just driving, driving back home, listening to the city as you go. Wind and dust cutting against your eyes, tears will form. You'll wipe them away. At red lights, you'll hear screams, laughter, the goings-on from other streets. Kids playing, running in the dark. You'll see a mom walking home with her son carrying the groceries. Bums already sleeping. Hooded figures walking purposefully. Headlights glowing in opposite lanes. The night air against the skin of your face.

You'll turn off El Dorado. Its shopping centers and apartment complexes giving way to houses, duplexes, a neighborhood park, a basketball game. The distance between lampposts will grow.

You'll think about the things you want to say to Ernesto, and about how long you've known each other. It's not that there isn't anyone else, but he's who you imagine telling, always. Because sometimes you think ma and brother know already, or should know, if they don't, and you start hating them too. Hating them worse than that fucking asshole. And Ernesto would rather move, put a seat between you. For what? Just another paisa motherfucker rocking a Jesus chain. Like he's that fucking good-looking. And anyway, you do like girls, it's just, not only.

In Ernesto's eyes, you'll know, it won't matter. You'll be a faggot anyway. And what about your brother, would he put a seat between you if he knew? He says the word. But who doesn't, around here? And your mother, would she go all Catholic, perform an exorcism or something? Another limpia, maybe, because the last one worked so well. The tip of your nub on your pinky will tingle. You'll rub it soft, against your chest.

You'll get home too early, lights still on. Won't want to deal with his screaming, getting upset over nothing and then starting up on how fucking useless you are. What good have you ever contributed to the world? Always wanting to turn it on him, ask him of his good to this family. You'll grab the Febreze from the back seat and spray the car down, yourself too. You'll sit for a while, focusing on your breathing.

Still thinking of that empty seat. Then you'll get out, taking your time as you walk those few steps to the house.

You'll fumble with the keys, like you've never opened a door before. When you stumble into the living room, your father will be there alone, a beer in his hand, laughing, watching as a man in a red superhero suit wrenches a man in the head for cutting in line, and when the man's girlfriend protests, the superhero will wrench her across the face too, then he'll take off running. That's what you'll want to do when he turns, sees you, a big smile on his face. He'll slap the sofa, tell you to come over. You'll walk away, turning toward your room. Getting angry, remembering last night, him belting you until you said sorry—because even with his hitting, he hasn't been able to make you cry since you were a child—and this morning, him still fucking pissed, taking away your blanket, and still, so easy for him to just forget everything.

He'll get up, grab your shoulder, and you'll squirm, try to slither away. You'll smell the alcohol. His buzz making him friendly. He'll pull you back into the living room, grind his knuckles on your head, pushing you playfully. Stop, quit it, you'll say. He'll push you again. Stop. Just stop. Sometimes he'll play-fight with brother, but he's never done that with you. You know it's 'cause he doesn't deem you man enough. Figures you'd go and cry to ma. But now, he'll stretch out his hand toward you, testing you, and you'll slap it away. He'll laugh. You'll push him back. Así, he'll say. Así, como pinche hombre.

He'll turn sideways, digging into you with his shoulder. You'll brace, dig back with your own. He'll put his hand on your head. You'll shuck him off. You'll try to do the same, and he'll push you back into a wall. He'll wag his finger at you, a smile on his face as he assumes a wrestling stance. You'll do the same. You'll nervous-laugh. Trying to keep it all down. The fear, the anger, the pain, how you can never express a goddamn fucking thing. Just like him. Just like fucking him. Why the fuck's he laughing? What the fuck is there to laugh about? Goldfish-memory piece of shit. Everything always on his terms. You'll charge at him, and he'll sidestep, but you'll pivot, dig your shoulder into his side. A ver, a ver, síguele, he'll say. He'll push you harder, and you'll slap his arms away. You'll push, keep pushing until he's up against the wall.

By this point, the sound of your feet and blows will have summoned ma, who won't say anything but will look on, also nervous. And her being there will annoy you, your head grinding against his. You'll put your hand on the back of his neck, hanging on him, making him carry your weight. You'll both be breathing heavy by then, the smile now gone from his face.

He'll step on your shoe as he pushes, makes you fall. He'll smirk and you'll get up and be on him again, your head against his, you'll reach for the back of his neck and he'll slap your hand down, but you'll spin and get behind him, climbing up onto his back, your forearm across his throat, you'll squeeze. He'll pull at your arm to relieve the pressure on his throat, he'll laugh nervously. You'll squeeze harder. He'll try to shuck you off but won't manage. He'll crash you into the walls and still you'll hold on, and in desperation he'll reach back with his hand and claw at you. Catching a lock of your hair, he'll tear it out, and you'll squeeze harder. You'll press your forehead into the back of his neck and keep squeezing.

Ma will yell for you to stop.

He'll be wheezing, nails digging into your forearm and then tearing again at your hair like a fucking bitch. But you won't stop, not yet. You'll wish you could see his face, that he could see yours. All the fear gone, and the rage, the rage about to crush his windpipe. Ma will keep pleading, pleading like a chicken about to get its head cut off. But because of her panic, she won't be able to move. You'll keep squeezing. He'll slow down. His grip on your forearm, loosening.

DÉJALO. DÉJALO. DÉJALO, ma will scream.

You won't want to stop. You'll know you can do it; you can end him. He will never hurt you again. He should die. He should die. You'll squeeze with every reserve of strength you have left. Your forearm like a fucking guillotine.

But then you'll see ma's face, her eyes on you, hands shaking as she mouths that word, *déjalo*, over and over. Absolute terror. And it's not him, after all their screaming matches, him running out the door, the engine revving on, it's not him. It's you. She's afraid of what *you've* become. You're worse than him, a freak beyond reason, a monster.

You'll let go. He'll fall to the floor, lifeless. You won't know if he's dead. And neither of you will move, she'll just keep scratching at her throat, mouthing that word, *déjalo*, tears streaming down her cheeks. Ma, you'll whisper. Your apology getting caught in your throat. You'll reach out your hand and take a step toward her. She'll backstep, her head tapping against the wall. And in that moment, you'll wish it had been him choking the life out of you.

This will be the longest minute of your life. His still, limp body lying next to you and the look on her face, she doesn't recognize you. She fears you.

His body will lurch. A long labored gasp as he picks himself up off the floor. He'll lean against the wall behind you both, catching his breath. He'll cough. Take in more air. And between breaths, he'll get out, cría cuervos—y te—sacarán los ojos.

You'll finally say it, your eyes still on her, sorry. He'll grunt disapprovingly, thinking the apology meant for him.

She'll turn her head away, and you'll freeze, not knowing how to get her to see how sorry you are. You'll be solely focused on her. You won't see him rush you. He'll grab your arm, twist it behind your back, hijo de tu PUTA MADRE, it'll snap. You won't feel it.

Not right away. He'll walk out the front door. You'll slump onto the ground. That will be the last time any of you will see him for several years. You won't know about the latest infidelity, about how he'd been slowly escaping into another life already. Your fight was just the final straw. Still, that night, slumped against the wall, holding on to your own broken arm, hearing ma cry in her bedroom, all you would know was that he was right.

    You're a crow.

HOTBOXING

We're supposed to be in class—summer school before senior year—instead, we're laughing. One of the hottest days of the year and we're whooping, slapping each other on the back, our knees. The whole car rattling like a tin can and we're high. Driving to Jack in the Box. Hotboxing. Six of us in a five-seater. Sardines. The four in the back shoving each other, passing the blunt. I take a hit, search for a CD to play. Ay ay ay, the road dude, Paisa says. I turn the volume up, Immortal Technique bumping and Paisa in shotgun just bobs his head with the beat.

Let's cut off Frenchie's head, Cuco says, bet he lives for nine days.

CÁLLATE PENDEJO, Frenchie says,[1] snatching the blunt away from Cuco. He inhales deep, hard. The windshield fogs. I squint, slow down, wipe at it and keep driving.

Damn, dude, Bighead grins, can't never take a joke.

Y'all just always be playing, Frenchie says. With a thousand-yard stare he mutters, fucking *South Park*.

Was that a stroke or a aneurysm? (Ay, turn this shit up.)[2]

Whatever. (Daaaaaaammmn, I want me a car like that.)

I want me a puta like that.

For real. They give each other props.

---

[1] We called him Frenchie 'cause he didn't pronounce all his letters. Some speech impediment. For the longest, we thought he was just lazy: too fucking lazy to finish his words, his thoughts, dude would make a good philosopher, if he could bother to tie his own shoes, who knows what that motherfucker might've said? Could've split the atom, for all we knew.

[2] Parentheses just mean it's one high motherfucker talking over another high motherfucker.

Cuco is the only one giving Frenchie shit.³ The rest of us are just cracking up, hotboxing. I guess I'm driving: red light, stop; green light, go; yellow, go faster.

Ay, Paisa says, we should do a mission later, hit up the meat market bridge (where they found that body? heard that shit fucking stunk), then do blow-ups, no fill-ins, and tags on other walls all the way back.

Man, Whiteboy says, it's too hot for that shit. He shoves Cuco for more space, keeps his eyes out the window. Always trying to do too much. (Damn, dude, straight coughing in my face. Probably what that body smelled like. Pinche puerco, brush your teeth.)

Ay, how come y'all never trying to do anything?

We going to Jack in the Crack, ain't we? (Nah, dude, that's just your mom on my breath.)

Ay, but for real, though, we should hit some shit up. Put our fucking names up, make people remember. (Can someone tell this dude to open his eyes? Gonna get us fucking killed.)

Dude, Bighead says, we getting some fucking food.⁴ (USE THE

---

3 Cuco's government name was Refugio, but everyone called him Cuco. He was in a car crash when he was eight, left him with a limp. Whiteboy knew him the longest, said he was different before. Then, that car crash. He got a morphine drip. Was Cuco after that. The first to punch out a window for laughs, but also, could just get dead quiet.

4 Junk food would sometimes remind me of things like steakandcheese.com, Bumfights, Indecline, and rotten.com. Brother introduced me to most of that shit. Some of it had an anarchist bent to it, but it was just too fucking obnoxious for me. I'd yell along with everyone else, for them to get back to the fights, the skating vids. Brother never did. Then his taste started to change even more, assloads of Rage Against the Machine, Immortal Technique, movies where someone was getting whipped or flayed, the New French Extremity, he called it. No chill, I called it. He said there's something that matters more than what gets tagged, what their lyrics are about, or even that it's political. They don't give a fuck about any sort of criticism, that's why they're artists, real artists. Have you listened to David Bowie yet, have you seen David Bowie? That's the kind of shit brother would say. Not that brother was that different, he laughed right along with us when we watched Rufus and Bling-Bling dive for bags of crack, beating the shit out of each other and the

FUCKING CAN, FUCKING DROPPING ASHES EVERYWHERE LIKE WE AT YOUR HOUSE.)

Who invited you anyway? Whiteboy says.

I did, I say.

Fucker, who invited you? Cuco says.

Whiteboy chuckles, then Paisa, then all of us. Hooting and howling and trying to keep the car steady. Driving on hard mode. Still, getting higher. Fuck.

At a red, a mom waits to cross with her two kids, groceries looped over the handles of a stroller. The AC's on full blast. I could fry an egg on top of that little homie's head.

How weird would it be to offer them a ride? Kick these dumb motherfuckers out. One of her kids asks her something, she smiles. Can't remember the last time I smiled like that at anybody. Maybe with brother, shit-talking, watching *Freddy Got Fingered* and *Party Monster* back-to-back while he was coming down from his mushroom high.

Green. It's green, dude. Green. (Greeeeeeeeeen. Greeeeeeen. Fun noise.)

I go.

At the next red, I take another hit.

Where the fuck am I going? Oh yeah, Jack in the Box, LOL. (Look at him, don't give him any more.)

My hands, they steer this way, then that, lift off the wheel, put the car in Park, unbuckle the belt, open the door, and let me out. Everyone else is outside too. Crazy.

Harold and Kumar turned this into an odyssey, shit ain't that hard.[5]

Bumhunter doing his thing and all that other crazy shit. Well, no one really laughed at the Bumhunter, but we watched it, we did. If I go to hell, I know who I'll meet there.

5 That scene where Kumar acts like he's married to a bag of weed and starts hitting her, that's still funny.

We run out of Jack in the Box before they get too extra and call the cops. Motherfucker behind the register looked like he was halfway to Saturn. Telling us we can't spark. Crazy. In the heat, my forearms feel like they're getting toasted, I roll them over, pretend they're on a spit.

What is you doing, bruh bruh?

He's cooking.

They join. Slow spinning in place, the sweat lingering on our backs.

We're laughing again. I don't know why. Too high to drive, though.

We leave my car and walk through the parking lot of strip mall after strip mall. Staying under the shade and most of us wearing long white tees,[6] looking like joints, except Cuco, he a blunt. We pass an AutoZone, Check 'n Go, DD's Discounts, Food 4 Less, Copeland's, Planet of the Vapes, and Michael's Pizza, the smell making me want to vomit. We go into a Big Lots.[7]

Now we're running out of that place too, security kept following us every step we took. We started playing with a Nerf football, throwing it across the store. Told us to knock it off, and we started throwing shit on the floor, then he got the bear spray out, now we're leaving, screeching and jumping like we're coming out of an NFL tunnel ready for the big game, making like it isn't 109 degrees out of the shade.

We pass a closed-down Kmart and S-Mart Foods on our way to the Sinaloa Market. We get some chips and are back by the Jack in the Box, peering into Copeland's. Not one skateboard left.

---

[6] Cuco got on the black slacks, black shoes. Same shit we all wore in sixth grade for multicultural whatever the fuck. Supposed to wear outfits that represented our culture. Had all this time to prepare, but we were clueless and decided amongst ourselves: white tees, black slacks, black shoes. Some of the teachers came up after, what do your outfits have to do with being Mexican? Don't y'all know anything about your culture? How the fuck we supposed to know what people in Mexico wear? We here. You think our parents talk to us? Tell me I'm winning the lottery tomorrow and I can stop doing my homework too.

[7] It used to be an indoor go-kart track. I tried to go once, goddamn pricey, though.

Y'all think Copeland's will open up again? (Dude, I gotta piss, open your mouth.)

Hell nah, all the cool shit closed for good. (Bruh, have you seen your teeth? Someone's pissing in your mouth.)

Even Paisa's gonna get kicked out, gonna turn his house into a Dollar General.

I remember when Golfland shut down and that place next to it, Frenchie says. The water one; yeah, I liked Golfland. (You take your girl there, and the sidepiece to Costco for samples.)

Least we got all these chains, though, Walmarts and pawnshops and Check 'n Go, everything we'll ever need, Paisa says. (Nah, nah, nah, nah, the other way.)

Hey, Bighead says, are you being ironic? Grinning like he just won big on a scratcher. (How you gonna do that to your main chick, though?) Maybe you and Whiteboy should pull your pants up, hang out with the hipsters.

Look, Paisa points at the stores, how many of them for us? ('Cause, foo, you already got her.)

You think DD's ain't for you? Have you seen your shoes? (That's grimy.)

Paisa side-eyes him, all I'm saying is where the panadería, the paletería, the shops with Spanish and Vietnamese and Hmong names? (This dude still talking? He gone kill my fucking high.) Shit that I can't read, some fucking Tagalog or Cambodian, where all that shit at?

And all I'm saying is, if you'd seen *Juno*, you'd know you'd fit right in.

Paisa gives him the Mexican salute.[8] Ay, you ever read *A Modest Proposal*?

---

[8] The way to do it: at an angle you curl your fingers into the middle of your palm, and with your palm facing whoever, you let them know: huevos güey.

Shit, who you think you is, homie? (BIGHEAD NEVER LEARNED HOW TO READ...Who the fuck reads anymore?) You gonna talk like Whiteboy now?

Ay, nothing like that, foo. (Paisa read at the third grade level.) It's about—

Blood In Blood Out, American Me, Boulevard Nights. Bighead stretches his hands out, gives Paisa a head nod. We chime in:

One Eight Seven.

Scarface.

Menace II Society.

Mi Vida Loca.

Ay, *Stand and Deliver.*

Fuck that bullshit.

I liked that one, his comb-over, Frenchie starts laughing.

Modest Proposal, ¿quién te crees?

Ay, it's about eating poor people.

Whatever.

We stop by One.[9] The one with no trees and the narrowest little windows at the top of each classroom. Bighead jumps, tries to peek in, yooo it's still there. He starts dancing and I go over to the side, looking for a spot to piss, find one of brother's tags, a huge blow-up, WARD, instead. We all go to the other side and piss before leaving.

We drive past Michael's Pizza as Frenchie asks, that or homeless people?

What you think the odds are they also taste like cardboard?

Ask Whiteboy.

Why the fuck me?

---

9 It was behind Copeland's, the continuation school Bighead and Cuco had gone to. Neither ever knew when to shut the fuck up. I never went to class, that's how I didn't end up in a place like One.

'Cause y'all like that.
Like what? (Ay ay ay ay, light up another one, let's hotbox.)
Weird psychos, what you think. (Fuck no, it's too fucking hot.)
But we don't beat our women. (Y'all motherfuckers smell like wet dog too.)
That's 'cause no one wants them. (Ay, we all gotta smell like something.)
Unless they're white girls named Becky too. (Yeah, like fucking roses, not wet dog.)
Same.
Same.
Same.
Same.
Ay, fucking culeros, I see how it is.
Oi nomás, taking it all personal and shit.
See, we need to be hotboxing. (You wouldn't?)
Roll up the windows.

I look in the mirror, it's like my fucking eyes are closed. Paradoxical, I know. Still, makes me laugh, now my eyes really are closed. Frenchie comes over, looks at me, and says, FUUUUUUUUUCCCCKK. I say, FUUUUUUUUCK too.

It's dark and the moon is out, still 93 degrees, I keep the AC running. We cut through Angel Cruz Park and we're outside Pulliam Elementary. We get out and I call a tree, Cuco goes up to a wall, and Whiteboy makes eyes at the gate. We piss again. Piss ourselves empty. I can smell the curly fries.

Paisa still trying to go on a mission.

He talks about our names and what they mean and the 209 and that article. Now in *Forbes* and *Time*: Stockton, the most miserable place in America.¹⁰ Paisa loves being a downer. Cuco turns away, scratches at the pavement with something. Bighead's on the phone, cupcaking. When the spliff makes its way back to Paisa, he hits it like he's never gonna hit another blunt again. Coughs so hard I think his lungs are mine. My chest on fire. Fucking baby lungs. I take a bigger hit. Whiteboy says if I smoke any more, I'll go blind. Cuco and Frenchie pass back and forth whatever the fuck they're using to write on the pavement, and Paisa just keeps on talking like we're hanging on his every word. He lays it out like he's fucking Escalante: number one murder rate (that's wassup), number three in car thefts (motherfuckers need to step their game up), biggest city to file for bankruptcy (ay, it wasn't a city, just Whiteboy's mom, I told y'all).

(Man, fuck you.) Shit, why you telling us? Cuco says. Not one of us goes around acting like we tryna get stabbed.

Ay, you feel respectable and shit?

I feel like a balloon.

I feel like I'm one step away from being a college boy.

Look at Bighead on the phone, he gonna be a businessman. (Un ejecutivo.)

Shit, maybe a pimp. (Yeah motherfucker, *a businessman.*)

How a city go bankrupt? Cuco asks. It ain't even a person.

---

10 The reporter from *Time* talked about getting her purse stolen. What kind of place did she think this was? I was in second grade first time I got jumped; Paisa, Cuco, Frenchie, Whiteboy, and Bighead all got that Stockton love too, eventually. You learn real quick what not to do, where not to go. The second time I got jumped, could only blame myself. You submit to one logic or another, hold yourself accountable to stop yourself from going crazy, or you submit to the chaos. Maybe that's what brother was trying to get me to see, what artists do, the good ones anyway. There are other ways to be, gentler ways, some are ignorant as fuck but not all. I don't know if that even matters with the reporter, but if she's out there wondering how people get on in places like this, same as everywhere else, behind the mask of anger, aggression, there's one thing really. Joy.

We should slap that bitch-ass accountant and say we ain't gonna pay. How you gonna take a city to court?

They gonna make all of us show up, except Whiteboy's mom.

Ay, y'all know that's not how it works. (You a bitch for that one.)

If they wait, someone'll murder the problem away.

Damn, Frenchie, stop watching Sangre's movie recs. Dude's a downer.

Ay, those movies the truth.

They be like 95 percent boring. (You be watching Lifetime with your moms, though.)

You seen *Martyrs* yet? That family can get it.

They got it, bruh bruh.

Ay, when the city goes bankrupt, and completely fucking fails like that, that shit don't occur in a bubble.

Man, you failed those classes on your own.

That's wassup.[11] Then the blunt hits for real and it's like I'm listening, caught in ellipses:

No one gives a FUCK 'bout that article, bruh, Cuco says between claps. Is we going on a mission or what?

Then blink:

We'll go to Paisa's place. Then—

Blink.

This is like meditative.

Blink.

You think I could put grass inside my house? To like, you know?

Blink.

FUCKING MISSION! MISSION! MISSION! (Can you imagine, tiny cows, grazing?)

Blink.

---

11 That was the last sober thing I said.

Ay, you good to drive, Sangre? (Like a cow being all small so I can put it on the table and it makes milk for my cereal?)

Blink.

Sangre, make a left. (Like you're milking it?)

Blink.

Sangre, it's green, fuck, this motherfucker gonna kill us. (Yeah, like squeezing its little teats. Ha-ha.)

Open the door, I'ma get out this bitch.

Blink.

Fucking chill. Chill, dude. We fine.

NO, WE NOT. LOOK AT HIM. HE'S LIKE A GODDAMN MORON.

Ay, you gonna walk from here? From Charter to Mariposa? You the fucking moron.

Blink.

Just fucking chill, all right. Goddamn niñitas.

They're gone. Gunshots in the distance. My breath, like I'm underwater. Alone, in my car. Everything I touch, like I'm doing it for the first time.

Hasn't been this quiet in forever, not since that time with brother. I was telling him another one of my Ángel and Misterio stories, this time, they're birds. And every morning they'd wake up and carpet-bomb this old man's house. Just to see him turn beet red, smash shit, and curse. But it's not enough. They want more. They need to go inside. So one day, they shape-shift, appearing to the old man as his adult sons. And upon seeing them, the old man is filled with an unjustified pride at having *raised* such fine young men, broad of shoulder and chest, never mind their skinny legs. Soon after, they begin working on their new plan, hiding turds. First, under the cushion of his recliner. Every so often, the stink hitting him strong, sending him into a rage. The old man doesn't find the turd for three days and fucking loses it when he does, and all the while, Ángel and Misterio just laugh and laugh in their room. He then finds one right next to the toilet, and hits the wall, screams until he tires himself out. Then another next to his pillow. He tears all his hair out. And the whole time, they pretend they can't see or smell anything. It's piling up, the old man says. I pick them up, flush them down the toilet, but they're everywhere. He pleads with them, for all the love you have for your father, tell me they're real. Well, they say, pointing at his nose, maybe this is what you're smelling, they scrape an almost microscopic spot of shit off the tip of his nose. They lend him some glasses so he can see. A tiny Hershey's Kiss of shit. He screams, howls, punches holes into walls, and they laugh and laugh and laugh and somehow that laughter making it impossible for him to strike his sons. He imagines it so well that he thinks he remembers: how they'd cower, plead, cry, and how he'd whip their asses all the same, because he saw himself in them, pleading to his own father for mercy, but the belt came for his ass anyway. But this laughter, it sets them apart from him. Makes him see, they're full grown, too old for lessons, and he screams to keep from crying. The sons let him scream himself into the ground, fetal, whimpering. They hunch over him, fucking child, pathetic, look what you raised, old man, and they show him, turning back into birds. Plucking out his eyes, eating them, then taking flight, flying through the kitchen's open window. The old man never gets up, never stops sucking his thumb, shits all over himself and dies there, more alone than he'd been before his sons arrived.

That story made brother laugh, I laughed too. He said, our father would never pick up shit, though. Dude never washed a dish in his life. Then it was quiet. The warm orange light from the closet made everything look, feel, delicate. I hadn't had a day that good in a long time. Forever. No one else home, just me and brother. For once, I could hold on to that good feeling long enough to tell him I wanted to die, had been wanting to for so long. Had already half tried years earlier.

But I couldn't tell him why. Still too embarrassed to admit how lonely I was, so lonely and for so fucking long.

How I'd been trying to escape that feeling by jerking off, over and over, but even that had stopped working. And in the meantime, he'd started taking tagging more seriously, got a girlfriend too, all this other shit to do, parties he couldn't invite me to, what the fuck was I supposed to say? In the end, I just said that it was hard, so hard to breathe. That was the first time, the only time, he'd ever said that he loved me. I couldn't say it back. Couldn't hug him the same way he was hugging me as he cried, saying no one was more important to him than me, that I'm his best friend and if something were to happen to me... and then his voice trailed off. He hugged me again. His best friend who he's got no time for anymore. That was two months ago.

Now I'm here. In a car, alone. On the comedown. My brother's painting, being an artist, living the kind of life that could be profiled on DVDs, like Indecline and Infamy. A vision that no one will fucking deny. And I'm doing fuck all. Should at least enjoy it more. 'Cause what the fuck will we all do after one final year of summer school?[12] What would brother say, what advice would he give? Get

---

[12] More of the same for me, guess that's what I thought. Didn't know it yet, but Paisa would leave for school. His and brother's going to college made me think about what was possible for me. Paisa said he's coming back, but I doubt it. When we talked about Cuco, he told me Cuco had been doing pills a long time, but when his mom died and Selena couldn't take his pills anymore, all in the same year, it all got to be too much. Didn't know we had that in common. Don't know what I could've said, but I should've called him. I'm sorry, Cuco.

free. Become an artist. An escape artist. Get somewhere. Anywhere but here. I've been seeing more and more of his blow-ups, WARD, he's going all-city.

A black sheet stretches over the sky. No stars. A hot flurry of air shaking every branch in that old oak tree. God, it's so fucking hot, even with the windows cracked. Sweating. I search the car for my lighter and spark up. I hold it on, and the flame: soft, steady, gentle; can't help but smile. Wherever my brother is right now, I hope he's having moments like this. Maybe this is what tagging gives him. Like what ma used to say when she cooked, like bad news. Got to get it out of you. Got to put it someplace else. How else can you let in the light?

They come out of Paisa's house and walk up on the car like they didn't just ditch me. Paisa has a backpack on and I can hear the paint cans rattling in between their shit-talking.

Look at this fucking psycho, I ain't getting back in there.

Then fucking walk, bruh, Cuco says between claps.

I play "Survival of the Fittest" and we drive to the meat market bridge. Past Tower Records, Mervyn's, 99 Cent Video, Hollywood Video, Circuit City, Gottschalks, Blockbuster, FuncoLand, These Are Alright Flowers, El Grullense, La Fogata, Pupusas Pupusas Pupusas, La Comadre, Terry's Noodles, Naughty Nick's, and the Donut Shop.[13]

At a red light, the 5.0 next to me revs its engine.

YOU GONNA LET HIM DO YOU LIKE THAT?

I rev back.

Damn, dude, I didn't know this was your grandma's car.

---

13 They'll all go out of business within the next couple years. Some a lot sooner than that.

I rev it again. Harder.

He revs it back. Harder and harder.

Ay, olvídalo ya.

The light goes green and we both peel out. Though I keep my foot on the brake, and he never even taps his. I let him win. He's already past the next light before it goes green. I let off the gas and we crawl forward.

Pussy.

HAHAHAHA CUUUULEEERO. CUUUUUULEEEEERO. CUUUUUUUULEEEERO.

I just keep driving. Focus on the road. Not making eye contact with a homeless person taking a shit on the sidewalk, victory enough.

Your car just looks like it go fast, huh, foo.

He never had a chance anyway.

Man, what's the point of slanging if you STILL gotta drive a bucket?

Ay, *we* never had a chance.

Shit, this ain't my car.

You in it, pendejo. (You don't even have one.)

Cá-lla-te.

We get as close as we can to the meat market bridge, we park, walk the rest of the way. We follow the train tracks: full moon, no clouds. Heat still in the high 80s. Maybe this is what the sky was like when brother crossed with ma. But that was desert, summer, must've been even hotter. Ma, you never talk about what that was like. Been less than a week since they found a body on these tracks. What the fuck did it say on channel 3? Unidentified. Unknown. Guess I never talk about shit either. Still, can't let that be me. I won't do that to them.

We take out a blunt and blaze. In the smoke and moonlight,

and the dim glow of the cherry moving between us, from where we parked, we must look like ghosts.

The rail vibrates under our feet, vibrations going all the way up, ringing in our skulls. The train a big yellow flare coming at us, its horn a tin bellow that bores into our ears like a hundred Lloronas.

We stand just off the tracks, take out the cheap Walmart cans, and don't even bother to replace the tips. We spray as the train goes by, too fast to write our names. Still, even if it's just lines, loops, zigzags, it makes us smile.

You think this right here is misery? Write an article about this, motherfucker. The hiss of the can, the smell of the paint, could turn even a motherfucker like me into an artist. What would be my message? Fuck you. The train pulls away.

We make it to the bridge and stop beside the creek to sit. Water trickles by. Paisa kicks the dirt with his heel, and the scent of peat and moss lingers in the air along with our intermittent coughing. We've forgotten how to talk, how to be. We pass another blunt around, smoke shining in the moonlight. After a while Paisa says, ay, tell us a story.

Y'all ever hear the one about the tugger? I ask.

Crickets.

There was this cow on a ranch, I say, needed milking constantly. Except no milk came out. Only blood. Blood that was then sold to a processing plant. Thing is, the cow wouldn't let just anyone milk it, and the first milker had died shortly after this cow had appeared. So the owner of this ranch made all his ranch hands try, but the cow wouldn't even let them get near. Quickly a rumor started, the ranchero had made a deal with the devil, and if anyone got near the animal, it would surely bite their dick off. Then this one guy came along, recently fired and needing to provide for his family. The cow never even fought him. He got the job. First problem though, when he milked it, the cow would bleat in pleasure like a goat. And loud. The whole ranch could hear it. Another rumor started, he was fucking the cow. Or letting the cow fuck him.

Anyway, hearing the cow bleat, all the ranch hands would laugh, and count themselves lucky for having a different shitty job.

Pretty soon, he got a nickname. Tug, Tuggy, Tuggerton. He stopped being real to them. The people on the ranch, in the village, they could only picture his hands. Scarred, burned even through gloves by the hot sticky sap of blood that would ooze from the cow's teats whenever he tugged on them. That was another problem. The blood came out so hot it would bubble on the dirt. And Tug, having been so desperate, he kept the job. Going around town, he bore the brunt, as they greeted him with, Tugger, Milkman, El Que La Jala. He knew no one would ever give him another job. Cursed to milk the blood cow forever. He tried to endure and did for a while. But he could only be called El Lechero so many times buying groceries with his wife, before he had to say fuck it, fuck this ranchero, fuck his deal, who does all the work around here? Who's the fucking man?

So, one day, he gets this idea. He walks the cow over to the ranchero's house in the middle of the night, sneaks it into his home, his bedroom, where the ranchero's sleeping with his wife. They don't hear shit, 'cause just the day before, there'd been an accident. The ranchero, wanting to seem like hot shit, gave his wife and baby a ride on a combine harvester, but he'd driven over a part of the field where they were installing a new sprinkling system. The ranchero didn't know until the combine started smoking and stalled out. He kept trying to power through, not wanting to look like a dumb shit in front of his wife. The machine made all these horrible grating noises, but the ranchero just kept pushing, until *BAM*, the fucking thing blows a gasket. Blows out their ears too. Doctor said they'd be fine, only it'd take a week for their hearing to come back. Tug didn't know this as he led the cow into the ranchero's bedroom, seething as he positioned the cow next to the sleeping ranchero. He got to milking it.

The ranchero woke screaming, hot blood coating his face, filling his open mouth, choking him as his face melted. And all the while, the cow's bleating in pleasure as the wife falls out of bed, crawling back as far as she can, hitting her head against the wall and still trying to push past. She can't get far enough away. And Tug continuing to milk the blood melting her husband's face. And the whole time she's screaming, screaming and screaming, she can't hear herself, can't hear anything, staring into the cold, dead eyes of the tugger.

She can't hear and she's too panicked to remember why, terror racing through her in a flush of heat, her screams becoming shrieks. Her vocal cords tearing, creating little rips inside her throat, blood curdling inside her too. Because she needs to hear herself to move, but she can't. She's frozen, stuck watching the tugger as he tugs and tugs hot ropes of blood onto her husband's face.

But eventually, she does. She moves. Goes on autopilot. Later, she'll remember only snatches, clothes, keys, baby, speeding all the way to the airport, awaiting the call that confirms her life has a new trajectory. All because of the tugger, whose name she never knew. She'll be sitting at the terminal, baby wailing in her arms, shaking his little balled-up fist. She'll lift her shirt, offer him her breast. A quiet comfort will come then, nursing him, tears streaming down her face. All she's seeing: her baby. Her son. But then they'll come back to her—the cold sunken eyes of the tugger. Staring at her—always. Reducing her to nothing as he just tugged and tugged on his blood cow.

Crickets.

Y'all wanna know what the story's about?

Crickets.

It's about what it's like. Living here.

Crickets.

I don't know, no cows in my Stockton. (Which part?)

No brain cells either.

Your goddamn brain is filled with shit. (Ay, it do be like that sometimes.)

Gross-ass motherfucker. (Thought Tug and the wife were gonna end up together.)

Where we at, though? (Did you pay attention at all?) And why it gotta be a farm?

We're surrounded by them. (Them together, that would've been the best revenge, though.)

So what happened to the cow?

Now, not really high anymore, I ask, when y'all were some little-ass mocositos running around with your dirty-ass faces, y'all ever wonder what you'd grow up to be?

Ay, artist, bro. Paisa takes out the Rust-oleum, replaces the tip, starts tagging the wall next to the bridge. I look farther down it and see one brother did, it doesn't look new, but still clear, every line clean. WARD. One day it'll get painted over. But it's here now. He's fucking doing it.

My cousin wanted to be a gangster.

What he up to now?

What you think, foo?

What about you? Doctor? Army? Bank robber? ¿Pollero?

I don't know, dude, stop asking dumbass questions.[14]

---

14 Frenchie will spend time in Alaska, won't ever talk about what he did there. He's got a kid now, another on the way. Paisa told me after the funeral. I'm not in contact with any of them, but Paisa drinks with Frenchie whenever he's in the area. He doesn't go by Frenchie anymore.

I wanted to be a race car driver.

You halfway there, Whiteboy.[15]

Shit, if only I was racist, I could be driving in circles right now. Making that schmoney.

We pass the blunt again while Paisa scans the wall, tries to pick his spot. Ay, y'all trying to paint or what?

Dude, I'm still too high to be doing all that.

YEEEEEE.[16]

Ay, you letting this fucking place make you invisible.

Shit, don't you wanna be? Could paint easier.

Ay, the most miserable. That shit should make you feel some type of way.

Shit, haven't been miserable a day in my fucking life.

That's 'cause you're fucking stupid.

Tugger or ranchero?

Tugger.

Tugger for sure.

Tuggerton all day.

Paisa paints the outline of a cow.

I get up, take the can from him. Y'all know what "most" means? I do a big outline of the number one.

WE WINNERS, PUTOS!

WE THE BEST!

WE CHAMPIONS!

NO ONE BETTER—

at being miserable.

Everyone gets up and goes to the wall. Fuck our names. We write our number.

---

15 Last I heard, he's a pharm tech out in Oakland.
16 Bighead will go to Sac State. His girl will go with him on the condition they come back. They will. He works for the city of Lodi, got two kids.

Cuco starts in a hushed voice, number one, number one, Frenchie joins, number one, number one, and we're all chanting, filling the starless sky with our news.

In the car on the way home, we'll roll up the windows and blaze. It'll be impossible to see, but still, somehow, I'll drive. We'll take El Dorado, go all-city, from Ponce de Leon to Bianchi, Miner, Lafayette, Eighth Street, hotboxing the whole way, and all of us shouting how we did it, we won, we're number ONE.

INVISIBLE

2016, last night at Finnegan's, I drank with Selena. Under the harsh orange lights, we sat in a corner, ordered a pitcher, fries. Celebrating my final days in Stockton before leaving, maybe for good, and the only way I could get her to stop asking about it—was I excited, scared, would I miss her?—was to make her talk about Cuco instead. They got close last year of high school. They got married, stopped hearing from her, from anyone for some years after that. Shit kept happening, then I reemerged. Four years later. She said, Cuco could make tying shoes entertaining, dude was just funny like that. He was different, could be anyway, when he wasn't on pills.

It's been three years since they found him hanging from a tree at Victory Park. His shirt mangled like two pit bulls had fought over it, and with cuts and bruises all over his body. Still, she said, that very day they found him, the detective assigned his case labeled it a suicide. I don't know who beat the shit out of him, but if I did... We were never really close. He still deserved better than being seen like just another junkie.

Maybe he did kill himself. Selena has never believed that. Either way, getting his ass kicked, in those final hours, it had to do something to him. I should know. If—or when—I kill myself, it'll be a private act. When I tried at twelve, it was. Nobody saw the closet rod snap in half or how I picked myself up after.

Anyway, with so many undeniable murders going on—2014, another year of Stockton on fire—of course the detective said suicide and moved on. In 2014, I was starting to leave my room again, for things beside school. I wasn't in contact with anyone. But still, was going downtown, catching a movie, and sometimes having to dodge stray bullets too.

In line, waiting to get my ticket, it didn't matter how often I had to duck, wait for the *clack clack clack* to end, I'd be back there again the following week. Movies kept me alive. And usually the shooting happened while I was inside. Only after I came out would I see the aftermath: Blood. Body. Bullet casings glinting. Any screams already having turned into wailing. Whenever I saw people hugging, burying their faces in each other's shoulders, I knew. I'd be there next week, catching another movie.

I don't know how I survived and Cuco didn't. Don't know if Selena still thinks everything happens for a reason. If I went missing, left some ghost blood trail from Victory to the port, would my family find a reason?

At least the way Cuco did it, you know he ain't never coming back.

Selena tried to show me a picture of him from right before their divorce, everything still happy, but I couldn't, didn't want to see if I could note the pain in his eyes. Death approaching. I think about killing myself too much. Of joining him. Cuco never even made it onto channel 3, she complained. All he got was four shitty inches on page 14b of *The Record*. It's more than I'd get, I think, but I wouldn't tell her that. Selena *wants* to remember. I told her she should move on, that ghosts just weigh you down.

She asked: Oh? And how's that working for you?

At Finnegan's, we have a ritual, at the jukebox we only play songs we hate, then dance to them, "Bye Bye Bye," "A Boy Named Sue," "Bidi Bidi Bom Bom." And last night, we drank, danced, and laughed until someone called me faggot. No time to wonder what the fuck could he actually know about before Selena was grabbing my crotch, climbing on top of me in front of everyone. I thought about drowning then, what the sensation would be like to allow myself to be enveloped, consumed, as with smoke. The laughter, the bar noises, and the music from the jukebox faded; the beer crashed over everything like a wave. I wondered how many times Selena must've tried to save Cuco before they tied a rope around his neck. That's when her tongue slipped into my mouth, tart, bittersweet. I closed my eyes and kissed her, kissed her until I was invisible.

KALOPSIA

Year One

In Berkeley, you dream a psychotic dream. A dream filled with smiles. A parade filled with onlookers, and those passing by in the middle of College Ave, holding knives at the ready just behind their backs, glimmers of light catching each blade. Each might blind you with their perfect straight white teeth before plunging the knife in. Though this is delusion and you know it.

It's just that the same tools that served you well in Stockton, the armor, the bravado, feel like they will sink you here among the Birkenstocks, the pajama clad, those who, at least during the day, are afraid of nothing. Though at night, off campus, being six feet tall, brown, dressed the way you are and seeing a woman alone, blond, a high ponytail, Lululemon everything, you go to the opposite sidewalk, not because you're an ally but because you know fear, what it can drive anyone to do. What it drove you to do.

Still, danger isn't omnipresent, and during the day, most you pass on the sidewalk tend to see you as just another student. Though sometimes you notice women smiling at first, but something about your face, the lack of a smile, you catch a flash of shock when your eyes meet, and then their eyes dart away, and they try to pass you as quickly as possible. Here, the face has different expectations. The ethics of physical morphology, was that not an elective you could take? The face, the body, perhaps you can combine the research you're doing for all your classes, hermeneutics of suspicion, privilege, the ethics of physical morphology, and gentrification. Because it all comes together in what is needed, in what people expect from you: a smile. Who the fuck smiles at strangers? The unafraid, the privileged, those who gentrify, students—what you're supposed to be. You want to fit in. Have friends different from the kind you had. Though that's not it exactly, they don't need to be different, just you.

So, in front of a mirror you practice smiling. Research, you tell yourself, praxis. Different expectations and all that—a kind of bodily code-switching. Never realizing before that there was a Stockton way of being, and—looking into their eyes you realize, there's an SF, a Fresno, a Wimbledon, and Moldovan way too—that your personality, stance toward the world, it might not be doing much for you since leaving Gateway. Walking down Telegraph with a practiced smile, you feel it bubble at times, a bitterness. For what? For other people existing outside of Stockton. As if you had it so hard. You also escaped the drive-bys, unlike Cuco, Selena, and Whiteboy. There's a reason why you're the one here now and not them. Over a decade since you've had that school bus–yellow government cheese. Stale bags of cereal. Maybe you're not the same as everyone here who has *summered* in Europe and gets birthday presents like 1,200 shares of Netflix stock. But who the fuck are you kidding? The worst that ever happened from someone breaking into the house was the garage getting trashed and the other time your dog getting cut under the eye. So you smile and try to be your own parade.

Funny how much easier it all gets after that first, second, third beer. Smiling feels natural as you walk from bar to bar, and not having to worry about someone running up to you, asking where you from, having already determined they like your shoes, going to take them from you. Because Telegraph, College, Shattuck, it's all good, safe, the thought makes you want to laugh like a psycho, even though the university emails and your eyes tell you to avoid places like People's Park. Though some students seem incapable of learning the lesson. Victim blaming, they can call it what they want, you know there are things one can do to limit one's danger.

Every city has its rules, and Berkeley's are legible. So never mind the banging on the bathroom door, what the fuck are they gonna do, stab you? In Berkeley? At Pappy's? They can fucking wait. You'll practice for a few minutes longer, looking at the mirror, showing your own busted teeth, so you can look at them and not haunt with that crooked mouth like a bad spirit. Trying not to be a sieve for others' kindness, malice—anger, frustration, compassion? Trying to just be. Beer helps with that too. In Berkeley, people smile at each other. Unafraid of a gun being pulled, only thing getting pulled in your new home is a Hydro Flask filled with beer.

After a few months, smiling gets easier. Grabbing a beer on your way to class because you can. At night going to bars, house parties, the kind without a bouncer hanging at the door. Drinking, laughing, slapping a bag of wine before chugging, your mouth overflowing and the bottom half of your face getting painted scarlet. Sometimes a guy looking at you across the living room, soft and inviting, with lips you want to bite, but somehow there always being a girl smiling as well, turning your head toward her, you forget about everything except her. After, still drunk, eating at Top Dog, Smoke's Poutinerie, or at Asian Ghetto, and walking home, smiling, no real threat except for the raccoons the size of large bulldogs. But then it's like a psychic whiplash, and it seems like no one else smiles, not down Shattuck or Telegraph, or even on campus.

Here's you, in your best I'm-not-a-serial-killer affect, smiling at people who would rather you not look at them at all. You came here to learn. You're even doing your own research, and couldn't give a shit about most professors; some are cool, some will write you letters even though you don't know exactly why they're so kind. That there can be in one place this many adults who simply care, it will leave you a little astounded, frozen, your stomach feeling fragile. Though beer can help silence that feeling, can help you smile as you keep researching as much as you can outside the classroom. Because discoursing on sustainability isn't going to get you laid. Or will it?

An individual's opinions on childhood pedagogy seem to matter to some Berkeley girls. What the fuck kind of place is this? Maybe. Still, smiling seems like a better start than some sweaty ask about literary theory. As does going to TAPS and drinking. You sit at the bar, smiling. A woman in round black glasses and green corduroy overalls sits next to you, intermittently looking over her shoulder for the next half hour while you talk to the bartender. She keeps looking at her phone, sighs, is about to leave, when you smile, say, give them another five, I'll buy you a beer. She hesitates, complains about the Berkeley scene, you buy a pitcher, ask what she finds romantic—or sexy at the very least. You smile. It feels like forever, but eventually she smiles back.

By the second semester, you have your spots, Kip's, TAPS, Pappy's, most nights you go home alone, which is fine, you're drinking, sometimes playing a game of pool, and rare as it is, when you can really relax, stay with that feeling the beer gives you, you can talk to anyone, like her, short wavy brown hair, flowy dress shirt, tight cream pants, and the kind of cheap skinny dollar-store sunglasses that only someone knowledgeable about fashion can pull off. When you're back at her place, you keep your shirt on the entire time, and she does as well, when sunlight filters into her bedroom, you're wide-eyed and soaked in sweat, you kiss her goodbye, not bothered whether you'll see her again, then catch the bus back home. You shower, turn in your paper, then help research gentrification in the Bay Area, going to the library, searching then scanning microfilm, old newspaper articles, looking for keywords like *urban renewal*, *displacement*, *revitalization*, before meeting with the other team members who all report to the postdoc in charge of you all. Though sadly, you realize this research has nothing to do with smiles. Still, you're a convert to smiling, and you walk with headphones on because you can, because it's safe, and "Black Hole Sun" plays in your ears. You remember the music video, all those manic smilers, and you think, one day you'll have a smile as big as theirs. At night, you go to Kip's and drink three times the amount that girl with the bright red lipstick and leather jacket does and she's impressed by your tolerance. You tell her what you're working on, a praxis of smiling. It will cover all the different variations of smiles. Smirks, grins, people's O-face. You're going to be a millionaire, she says. Indeed, but money is not the objective. Maybe you'll have to change your name to Johnny Dentist or something like that. She tells you to keep working on the name. You ask her what she's passionate about, and she says quilts. Her family is from Armenia, she tries to add something about what that means to her into every one that she makes. She says she grew up in a conservative family, but also, she says smiling, art was like another religion, they'd just never admit it, but it's true. There's a tradition of quilt making in my family, my great-grandmother, and my grandmother too, but I never met them, cause we moved when I was still a baby. You ever seen the AIDS Quilt? She pulls it up on her phone, you both talk for a while, and after when she gets up, and you do as well, you hug, embracing in the kind of way that looking into her eyes, she's asking you to lead her, and so you do.

The next three times you meet her it's at a bar, she comments, her voice less cheerful, how can you handle it, all your drinking? You wipe the beer from your chin and smile as you tell her, she's the endurance runner, she knows the importance of pacing. When you suggest another bar for the next date, she asks you to take her somewhere without alcohol, so you pregame alone, going to Pappy's and ordering a pitcher and though you're smiling when you show up, she says she's worried about you. That's how she says it. Worried. About. You. Her brother, she says, he was always drinking, and then she cries and twirls her hands through her long braids over and over. It's hypnotizing, the twirling, like the cylindrical sign outside a barber's window.

You tell her you're fine, there's nothing to worry about, never mind the bloodshot eyes, your brain feeling like it's got ten thousand volts running through it, you've just had a lot to do, lots of papers that needed to be written. All your efforts are starting to pay off: the smile stays plastered across your face. Besides, you know all-nighters are nothing new to anyone around here. Still, you assure her after she doesn't respond, you'll drink less. And you do. Cutting back more and more for a couple weeks, and when you realize you've still been drinking every day, you stop completely. But that next morning your head rings like crazy, like you've been out in the sun since the sun was a thing, sweating and shaking, and you know what it means, what you gotta do, and will but not yet, right now you just gotta get the whole smiling thing down. So you take a drink, and then another, and after a while it's not even practice anymore, it just happens to your face—you're smiling.

Year Two

When you have sex with her for the first time, it's at your place. Your roommate out. Nothing on your side of the walls, mattress on the floor, a plain blue comforter with no sheets underneath, and all your clothes in folded piles in the closet because you never bothered to buy any hangers. You take everything off except your shirt. But she insists, pulls at the bottom of your shirt and you try to take her hands off as gently as you can but she's persistent and you don't want to actually say no, and wish you hadn't shared all that you had, but still, she kisses you, says it's okay and eventually she wins. Then every story you've told is there on your body and she doesn't say a word, just kisses you, smiles a crooked smile and runs her fingers over the scars; only after, weeks later, back in your apartment, shirt off, sitting on your bed, does she tell you she wasn't ready to see, to think of you as that boy, the one in all the pictures she's seen on your phone. Smiling at four or five, a softness in your eyes, then older, smiling less, older yet, and not at all, eyes just like your father's. Hard, fixed, gleaming.

And then she grabs your pillow, hugs it and does what she had never done before, she stares at your hand, most of your ring finger and all of your pinky gone, he did that too, then? she asks. And before you can answer, say no, you did that to yourself? she asks, to that little boy? She cries while hugging the pillow. You look away, stare at the blank wall while she cries, over something that didn't even happen to her, that she kept fucking asking about. You put your shirt back on. You wait. Hide your hand for the first time since elementary. You hug your knees and wait for her to stop crying.

I'm sorry, she says. She wipes her eyes, careful not to run her mascara, eyeliner.

You keep staring at the wall.

Talk to me, please.

I'm sorry I told you all that shit. I shouldn't've.

But why? Look, I'm sorry. Can you look at me? Please. Just look at me. She reaches for your hand and you pull yours away.

This is what I fucking do, man. I'm a fucking curse. You look away from her, back at the blank wall. Your hands on your head. I think you should go.

I'm sorry, she says.

Just go.

She crawls along the bed and hugs you. Starts crying again, I'm sorry. Please just talk to me.

You don't hug her back, you wait.

I don't think you've done anything wrong. It was just a lot and—

Look, I'm sorry too. My whole fucking life I've known better. You let out a long, exasperated sigh, you get up off the bed, you think of leaving the room, but instead you just start pacing, hugging yourself instead of punching a wall. I wasn't trying to put all my shit on you. I'm sorry that that's what I did, I—

You didn't do that, I'm sorry, not what—

Can I finish, please? I didn't fucking just share all that shit out of nowhere, you asked and yeah, I should've known better. I'm sorry. I'm fucking sorry. But you asked. I wasn't trying to weird you the fuck out.

When you ask about my brother, what I've told you, does that weird you out?

No.

So why is it different for you?

I didn't cry when you told me that stuff.

A long pause.

She gets up off the bed. Takes a step like she's getting ready to hug you. Stops. Have you ever cried over any of what you've told me?

Why would I?

How much do your brother and mom know?

They know that this, you bring your damaged hand up, put it between you, this was my fucking fault. A stupid fucking accident, held a firework for too long.

And though you're in your bedroom, you leave. Leave your apartment.

Eating beside her at a bar, you think she's too nice, naïve, and you're just a mistake she's unaware she's making. But that can't last. And even though you know this, you pretend that it might. You drink. Then after you're with her. Buzzed. When she asks about your past, you obfuscate, keep mostly to the things you think are funny. But the way she reacts sometimes, you know you both are just lying to each other. Playing it all for laughs but half the time you're the only one laughing. She thinks you want to be different, but is that really true? Doing just fine before her.

You're on your bed drinking, telling her stories again, a smile on your face. You're showing her more pictures. Ones with brother, your father, and looking at them, their eyes, you wonder whether you don't all deserve each other. So few words spoken between you all, they could easily fit balled up into a fist. Silence, separation, just as bad as the real curse.

You remember how after the limpia, for weeks, you stayed in your room without leaving, or even talking to brother. Ma started staying in hers. Or maybe she always had? All you know is that after you were cleansed, no one ever talked about it again. It was understood: You'd been beaten but the beating had done you good. It had to. For everyone's sake. Or else what had it all been for?

That history held you all by the throat, never letting go. Your girlfriend sees a picture of you at fifteen, the last ever taken, she asks, where are the others of you at that age? You say you don't know. You really don't have any pictures after this? she asks. There might be a few, but in Mexico. My dad stole some pics of us when he left, his family in Mexico has them now. Why do you think he took those pictures of you guys? You shrug, would have to ask him. She smiles, begins to ask, you ever think of reaching out to—and before she can finish her question, or ask for you to take your shirt off with her eyes, her smile, you climb on top of her. Kiss her. Still, she does anyway, tugging at your shirt until you acquiesce, and then your pants, and you take hers off as well then close your eyes, you go in, her breathing sharpens, you know you're bad at this, but try to focus on the sensation, of being hugged, swallowed, taken all the way in by her body, her pussy wrapped around your cock, her hands on your chest, and wanting them to stay there. Though so quickly her hands start moving. She's touching the scars on your back, her fingers following their paths and just wanting it all to end, so pretending to come, and she does as well. You get off her, lie there next to her, feeling her eyes on you, and don't know what she's thinking or feeling. You keep your eyes closed and hope she can focus on just your smile.

Another month passes and you're with her under the soft yellow Christmas lights that adorn her bedroom, plants hung on ceiling hooks and on shelves everywhere, smiling, a tingling on your lips. She bites hers, and you immediately sense it, know what's coming, there in the way her eyes shift toward your hand, I'm worried about you. Have been. Wipes your smile away. The way you drink. You're hurting yourself.

Just stop.

I know what I'm talking about. I do.

I'm not your brother.

She turns away, hugs her childhood teddy bear and cries.

You put your hand on her shoulder, delicate and imprecise. She keeps crying, shucks your hand off.

I'm sorry, you say. You go in again, and this time hug her.

She shakes, shucks all of you off, I'm sorry.

No, you're not. She cries for a good while longer. Why am I always the one crying?

You don't know how to tell her that you never can. Or could? Crying, only ever really seen in movies. And that's how she looks, holding her bear, mascara running, she's in a movie. And you're the asshole, the bad thing that happens to her before the good comes her way. That's what you want, for once to be the good, and slow and hesitant you approach again, putting your hand on her back, and again she cries and you hug her, put your whole body into it. Holding on until her breathing calms, her body relaxes, I love you, you say.

She takes the beer away. From then on, she makes you leave bars and parties early. You stare down into her dumb religious smile and you don't want to hate all her joy. You kiss her, let yourself be infected by it. But by then you've already decided what you want to try to do, and if you're going to apply to MFAs this semester, you don't have time for withdrawals, therapy, medication that makes it impossible to come. Instead, promising yourself you'll get better at hiding the booze, and week after week of her not finding out, seeing you as clean, as good, it all gets so much easier because you've done it, you've become a natural, a smiler, it was what you were born to do.

During dead week, after all the applications are in, you tell her more secrets, soberish for the first time. How the worst always came when it was only you and him around. She tells you he had no right and though you know this, it's different when she says it—something in you, displaced—and it becomes hard, almost impossible, to hold her gaze, and still, she says it again—you didn't deserve it, it wasn't okay. And the only way out of the feeling is to defend him, you were a pretty terrible kid and don't know anymore what came first, the belt or your wretchedness. It seems so important to remember. She suggests starting therapy again, medication too, but you refuse, and expect another argument but instead she takes you to her church, makes you dinner, and everywhere you go together, looking into her big shiny eyes, you know as you say it, I love you, she won't catch a whiff of the beer you just had before seeing her.

In the final semester, both keep putting it off, the future diverging. She wants to travel, Asia, Europe, a year to start, and you don't have any money saved, it's MFAs or finding another kind of job. And as the semester rolls on, neither breaks up; both just drifting apart, you into the writing, your roommates, and her into the quilt making, her other friends, training for a marathon. The need to hide the drinking evaporates as does she, only seeing each other once in three weeks. But still, every time you see each other it's like nothing has changed, laughing and telling secrets, spending the whole day in bed. Hers.

She asks if you brought it, you say that you have, the writing you hadn't wanted to share, what you submitted for the applications. Unwieldy and full of violence, though not only, also there is that sometimes lust for men, and that word you've heard your whole life, faggot. She reads, and then, so, you're gay? she says.

No, you say. Standing up.

Why couldn't you just say so?

It's not like that.

What, you're bi? It all makes so much sense. The way you close your eyes when we're having sex. Don't try to tell me you're bi, you're not bi. You're just afraid.

You don't look at me either. What's that make you?

Don't try to make this about me. I didn't write this. Her hand balling up your pages.

It's just a story.

Yeah, they just happen to be the same ones you've been telling me, except in there you can actually do what you want and fucking blow a guy. You don't even touch my tits.

I'm not gay.

I think I want you to leave. I need some time.

You mean more?

She throws her teddy bear at you.

You go back to your place, roommates having a party, so you drink, glad she's not there to police you. Playing round after round of Rage Cage before in the middle of another round being set up, you tell the roommate with whom you share a room that you tried to kill your father. You laugh and she does as well and then you're both in the bathroom and she's on her knees, pulling your dick out above your waistband and don't know why it's happening this way when both your beds are only a few feet away. And you're too drunk to get hard but seeing her like that, eyes soft and wanting, her mouth full of you, you wish you could get hard, that you could come, but you can't and so you pull her up and kiss her. You hug and with her head on your chest she says, can I tell you a secret? Sometimes when you change, I watch you. I'm sorry, she says. It's okay. It's okay, you say. I've done the same. Can I tell you a secret? She whispers yeah into your neck. I wanna tell you all of mine. You pick her up and set her down on the bathroom sink, staring into her eyes, touching foreheads. You're wonderful, you say. And then she's gone and you're looking into the mirror—unrecognizable until you take a swig of Bacardi and smile. Then you're crawling out of the bathroom and everyone including your roommate is cheering you on, telling you you've almost made it to your bed.

When you wake up on the floor beside your bed, you're disoriented, finding clumps of vomit on the carpet and in your hair. As you get up, dazed, the smell—like tomato sauce and fish guts—hits you harder than the pounding in your head. Your shirt ruined. You take off your shirt and you notice your roommate looking at you. She has the same look she had after her boyfriend broke up with her. You want to tell her last night wasn't a mistake, that you remember everything, but your head's ringing and her eyes, there's no other way to read them, disappointment. You tell her you're sorry, you'll clean up the mess and she says, wait, last night, the things you shared—but you can't, I'm sorry, you say, the smell caught in your hair, the side of your face, it's making you shake, and the nausea, you have to go to the fridge, and do, and there's beer, you open one, and drink. And the headache goes away.

Year Three

In Blacksburg, VA, the beer is cold, cheap, and you smile with the best of them. You pretend, taking up the praxis, smiling, though most of the time no one's even looking. Never imagined having to drive to the next town over just for the shittiest, driest tacos of your life. They go down hard, slow, two whole beers just to wash it down.

But that's the Blacksburg, VA, way of being. Here, getting an MFA, reminding yourself, this is just a step toward that dream of becoming a writer. At night, walking back to the apartment, it begins to snow, and your jaw is sore. Head still fucking ringing. Kicked out, maybe for good. Smiling the whole time but it wasn't enough. Doesn't really matter. There are other bars. Everything spins and you try walking in a straight line but keep stumbling. Then you stop, kick snow off the curb, sit and breathe, heat leaving your body with every exhalation. You watch it go, packed in a small cloud, your heat, floating like it's on a string.

You remember chasing a balloon when you were five, men begging you to get into their car. That simple little demand, ven acá, by the one leaning against the hood, smiling in a teal tank top, gold chain, and a dark mullet. Though quickly those inside joined in, their windows down, whistling, and their necks, their arms reaching toward you, and the one leaning against the hood, his face, that leer, like he was taking off your clothes with his eyes, his metal tooth glinting in sunlight. You remember running away, balloon eclipsing the sun, turning candescent maroon like a heating coil ready to pop. You had nightmares for months after, pissing your bed, imagining him outside your door, balloon in hand, smiling, ready to take you away.

Remembering his face, you sober. And standing back up, you just hope you won whatever fight you were in. The taste of copper swishes in your mouth. You spit and watch it burn a hole through the soft snow. Nothing's changed. You're alone. Alone because you came here to write, trying to follow that thread. Sometimes you can see it—birds, blood, and shit-talking—other times, you can't. And it makes you want to get better, and it beats swinging a hammer, rising at five, crack of dawn, like your parents did every day of your childhood, your father swinging a hammer but not before going on a commute so long he's paid for just two-thirds of the time that he's away. And ma's work never seemed to end, cooking before and after her job, then night school. How the fuck could you ever even think of complaining? The MFA, writing, will always be better than that.

Doesn't matter that you're three thousand miles away from everyone you love. In a shared apartment though now with your own bedroom, again, mattress on the floor, nothing sentimental anywhere, and all your clothes, the eight shirts, two button-downs, and the three pairs of jeans, folded and packed into the closet floor. You imagine walking back home to your family, that at the end of this walk, you'll reach not your apartment but that house, opening the door on those three crazy-ass dogs jumping all over you, licking your legs, your arms, your face. You'll be asked about your day and won't have to lie. You'll answer in the present perfect, bien. You'll put your things away knowing you still have to write. But first, for a minute you'll bother ma, you'll see what brother's doing. And relaxing, you'll let them talk, listening for it in their voices. Love. There will be sunlight and barking and wagging tails and everyone will just smile. Still no calls yet letting you know that a mass was found during a checkup, leading to more tests, and though she didn't say anything more, you all hold on to the same hope three thousand miles apart. There will be no cancer. There will be no cancer—you say it as you pray over a rosary of bottle caps, corks, awaiting the results of ma's biopsy.

You've been here for four months, though since Halloween—seeing that group at a bar, sombreros, ponchos, fake mustaches, yukking it up, no one else paying them any mind—you knew, gotta get the fuck out of here. Four months seeming long enough to stop feeling crazy every time you step outside, trying to smile but noticing them. *Theatrical eyes.* Eyes that dance away from you like magnets repulsed—by your body, its charge. You want to neutralize it, always fighting the urge, then surrendering to it.

Because the glass in your hand always fits, drinking that amber, sweet, like pennies coating your tongue, and then a second, third, a few more after that, then you're in class, comparing your classmate's work to that lineage of comedy of manners, smiling, and before you hear their response, you're back home, then a bar, at your friend's place with your clothes off, someone knocking at the door, and she's rushing to put her own back on and your bare ass is halfway through her window and when you look back, it's not your friend's face, it's her mother putting on a shirt and you dress on the lawn and wake up in bed and there's a beer on your dresser and it's buzzing like an alarm, and you have to pop the cap to turn off, so you do, and it tastes like water.

Walking downtown you notice necks stiffening, eyes diverting, concentrating on anything but you. Sometimes asking yourself, why are you being such a fucking bitch? This is nothing. No risk of being stabbed, shot, jumped over a pair of shoes, or just because it'd be a good time. No one's fucking with you. You're just being ignored, constantly, unless you're with your friend, who's white, and then can see the math going on behind their eyes, like you stole her away or something. In California, you never knew how important it was, seeing your own kind, and now you feel like a fucking idiot for taking Stockton and Berkeley for granted. Days pass—a week once—without seeing someone, anyone, you'd even take an old lady who looks like you. You feel pathetic for needing it. And the more you're ignored, the more you wish it were dark, and everyone alone, that way at least you could rationalize the fear. Rather than what it is. But really you're usually the one walking alone, three thousand miles from home. You wonder how long it's been since someone's seen your eyes. Always keeping your sunglasses on everywhere you go, even inside, even at night. Not caring that you look like a fucking douche.

It makes it easier to pretend people aren't refusing to look at you. Only taking them off when you reach your apartment or one of the bars you're still allowed into. And in the bathroom, pissing in the urinal, a man, the same one you've been sneaking glances at all night, walks in and stands by the mirror, thumbs out his pockets, you keep your steady stream of piss going as you turn and look, he smiles, his big pink lips shining in the amber light. He walks over, pretends to go in the adjacent urinal, and after zipping up, washing your hands, he comes over, washes his, you're getting ready to say you could take him back to your place, get on your knees, but you notice him staring at your hand, and instead call him a faggot. He leaves. You think he was exactly your type, clean-cut and taller than you, but the way he stared, and though you know it isn't true, you tell yourself he'd know better if he wasn't fucking white. Outside, he's nowhere.

Your breath visible in the cold air and all you see is lampposts like checkpoints in the dark. You walk from one to another, like beacon to halo to lantern, every outpost of light carrying a beer to help you catch your breath before forcing yourself forward. In the dark in between, the wind cuts through your eyes and they water. Still, you keep walking and the distance between lampposts stretches, longer and longer, until there aren't any more, but you're warm now from the beer and keep walking through the dark, through gusts of wind until in a whirr of leaves a tree bends in the dark and a pathway lights up, Christmas lights switched on, you're at your friend's house and you knock and her mother in a pink negligee answers and she takes you in her arms. They wrap around you like snakes and your body goes limp.

You walk past the graveyard, the downtown bars, the bookstore where you can never get any help, on your way to class, head ringing in a sunlit daze. On campus, the grass white, frost on every blade. Wind shearing at you as you breathe the bitter air, eyes tearing but under control. And in class, at bars, grocery stores, you remind yourself to breathe, just breathe, turning it on, smiling when a classmate asks—what's wrong? But as the weeks progress, you start to always look down, because you can't hide it anymore, you're tired. Becoming a weird paranoid fuck while waiting for news from home, and for the bartender to come around, to tell her dealer's choice or whatever's cheapest. At Kroger you think people notice you, old men with old wives looking away and smirking, talking loudly with one another about cleaning their homes. *Spic* and Span. You keep walking, headphones on, telling yourself maybe it's all in your head, just let that shit go, and when you pay, you go to the same cashier, the young one with the long hair and septum piercing. He's seen your ID enough times that he's stopped asking for it, just smiles and tells you to invite him to the party and you think that's pretty cool.

Later when you're drinking at the Cellar, you see him at the other end of the bar, dancing, swaying, his long strawberry blond hair glowing, almost orange. He notices you, and the smile blooming on his face, it's like he wants to open you and you want to let him. Then you're dancing, pressing against him, laughing, drinking, his tongue of cigarettes and apples sliding into your mouth. When you pull away, you still feel him on your lips, tingling, your whole body gone static, waiting to be touched again, and then he's pulling you into the bathroom. And you're trying to slow it all down, can we... I don't live far... you attempt to say, but he's smiling, backpedaling as he tugs at your wrist and opens the bathroom door with the other. He pushes you against the wall, undoing the buttons on your shirt, running his hand over your chest, pressing his face into your armpit and breathing you in like a brown paper bag filled with paint, and he's kissing you everywhere, running his hand down over your pants, feeling you grow, harden against him.

And even though it's too much, too soon: Just once, you tell yourself, you have to do this at least once. You ignore your desire for this to happen anywhere else. You turn, press him into the wall. Unbuckle his belt and lick your hand then stroke, leaning into him. And he's just short enough that he fits perfectly under your chin. He nuzzles, kisses your Adam's apple, moaning softly into your neck, his sweet hot breath skimming across your chest, while your hand glides on his cock, up and down, up and down. Don't stop, he says, don't stop. His voice, a breathy pleading lilt, makes you want his cock, his come to fill your ass. And with your other hand, you stroke the back of his soft golden head before gripping fistfuls of his long blond hair. He lets out a small whimper as he comes, his cock pulsing and filling your hand; and all that heat, his come and heartbeat in your hand, and you don't ever want to let go. Though before he can reciprocate there's a banging on the bathroom door. He laughs, smiles, zips up. In the mirror, he checks himself, walks to the door without noticing—you, still holding out your hand warm and thick with his jism. Smiling. And before someone else can enter, you hear him say, he's sick in there. The door shuts. The noise from the bar slowly fades in. You wipe him off you with a paper towel. But his smell still there on your hand, sweet and biting, an apple dipped in vinegar, you close your fist like there's a wish there, one you're not ready to let go. In the mirror you look at yourself—there's a banging on the bathroom door again, still, you wonder—have you ever smiled like this before?

You're buzzed, out walking downtown, smiling because it's so cold your jeans feel wet and it keeps you moving toward downtown. Lips and fingers tingling, thinking of going over to Champs or PK's or Frank's. Then you get the call. Cancer. Confirmed. You think about your great-grandmother, she died when your grandmother was fourteen, your grandmother, she died when your mother was eighteen. You're twenty-five, and have been so lucky. You're glad she's lived long enough to see you prove her wrong, you aren't just like him, you can be rid of rage, able to hug her, and tell her you love her. You've stopped blaming everyone, have grown to listen, to let yourself be comforted. You, the kid who stopped crying and grew with rage, used it to swing aluminum bats at your own kin. Maybe that's still there, but at least she's gotten to see it isn't everything that's in you.

Sitting down on a bench, heart still pounding from the news. You imagine you and brother alone in that house. Her warmth, her random acts of joy, her gentle spirit and booming laughter, gone. You think of how different she'd been in that last year before you left, just as quick to flash her boobs for a laugh as she was to try to sneak up on you for a scare before hugging you and saying how much she loved you. How long until the sickness takes over? Dulls out her eyes until all her light is gone.

And you couldn't even be there with her when she found out. That's the kind of son you are. Walking back to your apartment, a woman with wet curly hair, bright red lip stick, stops you, questions you. She says she's from Puerto Rico. Wants to know where you're from, what language you speak at home. She looks at your clothes, rolls her eyes, do you think you pass? You don't walk away, she's caught you off guard, you answer her like she's your teacher from second grade, who said all men are cowards, and you're proving her right, pretending you're going to be a writer because that's easier than being back home, three thousand miles away when there's a mass growing in ma and you know, and in truth you're relieved for having a reason because none of this has been easy, has been what you expected. And this is it. As close to the dream as you'll get. You walk away from the woman and she's still talking at you, calling you names. But the choice is already made, and the only word out of your mouth—ma.

Year Four

Having failed at becoming a writer, you're back in Stockton, at Finnegan's, thinking about your friend who killed himself, wanting to do it too. Playing out scenario after scenario of how and where and when. Even as you smile at the woman with the three-inch lilac press-on nails, touching your hair, can I touch it? she asks. Oops, guess I already am. She sticks out her tongue, licks her upper lip, spreading the lip gloss onto her philtrum. Wow, it's soooo thick, you must be Native American. And you're thinking about brother's kitchen knife, the one he got when he thought of going to culinary school and using that to slash down your forearms. Mesoamerican? She stares at the ceiling, hands on her hips. Never heard of that tribe. How much money does Uncle Sam give you? She laughs, and the alcoholic stink coming from her mouth makes you get up.

At Dave's, you sit on a stool, drinking, and the guilt of your impending suicide swirls with the laughter, the jokes, the group of Mexicans, one in a black hoodie and tan steel-toe boots who keeps bumping into you every time he laughs. My bad, bro, his only reply. You think about the reason you're here at all and how you should be back home with them, brother, ma, how you've still got her—for now—but instead you're taking another drink at another bar, leaving a tip like penance. Walking home on Kelley Drive, passing duplex after duplex, the occasional rusted car on cinder blocks, and thinking about your aunt, the witch, how she'd said you had to love God more than your family, and how at seven, that made you an atheist, later agnostic, but not before you found mercy in drinking. And that's what you're hoping for, that there's still a six-pack of Modelo back home.

Entering the house, it's quiet, brother still out, working at the mall. His history books on the dining table. And ma sleeping in her bedroom. Resting on her day off from radiation and chemotherapy appointments. Tomorrow she'll have her fourth of five for the week. Week two of five. This is why you're here. Stage III cervical cancer. The doctor letting you and brother know that ma is going to need support from *everyone* for optimal recovery and though you hear the condescension in his voice, you say nothing. You do what is needed of you, driving her to and from, the migraine and shakes growing, until you can drop her back off, and you're out, staring at that amber glass perspiring, a candescent charge you drink until you pass out, wake up and it's Friday again, nothing else to do, you take another drink, and on your phone it says Wednesday, and there's a text from brother, a half dozen actually, the last saying, when you're home, we'll talk. And so you drink again and again waiting until brother is out working or at University of the Pacific finishing his last year, and you're coming home and saying—ma. She hugs you with her cold hands and you wonder if she can still generate heat. In her arms, it's like you're made of paper, and you try not to tear.

And somewhere between her radiation and chemo and all her resting, sleeping, you hand her off to brother, he cooks and spends any downtime on hold waiting to talk with one of the doctors, and you're leaving, getting hammered because that's what your father and his construction taught you: Every problem—every feeling—is a nail, and you're a hammer. Except he's Mexican, so he said: Cría cuervos y te sacarán los ojos. You parsed it out. You remember standing over him, hands like talons, body flared wings, accepting it, he'd raised crows. Still, because ma begged, you let him go. You've been thinking a lot about that day lately, wondering what it takes to be cleansed, to be free of curse. When you were seven it meant being beaten, and then at sixteen, beating *him*, he who had loomed like a shadow until you were nothing. That couldn't just be anymore. But what the fuck did it change, really? His absence wasn't a cleanse, hasn't freed you of any of it, and drinking won't either but if he gave you anything it was anger, and sometimes—that's a gift. So you take another swig and you wish he had cancer, not her.

You accompany ma whenever you can. Your fingertips sometimes shaking while you're driving her to look at wigs, grabbing her pairs of socks for better circulation, and getting her special gloves because the arthritis sometimes more than the chemo makes it hard for her to sleep the whole night through. And back home, in front of the bathroom mirror, she cuts her hair. She asks you to shave it and you do. You smile and try to laugh and she tries laughing back, and it'd be easier if you weren't buzzed and she didn't look so cold. The selfish part thinks, at least she hasn't caught on, too tired, and you're grateful she doesn't know, doesn't have to worry how much you drink. Looking at her body, twenty pounds down, terrified how much more she might lose.

She's sleeping and you wish you could give her your hair, could shave yours in solidarity, but you need it to cover the scars. How long has it been since you've started drinking without chasers? Another penance. But mostly you're just maintaining a buzz unless that tips over and then it's like what even is the point of drinking if you're not getting hammered in bars, telling people shit they shouldn't know, like how you used to fear your father until you almost killed him—then the fear went away. But not saying what replaced it, how, once he was gone, there was no one else to blame for how small you let your life become. Shutting yourself in your room for years before you came back out. Instead—saying it again, you tried to kill your father—showing them your hands, the ones you strangled him with, how steady they are.

Then in the kitchen with ma, she's taking off her gloves and every finger curved, the top joints bent and swollen, her hand like the rhizome of a ginger plant. And she coughs into her fist, a nickel of bright red blood in the middle of her palm. You wipe it off and smile.

She smiles back. And it's possible because you're buzzed, and she's sick, and each having learned that preserving this sense of normalcy requires a lack of truth. You help her into bed, bring her soup, lie next to her, watch TV for a few hours, just trying to forget how sick she is. She tells you she loves you and you remember all the times you didn't say it back, couldn't, possessed in a spirit of rage—you say it back now, te quiero mucho, and close your eyes. The spinning's worse when they're shut, but you let yourself spin, just listening. To her labored breathing, her pain.

You look at old photo albums with ma. Between coughing fits and naps, she points out all the uncles and cousins you never met. Mostly she keeps her eyes closed and puts her hand over the photographs and reads them like Braille, like memory textures the glossed paper and you start touching them too as you ask about the people in them.

And maybe just because you know before ma even says it, it doesn't matter that they're smiling, there's something pitiful there too, in the way they stand in the pictures with the Golden Gate behind them. Alone or in groups, it's the same. And the more pictures you look over, even their faces stop mattering, fading into background, like artifacts of the lens, like colored bokeh, and the only thing foregrounded is clothes. Their shirts looking like they've been on their backs since crossing the desert, maybe since they were born, growing with them, covering their frailty, their mistakes. All these cousins and uncles, she says, pointing them out one by one, no dejaban de pistear. Somewhere along the line, they stopped trying to hide it in thermoses, carrying coolers everywhere they went. Most, ma says, died young. More worried about their next drink than the clothes they put on. I felt so sorry for them, ma says. Everyone did.

That won't be you. You start to get up a little earlier than you want to, brush your teeth, comb your hair. Been this way for a while now.

Clean shirt and hair product and sunglasses on. Smiling where you can around town, though Stockton has never been for smilers. Still, you've stopped driving when you're buzzed, something all those cousins and uncles could never do.

You're DUI-free but somehow that doesn't help when you're back home, looking at ma as she sleeps, photographs blanketing her body. The dog curled between her legs. You put another blanket on her and wonder why she was looking at those photos again. You want to leave, hide, but you wait—you wait for that sensation that you're made of paper soaked in a vat of alcohol about to be torn, lit, to pass.

It's the end of June and brother is out, working, and you're fucking off, drinking, not even writing anymore. You told yourself you'd come back to care for ma. Sometimes you cook. But mostly just driving her to appointments, taking notes, ignoring as best you can the side-eyeing the doctor gives you. But as soon as brother's home, you're off drinking at bars, spending your dwindling savings from that job, the MFA. Mostly nursing beers, scoping out the large crowds at La Tropicana, El Centenario, Gordo's, La Flor, because there's always at least one person who doesn't finish their drink. Taking a swig and hearing snatches of conversation: Nah, you play too much... my man's coming home tomorrow... Playing billiards for a beer. Oh my God, who she think she is, ratchet-ass bitch... Ayyy, we was out there doing our thing, huh... Pissing in a urinal. Dude, he was hella funny... Steve Buscemi? What kind of a fucking name is that? Feeling the air thicken, everyone not involved backing up. Your pussy fucking stinks, bitch. Walking out before the first chair starts flying.

This year brother will graduate, become a teacher. Working full-time on top of being a student with a full course load. You don't know how the fuck he's managing, but he is and has been for years.

He chose to stay. Why? He was just as much of an escape artist. As soon as you could, you left. Now, being back, it's like being in a trap. There was only one way to be here and you can't be that anymore: hood up, head down, strides long and slow, fists clenched, ready to go. You're too tired. Too soft. Always were. Pinche delicado. You see that now. Fucking *Sublime*, never thought that album title would be your life. Never thought about the future, period. Still, if she gets better, or maybe even if she doesn't, this fall, you'll apply to MFAs again.

Early July, ma has just finished her treatment. She sleeps in her bedroom. And all you can do now is wait. And you are. Waiting and buzzed on the couch when brother comes through the door. He's greeted by the dogs, their jumping and wagging tails. He pets them, takes off his shoes, and sets down his backpack on the table.

He sits on the couch. Two of the dogs, Frida the German shepherd mix and Loba the husky, circle him. While Linky, the tiny mutt, sits on his lap. He pets his little red head as he asks, ¿Cómo está?

She's good, or all right anyway. She's sleeping. Just gave her some soup. We'll have to wait and see now.

Frida climbs on top of the couch, lies directly above him. While Loba rests at his feet. He kisses the top of Linky's head. Scratches just behind the mutt's ear as he asks, and how've you been?

I'm good, dude, just chilling. You lay your arms across the sofa, stare up at the ceiling. Pretend it's the old days, and you've just taken the biggest hit of your life, and the smoke, you're blowing it out and it's spreading, filling up the entire room.

After a while he asks, that story, how much of it was true?

Maybe if the paranoia didn't grip you every fucking time, you would still smoke, would be smoking right now. It doesn't matter, you say. All in the past. You keep your eyes up on the ceiling, the cracks and indentations, try to make out a face in it.

Brother will look over your head, through the window, at the car peeling out. Doing doughnuts. Burnt rubber rising into the atmosphere. Have you ever talked about that stuff with ma? he asks.

Honestly, you let out a big drawn-out sigh, I tried once, not even like the real... anyway, tried to talk about just Gateway, how we'd run around all day, only being home to eat. I didn't even bring up anything crazy. We were in the kitchen, I was chopping an onion and just smiling, remembering when we went with Ray to visit his half sister, the one who lived upstairs on her own. How she answered the door with a kitchen knife, and that shower cap with the blue ducks. And then her screaming and chasing us down the hall. Her waving that knife around.

Yeah, he smiles, she had mental problems.

Anyway, ma said that there's no way that was true.

Yeah, dude, it was.

I know. But I didn't want to get into it. And I didn't want to bring up all the other shit. She was busy working, I get it. But I don't know... you ever think about them growing up in Mexico, small-ass village, and then being here, and not knowing all the shit that was even available to us?

I don't know, dude. You remember when just the two of us went to Mexico and in the pueblo, whatsherface talked about E?

Yeah but they come from money. Anyway, what I remember about that trip was when we visited our dad's family, on those boats in Xochimilco, and all our aunts and uncles were openly telling our grandma that she abandoned them. And our grandma just kept shaking her head, all casually, just saying that wasn't true.

Yeah, but that's dad's mom.

I don't think it's that different, though. Denial runs on both sides of the family. And it's not like I'm holding a grudge, but also not trying to argue. She thinks that that didn't happen, us getting chased by a knife-wielding woman, like imagine what else she thinks didn't?

Silence.

Think you gotta give someone a chance, though.

Silence.

Well, now's not really the time for that.

Linky gets up off brother's lap and barks, runs out the living room, out the doggy door, and continues barking at the neighbor's dog.

You ever think about, like, what if all this shit, it doesn't work? you ask.

I can't think about that. The doctor said we gotta stay positive. Part of what's gonna help.

You ever google what she has? The survival rate for stage III.

Stop, dude.

It's not fucking good.

He gets up. Paces the room. I'm just trying to keep up with all the shit. And I can't.

Another pause.

She asks me where you go, he says. Did you know?

What do you tell her?

I say that you're dating.

Yeah, dating Modelo, Corona, Bacardi.

This shit ain't funny, dude.

Silence.

I'm sorry.

I don't want to lose her. I don't want to lose both of you. His eyes, gleaming, fierce. Lips pursed.

You won't.

Then fucking quit, dude. He cries. No noise, his breath hardly changes, but the tears are there and they keep streaming down his cheeks. Getting soaked into his beard. Slow it the fuck down at least. He wipes hard and fast at his face. Loba goes and grabs her favorite toy, a purple salamander, and brings it to him. He grabs it, and she starts tugging back at the toy with her teeth as he tries to hold on, all the while sniffling.

You get up, wanting to hug him, but then you both hear her moving around. Brother wipes his face, and the look he gives you, like he's pleading, scared, knows there's nothing he can really do. She calls both your names but only he goes to her. You leave. Another bar. Dave's. Gordo's. Finnegan's.

In mid-September you realize enough is enough. You lock yourself in your bedroom and you'll stay there, you think, until you've kicked it, the withdrawal. Three days of fever, night sweats, headaches—body shaking like you bit into a power line. You rise only to crawl to the bathroom. Brother brings you chicken soup. And you tell yourself you're doing it for her, not admitting you believe she'll die, that that next appointment is going to reveal how none of it helped at all. The mass, it's growing again, and faster than before and in the end all of it has only caused her more suffering. Because that's how it goes. And really, it's brother you're doing it for. With his bad kidneys, you know he'll be needing one of yours one day. And you just hope you haven't fucked them already, because if you have, you could never forgive yourself, and when he goes, there will be nothing left tethering you to this world. And those thoughts, your guilt, all of it tires you out. Until you can't really rise from your bed anymore. Drifting in and out of sleep, not even really eating anymore, and pissing yourself. The walls and the curtains start to shake. You hear that noise, a noise you haven't heard since you were nine, a wet squirming, a rippling under your skin, maggots. Maggots everywhere underneath you. And you vomit and you look for them in there but they're not. But Freddy Krueger is, like a giant worm sidling up next to you, licking your ear and laughing as your aunt, esa pinche bruja, watches with satisfaction as her talons grip the doorway.

You wake under sterile light. Hospital. Doctor saying you've had a seizure. Asking what drugs you're on. Ma and brother are there, eyes puffy and red, and you know you've undone every half-hearted bit of help you've provided over the last six months. You wanted to help ma but she's the one holding your hand. You're a wretched, selfish fuck. That's how you curse. You do it with a smile now, pretending you're different. But none of that is true. You're a crow, to the fucking bone you are.

In bed, you think about how long you've been pretending, putting on a front to get laid, have friends, anything to escape that feeling of estrangement. Helplessness. You've never found a home here. But escape hasn't meant freedom either: 40 oz. to annihilation. Erasing the parts of yourself that could never fully be. Drowning it all out in order to play at being human. Learning to smile. Nothing in you wanting to learn about humility. About crying. Especially around others. Ma is coughing, and all you want to do is sleep. She keeps coughing. You remember when you were a kid, hearing her cry sometimes when she'd lock herself in the bedroom. All the silence that existed after. The darkness too. Wishing for her to come out, for the silence to end, and for all the curtains and blinds to be opened, the light to pour back in. And you hate yourself for feeling it, but it's true, how much easier her crying would sound to you than her coughing does now. You get up and leave. Drive downtown. Bars everywhere. Could be recognized, could be coaxed inside. Still, you want to be sober, to remain sober. You keep walking and, eventually, hear the shouting, and the closer you come to it, the clearer it gets, shouts becoming chants, they're chanting, protesting. Calling for accountability. For justice. Another cop getting away with too much. You follow the protestors to the steps of city hall. No justice, no peace. Fuck the cop, set him free. No justice, no peace. Fuck the cop, set him free. When the mayor comes out, they call for his resignation. For everyone who has defended the police to step down. The mayor has a heavy face, stern, severe, but something pragmatic in it too. Fuck him! someone yells. Lying fuck! Bootlicking fuck! He smiles, with teeth, tries to calm the crowd, raises his arms, wanting everyone to quiet down. That gleaming educated mouth. Someone in the crowd shouts a joke about his wife. The crowd laughs and the mayor's smile fades.

When you open the door to the house, it's quiet, dark. Brother still not home. You toss the keys into the bowl, start walking back to your room, and then you hear it, hear ma's voice weak and calling out: Christian, Christian, Christian... You find her in bed. She's shaking and can't stop. You want to do something, anything, but the way she looks, the fear in her eyes, it freezes you. This is what a 106 fever looks like. You call brother and he calls the ambulance while you lie to her like the piece of shit you are, telling her everything will be all right.

You hold on to her and say over and over, vas a estar bien, vas a estar bien.

And she's shaking and helpless in your arms, every part of her rattling, sweating, you take the three blankets off her, but she grips the corner of one of them, frío, she manages to get out, her teeth chattering, and touching her forehead, like a heating coil, you say you're sorry but you can't, a tear streams down the left side of her face, touches her ear, and you repeat, help is on the way, they're almost here, and you hold on to her, thinking of what it'll mean if she dies because you couldn't be there for her, and that thought makes it impossible to say that other thing, what you want her to know, to know more than you being sorry, Christian, she says, and you can't say anything back. Brother should be the one here, that's who she deserves, you've been gone too long. And spit flies out of her mouth, tengo sed, she says, Christian, I'm scared. They're almost here, ya casi, ya casi. And she shakes, and shakes, and you don't know how much of it is also the fear, and as the firemen come, wheel her away, she says your name again, Christian. She's alive and shaking, looking at you as they stack her with ice packs, trying to lower her temperature. And you know that of course, that's what you should've done, but you couldn't, too fixated on your guilt. Your fear. Christian, the frailty in her voice the last thing you hear as they drive her away.

Year Five

In Irvine, you're safe. Never has a city been more sterile, so void of life, that crime itself seems to vanish as well. You should be happy about that, about being in grad school again and sober, and ma in remission, all healed from the appendicitis too. And yet in your apartment, you're sleeping with a knife under your pillow. For the first time in years. Like you never left for Berkeley. But there's comfort in touching it. The blade. It's like nothing ever changes.

You sleep. You go to class. Teach. Rinse, repeat. Nothing new. Nothing stretches beyond the ordinary. Days, weeks, months. Sleep. Knife. Class. Teach. Smile. Knife. Class. Sleep. Teach. Smile. Writing, something you used to do.

And then one night in bed, you hear a thud. You look out through the window and see it, a little black crow twitching under the sill, flapping its wings, trying to raise itself. By the time you get to it, it's stopped trying to fly away. You take it in your cupped hands, its little black beak opening and closing, like it's trying to speak. You wonder if you're dreaming. Its body hot, and its heartbeat pulses against your palm. Its eyes are closed and it's twitching like it's having a nightmare. You hold your breath, try to remember a lullaby. You wait. The baby crow's nightmare ends. The warmth of its body leaves.

You bury it in the community garden next to your apartment. Staring at the little mound of packed dirt, you wish you knew how to pray, how to bless it, this dead thing.

Back in your room, lying on your bed, you take the blade out, run the tip against your hand, along your arm. All it'd take is applying a bit more pressure and you might finally see inside yourself. Why can you do this but not cry? Can't ever cry. Not even once during her sickness. When a crow dies, you're supposed to make a wish. But that's what you haven't been able to hold. Hope. Not drinking was easy. But this, you know you'll have to go back, back to what was working before you left for Berkeley. Therapy.

A LOSING GAME

The First Approach

Christian was twenty the first time he told a therapist he wanted to kill himself. It was during their first meeting, the first thing he said. Still, she heard him out. She'd asked if he might consider going to a hospital and he had felt comfortable enough—because of her demeanor, the way she'd asked, and in her asking a degree of respect being shown—to answer simply, no, he would not like to go to a hospital.

She made him promise to come back the following week, made him sign a contract, taking numbers for his brother and mom. She was in her early fifties, older than Christian's own mother, but with the same full, round cheeks, and whenever she smiled, her eyes would close just the same. Christian had tried therapy before, when he was sixteen, but that had been for anger issues—ordered by his school—and he didn't tell that therapist shit. He'd been too immature, and it hadn't been of his own free will. Though it hadn't helped that the therapist was a very thin man with a long gray ponytail whose loose, colorful clothes made him look like a kite. One that, at any moment, the wind might carry away.

So this time at twenty was what he himself considered his first time in therapy. His first and/or last time, he'd thought.

He grew the courage to go by telling himself that if it didn't work, it might at least release him of his guilt, and *then* he could kill himself. Though this was pretense, and necessary only because he had grown unaccustomed to asking for or ever receiving help, but even still, looking at her as she welcomed him into her office, warm earth-toned colors all around, both of them sitting down, her hands resting on her lap, smiling, he thought of his own mother, and he said what was on his mind, though really every word that came out could've been replaced with that one word, *help*. Help with the part of him that wanted to die, grown larger over the years, like a tumor, taking over. But Christian being Christian, when he said it aloud, first thing out of his mouth, it came out casual, like he was ordering a burger and fries and a cup of water.

This, however, was not in fact how it occurred but the way Christian had remembered it until a week ago. At twenty-seven, a month removed from his second time forcing himself into therapy. Back in Irvine, in his apartment, lying on his bed, having just closed the door, refusing to answer everyone's questions. Though by then it was too late, after the fact of when it might've proved useful to remember how it had actually occurred. And that was that he hadn't actually said he wanted to kill himself until the end of that first session. He was right, though, about how casual he had said it. And the therapist, for her part, had been understandably caught by surprise by his casual mentioning of wanting to die. She hadn't taken his admission quite so in stride as he remembered. It had actually blown her hair back, her cheeks, her eyebrows too.

Christian had seen that look before, on his brother right before he'd blown up his own hand, and with his mother as she begged while he choked his father almost to death. If his therapist's reaction was a detail he'd willed himself to forget, it was because it filled him with a familiar shame. Still, she quickly recovered from her shock and did her job, kept him there, asked questions, ran over their allotted time, this happened often in their first months together.

But really, how depressed had he *seemed* then, to that first therapist? Tired, short on hope, sure, but ready to die? Christian knew he had a way of projecting, of obfuscating his emotions, pushing it all down then resorting to the kind of ultimatum that might solve an issue in its entirety. And so he wondered if perhaps, to that first therapist, it hadn't really *seemed* like he would kill himself. Christian will never be able to remember or even to imagine what he'd talked about in those first fifty minutes. Christian was no conversationalist. But still, somehow whatever he'd said had been enough to convince her. By waiting until the end of the session, he'd given her enough time to gauge him. And it was that length of time, perhaps, that made all the difference. Because she did let him go home, hadn't blown it out of proportion. Perhaps that was also experience, she must've seen a lot worse. If she had called the cops, made him go to the hospital that day, he would never have spoken to her again. Would've blamed himself for opening up to a stranger and, feeling betrayed, would've learned to play their game, and soon after getting out, would've killed himself. This, he doesn't doubt.

As for what *did* happen, we'll come to that soon enough, but first, you should know that that simple act of not calling the police, not committing him, had kept Christian coming back for years, until he moved away to Berkeley, having gotten a lot of his shit together with her help.

The Second Approach

This time, he was twenty-seven—and just a month and a half prior to COVID shutting everything down—when he told the therapist he wanted to kill himself straightaway.

He'd found a place online that took his student health insurance, then made an appointment for a couple days after. When the time came, he walked across the street from the UC Irvine campus for his intake appointment with a new therapist. She was young, about the same age he was. He'd said it, suicide, thinking they could keep talking, but immediately she'd interrupted, taken out her laptop and told him she had to summon the CAT team, so they could come and evaluate him. They'll come and ask you some questions, assess if it's best for you to go home.

Christian tried to ignore how much he didn't appreciate what she had just done, wanted to just talk, 'cause he was there and needed to really try to get better. He'd hoped she would listen, and remembering it afterward, he knew he should've tried to explain himself, but he'd been caught off guard, responding the same way he would when, as a child, his father took out his belt: He froze.

He sat there as she typed away, the blue glow of her screen making her look disgusting. Little squares of light reflecting from the woman's horn-rimmed glasses as she pulled up a questionnaire on her laptop, different from the one he had filled out in the lobby. She robotically began to ask him questions from it, ticking off boxes, doing her due diligence and so forth. For his part, he tried to ignore how she wasn't even looking at him anymore. Tried to tell himself he had to really try, if it didn't work, he needed to be able to say he fucking tried, he really had. Then he'd kill himself. So he answered her questions about drugs, family history, head trauma, and so on. She then asked if he had a plan to kill himself.

He told her he did. He wanted to be honest, though he was also embarrassed to admit it, embarrassed in part because she still wasn't looking at him, still typing away on her laptop, typing even when he hadn't said anything. By this point, he was already thinking about how to get out of there without causing her further alarm. But he couldn't help but feel that the question was condescending. Did he have a plan? Oh yeah, no, I just thought of killing myself but I didn't think about how, 'cause, you know, I'm a moron who can't finish a thought.

His old therapist must've asked the same question. But something about her demeanor, her gentle handling of the situation had, unfortunately for Christian's sake, been completely forgettable. With this second, younger therapist, Christian regressed to his teenage self, frustration taking over.

He just couldn't get over how fucking absurd that question was. How the fuck are you not going to know the how, if you're thinking of killing yourself? The fuck? But he played nice. Stupid and nice. Told her he'd take a knife and slash vertically down his forearms. He demonstrated the act, stupidly.

After that he knew, based on her previous questions, her laptop, her unwillingness to look at him, this wasn't going to work out. Not with her. Still, the questions continued. Do you have any knives at home? Are there any you can easily obtain? She must've thought he was the stupidest person ever to come through her door. If he lied now, said he didn't have any knives at home, he was sure she would tell the CAT team when they arrived and he would definitely end up in the hospital. So he answered, yes, I use knives to cook in my apartment. It wouldn't occur to him until much later that she might've been asking him, in her legalese, observing-protocol way, to lie to her. In the moment, he just thought she was being a condescending fucking asshole, asking obvious questions. He thought she thought he was stupid. He smiled now, lying on his bed, thinking that the way he'd responded, if she did think that, he'd only proved her right. He was. A complete moron.

He had to give bullshit answers no matter how absurd and impossible they seemed. And though condescension in authority figures was nothing new to him, his own frustration had blinded him to such a degree he'd seen only what he'd wanted to see. But he knew that was true of her too, typing away on her laptop. Christian still wasn't sure why she'd handled things that way. Couldn't even give him that hour. Was it fear of liability? Laziness? Indifference? Inexperience? Or fear of his own large dark brooding presence—six feet to her five four. Whatever her reasons, they seemed little to do with him. The whole thing—her rote and absurd questions, and calling up the CAT team—felt strangely impersonal.

The only other thing he would remember from that session was how, while she worked on the form, she'd given him this laminated sheet. A chart full of sad and happy faces; she couldn't find the one for adults, so she'd given him the one for kids. But still, she'd said, he should take a picture of it with his phone. She wanted him to try some basic exercises, identifying his emotions. It reminded him of when, as a junior having switched high schools, he'd been put—an oversight, his transcripts not yet transferred—into an ESL class. The teacher, wanting to assess his English level, had taken out a picture book, asking him to describe in full sentences, if he could, what was going on in the pictures. He'd just kept thinking: Do I have some thick fucking accent or something?

Hot Potato

Christian bided his time, understanding what the young therapist's jump onto her laptop was: a refusal to be responsible for him in any way. Why would the CAT team be any different? He figured if, hypothetically, they let him go and he killed himself just after she'd summoned them, it'd be their fucking job on the line. Though afterward, the more he thought about it, the more it seemed likely that at most it would just be more paperwork. Anyway, after the fifty minutes were up, she instructed him to wait in the lobby for the CAT team, saying it could take a few hours as she shooed him out of her office, preparing for her next client. It felt like being asked to wait for his own execution. Fuck that. He asked where the restroom was, she pointed down the hall, and he went that way, for the optics. Though no one was looking. He was being careful about all the wrong things. After the bathroom, he left.

Though he didn't think it was entirely his fault, he still felt pretty bad about running away, because though he was only out of reach for a few hours, calls were made, and it made his family fear the worst. He hadn't meant to worry them, but had turned off his phone, figuring correctly that the CAT team or that fucking therapist would call once she got out of her next meeting. He hadn't wanted to talk and pretend like there was any other possible outcome; he knew, much in the same way he had growing up, dealing with teachers, parents, aunts, whenever they asked for the *truth*, the *truth* had already been determined. The outcome—a slap, the belt, suspension, or just flat out being called a liar—could only be delayed. The outcome here, of being hospitalized, he wasn't ready to accept. He didn't realize that his being unavailable would get the police involved, reaching out to his emergency contacts, ma and brother blowing up his switched-off phone. Police blowing it up as well. Goddamn moron, was what he later thought.

Later, it would make him smile to imagine that word, MORON, tattooed across his forehead. But those hours he'd had his phone off, it turned out, would be the last good ones he'd have for a long time. He met up with Selena for lunch. She'd driven down for the weekend to crash. She hadn't wanted to talk about it, when he asked over text, you're really not gonna tell me? She had simply replied, like you tell me anything. He gave her his address and then she'd shown up a few hours before his appointment on his doorstep, a new look: short blue hair, a septum piercing, combat boots. He didn't dare ask about any of that either, he had simply hugged her and she had hugged him back. During lunch he didn't share anything about what had just occurred.

His running off, he'd understand only later, could be taken as proof of his instability—going off somewhere to kill himself. He was the one who'd brought up suicide, after all. But he was also the one who'd gone there. He was trying to not kill himself. And anyway, he wasn't going to kill himself after one failed session, he knew how long it can take to make progress. Though he was sure *progress* wasn't going to be with her.

When he finally turned on his phone, there must've been a hundred if not a thousand missed calls. That was when he knew he'd fucked up. Oops. He actually said that, to Selena. He laughed. They were in a restaurant, eating pho. All things considered, he was feeling pretty good. Not in despair anymore, just angry at the way the therapist had so quickly turned into a questionnaire in human form. But even his anger was beginning to dissipate as he bent over his steaming bowl. It was actually turning out to be a pretty decent day, he thought. Though that stupid fucking question still gnawed at him. *Do you have knives at home?* His response, no, as you can see I'm Mexican. An animal. I eat everything raw, whole. I use my crooked, mama-couldn't-afford-braces teeth to tear into meat, rip sinew from bone. His tongue, he thought, he should've cut it out with a knife before going to therapy. He was seeking help, sure. But he was also expecting to be treated like a human being. Fucking idiot. His father, he thought, was right about that, at least. Pendejito de primera clase.

He called brother first, told him he was fine. Christian could tell by his voice that he was worried, and rightfully so. He could only imagine what the cop must've told him. Fucking asshole. He listened to the voicemails the cop sent. A bunch of fucking lies. We're worried about you, we want to hear your side, if we don't find you, we'll ping your phone. Okay, so, you think I'm going to kill myself, and you can ping my phone to find me, but you'd rather I come talk to you first? Everyone thought he had half a brain. Maybe it was true. He finished his bowl of pho. Not that good, he said, we should've gone to Garden Grove, he made a sad face at Selena. You're soooo ridiculous, she said. He then told her what was going on.

She eventually convinced him to call the police officer back. But the woman's lies just kept coming, and that made him want to hang up on them, and he did, actually. Selena became the intermediary, negotiated time and place. The police station, in half an hour. Selena and him would go together. It was seeming less and less likely there'd be a way out of this that didn't end with him bound to a fucking bed, all drugged up and drooling, until someone put a pillow over his face, Randle McMurphy style. On the drive to the police station, she just kept saying, fuck, you're going to the hospital, huh? Christian kept nodding. Definitely.

It was this knowledge that led him to call his mother, he was glad when she didn't pick up, her being at work felt like a small blessing. He left a voicemail, told her he didn't know yet, but he thought he was probably going to end up in a hospital, but he was fine. I promise I'm not going to do anything stupid. I'll call you when I can. Te quiero mucho. Selena asked if he wanted her to come inside with him. He said it was fine, better if she didn't. She pulled alongside the curb of the police station on campus, students walked by. He looked ahead, not wanting to look at her yet, and said, you can stay as long as you want.

She smiled, some of us still got regular jobs.

I know.

Silence.

You think I'll see you again before I take off?

I don't know. You should come down again when... after a while, he hugged her. And she hugged him back.

You still smell like a lawn and Old Spice. Mostly Old Spice. How 'bout me?

Cocoa butter and honey lemon cough drops, is what he thought, but he said, smirking, like Wilson Way.

You know I have your keys, right?

He got out of the car and watched her speed off.

Inside the police station, he was searched, patted down, and then brought into a little room, where he finally met the big ole CAT team. One person. He was darker than Christian and just as tall. He wore his hair in a ponytail and stood just a little too straight. Christian watched as he clung to his clipboard as though without it, he might be confused for someone in distress rather than the person there, in uniform—khakis and a navy-blue polo, with white lettering over the heart, Centralized Assessment Team—ready to make a final assessment. His name was Miguel, but the business card he handed Christian said MIKE. Pinche traidor a su propia raza, no way Christian was going to listen to a word this fucker had to say...Apparently, he felt the same way about Christian.

The CAT Team Interview

It was Mike who'd decide whether Christian was hospitalized. So, Mike asked him the same questions, word for word, that the therapist had. He answered them. But still, he hadn't learned his lesson. When Mike didn't ask the kind of follow-up questions that would have invited Christian to elaborate and contextualize, Christian, proud and sullen, didn't volunteer any explanations either.

Where was the human? These were automatons following protocol, filling out their forms like little myopic medical fascists. He knew he needed to wise up and play the game. But he couldn't bring himself to truly understand the ramifications of them having no interest in his actual well-being. He thought they were simply playing a role, as was he, the noncooperative person on the other side, the enemy. He was the enemy. With the cop still there in the room, another half dozen lurking in the hall, Selena gone, and *Mike* across the table, asking him questions, Christian felt the dimensions of his life being processed and limited to what could fit onto a sheet. Everyone there in the room, and just outside of it, getting to live beyond the borders of that very sheet getting filled in his name. Outlining all that he is, six feet, brown, desirous of death, and all that he's not, powerful, sane, capable of deciding anything for himself. Whereas they were free from that outline, that facsimile of facts weaponized at their discretion. It all felt inevitable, just procedure now. Still, he answered truthfully, because fuck you, *Mike*. But really, it was himself he was fucking.

Mike had his form filled in six minutes flat. He then left the room for forty-five, fifty minutes. There were times when Christian could hear him just behind the door, talking with cops, maybe other social workers too, the occasional sputter of laughter. He wondered if that, too, was protocol, if Mike needed to kill time before he could make the call, so it would seem like Mike had really tried everything before taking Christian's rights away. Though who would challenge Mike's verdict? Most likely, he was just dragging out his job for the same reason anyone does. Shit job, shit pay. Another hour, maybe, and Mike could clock out, making Christian his last basket case of the day.

Anyway, when Mike did come back, he sat down opposite Christian, put on this sad serious face, and told him he didn't feel comfortable letting him go home. And that was that.

5150'd.

Christian's Moment

Christian sometimes remembered crying, even when he hadn't. He'd imagined he'd express his hurt just knowing that he should, though really, he never could make himself vulnerable. Not since he was a child had he really cried. Not off the meds anyway. Not when his ex dumped him in Berkeley, not when his friend died in Stockton or when his mother got cancer. And not then, at the police station, standing, watching as all control over his life was given to the State of California.

He had two options available to him in moments of such distress: He could remove himself from his body, excising all pain at the cost of his own lucidity, or he could, as was most often the case, turn that hurt into rage. And rage was what he chose then, eyes dry as he, calm and seething, cursed *Mike* out. Another mistake, but this time he didn't care.

If he could've cried there, he might've wondered about all the times he hadn't, about what getting his ass beat on an unpredictable schedule had done to him as a child, how it had affected, poisoned his idea of what it meant to be hombre. And that that was what his father had infected him with, the inability to let out soft and gentle, crying as a form of asking, not for help exactly, but to be held, to feel held. That not being an option meant he could only ever hold himself with anger, with rage, holding on only to inevitably explode. Instead, and because he hadn't ever really appreciated the medication, the way it had turned him into a crybaby, it had been three, three and a half years since he'd stopped taking them, stopped crying. But maybe there was some good that came from this inability to cry if only because of what followed.

Now, some dudes like having their balls crushed or being shamed for their little dicklets. If that's you—if humiliation's your kink—you might try getting escorted by police to an ambulance in the parking lot of a college campus in the middle of the day, in front of students, professors, passersby, being made to lie on a gurney while an EMT younger than you straps you in. Double points if you ask them nicely not to strap you down. Plead softly, try not to cause a scene. It won't help. But still, plead, so you can tell yourself you tried at least. You'll know you've pleaded hard enough when the cop gets involved, places a hand on your shoulder, the other on your wrist. Doesn't matter, they'll tell you, that you're not *that* kind of crazy, they've got protocol. And here's where Christian stopped resisting, because he didn't want any more people looking, feared someone might start filming on a phone. So after they had him up on the gurney, he focused on the ground, on their boots, rather than the gathering crowd. He noticed the EMT shuffle toward him, don't hurt me, okay? she said, laughing nervously, tightening the straps over his abdomen.

You'll wish you could disappear. And being distracted by your shame, you'll forget all about the reason why you were looking down at the ground. You'll look up and lock eyes with one of your own students. One of the few who comes to your office hours. And though she can't exactly know why, that's what you'll most fear, that she does, as her eyes widen, a shock of fear as she takes you in, the highlighter-orange Velcro straps over every one of your limbs, there's no doubt, you're completely fucking crazy. Don't worry too much, though, she won't be coming to office hours anymore. Anyway, for Christian's sake, let's keep this moving, shit was humiliating enough when it happened.

5150

For the uninitiated, this is what being 5150'd meant. A seventy-two-hour hold had been placed on Christian's person. He could no longer decide what the best course of action for himself should be. The problem now being that he would either have to wait the seventy-two hours for the hold to legally end, or he'd have to be seen by a mental health expert that could then determine whether or not he was mentally fit to make decisions for himself again. Though if it were to be determined that he wasn't mentally fit, this would add an additional two weeks to his forced hospitalization. Ad infinitum until deemed fit by a mental health expert.

In Transit

Once he'd accepted his fate, being 5150'd, Christian shifted gears, setting all his hopes on whatever doctor he'd see. Strapped to the point of immobility, hearing the rattling of metal shelves in the back of the ambulance, he took deep breaths and tried to lower his heart rate. He closed his eyes and listened to the distorted voices that came in over the radio. He resolved: He'd talk this time. He'd be proactive, sincere, explain how he'd misunderstood the early questions, thinking they were traps. Once he talked to the psychiatrist in charge, he was sure that with all their experience, all the patients they'd seen, they would understand right away how sincere and most importantly how sane and sorry he was. It really had been just an unfortunate series of honest mistakes and misunderstandings. All he had to do now was wait.

And so it was off to the nuthouse for Christian, except not really, not yet. The hospital *Mike* had chosen, as Christian would soon learn, had no psychiatrist on duty. Christian having been sent there for warehousing purposes only.

The First Hours

Christian didn't expect to wait too long. He thought, once there, it'd be thirty minutes, or fuck, and hopefully not, but maybe two, three hours tops before he saw the person in charge of his fate. Perhaps this unfounded optimism was just an anxious by-product stemming from the fact that he was not in charge of his own body, in any case, Christian had forgotten what health care for someone in his position was like, this was always going to be an uphill battle. He waited. On a hospital bed, but not even in the right kind of hospital yet, although he didn't know it then. No shoes, no phone, no clothes. Even his underwear they'd taken from him. He'd wanted to fight them on that last point, but when he imagined resisting, being pinned and stripped of them, it took all the fight out of him.

He kept his socks and was given a hospital gown as Nurse Fuckup, as he came to call her, stared him down. She was rail thin, with an accent he couldn't pin, and these bugged-out eyes, like she injected caffeine right into her corneas.

Don't you dare leave that bed, was what her stare said. She'd already fucked up twice that month, Christian would learn, hearing some of the other nurses talking about it: how she'd let a patient get all the way to the parking lot and would have lost him completely if he hadn't tried to hitch a ride from a passing cop car.

You will not jeopardize my job, you'll lie still on your bed, you'll ask for permission to breathe, you will fold yourself into the pillow, was what her eyes said to Christian. Stay in your fucking bed. She of course didn't actually say this. What she did say was that he had to ask before using the restroom that was right next to his bed. Both of which were on the opposite corner from the nurses' station, which stood right next to the only entryway in and out of the psych emergency room. Still, she insisted he ask, who knows what the insane might get up to in there. He might piss, and seeing his piss, yellow, might remember standing atop a building, a solid and heavy stream streaming all the way to the ground, and that puddle from up above, reflecting the sun, a passing school bus, might seem like a little slice of heaven, and he'd want nothing more than to jump. He might then try to kill himself in the bathroom. This is what she was trying to avoid. His hero. That's why whenever he'd get up, stretch, pace in his little curtained-off section of the psych emergency room, she'd be there, telling him to get back into bed. Her eyes—always her eyes— seemed to communicate: You can kill yourself on someone else's shift, not on fucking mine.

For the first couple hours he waited for the psychiatrist, whose voice of reason he could already hear, to come and restore his rights to him. He waited for hours before asking the charge nurse when he'd be seen by the psychiatrist. He waited because he wanted to give the impression that he was sane, decent, and proper. Wanted to offset the way he'd come in, strapped to a gurney, the EMT—the same one who said, please don't hurt me—reading his vitals, flipping a page on her clipboard, then reading off *Mike's* form, 5150. (*Psst pssst, watch out.*) She hadn't said it like that, but Christian was self-conscious about it.

So even though no one told him anything about his current situation, he waited because he didn't want to be seen as a threat. He hoped the waiting was also part of a test, all his reactions and behaviors relayed to the psychiatrist. And although logically he knew it wouldn't play out like this, he imagined sitting in front of a panel composed of a team of nurses, psychiatrists, *Mike*, and all of them talking among themselves about him before peering over their giant table covered in forms and notes and then saying, all in unison: DENIED. So he did what he was told. He stayed in bed, biding his time, while Nurse Fuckup made her rounds.

But yeah, after three, four hours like that, he just got up and asked, which was when he learned: he wasn't even in the right hospital for the psych eval that would restore his rights to him. He wanted to scream. Why the fuck had they sent him here?

He didn't, though. He stayed calm. Couldn't afford any more fuckups. The charge nurse said there weren't any beds available, so they'd brought him here. Wasn't there a psychiatrist, one at least, in this whole hospital? he asked. They're on the third floor, the charge nurse said, but they can't come down. You have to wait till you're transferred. It's protocol.

He remembered holding his father by the throat, his mother's pleas growing ever more desperate and how her eyes, the sheer terror in them, had broken his resolve, his grip relaxing almost despite himself. That was how this felt. He couldn't even make eye contact anymore, his words coming in a whisper, asking, when could he expect to be transferred? Could be an hour, could be tomorrow, the charge nurse said. Or he might have to stay here, on this ward, for the rest of his hold.

Christian went back to his bed. Nurse Fuckup was waiting for him. He could see it in her stare: She hadn't liked how he just got up and spoke to the charge nurse. She told him it was getting late. Christian had no idea what time it was, there were no windows, the room lit only by fluorescent lights. If he got up again, Nurse Fuckup said, she would give him something to help him sleep. She said it stern, looking him over. At the time, he told himself it was only his paranoia. But the more he thought about it after, the more real her threat seemed. He remembered how her thick eyebrows furrowed.

Remembered the sharpness of her breath as she spoke the word *sleep*, like she was casting bullets. She wanted him to know her power. Stay in your fucking bed or I'll make you catatonic, puto.

He considered rebelling, becoming a fucking handful, getting himself sent to the third floor. But he knew going up there like that wouldn't help his chances. The hopeful/delusional part of his brain told him this was all part of the psychiatrist's test, the game. Be good, pass, they'll let you go. This thought helped him maintain a certain level of dignity. And a false sense of control was better than no sense at all... And actually, by this point, they'd done their job. He was cured. Didn't want to die anymore, but he would've been glad if some of those fuckers did. He didn't care if that thought made him an asshole. Better to be an asshole than crazy and stupid.

He played out different scenarios: If he ran away, hurdling past the nurses' station, dick swinging in the air, pushing past nurses, breathing fresh air and running toward his apartment, running through traffic, police giving chase, a ghetto bird overhead, he'd never make it back. Or he could run to the third floor, sneaking past the nurses' station, waiting by an elevator, looking straight ahead, sweat forming, deciding to take the stairs, talking to a compassionate nurse on the third floor, then a psychiatrist who hears him out, being told they understand the misunderstandings. But then the nurses he had escaped from come charging through the door, rage in their eyes, holding him down, a needle puncturing his skin and the last words he'd hear would be the psychiatrist telling him, this is for your own good. What if he screamed and screamed? He could start knocking shit over, other hospital beds, slamming his head against a wall, telling them to let him go, getting dumped out onto the curb. He'd seen videos of this happening to homeless and senile patients. Though he knew the likelier outcome, as was the case with all these scenarios, was him alone with straps, forced sedation, and catatonia.

There was a girl in the bed across from him. A curtain obscured her from view but he could still see her through the gap, doped up and drooling. Fuck that. He'd kill himself before letting anyone do that to him.

Hours/Days

Time can escape meaning. It begins with the lethargy of a room, within a floor, within a hospital. Everyone awash in the sterile light, something green growing under the skin. Something bacterial. Beauty having been erased. Just like the clocks. Time escapes. Seconds. Minutes. Hours. Passing like a conspiracy that cannot be named, still, it is there, and it is happening. And in the middle of it all, you are there, in your bed. Bed 9. Marooned. Cast off from the nurses, the other patients (one other patient for the moment), and the rest of the goings-on of the hospital. Trapped. The bed, a settlement—a small island colony within that greater imperial dependency—upon which you have very little say. The goings-on of Bed 9 decreed by the Hospital. Overhead, the incessant buzz of the fluorescent lights begins. Continues? What's the expression, "Time is a flat circle"? Oh, time is the expression of transition, and you are outside of it. Existing in a continuum of waiting, of psych evals, of no rights, a hospital gown, scratching your skin from where you were strapped down (wait), Bed 9 barely big enough to lie down (wait), what do they do with the tall people? And as hunger begins to pang (wait), and as Nurse Fuck-up leaves, her shift ending (wait), a new nurse coming by, your pillow over your head, eyes closed, trying to mute the incessant buzz of light fixtures that erase time. (Wait.)

Alone. A notebook and pen given. Then left alone. The scratch of pen on paper, the black ink drawn, an existence outside of yourself. Still, the conspiracy of time continues. The lights overhead erasing not only the night but high noon from dawn. Time erased, replaced by noise, the electric buzz, creating its own heat, something sweltering in it. On the back of your neck you'll feel the prick of a mosquito, will slap yourself, but there will be nothing, just the noise, the light, the heat, all of it, growing. Just like the hunger pangs, striking again, sweat forming on the back of your ear. (The conspiracy of time continues.)

Tired. Pacing. Light disavows rest, rest requires darkness, still the light is double-edged, as vigilance is paramount. There's a game to be played, one that exists outside of that notebook where you're logging everything that occurs. Out of view, at the frayed edges of the floor, someone screaming, pure terror. White coats will run past the psych ER, toward the real one. Someone's dying. Nurse Fuckup will return. (The conspiracy of time continues.) She will look at you, those same intense eyes, frog-like and furrowed, asking, why are you out of bed? What is that? she will seethe, looking on at notebook and pen. You'll jump back into bed, putting yourself between Nurse Fuckup and your notebook. The hunger pangs striking again all through the staring contest. Eventually she'll ask, why haven't you eaten your dinner? Only then the tray magically made visible (the conspiracy of time continues): a turkey sandwich, an apple, a deep dark red, vibrant and whole, everything you are not. How could you eat it? Sweat will drip down your back and in between your nalgas. Heat waves will rise from the tray. She'll menace you. Menace the food. Scowling at you before stomping back behind the nurses' station.

Sleep. The unfelt kind. How much time has passed? Breakfast will be wheeled over. Pancakes, orange juice, and breaker eggs. The eggs, a dull yellow, no real life in them. They're wet. Leaking. The nurse will linger. The assessment is never-ending. Her tight high blond ponytail, the same color as the block of eggs leaking into the pancakes. You're sweating everywhere. Her eyes, they don't seem accusatory, not yet. You slide the tray over, open the plastic wrapper with the spork and napkin inside. She leaves. The eggs. For a second they taste like hair. You dry heave. Collect yourself. Go for the pancakes instead. Eating them without syrup. The buzz of the light fixtures overhead continues. Drenched in sweat. The light, it's like a heat lamp. There's something rank in the air. You work through the pancakes like some dull, unfeeling animal. And the smell, it's there every time you shift, in every bite of food brought up to your animal mouth. Wafts of yourself. It's reptilian. A lizard smell. Perhaps you're becoming a lizard. Sweating all through that unfelt sleep. All through this heat.

Other patients arrive. Ponytail leaves. Fuckup returns. Everyone their own island. A woman in her fifties arrives. She's dark the same way Selena's mother is, like an old gnarled walnut tree. Her hair a tangled mess, salt-and-pepper down past her chest. They put her in a bed diagonal from you. Her voice is a rasp, but the tone and quality are childlike. She grabs her head, anguish stretches out her vocal cords. Like a baby bird asking for food. She pleads to be left alone. She's on an island. She's already alone. When you wake up, she's talking with the charge nurse. All you hear is the rasping whisper of a question being asked. A child asking for reassurance. You try to sleep. Put the pillow over your head and do.

Someone has brought dinner. A cup of soup, a sandwich, saltines. You take the notebook out from the pillowcase. Read what you wrote. Somewhere back there in time, it had made sense. But now the words and the rhythm of the sentences themselves are unrecognizable. Every consecutive letter shrinking and deviating more and more from the line. By the time it's completely illegible, the only way to keep from vomiting is to rip out those pages. Then getting up, breaking for the bathroom, and ripping them as fast as you can before flushing. Nurse Fuckup then knocking, wanting to break down the door. What are you doing in there? Open this door immediately.

You turn the faucet on, sit on the toilet, and flush again and again, drowning out her knocking, her commands.

When you finally open the door, the anger of her bugged-out eyes is not unlike your father's. She grips your arm, drags you back to your bed. Bed 9, sweat stained, implacable. Still, you get in, turn away from her, and try to sleep. Eventually you hear her footsteps get farther and farther away.

Another patient arrives. A high schooler. She's in the bed adjacent to yours. She talks to Ponytail, a cop, her mother is there too. She says she doesn't want to die, not really. That that other time, it was because of her brother, how he would hit her, he doesn't live with them anymore. That was a long time ago. Sometimes she still sees her brother, he's doing better too.

I just took too much E, that's all. I panicked, I felt really bad.

She repeats that over and over. The cop wants to know where she got the E. She says she doesn't know, she was just at a party. Ponytail asks her again if she's feeling suicidal. I just feel really really bad. Just want to be hugged, want to be real. She's crying. The muffled crying of someone being hugged. In broken breaths, she repeats, just feels really, really bad. You blink. A psychiatrist is talking with her and her mom. She's getting transferred to the third floor. Your dinner is still there on the tray. You stare at the cold soup. Soaked in your own sweat. You sleep some more.

You awake to that lizard smell. Imagining a shriveled-up lizard splayed and put on display. If that happened to you now, how could you tell the difference? How could you smell any different? Moving around in bed, you catch sour whiffs of yourself, your eyes water. The woman with the childlike rasp and migraines is tying her hair back into a ponytail, she takes off her gown, and before you can turn away she notices you. She looks disgusted, sees you as this leering man taking in her body. She gets up and closes the curtain entirely. Finally protected from the leering stink of a Mexican.

You sleep and awaken perhaps in the same breath. Looking around the room, bare and still, you again become the only patient awake. The nurses' station empty. Nurse Fuckup and Ponytail—gone. Something has been erased. A capacity, a station of life. Anywhere where action meets time. How long can this go on? You cannot let yourself spiral, you must find, grasp for the immediacy of time, of action. Though nothing in the room seems to move or otherwise mark time. You close your eyes and let yourself wander out of the psych emergency wing, wandering until you hear it, footsteps down the hall. Stilettos on tile. A telephone ringing. Papers getting shuffled. A lone phlegmy cough. Then the slow steady hum of a vending machine, metal spiraling, pushing out a soda can, its *plunk*. Life is approaching. You swallow your saliva. Thick and stale, still, it's movement. You hear the strikes of a keyboard. The consecutive rush of footsteps, a parade of doctors, nurses, janitors passing by. And then it's there over the intercom. The warbled distorted voices of doctors being called. Nurses and patients too. Everything happening over a checkered tile floor. Wheels approaching. At least one of which is loose, is swiveling, getting louder and louder. Ponytail rises from behind the desk. And Nurse Fuckup is coming out of the bathroom. Someone sneezes. Coughs. Retching. The footsteps and wheels getting louder still. Rolling and rolling, until they're there, attached to a gurney and accompanied by the same ambulance crew that brought you in. Just gonna put these on you again, the EMT says. The EMT smiles sheepishly this time, you notice her braces, freckles, her auburn bob haircut, all the brightness in her eyes.

Of course, for her, you've ascended, are one of the good ones. This time, she tries making conversation, talks about books. You talk for a bit, learn she's into Percy Jackson. She'd be better off watching reality TV. Still, there's something else in you now as you're being transported, is it happiness, relief? You feel magnanimous. You keep your Percy Jackson–level thoughts to yourself.

Hospital atop Hospital

During the transport, Christian got to put his own clothes back on, it felt good. Made him hopeful. But because he was brought to a transitional psychiatric facility, holding patients for no longer than seventy-two hours, he had to relinquish his clothes again, don a hospital gown instead. They offered him a pair of white socks, and though they were freshly laundered, the inconsistent dark spots made them appear mildewed; he chose to go without them. He watched as his phone, EpiPen, car key, and wallet were placed in a ziplock and handed over to a nurse, who placed it, labeled with his name, into a filing cabinet. To keep his shit together, he told himself that it wouldn't be long now, all he had to do was wait for the psychiatrist. He could do that, he would do it and more—whatever it took to demonstrate he was a good little puto. He would say yes when that was what was wanted and no when it was no. Well, no sir, I do not have knives at home. Oh no no no, I don't cook. The times I do happen to eat some carne asada, bistec, a chuleta, well, I just tear off pieces like a dog. See, look at my teeth, they're quite sharp, huh? He'd give them a nice big smile, his bottom row throwing gang signs. He was ready to play their game, to sit quiet and patient, hands on his lap in the common area. Just like they told him.

Interview Retry

As it turned out, the psychiatrist—hereafter known as the Expert—was the biggest fucking asshole of them all. Christian would have to wait several more hours before seeing him—nothing compared to the wait at that first hospital. After, he'd grow sad remembering all the patients waiting there with him, most of whom had looked like

Christian, or darker. While he waited, he saw the Expert scream at one of the patients, Christian didn't know the reason, how *justified* the Expert might've been, but doubted the patient deserved it. The Expert had an angry little sore at the side of his mouth and glasses just like his father; in fact, when he screamed, that's who Christian imagined. His father. He mocked the patient to his face, did the kind of shit Christian and his friends would do when they were eight, still calling each other retards. After, the Expert just ignored the patient, closed the saloon doors separating them. Though both sides could still see each other, both being quite tall, six five, six six, the gesture just letting the patient know, you see this issue of *The Atlantic*? Yeah, of course this takes precedence. When the Expert flipped the page and laughed, at some ad in the magazine, the booming shrillness of it, the performance of nonchalance, Christian's stomach felt unsettled. So this is the guy, he thought, who gets to decide if I'm sane or not?

Most of the other patients, Christian noted, were sedated, practically asleep though they all had their eyes open, sitting on couches, silent, the low prattle of the TV the only sound. *Dr. Phil* played. Christian was among the small handful who weren't catatonic. But he'd only just arrived. Suddenly, he had no confidence in his ability to handle the situation. He was already seeing himself different. Just another poor stinking crazy person. And legally, they could do whatever the fuck they wanted with him. He had no rights. He could see his father smirking, saying, ¿ya ves? ¿Qué te dije?

Before he was taken into a little room in the corner of the facility—windows looking out on the rest of the common area—to be evaluated, Benjamin Ramirez, twenty-six, six two, and 235 of unadulterated muscle, proceeded to walk around the common area, hands clasped behind his back, giving a long-drawn-out whistle before going in on the patients lying on the couches. His smile, the pure brightness of it, the way his eyes closed and the vein on his neck pulsed when he cackled, it reminded Christian of his brother.

Benjamin walked around from one couch to another, saying, you pathetic fucks, hey, look at what a beautiful day it is outside, come on, guys, let's wake up, let's fucking try to do something, his voice ending every phrase on a higher octave. Why the fuck are you in here again, you should be out there raising your daughter, you're so fucking pathetic, fucking deadbeat piece of shit. And as quick as he began, he stopped. Benjamin instead turning his attention to the ceiling, staring as if he were seeing through it, looking at a patch of sky. Beaming in delight. Then the laughing fits began: him covering his face, his shoulders rising and falling for minutes, then uncovering his face and smiling, looking at one of the nurses and whispering, I'm just fucking around, before going back to laughing, covering his face. Then Benjamin clapped his hands, like two legs of ham crashing together. Come on, guys, wakey wakey. Before going nose-to-nose with another patient, what the fuck are you doing here? None of the staff paid him much attention. Christian wondered if this was mostly because of his size or if it also had to do with lunch having just been served. In between mouthfuls, most of the staff were busy talking with one another. A few, like the Expert, were reading something. The only on-duty nurse was planted on a yellow plastic chair in the patient common area, nodding in and out of consciousness.

As the staff resumed their work, the Expert came over to where Christian was sitting. He had a tray of food in one hand and Christian's file in the other. He told Christian to follow him into the room in the corner, with the windows looking out.

Once they'd both taken a seat, the Expert facing the window and Christian staring at a mostly bare wall with a camera up in the corner, the Expert said, shame you got here after lunchtime. Might still have some in the office. He gave Christian a once-over.

Christian knew this was a lie, did the Expert think he was fucking blind? No, not blind. A dolt. And so, even though he was hungry, he didn't say anything. With his hands on his knees, bracing himself, he stared blankly at the sore around the Expert's mouth, saw as it moved, jiggled, while he smacked on a piece of gum.

Well, the Expert said, taking the gum out of his mouth and sticking it on the corner of the tray. He then grabbed the apple and took a nice big bite out of it. You hungry?

I ate right before I got here.

Really? Breakfast or lunch?

Breakfast.

Must've liked you. Tell me something, you think the food is better here, or over there?

I don't know, haven't eaten the food here.

Precisely. He gave Christian this exaggerated smile: eyes bulging, neck craned, body perfectly still.

Christian knew this game. Recognized it immediately. The sort his father liked to play, pushing and pushing Christian until his back was up against the wall. Until he had no choice. He'd played all right, destroying his family. Christian knew he could look down, away, from the Expert or meet his gaze, smile right back at him. He did the former, trying to assume a dull, defeated expression. One that said, I have half a fucking brain cell, so sadly, your game will not register. I'm a naïve moron who thinks everyone is just trying to help.

Okay, the Expert said, opening Christian's file. So, you want to kill yourself?

No.

The Expert stared at him, a staring-contest length of time. Christian lied and knew that he would know, but this had to be done. With a single finger, the Expert tapped his file. Tapped and smiled.

Says here you've wanted to kill yourself before. Christian's stomach growled. Hearing it, the Expert rearranged the food on his tray:

chicken pot pie in one corner, a carton of milk in another, plastic spork teetering on the rim, and the apple right in the middle. He slid Christian's file aside. You know, I could give you some of my food here…

Christian said nothing.

But no, no no, never mind, against protocol, have to set a good example. You understand.

Yeah, no worries. Christian placed his hands on the table, one covering the other. He smiled. Good-boy routine activated.

The Expert took another bite out of the apple, the juice trickling over his sore and down his chin. He wiped his mouth with his fingers, and his fingers with the file, rubbing his wet thumb over the label with Christian's name.

He asked Christian the same questions the therapist and Mike had, word for word. But this time, he thought about it: Suicide? Me? Could I ever? I mean, as a sane person, to have a thought and then imagine possibilities to get me there, well, that does sound insane, and sooo unlike me. But really he just said no, he had no plan. The Expert then asked, like the others before him, if Christian wanted to harm anyone else. This question didn't anger Christian. He understood. All the mass killings going on. But goddamn, did it hurt. The frightened laughter of the brace-faced EMT played in his head: Just don't hurt me.

The Expert took a big gulp of milk, then pointed out through the glass at the patients in the holding area, said, you see them out there? It's like they're sleeping. He wiggled his fingers like he was sprinkling a sleeping dust over them. He smiled. But some of them aren't. Which ones do you think answered the way you did?

I'm not trying to lie. It was all a misunderstanding.

The Expert shook his head, chuckling, misunderstanding?

I'm not saying it was anyone's fault or anything, but I think, sometimes, people get busy, things get hectic, and they have other jobs, other responsibilities that—

Are more important than you?

It was just a misunderstanding.

But it's happened before. You've wanted to die before, right?

I did. But that was a long time ago. Right now, I'm just going through a hard time, that's why I went to therapy.

Is that what we're doing now? The Expert looked around the room like he didn't know where he was. He smiled.

I don't know... I'm just trying to get better.

Why'd you want to kill yourself *so long ago*?

Christian didn't want to explain, it was complicated, so he gave a shorter answer. He told the Expert about his father. How it had been growing up.

Ah, the Expert shook his head, I don't know why they do that to their kids. He raked the surface of his chicken pot pie with his spork. It's a cycle, always a cycle. You know, fathers do their best. Sometimes you have to forgive them.

I have.

He looked up. He seemed, for the first time, more interested in Christian than in his lunch.

After a while, he asked, so what do you do? Got a job? He smirked, exhaled, then smiled.

I do. I teach. I'm a grad student.

Oh, what do you study?

Creative writing.

The Expert finished his milk. Made a satisfied sound. Writing, is that a good outlet for you?

It is, sometimes.

You ever think of finding another? Sports, maybe?

Yeah.

And school's not too much pressure? What about your friends? Have any?

I do fine, school's not really a problem.

Not connected, okay. Most of the time, when we get kids your age, they have a project or a test due. You have any big assignments coming up?

No. It's not really like that.

What school do you go to?

UC Irvine.

The Expert took out a pen, it looked like a Montblanc, black glossy finish with gold detailing at both ends. He then reached into his pocket and took out another one, the kind they chain up at banks. He put the fancy one away and started writing things in Christian's file. He did this for about a minute, and without looking up he asked, are there any *big* authors that have come out of there?

Christian cited the few he knew.

Huh, never heard of any of them. Strange, huh? He yawned.

Yeah, I don't know. He glanced at the camera above the Expert's head.

I'm a reader, you know. Read all kinds of things. Irvine, good program?

I don't know.

You read *The New Yorker*? The Expert asked, still scribbling away with his bank pen. Love *The New Yorker*. But I don't bring them with me, 'cause, he pointed—without taking his eyes off the sheet—behind Christian with his pen, at the patients. When Christian turned back to look, he caught a glimpse of Benjamin, his shoulders rising and falling; he couldn't hear him through the glass. You ever get published there? He put the pen down and picked up his spork.

The New Yorker?

Yeah. I didn't see anything about hearing problems in your file?

Can't say I have.

Really? The Expert going to town on his chicken pot pie. My nephew, he's your age, a little younger, he just had his first story in *The New Yorker*. Could be your next professor.

That's great for your nephew. Must be really proud of him.

Well, *anyone* could get a story published in *The New Yorker*. I bet you could right now. I wrote a poem, *The New Yorker* took it. First poem I ever wrote.

That's cool. Sounds really noble, this job and all that. Christian smiled so wide the corners of his eyes wrinkled.

The Expert acted like he hadn't heard him. Went back to eating. Milk. Apple. Chicken pot pie. Apple. Milk. Apple. Chicken pot pie. Milk. Again, wiping his fingers off on Christian's file.

So, your father, you see him often?

No. He passed a few years back, Christian lied.

Sorry to hear that.

Thanks.

Have you grieved him?

What?

Were you able to grieve him? Or did your anger prevent you from—

No. I'm sorry if you misunderstood earlier, I'm not the most articulate, but—

But you're a *writer*? The Expert chuckled.

He placed both his elbows on the table, clasped his biceps like he was getting ready to take a nap. My old therapist, she told me all the time how much I'd improved since being suicidal. She was the one who encouraged me to try—

Trying and failing, that's life, isn't it? Do you find it hard to accept your failures, Christian?

Sometimes. Still trying, though. He lowered his head for a second, then raised it back up. Kept his hands on the table.

You know, he said. He looked at his watch, at Christian's file. It's been sixty-two hours since they placed you on this hold. You could be free in ten. Could be free right now. Unless you're not well enough.

Sixty-two hours. Christian was confused. Was it a test? Had he really spent two nights at the other hospital? He remembered eating dinner only once there. If true, it explained his hunger.

I think I'm okay, he said, trying to focus. I know I fucked up. But I'm okay, I'm trying to get better. I know I should make more friends. And I went off my medication. I shouldn't have done that either. I really do think it was just a simple misunderstanding, I could've phrased things differently. Christian gave this inoffensive little smile, the kind he first learned in undergrad, his praxis still paying dividends. All that could be gleaned from his smile, from the way he scratched the back of his head, was that he was embarrassed at how simple it all was.

So, it's on you? You know—and for the first time, he noticed Christian's damaged hand—in my experience, he pointed at his hand with the spork, a little chicken pot pie still wedged in the back of the spork's prongs, when things like that don't show up in a file, someone was very negligent or... He paused for a long while, smiling as he stared intently into Christian's eyes. Or, he said, someone is very good at hiding, and those that hide, well, they can't be helped.

Christian answered instinctively, because he had to.

Yeah, no, I know what you mean. He let the tone, the affect he was putting on, soothe the impulse within himself. A death-driving impulse to reach over the table, slam that tray across his face, then as he stood over the Expert, bring it down like a guillotine right in the middle of his face, over and over, until, well. He couldn't keep all of that out, but enough, enough to continue piling the shit on.

I know people like you are only trying to help.

Saying this cost Christian something. But being there, in the hospital, forced to reckon with just how stuck he'd been, his pride, anger, always the fucking anger, pride and anger, driving him to make all the wrong choices. When he really considered it all, he saw that he was not that different from his father. Maybe the only real difference between them was that, unlike his father, Christian fought those feelings in himself. He was always fighting himself, like a coward. He could reach across the table and do exactly as he envisioned. But he didn't want to act on his anger, or to feel it at all. It was just always there, and he didn't know what to do with it. And because he didn't want to act, he would freeze, go cold, like he didn't give a shit about anything. That's what was always in him, at his core, beneath the anger, the sadness. Fear.

He covered his mutilated hand, another reminder of his anger. But quickly thought better of it and laid it flush with the table. He then began tapping in a repeating rhythm, starting with the pinky, the nub anyway, then ring, middle, and index, again and again, creating a solid thud that resembled a heartbeat over the table. He smiled and imagined using both hands to wring the Expert's fucking neck. He could keep swallowing his pride this way, could keep lying without shedding a single tear.

Everyone's been so nice, you know, Christian was saying, I really appreciate it. I know my family will too. I haven't told them yet, about any of this. Don't want to freak them out.

The Expert was scraping at the bottom of his chicken pot pie, remaining nonresponsive. If Christian repeated himself, he figured the Expert would sense his anger, or perhaps even his fear, and sensing it, would push him. Push and push until he got the correct reaction. Christian tried not to focus on him, let his eyes wander. But the window wall was behind him. He'd have to turn to look out. So there was nothing much to see. Just the camera, the earth-toned walls, the sign that said, DOOR MUST REMAIN CLOSED WHILE IN SESSION, and taped underneath, a sheet of yellow legal pad that read, SLEEPING IN THIS ROOM WILL NOT COUNT TOWARD POSITIVE BEHAVIOR.

When his and the Expert's eyes did meet, Christian smiled. Stayed calm. Making like he was sleepy, he yawned, wiped his sweaty face with his palm, kept reminding himself, don't shake your fucking leg.

Stay calm, asshole. Calm. But by then the Expert had already reinitiated his fascination with his tray of food. Only after finishing his apple and milk did he consider Christian. He stared and wiped his mouth with one hand, then the other. He looked down at the file. Could've had a whole other meal in the time he spent staring at it. He flipped it over, looked at the back, then flipped it again, like he was expecting something to magically appear the next time he turned it over.

The Expert dug into his breast pocket, pulled out a green gumball, popped it into his mouth, then got up and walked out the door. Christian wanted to ask, what about me? Can I fucking go? But he kept his mouth shut. The Expert closed the door behind him.

Christian figured he was fucked. He thought about making a break for it, but looking up at the camera in the room, he knew he had to remain calm. Had to keep his breathing as quiet and even as he could. He turned back and stared out the window, at the heads of all the patients on couches, sofas, chairs. All of them so still. That could be him. It will be. That's what he kept thinking.

For another hour he waited in there. No one came. Then finally he realized, no one would. He got up and walked to the door, tried the handle. It opened. He stood there at the threshold, wondering if this was all a trap. He didn't know what would happen, maybe the Expert had seen right through him. He stepped out. No one came. There was an unoccupied yellow plastic chair in the opposite corner of the common area. He took a seat.

Holding Pattern

That's when the woman was dropped off. The woman that had been lying across from Christian, drooling, doped up in that first hospital. They placed her in a wheelchair. She had thick bird-nest hair, a thousand-yard stare, and still, it was clear: She was young, younger than him. Her eyes had a youthful quality. Dull as they were,

Christian could see, faint behind the fog of drugs, a tender light. Most people, especially old people, didn't have that, he thought. As the paramedic read off the form—vitals, medication given, name, date of birth, last known address—Christian listened: Tracy Chapman, 10-23-1998, 227 Clay Ave., San Diego. The staff doing intake began to whisper, like they were trying not to wake her, though that seemed impossible given the state she was in. There must be some other reason, he thought, for their whispering.

After she had been officially transferred and the paramedics left, both the nurses—the first guy had a neck tattoo in fading cursive, ANGIE, and the other had acne scars across his right cheek—stationed at reception walked past the saloon doors and wheeled her off into a separate room. When they came back out, they closed the door. Acne Scars reached for his key card as if to lock it, but Neck Tattoo looked at him disapprovingly. They then returned to reception past the saloon doors.

That's when Benjamin emerged from the bathroom. He was smiling, a look of total satisfaction on his face. He walked right up to the saloon doors and craned his neck inside.

Hello? Dr. Gumball. Where's Dr. Gumball? He grinned. I'm gonna start yelling. He stretched his hands, neck, his lower back, as if to prepare.

One of the nurses at reception started to stand, but stopped when another came through the entrance, she had on a gold chain that peeked through her teal scrubs and a pack of menthol cigarettes in her left palm, she was just getting ready to start her shift.

Hey, Benny, the new nurse said, how've you been?

It's Benjamin, he replied.

Ben-ya-meen? What is that, Dutch?

It's smart is what it is, he said, you know, like the philosopher.

The who?

Oh, don't worry about it. Go over your pretty little head.

Don't start now.

Just a friendly joke. He put his hands up, showed that they were empty. Hey, can you get Dr. Gumball for me?

Now, why should I do that?

I need some reading material, girl. I was just in the shitter, all I had was my thoughts. You know how bad that can be.

Yeah, well, you got plenty to read over there, she pointed at a wall filled with magazines directly behind Christian.

He turned to look. Oh, you know that's no good. He was smiling at Christian, even as he continued to speak to the nurse. Dr. Gumball gives me the good stuff. He winked. *DR. GUMBALL.* For a moment it looked like he was on the verge of another laughing fit, but then his eyes got all big and he exhaled, slow and steady, shoulders relaxing.

All right, all right. The nurse sounded tired, let me see what I can do. Just wait there, all right?

Christian hadn't meant to stare, but once their eyes met, he couldn't look away.

Benjamin broke the silence, the fuck you looking at? He smiled.

Christian stared for a while, he considered how to respond. He raised his empty hands just as he'd seen Benjamin do with the nurse.

The nurse then reached over the saloon doors, here. It was an old issue of *The Atlantic*.

Benjamin grinned, bared all his teeth. Thanks. Thanks. He bowed to her, opened the magazine, held it up just inches from his face, and slowly started walking toward the hallway.

The Commotion

Another hour passed. Unlike the previous hospital, here no one seemed to care about his movements, Christian realized. As long as he didn't try to get past the double door entryway, which he'd need a key card for anyway, he could wander as he pleased. Yet there he'd sat, in the child-sized yellow plastic chair, because of his fear. Christian wandered down the hall, the door to every bedroom he passed had a window and through it he could see each room had two beds on opposite sides. He didn't consider avoiding Benjamin until there he was, in one of the rooms, lying on a bed. He was taking a break from his magazine, hands cradling his head, legs crossed, whistling to himself. When Benjamin noticed Christian at the door, he sat up, smiled, waved. Christian turned, walking back out toward the common area. He remembered the room they had put that girl Tracy in, right beside the nurses' station. Christian figured there would be two beds in that room as well. Figured she'd make for a better roommate than Benjamin. But as he made for the door, a nurse yelled at him, hey what are you doing? That's off-limits. The nurse—the same one who'd wanted to lock the door—pointed down the hall. Take any one of those.

Benjamin had followed Christian down the hall. He'd heard what the nurse had said about the room being off-limits. And so, right away, of course…

Hey, hey, Ramirez, you can't go in there. Don't go in there. Ramirez.

But Benjamin was already turning the knob.

Trace? He said, rushing into the room, Trace? Tracy fucking Chapman, is that you, why you hiding from me, girl?

The nurse with the acne scars, who had been trying to prevent this very scenario, came out from the nurses' station, calling the other nurses out with him. It was clear from his expression that he knew where all of this was headed. He'd seen it before.

Benjamin was in the room now, by Tracy's bed, losing it. What the fuck did you guys do to her? The four nurses were at the threshold.

Benjamin set himself between Tracy and them. What the fuck did you do?

The nurse with the gold chain who'd greeted Benjamin, got him

The Atlantic, stepped forward. It's just a higher dose of haloperidol, that's all it is. Benny. She's gonna be fine. Don't do anything stupid.

She edged a little closer to him.

Benjamin backed up.

She's gonna be okay. She's okay. She tried edging closer but Benjamin, as gentle as he could, pushed her back into the rest of them.

He was strong, stronger than any one of them, but they had the numbers.

The nurse regained her composure, edging forward again, the other nurses flanking her. He backed into the railing of the bed. The nurse edged closer, reached out her hands, tried to lay them on him but he dodged, sidestepped, climbed on top of Tracy's bed. He lifted his gown up and over him, pointing his dick at all of them like a loaded weapon. Don't you fucking get near her!

Grimacing, he shot a short quick stream of piss at them. All four nurses backed up, each wild-eyed and with their hands at the ready to defend themselves. Their look gave Benjamin all the courage he needed. He shot out more piss and smiled, then started to laugh. YOU'LL NEVER TAKE US ALIVE. The nurse with the acne scars had wanted the door locked and he'd had enough. He lunged forward, catching Benjamin around the legs, pulling him down off the bed over Tracy's limp body. Benjamin struggled to stand while the other nurses dogpiled him as well.

Christian saw an opening. He walked back toward the nurses' station; it was empty. He went in through the saloon doors, opened the filing cabinet, grabbed his ziplock. Saw another, Benjamin's. In it, just a packet of cigarettes, a lighter. He grabbed it too, rummaged around the desks, drawers, until he found a key card. They were still dealing with Benjamin and his flopping dick, squirts of piss flying across the room as Christian strode back out of the nurses' station and used the key card to get past the first set of doors. At the other end of the hall, another set of doors. The key card still worked. He was out in the lobby, the ground floor. And before him stood the sliding doors to the parking lot, freedom. Perpendicular to them stood an elevator, its own door open, waiting, a sick orange light flickered within, it seemed to beckon him. Christian weighed his options: Freedom or elevator. Freedom. Elevator. Freedom. Elevator.

He hit the button with the highest number, 18. Found a staircase with rooftop access. He removed a cigarette and wedged the pack in the door to keep it from closing.

The gravel crunched, rolling under his bare feet. He thought of the texture of Legos, marbles, and plastic army men when you stepped on them. Above him, the moon shone brightly across the gravel to the ledge of the building, waist high with an eighteen-inch-wide lip. Christian calmly walked along the edge before climbing atop the ledge and straddling it, one leg in, one leg out. Far below, in the lot, he saw two pairs of cops hurrying into the hospital. He turned his phone on. Lit the cigarette and took a drag. The nicotine entered his bloodstream, wired him, sent a tingling down his arms. The phone buzzed with messages. He pulled on the cigarette again and saw: missed calls, message after message from brother and ma. Though the two earliest had been from Selena, she thanked him for letting her crash, wished they talked more, and ended by writing, hope you're okay. Her second message: Left your key under the door mat btw. He knew he didn't have to respond, not right away, not like he did with brother and ma. They'd want updates, he supposed. All he had told them was that he was probably going to the hospital and would be out of reach for a few days.

He put the phone down, looked back down over the edge. An ambulance had pulled in, its back doors propped open, a gurneyed man was unloaded, a square orange brace around his head. Christian squinted, trying to make out the man's face, its expression. Was it pained, frightened, unconscious? He was too high up. He watched as the man was wheeled into the building. Christian took another slow long pull, tilting his head up before exhaling, trying to cover the moon with his smoke.

He scrolled through the messages on his phone. Hey, we love you so much. Haz lo que te pidan. Estamos contigo. Siempre. I know you know this. Hey, call us when you can. Will you call us? Please call. An increasing urgency to them. He looked at the time stamps on those final messages, six, eighteen, and twenty-four minutes apart. It made him uneasy. They knew where he was. Was there some other emergency besides his own?

He put the phone down, took the cigarette from his mouth and examined it. The cherry glow, its ruby brightness, he flicked the lighter on and compared the flame with the ember, the difference in light, in intensity. How odd, he thought, that he should find the cherry, which was burning out, smoldering, so much more beautiful than the flame itself.

He stood up on the ledge, looking down at the ground eighteen stories below. Heights had never really scared him. And this would be quicker certainly. It beat letting them turn him into Tracy. He wished he'd known what to say, to play and win the Expert's game. He'd lost, that much was clear—or so it seemed to him then, hungry and tired as he was—he wasn't ever getting out.

A powerful wind buffeted him. He grabbed his stomach with his free hand to brace himself, to keep the gown from whipping up, but still, his cock and ass were bright with cold. He might never have to feel the cold again. His phone buzzed, same message. Please call.

He walked along the ledge, playing, balancing, the way he'd do on walls, fences, branches as a kid. He brought his foot out past the edge, let it linger there. Trying to see if he could feel the difference between the two choices, testing the emptiness, as he'd test water. He sighed, sat back down, straddling the edge again. His cock and balls against the concrete, cold and warm all at once. He still had half his cigarette, he put it out, then called his brother.

Hey, are you okay, are you still at the hospital?

Christian paused, he considered how to answer before saying simply, yeah.

His brother waited, expecting Christian to say more. He didn't.

His brother sighed, look, there's no easy way to say this… He stopped. Are you sure you're okay? What's going on, dude?

Dude, what the hell. You can't just do that. Dime. Is it ma, is ma okay, where's ma?

She's fine, she's right here. You're on speaker.

Ma? ¿Estás bien?

Sí, estoy bien. She sounded congested, he could hear it in her voice, that tender scratch. She'd been crying.

Christian didn't know how exactly, but intuitively he understood. That her crying hadn't been for him. Something had happened. He felt his stomach drop. Held on to the edge. Braced himself. A lump in his throat. He coughed. Phlegm. ¿Qué pasó?

Tu papá, there was an accident, se murió.

What? he said.

There was a fire, his brother said. He died. He's dead.

What? When?

It's been a couple hours. The cops just left.

He was there? He died at the house?

No, he wasn't here, but ma was his emergency contact, I guess.

What the fuck happened? Christian was surprised at his own voice, the way it cracked. Shocked at his own pain. It felt like betrayal. He grew angry. He asked again, voice taut, shooting out like a rubber band, what the fuck happened?

There was a fire. Don't know yet how or why, but there was a fire. It was smoke inhalation. They didn't suffer.

What do you mean *they* didn't suffer? Who the fuck else died?

You know who, dude. That woman, her kid.

Jesus fucking Christ. Christian covered his mouth. He cried then. Like a helpless child, he did. He lay down on the ledge, resting his cheek against the concrete, raw, porous, and so cold it burned.

After a while, his brother said, we're sorry we're not there with you.

Te queremos mucho, their mother added.

Christian was numb, it took a long time for their words to register. I'm the one who's sorry, he finally said. Don't worry about me. It was just a misunderstanding. I'm fine. I'm okay.

What happened, though? How?

Just misunderstandings. I'll tell you later.

¿Pero deveras estás bien? she asked.

Yeah, I'm really sorry I'm not there. As soon as I get out, I'll drive up.

There was a long silence. Christian was unsure how to take it. It unnerved him. Finally he said, I'm not really supposed to have my phone, but they let me have it for a quick call. I have to go, actually.

Okay, but call us as soon as you can. Let us know if you need us to come down.

I will. Los quiero mucho.

Yeah, love you too.

Te queremos mucho. Cuídate por favor.

A Choice

For a long time, Christian didn't move. Just lay there on the edge, limbs dangling off either side of the building. The edges pressed into his thighs and shoulders, obstructing his circulation, sending tingles down his limbs. He was crying still. His forehead pressed to the concrete. He could see where his tears fell, splashing, darkening it, and then drying out, disappearing as the concrete drank them up. He heard shouting down below, peering over the edge, two cops were escorting Benjamin—his hands behind his back—and placing him in the back of their patrol car. They drove off. He counted the floors, eighteen. He counted them again and again. He imagined falling, letting himself fall, his body breaking against the ground. He imagined the asphalt absorbing him, drinking him up.

He thought of his father's body then. What it would become, was already becoming?

In the last ten years, he'd seen him only once. A few weeks before Christian left for Irvine, he'd shown up at the house and they'd all sat down for Sunday breakfast. Chilaquiles. What would he have done differently if he'd known it was the last time he'd see his father alive? Everything? Nothing? How could he fucking kill himself now, though?

He'd have to face the Expert. He sat up, shaking the blood back into his arms until he could move them freely again. He brought his outside leg in and stood. Picked up the stubbed-out cigarette, relit it, took a drag, and stared up at the moon, that cratered hunk of rock.

Crazy, he thought, worn down, beaten, all that damage, but still, or almost despite itself, it glowed.

A FAMILY ON FIRE

I'll be on the roof of a hospital—basking moonlight, taking occasional drags from a cigarette, red neon pulsing, looking at moon, horizon, everything underneath—when I hear the news, you and your other family dead in a house fire. I'll look over the edge, gusts lacerating my hospital gown, laces flapping, twisting, snapping against air. The sound, almost electric, opening a sonic slipstream into the past. The whip-whip-whipping reminding me of your belt, your favorite object. An objective correlative that could stand in for you and your parenting style. Hate and leather unlatching and uncoiling, slithering past belt loops to land and land like a viper on my back, my legs, sometimes an ear, a cheekbone.

What would've been different if instead you were just a belt?

Of course, this reduction of you, your personality, to volatile anthropomorphized leather is an exaggeration and not everything I believe you to be. Still, when I first learn of your death, I'll try to contain you within that history; I'll be glad thinking of the coming days, your funeral, burying you, a prospect that will keep me going as I descend the elevator, bracing for whatever punishment the Expert has in store. I'll imagine everyone crying over the tragedy, the sudden violence of your death, the house filled with people in black clothing, all their rememberings spoken somberly in the living room, the kitchen, everywhere inside our house. When it's all over, you'll mean something new to them. Of course, what that something is will depend on which, if any, of my own rememberings I decide to share.

Still, the generational impact you've had on all our extended family, all the relatives you've sheltered and fed, the jobs you've secured;

who the fuck am I—I have trouble helping myself—to say what you did to me weighs more, in the balance, than all those lives you helped change?

While you were suffocating in your other house, I was downstairs, probably, lying, refusing to play the Expert's game. How different would everything have been if I'd refused to play *your* game? If instead of fighting you, I'd made you talk to me? Where would I be then? Perhaps I'd never end up at the edge of a roof, smoking, giving myself vertigo, having momentarily slipped away from nurses, codes, protocols, Velcro restraints, all the bullshit designed to keep me from deciding things for myself. Did you visit me then, on the roof? Naked except for a hospital gown, butt cheeks getting colder by the second. If you did, were you a spirit or a ghost?

It's been almost a year since you died. Since I was hospitalized. But I don't want to write you from that distance, in part because I'm as conflicted now as I was then. My conflict: how to remember you. It seems in keeping with this conflict that I should write it as if it has just happened, is still happening.

And at the same time, I know it's what I'm resisting, because I still find it hard—to go there, to let myself feel everything. When I drove up to Stockton after my release, spent time with brother and ma in the days leading up to your funeral, I was numb. Perhaps in part because I was back on the meds, a higher dose.

Whatever changes I make between this draft and the final one, I know this is how I'll have to begin. First, in English, to keep my distance. And second, with small lies, deviations. For narrative convenience. Both narratives and lies, I think, work by compression, collapsing distances, opening paths to clarity, forgiveness. Took me so long to have any measure of either of those things. In the final draft, this lie, a change in setting, will smooth out the telling. For my character, it will be *events*—coincidences, miracles—that give rise to this, your remembrance.

Do you care to know any of this? How the changes I make to the story might shift the focus, color your remembrance? I'm making your death about me. Milking it for self-revelation. I know how gross that is. You deserve better. But also, you deserve *this*. You deserve anything I give you. And really, I don't know if you'd care. The man I knew, the one you were to me, wouldn't. But maybe you'd changed. Who were you, in your final years, days?

Because before you become funeral, mourners on grass, sky full of crows, no one saying a word; before I carry your coffin—the weight of it, your corpse, biting into my shoulder—remembering the night everything changed between us, the night we fought; before I put you down by your hole and watch as you're lowered into the mouth of the earth; before ma and brother and medication; before revisiting old places and new ones too, your other house—the one that burned, nothing there for me at all; before driving to your funeral alone; before all of that, you were alive, and everything between us still held potential. We hadn't been in each other's lives in years, but the possibility remained—do you think the finality of it all, is that the thing I should mourn?

Anyway, I'm conflicted. How to write you, me, our story? To start, I choose: a roof, your death, to further catalyze my character's internal crisis, his loneliness, to give him a vantage, storm-eye calm, from which to reflect, speaking from the midst of a forced hospitalization, flirtations with the edge. Feelings, tendencies that were real then but gone by the time I began to work on this, your remembrance.

I was surprised how many people seemed to care, wanted to help, after I got out. I only go to therapy once a week now. Still psychotic, I guess, but in a lovable way. I'm not suicidal anymore, not even on meds. The only edge I go over these days is the kitchen island, visiting brother and ma, leaning far out over the counter to play with their dogs, making them roll over, jump, then taking their paws in my hands to dance.

Do you remember the first dog you gave us? You'd seen a German shepherd puppy wandering around one of your job sites, put her in the truck, next to you, not in the bed. She was too small, too young for that. And she pissed all over the seats but you didn't hit her, you even laughed about it over dinner. You never laughed when I pissed my bed. You would say, ay, pinche inútil, allí está el pinche baño, your eyes bulging out of their sockets. Maybe someday I'll decide to piss on your grave.

Nah. Out of all your many flaws, I don't rate this one too highly. You had to kill the fear somehow.

In the final draft, when I make it back to Stockton, there'll be a scene with ma in the kitchen. She'll be grieving and will want me to grieve with her, and she'll be saying, over and over, tu papá, tu papá. And all I will think is, not *my* dad, haven't had one for years. Not since that night. And even before, I'd wished I didn't. You were dead to me from that moment, when ma pleaded with me to let you live, when I granted you mercy. More than you deserved or ever gave to me. Thank ma for those ten extra years, wherever you are.

I do still wonder, still struggle with all that I can never know about you, can never ask. Whether you changed in our time apart. I'd be glad for you if it were true, but even if it were, it'd have nothing to do with me. With *my family*.

Perhaps better, in that final draft, when I make it back to Stockton, finding them in the kitchen, both crying over your death, I'll hold them. As you never could. I don't think you hugged me once my whole childhood. If you did, I'm sure it was stiff, mechanical, arms not used to holding, or to any motion that wasn't a swing.

I remember when you told me and brother, as teenagers, how you regretted the way you'd treated us when we were kids. You weren't going to hit us anymore, you said, because you knew the harm it did, the resentment it spawned. That's when you started the play-fighting, wrestling with brother. I hadn't put it together back then, that this was your way of trying to be different, I was just glad for the reprieve, and a little resentful that you'd never tried it, that play-fighting, with me. At least until the day you did, the last day. And how did I react? Like the crow I am.

I must've been thirteen when you shared your regrets with brother and me—already too late. All I thought was, what fucking world did *you* live in? Felt disgusted, and pitied you for thinking there was still a chance. When you did walk out, I was just glad you'd left.

In the final draft, perhaps I'll tell of how your own mother abandoned you, left you with an angry father who doled out abuse. Use those details to then laugh at you for perpetuating a cycle of pain. Because before you could even consider leaving us, you first had to loathe coming home, make it so we all did as well, when you did. Then all those years later, you finally burned. All those years we spent down in *your* hell, held hostage by someone who just wanted out. Why couldn't you just skip everything in between and fucking die when I was a child? I could end that scene saying, I hope you're down there now, still burning.

Because to me, you were vile. And only now, after all these years, have I begun to understand why you were who you were. How broken you were. Maybe if you'd had more time, you would have reformed certain ideas you held about your own masculinity, about being hombre. Maybe you'd have been a father not only in fact but in verb. I wonder: That new kid of yours, were you *fathering* him before you both burned? What did he know of you, I wonder—what softness, what patience—that I never would?

How much yelling could you have done in your fifties? Did you beat him for being loud, the way you did us? Or did you communicate? Had you realized, on your second try, that all those times you'd yelled at us, you were the one acting like a fucking child? You couldn't talk normally to us because...what? Why couldn't you?

Only now can I see how scared you were. Scared not knowing how you'd pay the rent. Scared of our having to go back on welfare. Scared that you and ma and brother, all undocumented, would be deported. Scared to death. And all that stress and fear building and building and instead of talking about it with ma, you let it gnaw at your heart until it was hard, thin, flat—pliable as a belt.

You were frustrated at the way things turned out. And still, you were a father and had to be responsible, because no way would you let yourself become your mother. That deserter. Staying, I see now, must have cost you a lot. Did you think everything was on you? I think of all you couldn't let yourself see when we were young. Like the time I was nine, alone at the park. You were supposed to pick me up but forgot. And when you did finally show up and saw me, how pathetic I looked, with the sun still out, standing under a tree, alone, with a fear I couldn't hide, you said you'd had enough of your son portándose como puto—telling me as I climbed into the truck, ¿y ahora qué tienes, pinche niñita? ¿Qué piensas que te va a pasar? Tú y tu pinche miedo, but by then you weren't looking at me at all, too ashamed to look, to see the fear of a boy thought abandoned, waiting for his father, waiting to be rescued.

And there was your fear that I might never belong because I scared too easily. Would never be able to take care of myself. All my strange sensitivities. Delicadito, you'd say around ma but I knew what you were really thinking: faggot pussy son. And that was another reason you couldn't look at me that day, driving home, staring ahead, grabbing fistfuls of sunflower seeds, chewing and spitting, while I looked down at the floor covered in your shells. When we made it back, you dragged me out of your truck and into my room, smacked me across the face. I fell and you pulled me up by my arm as if I were a doll, not saying anything as you smacked me across the face and again I fell, and only then did you think it would be easier to just take off your belt and whip me, all over, like a dog. I went fetal then, feeling the whip electric on the back of my neck, my knuckles, the crown of my head—and you were silent, not making any sound at all, just staring at me with those remorseless bitter eyes of yours.

I feared you might kill me if I made a sound, so I didn't. I never did.

I remember feeling dizzy and vomiting afterward. From pain or fear, I don't know. I couldn't hold myself up, ears ringing, blood pounding in my face, a sensation I wouldn't experience again until after you'd left, out drinking with friends, still sixteen; or not drinking really, but *leaning*.

My first time on the stuff, I was laughing, scared as fuck but laughing and trying not to fall. Unable to talk, my equilibrium shot, I fell, splayed on the ground like a dying bird. The sky dancing, a smile on my face, and everything seeming to stretch and spin before me in a loop, my friends, the sky, and you. Somehow you were there, and the shallower my breath grew and the quicker the sky looped, the more I saw you, your face: cold and uncompromising, staring down into me.

Based on all you instilled in me, I'll decide what you thought made someone a man. Is that fair? Regardless of what I think, our history, everyone should have the right to surprise others. What were you thinking—what secret histories were running through you—all those times you took off your belt?

I don't know how much of you I can disguise through fiction.

I've kept so much from brother and ma, for so long. Not wanting to burden them with the knowledge of how you beat me when they weren't around. I don't lie to protect you but to feel closer to them, afraid that the truth will create distance. Of course, a lie is its own distance, and I've lied a lot since you left our home.

When I was a boy, you thought I was a bitch, tried to toughen me up. Made me another one of your home improvement projects. And I am now. Tough, I mean. So be proud of your son. Behold the cold compartmentalizing motherfucker you helped me become. In terms of your remembrance, your paper funeral, it'll mean that I'll emulate you, the way you acted when you learned your own father had died: tearless, shrugging.

Maybe I'll even resurrect you, beat the shit out of you all over again. Come on, old man, put them crispy bones up! Square up one last time before oblivion! I'm kidding, but I do wonder, for you, was it easier to hate him than to grieve him? Maybe I won't grieve you either. I'm a man, after all.

I hope you can see the stupidity of everything you tried to foster.

The days after coming home I felt a kind of motion sickness. The loss meant something different to me than it did to brother and ma, it set me apart. It isolated me. I was useless. The most I could do was hug them, listen as they cried and told stories about you. Often, I would leave to walk the neighborhood alone, remembering all those times you stormed out in a fury. Did you always leave with a plan? A destination? Another woman? In the final draft, you will, because I have to compress it, smooth out the wrinkles, the mess of reality. In the early days, just after your death, I didn't have anywhere to go. And still, leaving was a relief. But unlike you, I didn't slam any doors.

When I was walking down the street, toward the old folks' homes, the leaves changing color, the sky gray and severe as if it might rain, your death seemed to me like another world entirely. I was still just glad not to be contained in that hospital anymore. What was it that kept you all in that other house, dreaming, as the fire spread? Was it still your birthday when it began? Or had midnight already struck? Were you still drinking? Were you all drunk? Is that why no one woke up? And that kid, dead-drunk as the smoke darkened his room. How old was he? Eleven? Twelve? Same age I was when I started drinking. Did it happen to you, did your tongue go black from the smoke?

I hear they sew you up when you're dead, glue your eyes, pack your ass with gauze. The limit of a life reached, outlined, then closed off. I wondered if anyone else would think of this during your funeral; the way a body is treated once the spirit is gone.

Maybe I'm the bad one for not remembering enough of the good. Like how hard you worked, but if being a hard worker were enough, I'd have been the one cast out, not you. I could karate chop my way to China or work at being a writer and they'd still love me more than they did you.

Now, a year after your death, whenever I visit brother and ma, I walk the dogs. And sometimes, walking them, I'll make believe I'm a plane, stick my arms out and jog like I was taking off, lips humming like jet engines, air getting heavier and heavier against my wings until my shoes glide up off the pavement and I'm weightless, flying, the dogs chasing after me while I try to get back to where you and ma were born.

You never saw that about me. How playful I can be. Would you believe that's how I got my first girlfriend? Just being a complete fucking idiot. Was any of that playfulness in you, however latent, untapped? Or was angry robot your actual personality?

You know what's manlier than angry robot mode?

Alive mode.

I'm just kidding. No hard feelings. Can you believe I was hospitalized? Yeah, me too. Me too.

You just wanted to harden me, to make me impenetrable, make me like you. But you were closed, and it closed me off in turn, made me into something I couldn't stand.

But my isolation isn't on you anymore, hasn't been for a long time. I have to be a man now, acknowledge you had good intentions. You stayed, didn't you? Went to work, made sure we had the essentials, that ma could better herself, go to night classes, learn the language. You stayed until I made it so you couldn't. You weren't evil, just broken. Who wouldn't be, having gone through all the shit you had?

Since you've died, I've started to ask ma about how you both grew up: dirt floors, sheet metal roofs, dead siblings, parents dead or violent or deserting, and years and years of loss, pain and stress mounting, culminating in the horrifying events that led to ███████ ████████████████████████ and then your mother came home. Did you hug her when you saw her? Did she hug you? Did you two ever talk about everything that had happened while she was away? Sitting here now, writing to you, I hope that you did.

At dinner on the night before your funeral, we put a place mat down for you, though it had been years since you had dinner with us. We ate in silence at first, forks clinking, providing the only conversation. When we spoke, it was only to ask for things to be passed—salsa, sal, limón, another tortilla. Then I reminded them about the time we were all eating spaghetti and you asked for a tortilla, hella Mexican. Hella ridiculous, brother said. We laughed softly. And then ma, holding her smile, told us how you could never use Mexican washcloths, the real rough ones, because you said they hurt too much. So instead, you'd use those baby-soft American ones. This made us laugh. Made us look at your place mat. She said you didn't want us to know about that, that you'd told her never to tell us, and we laughed even harder. All hombre and shit but the loofah too rough? This told us more about you than we ever knew growing up.

Afterward, we washed the dishes together. We'd never done that before, all three of us. All squeezed into the corner of the kitchen, not saying much, but just giggling, uncomfortable as it was, all the dogs lying down practically at our feet. We didn't mention the next day, what clothes we'd wear or how we'd feel, and everyone—everyone who wasn't stuck in Mexico—who would come to remember you.

I think we were all wondering about your other family's family too, whether they'd show up. Though you should know, in any draft hereafter, that woman and her kid will remain more or less as absent as they'd been before you died—we never cared to talk about them, still don't. And when the dishes were done, though it wasn't that late, we all went to our separate rooms. Slept, or tried to anyway.

On the day of your funeral, I left early to drive around. I told ma and brother I'd meet them at the church, but really, I was still contemplating whether or not I'd go. I drove around, not paying attention, taking turns, lulled by ambient sounds, the wind of cars, sirens, AC humming, the occasional clicking of the turn signal, my own breathing. Of course, some part of me knew where I was going, but I didn't even think about it until I was coming up on the address. Saw the house. Burned but still standing. I parked.

The whole structure wrapped in caution tape and charred through.

I got out of the car and the closer I got, the more I felt it, a dark heat, as if the house were still burning: the smell of smoke in everything, paint chips, blackened wood, broken glass, the front door and a part of the roof lay like hot coals on the grass. Standing in the yard, drafts of ash air breaking against my skin. My eyes watered. Like smoke was still rising, everything still molting from the house. The night it all burned—as you breathed in the smoke, your tongue turning black—did you ever open your eyes? Did you really die peacefully, in your sleep? Did you not fight death? It doesn't sound like the you I knew.

Being there, in front of your house, any fantasies I had about starting the fire evaporated. Though it occurs to me now that I haven't yet written that part. In the final telling, if I'm more of an asshole, I'll be wishing I'd caused your death. Because in the story version, I may need to be someone else, to hate you more at the start, so that I, *we*, can have an arc.

Otherwise, there's just me, alone, with this loss.

I passed the threshold, my eyes adjusted to the dark, the soot everywhere. I coughed and coughed. The walls stained by the pressured water of the hose, carpet so soaked it seemed half alive. Every step I took I feared somehow that what I was stepping on was you. Though part of me was also relieved at not having to see the house intact. The photographs that still hung were almost completely black, though, in one, your mouth was visible. You're standing beside your mother, smiling. She's ninety, all wrinkles. I never knew you had gone back to visit her—you were already a citizen by the time you left, but since you hadn't gone back since I was a child, I assumed you hated her. Staring at the picture, I felt the need to look for you, to find you in the ruins, tell you, I'm sorry. I proceeded into the kitchen, maybe because I never saw you step foot in one, but beyond the linoleum curling up off the floor, cabinets black and warped, everything looked so ordinary and it hurt.

Who were you *here* when you came home after work? Did you have that kid take off your boots, like we did? Did you throw them when you were having one of your tantrums? Do you remember once throwing your boot and it landing on cousin's plate? Fideo splashing everywhere, and no apology from you, instead you came up to me, I sat frozen, you gave me a look like you'd deal with me later, then you ran after brother, who had already escaped the table and run upstairs. Cousin's face glistened red from the soup, he was scared, we sat there staring at each other as you climbed up the stairs, heard the belt smacking brother's ass, then he started to cry. I massaged my neck, then went up the stairs, grateful they were still intact.

Hair. Your hair, that's all I could smell when I found the room where you slept. The scent of you, somehow, everywhere. In the walls, dressers, curtains and blinds, and strongest in the thing I least wanted to see, the thing I kept dancing over—your bed. The sheets were bunched up in such a way that I thought, if I peeled them back, I might find you underneath. The fire had burned holes through them in a few places, left sunburst coronas where the flame hadn't completely burned through. I couldn't bring myself to peel the sheets back, too afraid of what I would find—the indent of your body there. If I hadn't forced you out of our lives, you might still be living. Could it really have been peaceful?

Standing in your room, I called out to you.

Your closet got it the worst, the fire had eaten a hole through the ceiling, all the racks on the floor along with your clothes. I didn't know what I was looking for as I sifted through them, but the longer I searched without finding it, the clearer my object became; I was looking for one of your belts. I couldn't find a single one. Did you not wear them anymore?

I'm ashamed to admit it, but I did. I went into the kid's room. I had to pry the window open to see anything at all. I touched everything, searched in a hurried way for some sign in the blackened posters plastering the walls, the cheap plastic trophies melted on their stands, drawers filled with drawings, colored pencils, charcoal and pastels, homework covered in doodles. And clothes, so many clothes. I looked and I looked but it was all so ordinary, so good. No knives or beer bottles or bandages or gauze or rubbing alcohol or lighters or glass cups—nothing there I could relate to. Not even a belt. I knew you'd changed. I knew you'd changed. Ma told me you had. And still, I couldn't cry, and I hated myself for it.

Maybe in another version that scene will be where your story ends. Where it should end. But this has to be more than your remembrance. And after that moment, I went to your funeral, sat next to brother and ma. I had no missed calls from them. If they were mad about my absence, they didn't show it. Ma commented on how I smelled of smoke, looking at me like she wanted to ask. But she didn't. Instead, we hugged. Then your ceremony began.

I could tell you it was solemn and that people cried—they did. I could tell you it was poignant, but that wasn't my experience. A somber carousel of mourning that I wasn't on. Maybe too much of a show for your taste, but I think you would have respected it. I just sat there, watching, as ma and brother and others went up to speak about who you were. I thought I should but didn't. Perhaps in the final telling, I will, maybe I'll even cry up at the podium, end it there. But in reality, when it counted, I couldn't. I froze. Sure that anything I said about you would be a lie. But no one seemed to expect me to say anything. Maybe brother and ma were even hoping I wouldn't, knowing the state I was in, and where I'd just been. God forbid the crazy spirals out again. But probably they weren't thinking about me at all, each caught up in their own grief, their own remembering.

Shouldn't funerals be cathartic? When yours wasn't, I set my hopes on your burial, on my carrying you. I'd already started writing you then, seeing you as character, a story, rather than my father. I still didn't know what I wanted to say to you, how to begin to talk to you. So instead, I wrote about you. Even as I was carrying you, I wrote the moment in my head, the pain in my shoulder, your coffin much heavier than I expected, digging into me, and the whole lead-up dark and sullen.

In one draft, I wrote it all as a joke. Superhuman, I toss your coffin into the grave by myself and as soon as I do, the sun comes out, so bright I put my sunglasses on. And as I turn, your grave explodes behind me, a bomb. I don't look back, I keep walking in slow motion, the wreckage growing smaller and smaller behind me. But then, the credits of your life roll across the screen, the page, whatever— covering me, my image—and instead of music, a voice, yours, plays: Mamá, ¿adónde te fuiste?...El desierto que yo pasé...las muertes de mis padres...mis hijos...la que quiero...y la que quiero hoy...la de mañana...y antier...¿quién abandonó a quién?

A stupid idea but it made me smile. Maybe all I want in remembering you is to feel covered by you? The whole atmosphere full of you, blood sky crying down with you. Only covered can I forgive you.

Gripping your coffin's edges, the pain in my shoulder radiating to my fingers, I buckled. Thought I'd drop you, but then I found it again, my balance, and your death was a real death after all. It rained and there were no umbrellas because it hadn't been in the forecast. It seemed a cruel joke, all that water rushing down over you now, enough to put out any fire.

And then it was over. You were buried.

And I still couldn't cry for you. Not since the hospital rooftop when I got the call. And was I crying for you then? Or for myself?

Maybe in the final draft your remembrance won't be literal but symbolic. You'll be a cow and I'll be a farmer with chain saws for arms, your bovine eyes widening with fear as I approach. Revving my arms, demanding milk. How much blood will it cost you? Will

I hear you crying out as I squeeze on your teats? Will I be able to stop my chain saw arms from ripping you apart? Will I feel that revving in my heart and want to transfer it into my arms? All those little metal teeth, the hunger in them. The rage inside me. Flashbacks clarifying that this is a revenge story, but also a remembrance—colored by the author's conflict re: the one remembered—and the whole thing shot through with grotesque humor, violence, the author, me, intending to represent the suffering of each while also commenting on the ethnomethodological roles we all assume: that is, the cow first as a father, and the farmer first a son. Who are we to each other? And why have we treated each other so?

Ultimately what the story reveals is that cycles of violence are doomed to repeat themselves. But really, I'm alive because I have hope. And I've forgiven myself for what you did to me and I'm sorry you suffered all that you did.

Still, you should know, there were moments during your funeral when I wanted to laugh.

I could tell you it was a whirlwind. Maybe that's how I'll write it in the end: the tension mounting, building toward catharsis. In reality, the rain let up. The rest of the day was quiet, clear. I heard and saw you everywhere. On the drive home, we passed a school with its playing field, and I remembered the first time you took us, on a day after Christmas, to Stagg's baseball field.

We played in the parking lot with our new toys while you, on the grass, set aluminum cans atop a fence, shooting them with your BB gun. Brother quickly took away my purple windup flying action figure and ripped the cord so hard that my toy flew up and got stuck on the roof of a building. And to keep me from crying, you taught me how to shoot. I remember liking it, the pop of the BBs and the feel of the handle, your big-ass metal gun. I remember walking with you to the fence to see the cans we'd hit on the ground, the holes in them. And I remember asking if I could have it, your gun, and you laughing without condescension. You said I could have it when I was strong enough to load it myself. Where's that BB gun now? Maybe in that other house. Perhaps in some other draft, the objective correlative of your belt will come to be replaced by your toy gun. I'll find it in the ruins of that other house and fire it off.

I know we shared good moments. When I look at certain photographs, I can see it in us, our faces, our bodies, smiling and at ease. But I can't remember it on my own. Only now that you're gone can I even remember Stagg, the BB gun. If I can see you now, it's because you're gone. I want you to know I haven't finished remembering. Though the good memories are still eclipsed, mostly by what I remember every time I take off my shirt.

Back home, we held your reception, people huddled in quiet circles, tías asking ma now and then if she needed anything. But mostly, everyone was quiet at first, talking in hushed voices, still adjusting to it, your death, your being gone. Then, slowly, the voices rose. Little kids started to run, babies and toddlers to wail, and your wake was turning, not a party exactly, but with so much of the family there, together, holding one another, it became festive. All the adults gathered around the dinner table, the one you made yourself, twelve of us squeezed into chairs, the rest standing, telling stories: about you. A cousin remembering how, back in the early nineties, you would all street race on the weekends, just for fun, the reckless freedom of it, until someone's younger brother died losing control, crashing head-on with a utility pole. Ma remembered how once, not long after you'd first started driving out to some hill or mountainside in the Bay for exercise, you'd called her, your voice winded, pained. You were running, you'd told her, when chinga su madre a fucking cow charged you, ran you over. A fucking cow. You told her not to tell us. And that made everyone laugh even harder.

But it wasn't at you, can you understand? At your age, to be trampled by a cow. If it was me, wouldn't you have laughed?

You were a fool not to share these things, always hiding, presenting an image of yourself that in our eyes only diminished you. Though you were different with brother. Hit him less because he wasn't your blood? Had to be more careful with him? One day he'd know, as he now does, and what would you be to him then? If this fact had any bearing I cannot, nor care to be the one to say, but regardless, I'm grateful. You were and are his only father. You know that, right?

Or did you spare brother because he was more masculine, and you saw more of yourself in him? Or at least wanted to see more, was that it? Did I remind you more of you? Your own softness? Beating me, were you trying to save, to protect not only me but the boy you'd been? To spare me by hardening me, remaking me in your image of a man, the sort you wished you could've been? One who never cries, hardly feels, not hiding fear but immune to it.

You tried to kill all the parts that didn't align. I don't think you did it out of malice. I used to, but I can't pretend you were some devil incapable of love, compassion, joy. I can't pretend any of that shit anymore, not in the face of the stories the people who loved you told, remembering you differently. Yet even during their stories, I kept thinking—after every remember, every te acuerdas cuando—about that day. The day I almost killed you.

Which, you should know, I've already written about. Wrote it as I remembered it. Except I cleaned it up, making my own mistakes and regrets the focus of the story. Because I couldn't stay with the whole truth, how, as you pulled my arm back, snapping a bone, ma just stood there. She was there and didn't do anything to stop it.

Couldn't. I can't blame her for the times she never knew about, the things she never saw. But that day she was there. And after you left, when it was all over, she didn't take me to the hospital.

Was she covering for you? Did she know about CPS, about the time I'd reported you? I never felt more alone, like more of a freak, than I did lying on the ground of our living room after you stormed out. I stayed there wishing, hoping she'd come to help me up. The arm healed on its own. Though sometimes, if I move too quickly, bend at the wrong angle, it still hurts. Flashes that make me remember that day.

Still that night, it wasn't only your life ma saved, it was mine too. Because of her, I'm not judged, condemned. Because of her, I got to keep going, keep learning how to understand others, understand you. No fairness in it, just luck. That's all it was. A chance you never got.

Seated at the table you made, ma was still remembering, sharing just then about the year of my birth, recalling how you stole diapers for me when we didn't have money for them and how, every night, you'd rock me. Only in your arms would I sleep.

How you'd work weekends, two whole days of construction for a hundred dollars so we'd have enough to eat. You never complained. I wish you had. Maybe if you'd shared, you'd have exploded less, or not at all. You could've been more than a monster. But you did your best. And because of you, we were able to get out of Gateway. All this is worth remembering too. It's the reason I want to remember you at all.

And it's what I'm choosing to remember now. Not a lie. All of it true. We were a family, but we were also, each of us, alone mostly. Closed off, in our own rooms.

And not knowing how to face it, my own loneliness, I tried to kill you.

All the shame and guilt of that night, I still carry it.

And brother and ma may be imperfect, just as I am, as you were, but still, it isn't a lie. Their love. One day, I know, we'll have to face it, to talk about it. The shame and the guilt, not only mine.

Seated at the table, ma on my left and brother on my right, I listened, silent, while they spoke, remembering you into the night. A chorus of voices, laughter, toasts. In everything shared, their love for you rang clear. But I still couldn't do the same. So, I'll say it now: As much as I do brother and ma,

te quiero mucho, pa.

PAST, PRESENT, CONTINUOUS

[They hug and then each takes a seat.]

Therapist: It's been a while.

Christian: I know. [He smiles. Grabs a cushion and places it on his lap.] Like seven years, something like that.

Therapist: Well, it's so nice to see you.

Christian: It's really nice to see you too.

Therapist: How are things? Is everything okay?

Christian: Everything's okay. Everyone's good. Well, actually... wait, can I just tell you what I've been up to? Otherwise, this is gonna feel weird to me.

Therapist: [Nods her head in approval.]

Christian: [Recounts, with some back and forth: graduating, applying to MFAs, his mother's illness, her treatment, returning home, his drinking, transferring, getting hospitalized, his father dying, and his recent graduation from the second MFA.] So, really, I just got back. It's been two months.

Therapist: So, how are you adjusting? To being back?

Christian: Oh, it's okay. I don't know really, how long I'll stay. Love my family, but it feels weird, I'm already getting this feeling, like I'm scared... that I'll end up stuck here.

Therapist: And what does that mean, what does that look like to you, to be stuck here?

Christian: I don't know how much of it is just my associations of where I was the last time I was here. But also, I don't know what I'd do. Get a job. I'm gonna get a job but that also seems easier to do if I left. But right now, I'm finishing a novel, almost done, but stuck on that too. Anyway, I don't really know how sustainable the kind of life I want to live is here. In part, 'cause

I'm used to my family seeing me a certain way, and I don't know how to just be different. How to just be how I want to be. I'm also thinking about the ways that it'd surprise them. For instance, I'm bi. And I think my family would be totally supportive, but still, it feels weird to try to be that way here. Or, you know, just being single, trying to date when I'm living with my family. Anyway, that's not really it. I just feel stuck. Like the way that I was, used to be, has a kind of gravity, and it'll pull me back into it. [He turns around, peeks through the window blinds, looks at his car for a while.] Being stuck, it just feels like this negative force is being exercised on me. [Pause.] I ever tell you how I was cursed as a kid?

Therapist: No, I don't think you ever mentioned being cursed. [She writes a note on a legal pad.] Have you shared any of these concerns with your family?

Christian: [He smiles, looks away.] No.

Therapist: Why not? You say you know they'd be supportive.

Christian: Guilt, I guess. I don't want to stay. I want to be in a big city, in an *actual* city with everything that can offer. I wish they'd come with me, but they got their lives here. And Julio, my brother...

Therapist: Yes, I remember.

Christian: He's been a teacher for a few years now. He's settled. I never really had that here. Seems easier to try somewhere else. Give myself a fresh start. [He pauses, sighs.] You know, all that time I was away from Stockton, at its core—it was running away. Maybe that's what I want to keep doing.

Therapist: What do you feel you need to run away from?

Christian: [He brings his knuckles up to his lips, covers his mouth.] This place fucking sucks. [Brings his hands down.] That's not really true... Just have all these shit fucking memories. I know it wasn't all bad, but when I try to remember, that's all that comes up. How it just fucking sucked.

Therapist: Do you think that's true for Julio? For your mom?

Christian: I don't know. I hope not. [Pause.] I want to say no. I want to say that's part of the reason why they're still here. Like I've brought it up to them, even before I came back. Leaving Stockton. And they entertain it, but it also seems like it's just always hypothetical for them. I'm sure all their associations aren't good ones, but they do have them, good associations. I've tried, really, to remember good times, but I can't. Growing up here—growing up period—it was just fucking shit.

Therapist: Have you tried writing about it?

Christian: [He lightly laughs.] Oooooh yeah. It's *all* I write about, actually.

Therapist: I mean, writing about the good times.

Christian: Nothing really comes up. Like, nothing that feels substantive.

Therapist: What do you mean when you say "substantive"? Why wouldn't it be? If it's a happy memory.

Christian: The small stuff that does come up, it seems insignificant. Things that are crushed by the weight of all the bad. [His voice cracks.] Just doesn't seem worth it.

Therapist: It sounds like you're being protective of the good things. It makes sense. But there are ways to be protective without negating them. [She pushes the tissue box closer to him.]

Christian: I know. I know. [He takes a tissue, twists it in his hands.] It's just weird. Like I know I'm not as fucked up now, like not even close, to how I was, but I still feel so negative when I try to remember. Just think of how bad it was, all the ways I failed. How I couldn't protect myself. Couldn't just speak up. Even when I got older, I couldn't. It makes me ashamed.

Therapist: But there doesn't have to be any judgment. Or even any commentary. Whoever you were, that isn't who you are now. And whatever happened to you, it isn't happening to you now.

So can you just hold it? All of it, I mean. In memory. The good and the bad.

Christian: I wouldn't know where to begin.

Therapist: Anywhere.

Christian: I'll try.

Therapist: [She smiles.] Don't try.

Christian: I know, I know. I remember.

1999. Gateway. I dream of an auditorium. Everything quiet. I'm five years old and onstage under the spotlight. Music plays: deep, resonant. I dance, heart on fire. My breath powerful. I send it gusting out into the crowd. Brother and ma are mouths open, amazed. Everyone we know is there in the crowd behind them. I spin like every part of me is on fire, and I want the flame of me to burn, burn, reach out toward them, and they see my burning, moving, swaying from one end of the stage to the other and they can't help it, they're cheering, clapping, the waves of adulation crash over brother and ma. Brother whoops, punches the air, and ma throws me the first rose. I'm catching my breath, smiling, waving to the crowd, my sweat brilliant in the spotlight. Encore. Encore. Encore. Once more, I dance. I'm dancing in my room until I can't anymore, tired. Breathless. Basking in the fantasy, and splayed on the ground, smiling, pretending to be covered in roses. As I shine in the daylight coming through the blinds, blue eyeshadow over my eyes, red blush on my cheeks.

I hear stomping on the stairs. My father, annoyed. He's yelling, WHAT THE FUCK DID YOU DO TO THE TV? I think of hiding under the bed, in the closet. The bedroom door swings open. And for a moment, we're frozen, both taken by surprise. Neither ready. There will be a before and an after from this moment. Time marches on. And then his face wrinkles in disgust. He takes off his belt, steps in, slams the door shut all in one motion. Showtime.

2012. I'm in my car with my shithead friends, hotboxing in a hotel parking lot. It's night. We're waiting for a text from Ernesto's cousin—room number for a party none of us are invited to. That's when I see her. Ma. Standing outside the same hotel with one of her friends. They're high, lost, looking around. They brace against a lamppost, ma staring at the ground as her friend rubs her back. The friend says something, and they both start laughing. My throat tightens. I fear they're headed to the same party we are. I slide down my seat, keep my eyes just above the dashboard.

The way they blink their eyes, dazed and looking out like everything is new; they're high for the first time. And all I can think is that they need help—food, water, a bed. When my friends spot them, they start with the jokes.

Two old moms out here tricking, sucking pipe for a washer-dryer.

They don't know they're talking about ma.

Hey. Whiteboy, why don't you buy her?

With the tits?

Yeah, ain't titty-fucking your thing?

Yeah, but not old tits, man.

Shut the fuck up, I say. But they don't. The jokes keep escalating as we wait for the text.

Bitch is so high, you might even get it free.

Wouldn't do her even if you paid me.

Old bitches gross me out.

It's too late, feels too late to say, that's my mom. I swallow and the spit goes down the wrong hole, I cough uncontrollably.

Dude, that's what paper bags are for.

I'd need a bag as big as her body. A body bag, that's what I need.

I grip the wheel tight like it's a life buoy. And the only thing stopping me from rushing out, yelling at her. I fucked everything up. Ma's out here high, and it's because of me, what I did. Get the fuck out of my car, I say. Now.

You serious?

All of you. I wring the leather of the steering wheel cover. I'll drag you all the fuck out.

Chill, dude, damn.

Getting all fucking butthurt. Wasn't even talking about you.

I clench my teeth so hard I think my jaw might shatter. They exit the car, doors slam.

They all disappear into the dark. It's the last time I'll see any of them until Cuco's funeral. Time passes. It gets darker. Quieter. They're still there, ma and her friend, under the lamppost. Looking at their phones. Whispering to each other. Lost. They're lost. I won't be able to take it any longer. I get out of the car. I walk toward them. I want to say a million things. To tell them, come on, let's go, I'll take you home. But something about the way she looks at me, once she's spotted me, defiant, annoyed, instinct kicks in and without intending to I say:

Y tú, ¿qué haces aquí?

No me hables así, she replies. Éste, Mr. Tough Guy. She rolls her eyes.

My stomach like it's being held in a Vise-Grip and I'm trying to keep the vomit down, if I don't, it'll all be there, all the food she's ever made me, my whole life, right there at her feet. I want to say I'm sorry, I fucked everything up. But instead, I look away, back toward my car.

I was just around.

Aha, she says, pues yo también, ah-round.

I can't look at her but can't leave either. I want to start over. Ma simply says, apestas. Not mad or disappointed, simply dismissive.

Apestas, she says, sniffing the air. Ya sabía. Chree-stee-an no asistió a los periodos...

Back home, in my bed, all I can see is the annoyance plastered on her face, her dilated pupils, red eyes. Lipstick same shade of red as my car. In the morning, I look out the window and don't see it, my car. There's a scratch at the back of my throat, and my eyes, my whole body is sore. I try to collect my thoughts, remember how I got home, how she did. Is she home? I don't remember driving. And all I can picture is her hair, the same color of asphalt, a tire, her hair, tangled under my car. My heart's pounding. What if I ran her over? I get out of bed, scramble, trip over my shoes, run into her bedroom. She won't be there, I'll run all over the house, calling out, ma, ma, MA, MA, MA. She won't be anywhere. Chills, a cold feverish anger, breaking over my body, I take one of her potted plants and smash it on the ground.

Hours later. The front door opens. I'll look ma in her eyes. She'll toss the keys at me. They'll hit my bicep. I'm sorry, I'll want to say. But the words caught in my throat, chest pounding. I'm in a nightmare. This is a nightmare. She'll step right over the plant. Bárrelo. Her bedroom door will close. I'll get the broom. My body shaking the whole time. I'm a freak. I'm a freak. In my room, lying in my bed, I'll remember: My arm tight across my father's throat. Ma screaming.

I'll watch the light change through the blinds.

Sunrise.

Sundown.

Sunrise.

Sundown.

Most of what I'll do for the next year will be to sleep.

2005. There's a door, I remember well. To a broom closet in the hall of our first house. After Gateway. When I remember that door— the brassy dented knob with the paint scratched off by the dog, surrounded in darkness, as if it existed separate from the rest of the house—like something from a dream.

In the dream, the memory, I'm in it. The closet, the darkest spot in the house. I'm on the floor. It's carpeted, the weave both rough and delicate. The way hands can sometimes be. Just a thin band of light, faint but warm, reaching me under the slit. In the dark of the closet, I study it. That band. It wants something. But what? What can light want? To expand? To spread?

Like warmth. Warmth in me, wants to expand. My blood. I imagine I'm bleeding. The room I share with brother has wood flooring. Only this floor is carpeted. I run my hand over it. It scratches me. The way a knife's tip does when I run it lightly, and at just the right angle, over my palm, slow and steady, my skin and the blade making a sound where they touch, soft and high, like a bird's chirping or a grindstone's whistling.

I play with a knife in the dark of the closet, listening to the sound it makes on my skin. A high scratching that makes me want to press down, to run the edge faster, deeper. So I do, my flesh giving, opening, blood spilling out.

To let blood out is what knives do, what they're for. Everything wants to be let out of itself. Air from a tire, blood from a body. I think of my father's sighs, hard, exhausted, his breath scratching its way out. Long-drawn-out sounds as the feeling escapes him, leaking.

I sigh. The air just keeps coming, more and more. I'm opening, leaking, emptying out.

I want to run and hide, afraid that if I let it all out, all my blood, my breath, I'll disappear forever. But I want to keep going too. Because letting it out—blood, breath, feeling—reminds me I'm alive. I should be running for help, the way my palm's bleeding, but it's dark and I'm just waiting. To be empty. Wiping my hand on the carpet, lying with my cheek to it, I breathe and bleed and wait. To be empty or for the closet door to open. Whichever comes first.

The door opens and a shadow stands over me. Something in its hand flickers.

Then the dream, the memory, cuts.

2013. A year removed from graduating high school. The fifth house, the one with the sycamore with the white bark in the front yard. I'm in bed. Earbuds in. It's dark. Still. Quiet. I play some Rage, dark and heavy, turn the volume up. Try to match my breath to the rhythm. I feel my heart against my chest. Move. Move, I tell myself. I can't. I take the earbuds out. His body. His chest. Twice my size, he must've been. How old is he now? How old was he *then*? I put the earbuds back in. I search for something else to play.

My door opens. My back to it. I close my eyes. Feign stillness. Like an animal, playing dead. Someone comes in, goes to the window, creaks open the blinds. It's brother.

    Dude never leaves his garage, he says. Think his wife loves him?
    Brother paces. I stay dead.
    I'm going to work, he says. And to Rem's after.
    A car goes by. A bird, singing.
    I'll see you when I get back, he says.
    He closes the door behind him.

When I hear his engine, I open my eyes. His headlights flash against my window. A tree's shadow playing over the wall. Leaves rustling like the feathers of a bird. I search for a song to play. Close my eyes.

My door opens. Silence. I sense her weight at the edge of my bed. Are her hands folded? Resting on her lap? I never look at her. Sometimes I think I hear her muttering, sometimes I want to open my eyes and turn around, but I don't want to know what's there in ma's eyes. She gets up, goes over to my desk. I hear the pencils clink against the cup, the crinkle of a water bottle, papers shuffling. If I made more mess, beyond the desk, she'd clean that up too. But the desk is all I can really manage. She sits back down on the edge of my bed. Grabs my foot. I play dead.

She stands. I hear the door close behind her.

Sometimes I wonder what she'd say, what she'd do if she knew about the knife under my pillow. My head resting upon a blade.

2000. I'm six. Brother is eight. The game starts near the plum tree, heavy with fruit. Plums everywhere over the ground, rotting. Brother and I want them fresh, from the branches. We claw at the loose bricks in a crumbling wall, ones we haven't hurled yet at lizards or crows. Let's make a pile first, brother says. But I don't. Instead I bring my brick with me under the tree. Brother makes his pile while I stand idle, looking up, searching the branches for the best plum, one that will burst when squeezed near brother's face. A breeze flutters the leaves, the purple light off the plums dancing on my skin like a dream. I wish I could lick the light off my hands.

All right, I'm ready, brother says. Move.

No.

Just get out the way. He balances a brick in one hand, raising it over his head.

I don't want to... Say please if you want me to move.

Why the hell should I?

I throw my brick down, cross my arms, lean against the tree.

Fucking move already. He assumes a throwing stance. I'll throw it, he says.

Do it, then.

His eyes narrow, and he does. The brick sails up into the tree's canopy. And like a game of pachinko, it hits branch after branch, ricocheting all the way down. It misses me by a wide margin.

See, I tell him, didn't have to move. A few ripe plums hit the ground.

Fine, he says. He picks up another brick and as he throws it, I stare at him, grinning, sticking out my tongue. I hear it ricocheting down against the branches, and I'm still grinning when I feel it. A thud. Brother's eyes go wide. I blink. Brother is standing right in front of me, almost against me. Dude, he says. Dude. A wetness warms the crown of my head, dripping down onto my forehead. I wipe. Blood on my fingertips. I get dizzy, sleepy. I blink again and again.

My arm is draped across brother's shoulder.

Oh shit. Shit, he says. I blink again. Why didn't you move? You could've just moved.

He keeps muttering to himself, and between blinks, I can feel the blood still trickling slowly down over my head, my face, my mouth. I blink and we're by the public pool. I blink again and we're in the second parking lot, getting closer to home. He keeps muttering. I glance at him, my eyes so heavy, an urgency in his. They just keep scanning.

Why is it so quiet? I ask.

I mean I didn't think a brick would sound like that, like a fucking walnut being cracked. A dragonfly lands on brother's hand. You got a goddamn walnut for a brain now.

Where is everybody? I ask. A sudden shiver as a gust of wind climbs up my shirt.

People only use ten percent of their brain anyway, right?

I blink again, and we're by the rosebushes close to our apartment. I look up at the sun. It's so bright where it is, it seems permanent. I don't think it'll ever move again.

What the? What are you doing? He lowers my head. I got your fucking blood all over me now.

I blink again, and we're back.

MA! brother screams. MA. MA. PA. PA. MA. PA.

He drags me up the stairs and still, in his eyes, that urgent scanning look. He lays me on my bunk. Just fucking stay there, okay?

He runs out of the bedroom, I can hear him rifling through the linen closet as I look up at the bottom of his pilly mattress and take in its fabric: stars, meteors, moons, distant planets. Look at all these stars, I say.

What'd you say? He lifts my head, puts a towel under it, another on top of it.

I point at him. You, I say. Smiling.

He grabs my hand, puts it on the towel. Pressure, he says. Gotta keep that walnut juice in.

Good night, I tell him.

Yeah, hasta mañana, he says. Stupid-ass.

1998. I'm four. With my parents, brother, along with an aunt, an uncle, and two cousins. They've decided to take brother to see a therapist. It's mostly for brother, because he can't be still. A real troublemaker, our parents think. But since I'm there, the therapist sees me too. I don't remember what she said about brother's session but when it's my turn, he's there in the room, with the rest of the family.

I look back at ma, my father, aunts, uncles, cousins I barely know. They're all watching me. I want them to go. I look at ma, want to tell her. Please, please, make them all go. The therapist asks me something, but I can't make it out. She repeats her question. She smiles, just her lips, nothing else moves, her eyes don't crinkle the way ma's do. I wish she wasn't behind her big desk, that I didn't have to look up over it at her. Ma chimes in. Tells her I won't eat grapes that have seeds in them.

Oh, is that true? the therapist asks. And why's that? My heart starts to race, I look back again.

It's okay, she says. Take a deep breath. In—and out. Good. Again. Eyes just on me, okay? Try for me, okay? Why don't you like grapes with seeds in them?

They're not easy to eat, I answer. And I have to peel them. I have to be careful, breaking the skin open. Like mine. Soft, and so easy to break. And when I eat it, I think of a giant doing that to me. Sucking my bones clean and spitting them out, like I do the seeds.

I see, she says. That's fascinating. But the way she smiles, I know she's lying. Lying the way grown-ups always do. Eyes on me, remember. Tell me, what do you think a giant looks like?

Soon, I'm not there anymore. Though my body is, I'm outside of it. I see myself. See my lips moving, the therapist nodding, and my family, all of them, behind me, my father standing with his arms crossed, brother tying his shoes slowly. Getting back to his highlighter-green Game Boy Color. More questions are asked. And I'm answering but I'm not really there anymore.

After, in the lobby, the therapist won't acknowledge me, talking about me as if I'm not there, as if I can't hear. She'll say that brother is fine, a normal kid, but this one—meaning me—you need to be careful with him. You should take him to a therapist, one that accepts your insurance.

They never will.

Maybe, I think, I was always broken.

2001. Me, brother, Selena, Moco, Roberto, and Cuco. We're playing dogs. Being dogs. In Moco and Selena's apartment. On all fours, tongues out, barking. I howl and Selena laughs.

That's not how you howl.

Yeah-huh it is, I say.

It's more like this, she says. Moco gives it a try.

That's weak, let me show you all, brother says. Selena smiles.

Y'all so good, show us.

Yeah, show us, Roberto says. A chorus of yeahs.

We do. Me and brother crash into each other. Grind our heads. Bare our teeth at them. We run around the living room, see who the fastest dog is.

Do a trick, they say. Do a trick.

I try scratching my head with my foot and I tip over. They laugh. Brother bites at my shirt and I bite at his. Everyone joins. We're all yanking at each other's shirts with our teeth. Growling, barking, howling. Moco biting the head off a green plastic army man. Grinning. Then brother bites down hard, thinking he's got a button but immediately I scream. I cry, stand, lift up my shirt, there's a trickling of blood from where my nipple was. Gone. A skinny trail of blood snakes down toward the waist of my jeans.

What are nipples for? I picture myself at the pool, taking off my shirt, a freak. Brother brings a square of paper towel and a Band-Aid—the smallest Band-Aid I've ever seen. Brother presses the paper towel over the little wound where my nipple should be, sponging the blood away. Then he sticks the Band-Aid on me. Selena gives me a cup to drink. Something very bitter. She says it's what her ma gives her when she's hurt herself. I drink one, then another, another.

We're outside and I've stopped crying. I keep trying to meet brother's eyes, but he avoids mine. Cuco, Roberto, and Moco are having a kicking contest, seeing who can kick the highest lime off the lime tree. I'm sniffling and casting about—running my hand through fences, tree trunks, rims of cars—looking for somewhere I can pee. The sun is directly overhead. No clouds. It's spring and the breeze whips my shirt against me. The paletero comes driving by and brother waves him down, buys a couple kites. Mine an eagle, his a wolf. He helps me fly mine first. When it's in the air, every couple minutes I unspool a little more of the string. Everything gone silent. Dreamlike veneer. Just gusts of wind, swaying trees, and my eagle kite getting above the tallest tree. When I'm out of string, and feel a little tug from the kite, I bite it in two and watch as my eagle kite ascends, soars, blocks out the sun, is blocked out by it. It'll start to burn soon. Until then, it's free.

2002. Gateway. His open palm strikes my face. No one else is home. The stinging heat of his smack—what did I do? I search his eyes for an answer—he smacks me again. Takes off his belt. I slump to the ground and cover my head, heart pounding in my chest. I haven't pissed my bed all week. My mouth is so dry there's no way I could scream or even cry.

Get up, I tell myself. Get up.

He grabs my wrists, pries my arms apart. His eyes, he wishes I weren't his son. I look away and he grabs my face. I did my homework, I always do. Not like brother. He smacks me again. Grabs the collar of my shirt, balls up his fist, rears back, and punches the wall beside me. I put my hands up, try to defend myself. He crushes my fingers, grinding them into each other until I'm writhing. Nothing in his eyes now. I haven't cried in forever. He presses his palm flat and heavy on my head, crushing me down into the floor. The pain, I'm doing everything I can not to make any noise, squirming instead, under the pressure of his hand. I focus on keeping my mouth shut, making animal pain noises as he smacks me again. He stops. Lets me catch my breath. When all I'm doing is breathing, shallow anxious breaths, he begins pinching the flesh behind my knee.

I don't know how I'm not crying. Sometimes looking back, the not crying will make me doubt the severity. But the pain, the pain I felt. I can't quite stay with it anymore. He keeps pinching like he's tearing off chunks of my flesh, and I stop being there. Stop feeling it. I float above, and I can see him, what he's doing, my body writhing, making stifled animal noises as he grinds into me like a pestle into a mortar, pinching and screwing his fingers into my flesh.

When it's over, he simply gets up, walks away. I lie there, curled and turned toward the wall. Soon I will sleep. But first, I will think there's something I can do, a way I can be to avoid this punishment again. There won't be. It never was about me.

2004. Last year in Gateway. I have cow Tamagotchi; brother has frog. I wanted frog too, but they were out. I had to choose between dog, bird, monkey, or cow. Brother gloats about getting frog but I know I've won. I have cow. Cow, more than all the others, has something precious in its eyes. Like it's saying, asking, do you know where I live? What I'm about? This field, grassy, wide-open, even on the little pixelated screen...I know, cow. I see. You're how I want to be. An open, wondering face, just waiting for me to push a button, to give you something.

Back home, brother holds his Tamagotchi close, like it's his baby. We look down into their tiny digital faces, calf and tadpole, feeding them until they start to grow. We don't know how much food to give them so we do what ma does with us—feed and feed and feed. They grow and grow. But at night, something happens. When we wake, they've sprouted wings—little cow and frog angels. We don't know why but it's the nights that kill them.

A fresh egg replaces each angel. New offspring that we promise to keep alive...for longer. Eat, eat, eat, we say. And they do, everything we give them they take. I feed my cow and the Tamagotchi beeps. Again, again, brother says over my shoulder. Feed yours, I say. I did, look, it already has wings. We want to make them angels. That's the game we play.

Yeah, my little guardian, brother says.

Christian: I tried to write, like you asked. [He pauses, and looks away.]

Therapist: [She laughs, makes a rolling motion with her hand.] Well? Go on.

Christian: There were some happy moments. Like my brother landing a brick on my head, biting off my nipple. Flying a kite with him after.

Therapist: [Sighs. Pinches the area between her eyebrows.] Well, it's a start, I suppose. And what makes them happy moments for you?

Christian: [He looks across the room at the picture of her son on her desk, in military uniform, American flag behind him, remembering what she'd said—how so many Samoan kids end up in the military.] We fought a lot as kids. When we were older, we stopped, but he was also just not around anymore. Remembering felt like a recalibration. More good than miserable, it's been a hard perspective to manage.

Therapist: And why do you think those memories, with your brother in them, are the ones that came to you first?

Christian: He always had some plan, some adventure. He was also, always, best he could, looking out for me. Sometimes he was the main reason why I needed looking after, but still, he did. And he never really thought about consequences, or at least, never let that stop him. That made him different from me. Not so serious. More joyful. [Pause.] Most of what I remembered, what I wrote, wasn't so nice. I think I have trouble speaking up for myself. I have a lot of shame around that.

Therapist: And where does that shame come from?

Christian: I know. I remember. Our talks. Feeling ashamed about how I responded to things as a child—it's not really logical. Responses I'd never judge any kid for. But sometimes, emotionally, it's still difficult to accept. [Pause.] Anyway, I was remembering how I started coming here. I was basically a shut-in for a few years after high school. 'Cause of my shame. Was remembering that.

Therapist: [She reaches for her notepad and writes.] I'll check my notes, but I don't remember. And what did you do? What do you think that was about?

Christian: Oh, a lot of things. [Pause.] That period—the shut-in years—kind of reminds me of ma. How she wouldn't leave her room for long stretches when we were kids. She'd just shut down. That stopped when we got older, but I remember it always freaked me the fuck out. I wanted to help, but didn't know how. I can still see brother and me huddled outside her bedroom door, wondering if she'll ever come out.

Therapist: What changed? For your mother, I mean.

Christian: I don't know. Never asked. And she never brought it up. But she's got better coping skills now. [Pause.] And I wasn't thinking about it then, but that's how I started writing in the first place, just to distract myself from my own loneliness. Spending all day in my room. I had this recurring character, Tom Hanks—different stories, different worlds but always him. Something was always going wrong. The fulcrum of all these stories would turn on one person, or a group of people, coming together to make Tom Hanks's life miserable, apropos of nothing. The stories were always supposed to be funny. You were never meant to feel sorry for the big TH, even though he'd done nothing wrong. You were supposed to laugh at how angry he'd get over everything he couldn't control. That was the point. How he couldn't let himself laugh, ever. Was never in on the joke. Had this little equation: chaos plus denial equals humor... for someone else.

Therapist: Do you think that's true?

Christian: The equation? I don't know. Probably.

Therapist: Do you see other parallels between your situation and your mother's?

Christian: [He looks at the diploma on her wall, Biola University.] I don't really remember talking to ma much growing up, like not much outside of: clean your room, how was your day, have you seen such and such movie, that kind of thing. But later, before leaving for Berkeley, we could. Talk. She'd share a little about growing up, witches, nahuales, riding horses without a saddle, just holding on to their manes, hailstorms, how little food they had, being the youngest of thirteen—hungry, often. Ma could tell some pretty wild stories. Anyway, I don't know why talking wasn't possible when I was a kid. There was my father, and my being cursed, but that also doesn't feel like the whole story.

Therapist: You mentioned that last time, getting cursed. What happened?

Christian: [He tells the story.] Sometimes I think about why my aunt—la puta bruja, my family called her—chose me. How I was the youngest, smallest, not the real target—she and ma had problems going way back—but I was just an easy way in. A weak link. That has always felt true about me. Defective. Like I'm this fucking black hole that sucks everything, and everyone, in. Part of why I stayed in my room those years I was a shut-in. It was my shame for sure, but it also felt like the sort of punishment I deserved. Sometimes I think the curse only worked because whatever a curse is, the opening it needs, that was there inside me already. Even before my aunt cursed me, I was already fucked up. Something about me broken, defective, even then, at seven.

Therapist: Do you really believe that?

Christian: I mean not now, maybe, but I did. For a long time. I'm trying to think differently, but. [She pushes the tissue box toward him. He lets out a long exhale.] I'm trying.

Therapist: You're not trying. You're doing.

Christian: [He looks at her diploma on the wall again.] I need to find my own way to pray. My own kind of prayer.

Therapist: Or you could just go to church, open up a Bible. [She smiles.]

Christian: Well... [He puts his hands up in defeat. She brings her hands together, in prayer. He laughs.]

Therapist: Keep going, okay? With the writing, I mean.

Christian: [Nods.]

2004–2005. During the years I'm in fourth and fifth grade, there's an uptick in raids. Warnings playing on the Spanish radio as ma drives us to school—all the places getting hit: corner of Hammer and West, downtown, car wash lots, grocery stores, La Superior, Rancho San Miguel, Gateway (our old apartment complex, always). ICE has taken Cuco's dad, ma found out from Mari. When I hear the radio warnings, I imagine him crying, alone in the commons of Gateway, a lizard scurrying behind him. I don't know why, but I imagine him in his underwear, snot dripping from his nose.

His aunt is taking care of him now, ma says. I'm the only citizen in my family. I'm aware that, at any time, I could become Cuco. Alone. Next week. Next month. Tomorrow. A year from now. The thought is never far. I spend countless hours daydreaming a different reality, one where ma didn't have to go to work or brother to school. I think of hiding them away in the house, always. Like toys in a drawer. I imagine them under the house, cramped, in the dirt, but safe there, stowed away. Doing what is necessary to wait out the raids. I'd bring them food and water, news of the world. Both a fantasy and a nightmare.

During one of these days, in fifth grade, ma drops brother off first, at the middle school, Webster. He jumps out of the car, slips his backpack on, closes the door, and walks toward his class in one motion. Ma tells me to finish my breakfast sandwich. I gag. ¿Otra vez? Respira, she says. But I do the opposite, it's my ritual. Every day after she drops brother off, I hold my breath, hoping to see them both after school. The schools are not far. Webster to Tyler is a two-minute drive. When we arrive, ma says, bye, pórtate bien, te quiero mucho. She smiles. A commercial plays, Rancho San Miguel, where we haven't been going anymore. I open the door with one arm, hug ma with the other, yo también, te quiero mucho. Always the same wish: that Border Patrol takes someone else's mother, brother, instead.

That day, my teacher asks my father's name. I don't know what I'm supposed to say. He has two names, two identities. I pretend not to hear her. But she asks again, in front of the class.

What's your dad's name, Christian?

Everyone stares.

I don't know, I finally say. Feeling the heat radiating off my back.

What do you mean you don't know? she asks again. Almost laughing.

I don't know, I say. My voice sounding like it's far away, underground. I put my head down on the desk. Pretend I'm in the crawlspace underneath the house. For the rest of the day, I'm terrified she knows the reason I can't say, that she'll call Border Patrol on my family. And it will all be because of me, my stupidity.

During lunch, there's a policeman in the cafeteria, we share a look as he talks to the radio on his shoulder. He starts walking toward me, and I vomit all over my classmate's lap, my shoes. At the nurse's office, I don't say a word. I just wait. Hope that ma can come rescue me.

2005. That first house, green roof, and a giant walnut tree in the backyard. I'm playing, chasing someone in the hallway, it's one of my parents' friends. She said, Deditos, ven por mí. Deditos. I can't see her face at all but she's tall. And by her clothes and the cold trill of her voice, I know: She's the same age as ma. She's hiding and wants me to look for her. I do. In my and brother's bedroom I look under the bed, in the closet, behind the door, I even climb up onto the dresser to peer into the vent. I hear her laughter. She's somewhere but I can't find her. I play her game, start looking in places I know she can't be, under the pillows, the mattress, in dresser drawers, and all the while she's saying that nickname, Deditos, laughing, and only when I've given up does she hug me from behind.

There's a man in the room too, drinking beer. The brown bottle shines as he tips it to his mouth. He's laughing. There's a party going on in the rest of the house. Music, laughter, footsteps—he locks the door. They're leering down at me, his Big Bad Wolf grin and her Little Red Riding Hood eyes, then at each other, both laughing. He passes the beer bottle to her. She takes a swig while he turns the TV on, pushing the button until the volume's all the way up. It's *Sábado Gigante*. Everyone in the crowd clapping and cheering, mimicking the sound just on the other side of the door. Little Red Riding Hood rumples my hair, caresses my cheek. They're smiling, making eyes, talking to each other. When they talk to me, it's like they're not really seeing me, instead I'm just a big cut of ham. And I can't really hear what they're saying over the sound of Don Francisco, his baritone voice announcing the contestants for some game. It's like I'm ghosting away from my body. The Big Bad Wolf comes closer, asks in Spanish if I know how to please a woman.

Little Red Riding Hood laughs.

You know how to suck a tit, don't you? he says.

He slides a tank top strap off one of Riding Hood's shoulders, then the other. Underneath she wears a dark blue bra with an intricate lace pattern. He opens it from behind, peels it off.

Look at these tits, he says. Licking his lips.

He takes another swig of his beer. She smiles and fondles her own breast while he licks the tips of his fingers. He squeezes her thick brown nipple. And the way Riding Hood's face, mouth, opens, it feels too private. I want to leave. But somehow they can sense it, because then the Big Bad Wolf is standing behind me and I'm trying to turn to him, not wanting him where I can't see him, but Riding Hood turns my face. And her teeth, they're perfect, straight, and pearly white, and when she smiles, her gums are exposed.

Don't be shy, she says as the man lifts me off my feet, pressing my face to her breast.

Go on.

I do what they say, wrapping my lips around her nipple.

Suck, the man orders. I do. She moans softly.

Harder, the man says. She moans a little louder.

Use your tongue, the man says. I close my mouth, purse my lips together, but she just presses her big thick brown-purple nipple onto my mouth as he digs his finger in between my ribs. I relent. Use my tongue. She lightly moans again and then they're talking to each other and again, everything happens at a distance. I hear El Chacal on the screen; he's playing his trumpet, the whole crowd screaming, ¡FUERA! ¡FUERA! ¡FUERA!

Ay, niñito, you're not so good at this, she says.

Pinche Deditos. The Big Bad Wolf sets me down roughly.

The woman puts her bra and shirt back on while the man stares at the TV, beer bottle still in hand. He changes the channel until Courage the Cowardly Dog is on-screen. All the cheering and laughter being replaced by that screaming purple dog. They leave. Close the door behind them. The volume is all the way up and though I can't hear it, I know it's there, on the other side of the room, the party still going on. My lips, my tongue, I can still feel the fleshy rigidity of her nipple everywhere inside my mouth.

I don't know how long I stand there, staring at the door, but eventually, it opens. Ma turns the TV off.

Party's over, she says.

2003. I'm eight or nine and have already become legend. The whole family knows I'm cursed, and I don't play well with others. No one says it to my face, but when they think I'm not around, I hear them talk about me. La mosquita muerta, they say. When they're bold, when they're drunk, when ma isn't around, they call me Deditos. Aunts and uncles, and grown-up cousins too. Though they all tell their kids not to try the same with me—better if they just stay away. Because when the anger takes over, I'll hit anyone, any kid, no matter how young.

At every party after, ma always comes over, says, cálmate ya. Grabbing my wrists, holding them in front of my face, pórtate bien, o si no... she threatens me with anger management classes. She never follows through. Though either way, there's no class to teach away what I have, a curse. So I scream, punch walls, become exactly what they say. A plague.

At parties I'm left mostly to myself. Spending hours holed up in the space behind the couch, playing with the green plastic army men, Hot Wheels, and marbles, bags and bags of them. Brother and all the kids our age, either outside or upstairs playing video games, while I hide away, make up stories. Marble, car, army man, it doesn't matter; the stories are the same: They'll be on the run, escaping.

They have superpowers: telekinesis, fire breathing, concrete manipulation. It's because of their powers that everyone is after them. They run and run but they can't run forever. At some point, they realize, if they want to live, they'll have to stop, turn, face it. Violence, the only path to freedom. They fight, kill all their enemies. Make themselves free.

After parties, it's always the same, brother comes down. He peers down at me over the back of the couch.

I beat *Diddy Kong Racing*, he says. It's easy when you're not around. Just stay back there forever, okay? He laughs.

I get up. Scream. I start chasing.

2005. The weekend. In that first house, I wake to the sound of maggots. They blanket the bedroom floor and are writhing. Their writhing, I hear it so clearly, like there's some in my ear. I can't scream. Afraid they'll get inside. Brother still using his superpower, sleeping. His bed is closer to the door—we're not in bunk beds anymore—but luckily, last night, like most nights, I pushed my bed against his, because of the nightmares I've been having.

I stand up on my own and jump onto his. He awakens then. I point and he screams and ma comes running. I'm in only underwear and staring at the maggots; I feel them crawling all over me. I clench my butt cheeks as hard as I can. Jumping again and again on the bed, like I'm trying to escape my own ass. I dig my hands into my ass but can't feel the squirming anymore. Ma yells, tells me to stop. Get out of there, she says. I jump from the bed, out the door. Brother does too.

We stare. A huge white vomitous mass, writhing and writhing. The squirming needling into our ears. And I think I feel it again, a squirming in my ass. I worry it's too late, they've burrowed up in there. Are laying eggs. They'll hatch, and that writhing mass will explode out of me. Rip me in two. I have to get it out. I turn, head toward the kitchen for a knife. Ma grabs my wrist. Bring me the mop, the bleach, she says. Brother stares for a few seconds more before saying, I'm getting the fuck out of here. He runs out the front door.

The bleach will burn them, like fire, she says. I watch as she douses it over them and the sound they make, a wet screeching. A piercing sensation runs all across my skin. I clench, try to close all the holes in my body.

Sometimes I'll wake up in a sweat, thinking they're inside me. Like fire.

20...? I'm eleven or twelve or ten, I can't remember exactly, except I know the house, the broom closet where it happened, where I was raped. Gateway was in the rearview. This was the first house I lived in. Extended family lived with us too. Though I don't know who it was, it was there in that first house where it happened at eleven or twelve or ten in the broom closet. A man put himself inside me. I have no memory of how I got there, of how we both got in that closet. When I remember, he's always already got me. His breath over the crown of my head, rustling my hair. And my legs, without my wanting, wrapped around him.

There is no pain. I can't feel it anymore. Can only see it. His arms pressed into my back, his hands clutching my head, and his chest slick and pungent with his sweat, staining my lips. I taste him, his salt, bitter and acidic the way an apple can sometimes be. I want to spit him out, but I can't, I'm too afraid.

And despite all my fear, I'm still there, pressed against him, when I look up and see the sweat streaming down the sides of his face, his chin, he drips into my eyes. My arms are wrapped around him too and I don't move to free myself though he's only holding me up a few feet off the ground.

It doesn't make sense but I fear I'll shatter if I let go, if I'm dropped. There's a part of me, the most childish part, that thinks he'll be the one to comfort me. Years later, this is what will shame me, haunt me most: how in my fear, I clung to him. Desperately, urgently, as if what I needed most was something he could give me.

In time, I'll come to see this as the moment of my profoundest self-betrayal—grabbing on to him harder and harder as he thrust harder and faster into me, making me a ghost, driven out from my own body. Though still, I'm there, within the broom closet, floating above, and looking on at the doll of my body being used. I don't know if this was a cousin that came to live with us, there were many. But he's six, six two, maybe five ten, with a light complexion, and sturdy, and I'm eleven or twelve or ten and a doll.

2019. A little before I moved out to Irvine, my father came to the house for Sunday breakfast. He came because ma was doing better. During her illness, they'd gotten back in touch; he'd helped out when he could, driving her to appointments when brother was working and I wasn't around. But they'd also spoken on the phone, just catching up, sharing what each had been up to, reminiscing too, probably.

So then, less than a month before Irvine, he was there, at the door. He was wearing calisthenics gloves and a blue runner's headband with a reflective strip that pressed his thick gray hair back into a pouf. Dressed more for a 5K than for Sunday breakfast. He hugged me the way a father does, no hesitation, all smiles, like he'd forgotten how long it had been since we'd last parted, and under what circumstances. I hugged him back out of sheer awkwardness. As we separated, he grabbed me by the shoulders. He opened his mouth like he was getting ready to say something, his eyes softened. He closed his mouth, smiled, and simply let go.

He strode past me into the kitchen like he still lived there and greeted brother and ma. Hugged ma longest of all. Ma and brother hadn't even started on breakfast, it was early. He was early but he didn't care. Apparently, he'd gotten on a health kick, started exercising, losing weight, watching what he ate. It was strange to see him interact with them while I stood apart. Kept thinking how natural it all seemed, except for my being there. I had the nagging suspicion that they'd been seeing each other while I was away, that seemed like the kind of thing that could go unmentioned unless I'd asked directly. They were too casual, too familiar with the last nine years of one another's lives. But I wasn't angry, nor paranoid exactly. I just felt the way I sometimes have in dreams—in thrall to a peculiar logic, one that works just so long as I don't think about it too hard.

Breakfast with my father.

He didn't offer to help with the cooking, and this alone seemed grounds enough to believe he hadn't changed. Couldn't have. Not much. I don't know whether it was my own defensiveness or spite, but I had to tell myself he was the same, to hold him at a distance that way, as the man I had guarded against my entire life.

He wondered aloud, sitting at the kitchen island, if he had enough time to get a quick workout in. Ma said he did. It would take about an hour for them to make the chilaquiles. He asked me if I might want to work out with him. I felt my body stand at attention. My fists curled inside my pockets, my jaw clenched. I was aware of everyone's eyes on me. And it was true, I wasn't helping either. I felt my heart start to slow. I couldn't think of an excuse, so instead, still surprising myself, I said, yeah, sure, I'd work out with him. Out in the front yard, he told me he'd just been for a run and really just wanted to cool down. To do that, he said, he'd usually just take a walk, stopping intermittently to do push-ups. I said that that was fine and so we set off.

It was the end of summer and early morning, early enough that the heat was still bearable, high seventies. I didn't know where to begin, what to say to him. Our last encounter was all I could think about. Nonchalant as he was, that must've been true for him too. He was swinging his arms back and forth across his chest, looking up at the sky and smiling.

You know, he said, my mother could predict rain just by looking at the morning sky. Maybe that doesn't seem so impressive, but sometimes she'd predict rain even when there were no clouds, and she was always right.

I looked up at the blue blue sky, electric and uniformly bright, like paint. I asked him, is it gonna rain?

He chuckled. I don't know, she never taught me how. She said she would if I didn't leave, but I had to. He stopped, dropped, and did twenty push-ups. Then he got up, gave me his gloves, and I did the same.

We kept walking. I asked him how it was for him, before he crossed over, and he told me about moving from the village to the city, living in a bakery, sleeping on a cot in the back, going to accounting school.

I wanted to ask how that worked since I knew he hadn't finished high school. Flunked out. He and ma would joke about it when I was growing up. But I didn't ask. Every time I glanced at him, had this feeling, something happening between us, and I didn't want to interrupt whatever that was. It was strange: after all those years, walking next to him, doing push-ups with him, seeing him smile every time he looked up. It was like he was expecting some change in the weather, and so each time he looked, finding the sky as blue as ever, he would smile.

He told me about finishing near the top of his class, how he liked it, accounting. Numbers made sense to him. Made the world feel smaller, more tangible, more legible. With numbers, the world could be tallied, systematized, defined. After school, he got a job, he said, working for a small electronics business. It was the first time he'd seen a computer. After a few months, his superior went on maternity leave and he got better pay, more hours, was able to leave the bakery, get the smell of flour out of his clothes, his hair.

When his superior came back after having her baby, she was promoted, and he was going to be promoted as well, but it wasn't what he wanted. He spoke then of summers in the village, when all the older guys would come back from Texas and California with money, cars, gifts for their families. He knew if he didn't go young, he likely never would. The bump in his pay would've been okay, but not great. And anyway, he'd always wanted to go, to be one of those guys, to come back bearing gifts, a small crowd gathering around him eager to hear stories of life on the other side. And so he left. And by the time he had the money to come back, he said, things had changed. Crossing wasn't the same.

Still looking up at the sky, he smiled again, did his push-ups and passed me his gloves, still warm from his hands. Somehow, the routine of the workout held our whole history at bay. As we walked, did push-ups, both growing more tired with every set, I seemed almost to forget how it had been to grow up with him, how scared I'd been. All of it gone, and only the ordinary awkwardness of conversing with a stranger, the discomfort of not knowing this man, my father.

And yet I suspected that the same couldn't be said for him, how he felt about me. I didn't sense any awkwardness in him, not in the way he moved or talked. It was like we were old friends. He was comfortable. I wasn't. It makes me think now about how charismatic he was, not in a boisterous, holding-court sort of way, but with that cool confidence of a guy who belonged wherever he was. I think that's what made the whole thing feel so weird to me: his ease. And implicit in that ease: a refusal to acknowledge any of the things that had happened. The things he'd done to me. He'd just put it all behind him, apparently.

Was that charm, charisma? Sociopathy? Strange to consider how easily I might have done the same, if I'd been another person entirely. On our way back, after our last set of push-ups, I kept asking him questions. I was genuinely curious but also weirded out by the situation, still aware of the possibility that perhaps, in silence, something harder, more painful, would open between us. And I didn't want that—I don't think he did either. Though when we did lapse, finally, into silence, it was a soft, an easy one.

Walking in silence, it was surprising to me to realize that he hadn't asked me a single question. I'd kept the conversation going, focused on him, but still, there were lulls, and now this silence. It was something to do, I sensed, with who my father was at his core: how at ease he felt with a one-way line of communication. What it truly meant, I wasn't ready to acknowledge yet. I was just glad about how tired we both were after that final set, glad that, because we were tired, we could walk the rest of the way back in that easy silence, no danger hanging between us. When we reached the house, he looked up at the sky one last time. Guess I was wrong, he said.

He smiled at me, opened the door, and went in.

2006. We're fishing in the Delta. Me, brother, and two older cousins. Only boat on the water. Midsummer and we're getting cooked. The water's dead calm. The boat only rocks when my cousin moves to grab a beer from the cooler. The water fucking stinks.

What kind of fish live in this water? I ask.

I don't know, brother says, probably fish with faces like yours. Both cousins laugh.

Out here in this backwater, a fish with a human face, human

teeth, sounds about right. Brother keeps his eyes closed. His turn to hold the rod we're sharing. A toy fishing rod, transparent orange, with a Taz sticker on the reel. It belongs to one of our cousins' nephews. I don't know why that nephew isn't here instead of us. The boat tips as I clomp around looking for sunscreen.

You're scaring all the fish, my cousin says.

Do fish have ears?

What?

Can they hear?

Nice try, the other cousin says.

Think we need better bait, brother says.

That's why y'all here, our cousins sneer.

I look over the side of the boat, trying to find my reflection in the murky water, and a comeback for the cousins calling us bait, a masturbation joke in there somewhere, surely, but I'm not finding it.

Hours go by. Brother hands me the fishing rod, I hand it back. We do this about four times. No bites. My legs start to cramp up with how little space they've got. What if we did catch something? Barely room for the four of us, where would it go? My lap? A big container ship crosses our path on its way to the port. The ship's wake sets us to rocking. Four lonely krill. Our cousins are fucking hammered. They tell each other the same kinds of jokes I've heard for years. What's black and blue and red all over? my cousin asks.

A newspaper, I say.

No. Mom, after asking pops a question.

How do you know when a chick is on the rag?

When she drinks a lot of water and—

He doesn't know what that means, brother chimes in.

What the fuck you answering for?

All right, how 'bout this one, what's the difference between a big dick and a small dick?

I don't know, a few inches?

What's wrong with you, ain't no one ever tell you a joke? All you gotta say is what.

Okay, what?

Forget it.

I cover my head with my hands, try to keep the sun from cooking my brain, after a while I have to take them off. Should've brought a hat, brother says. I don't know how he can tell what I'm doing, his eyes are still closed. Freaky. Then the reel from brother's rod starts singing, unwinding fast. Hold it hard, they tell brother. Con huevos. And he's a natural, he pulls the rod back and side to side, one foot against the rim of the boat, the muscles in the back of his neck and arms straining.

The boat starts rocking but we all do our part, bracing against the frame to steady it, give brother his best shot. He starts reeling it in. He's struggling, each turn of the tiny wheel a little slower than the last. He fucking yanks on the rod, then reels in a little more of the spool. What if it's a shark, or some great big fucking whale? We could be famous. We could be on the news. Channel 3, our big fucking catch, little letters scrolling across the video screen: four fishermen and the catch of a lifetime. He reels and reels, the line covered in muck and then, and only for an instant, it's there, by the side of the boat. Like nothing we've ever seen. Black, pink-tipped spikes all over its back. I recoil, it's about the size of my leg, though luckily we're without a net and as brother tries to reel in that last bit, lift the fish up, the toy rod snaps in two. Oh fuck, brother says as the boat rocks again, almost tipping us.

What kind of fucking fish was that? my cousin asks.

Delta fish, the other responds.

Ya casi, ya casi, brother says.

And the whole drive back, brother just keeps grabbing me, excited and asking, did you look at its eyes? Did you see those spikes and that fucker's eyes? Those fucking eyes. And the way he says it, his hands on my shoulders, shaking me like maybe I'll transform into that fish, I know how its eyes looked, because I'm looking at his.

2019. Sunday breakfast. With my father that day we ate in silence at first. If we talked, there would be no way to get around what no one had ever acknowledged in all the years in between, the four of us were no longer a family. Maybe never had been. The first to talk, it seemed, would have to admit this. So we each awaited our turn to scoop the chilaquiles, to pass the bowl of cotija and onion and the plate with the sunny-side eggs. We didn't talk. We filled glasses with orange juice instead.

After a while ma finally asked, had we heard the one about the witch who gets stuck in a tree? Ma was wearing a wig. Her hair was already growing back by then and she usually didn't bother with it unless she was going out. But on account of my father being there, she had it on then. I was struck by how fragile it made her look. Seeing ma in her wig, asking that question, I couldn't help but think about all the questions she wasn't asking.

I didn't know what I was supposed to feel or think about all those unasked questions, but in my head, I was asking them: How was everyone doing? What was everyone feeling? What had my father been up to? What had we? What all had changed since we'd last sat at this table together? And maybe because whatever changing we'd done, we'd done separately; we couldn't come together and be those new selves of ours. We had to be the old ones, be whoever we'd been the last time the four of us had found ourselves at the same table. But at the end of the day, the kind of intimacy I was after—am after, always—is the kind that's possible only between people who trust each other. And this breakfast wasn't it, not for me.

How much can four estranged people, even family, see one another as the new people they've become? So much colored by memory. It'd have been different, obviously, if my father wasn't there. Ma, brother, and I lived together, after all. If it had been just the three of us, as it so often was, it would've been less awkward, certainly, and more sincere. But more honest? I don't know. Our guardedness still needing to change. Ma played peacemaker best way she knew how, told a story. Hers:

A witch is on her broom, screeching through the night. Not clear what she wants. Just to fly around and wreak havoc. She's going into people's houses, stealing locks of hair, toenail clippings, sweat from the rim of a toilet bowl, cackling, so that everyone in the village knows: Those people are hers now. Hers to control. To curse. To fuck. She could do whatever she wanted with them. Only one hitch: She had to be home before the sun rose.

But night after night, she grew more and more arrogant, reckless, relishing her trophies—brown fetid toenail clippings she'd rub against her lips, a rag soaked with the sweat of nightmares, which she'd huff, getting buzzed, drunk on the scent of fear. So drunk one night, she crashes into a tree. Gets herself stuck. She tries and tries to untangle herself from the branches, but then the sun comes up. In daylight, she has no power. And the villagers she's been terrorizing seize upon her. And she dies as all witches must. A pitchfork through the eyes. The villagers seal her eyes into a jar and they become a kind of anti-relic. They drop the jar into the pit of an outhouse and day after day proceed to bury it under their own excrement. The witch's eyes entombed, slowly, with shit.

But as the eyes are buried deeper and deeper, the villagers begin to forget about things—they don't keep up their homes or jobs, and finally, they forget even their own names. They all congregate around the outhouse, waiting to shit upon the witch's eyes, taking turns. Soon after, even the name of the village is lost. It comes to be known in neighboring towns as El Pueblo de los Tres Ojos. Three Eyes: the eyes of the witch and... what's the third eye, do you think? ma asked.

We shrugged.

The shitter's asshole, she said. And then laughed. The only one who did at first. There was sunlight coming through the window behind her. And hovering just within the frame, a hummingbird. Our father was second to laugh. And brother third. Then me.

She was doing better. That'd been clear for months. If I withheld my laughter for longer, it was only because ma liked to give me shit when I told one of my stories.

I've got one too, I said. It's only a story because it's true. It's about a video I saw once.

My story:

There was a man who called himself a pig with tits. He had a tattoo, PIGSLUT, across his forehead. He was a veteran and had been a real estate agent but was now happily retired. He spent all day streaming videos. And he was doing this live stream to an audience of three.

And you were one of those three? interrupted brother, snorting.

No, I said. The recording went viral. I saw it after.

Anyway, in the video, I continued, the guy was naked. And fat, his gut so big it covered his little dicklet. His word for it. Anyway, he'd recently moved to Canada and become a big fan of poutine. He decided he was going to put on a show for his audience, his own pig-with-tits version of poutine.

Ma begged me to stop, which made brother laugh. Our father looked on confused, both disgusted and curious about where it was going.

By then I couldn't help myself. It gets better, I said to ma, trust me.

Pigslut lifted his gut and aimed his dicklet at the bowl of poutine. After pissing into it, he raised it to his nose and described it for his audience: the smell of poutine and piss, the way it frothed. And still, the stew wasn't thick enough. He set the bowl on the ground and squatted over it.

Oh no, stop, ma said. Christian, we're eating.

When I tell you he didn't wipe his ass, does that surprise you? I went on, smiling. Somehow it surprised me, but I couldn't stop watching.

Of course you couldn't, brother said, shaking his head. Where do you find this shit?

Well, even though I knew what would come next, I kept watching. He got on all fours, called the bowl of poutine his blessed trough, then stuck his head in there. And the noises he made... at that point, I couldn't even finish the story, because of the memory of the video, how it had played over and over in my head. I gagged right there at the table until I had to get up and run to the bathroom. As a teenager, I watched a lot of videos like that. I watched them to laugh, to set myself apart, to confirm that nothing could faze me.

Brother was still laughing when I got back, why would you tell a story that'd make you sick?

All those chilaquiles. What a waste. Ma looked horrified, almost annoyed.

I thought it was crazy, I said. Just wanted to share.

Well, thanks for sharing, brother said.

No, no te doy las gracias, ma said.

Then brother recreated the face I had made by the end, when I had to run to the toilet. Then the three of us laughed while my father looked on, amused at the story, or at us. The way we were with each other. I wanted to ask him, what exactly did he find amusing? And the only reason I didn't is because when I looked at him, his hands on the table, pushing himself back, a half smile, with eyes soft, tender, he seemed a stranger in our midst.

2005. The first house. It'd been close to ten years since my father first got married to one of ma's friends, a $5,000 investment in order to begin the process, the path to citizenship. When he finally gets a letter in the mail, a date given for his interview, he still has until early next year to study for his test.

I press Record on the tape recorder and then I pull a flash card, what are the three branches of government? I ask.

The legislative, the executive, my father pauses, closes his eyes, and the judicial.

I nod, then pull another, how many amendments have been made to the constitution?

Twenty-seven.

What's the Bill of Rights?

The first ten amendments.

Who's third in the presidential line of succession?

The Speaker of the House.

It's the vice president, the Speaker of the House, and then...

He sighs, he pinches the bridge of his nose, the Secretary of State.

It's the president pro tempore of the Senate.

We continue for another hour. And every Sunday for the next eight months. He recites the Pledge of Allegiance, the beginning of the Declaration of Independence. What is the supreme law of the land? Why did colonists come to America? What are the *Federalist Papers*? What was their significance? Though in truth we know these questions may or may not help him. He'll also need luck. Sometimes the governmental case manager asks three, four simple questions, and you're done, you pass, you're a citizen. Other times, you're grilled for over an hour, up to three, questions designed to confuse you, and all the studying in the world won't help you then. It all depends on which case manager you're assigned. Luck of the draw. I've heard ma say as much. She's heard from friends. Still, he has to study, and so I help him.

The day of his interview, we all pile into the car. I'm in the front seat, still helping him study. For the first ten minutes, I ask him questions and he answers them. Then he tells me, stop. He's sweating. Driving toward the freeway, every tree we pass has already turned—orange, red, yellow. He wipes the sweat off his nose. Turns the AC on. We'll be in Sacramento in less than an hour. He turns the music on for a while. Then turns it off. No one says anything for the rest of the ride.

When we enter the lobby, he tells the receptionist why we're there. She's surprised, annoyed. He's early. The way she arches her brow, like she wishes it were up to her. If it were, she'd deny him on the spot. Instead, without blinking or moving her face at all, she points us to the elevator, says it's the third floor.

We wait in a small office. Everything in it either gray or blue. A large American flag in the corner. Security officer standing by the door. What does he do with the people who fail? I stare at his gun until ma sees me looking and tugs at my shirt. There are no magazines. None of us talk. I lean forward, glancing at my father. He wipes his forehead. Cracks his neck. Starts tapping his leg. Ma rests her hand on his knee. He stops. She stares at me and I lean back. Close my eyes. An hour later, he's called.

We sit and wait. It takes less than five minutes. When he comes out, he's smiling, looking like he just ran a marathon. One down, two to go.

2001. Gateway. We're getting ready to go shopping. Brother and I doing handstands, putting our clothes on, practicing tae kwon do. Ma is counting the Christmas money. She places it on the counter and pats herself down, making sure she's got keys, coin purse—no coin purse. She goes searching for it, leaving the money on the counter. No one sees what happens then. We put it together after; ma looking for her coin purse, yelling at us to put on our shoes, brother and I looking for them, but finding green plastic army men, Hot Wheels, and Tamagotchis instead. Somewhere in all of that, our dog, Canica, comes into the kitchen, jumps up onto the counter, takes it and eats it. All our Christmas money.

Now no Christmas. Christmas canceled. Brother says we should cancel Canica now. Put her down. We don't have money for that either, ma says, smiling through her despair. Sometimes we call Canica La Aspiradora, because, like Moco, she'll eat anything if you leave it out. But Moco wouldn't eat money, at least I don't think. Who eats money? La Aspiradora, of course!

Brother and I take her out for a walk and we see it sticking out of her poop, Benjamin Franklin's head and other green bits, shredded like confetti. Guess Canica wanted to get into the Christmas spirit too. But it's not even a big turd. It's small, smaller than her usual ones, but somehow all of Christmas fits there: party, pozole, tamales, cake, new clothes, *Donkey Kong*, perfume for ma. All of it, gone to shit.

Dad still doesn't know. He's at work thinking there's still gonna be Christmas. Brother is mad, but not really; ma is mad, but at herself; she calls everyone, tells them the party's off. As for me, I'm just looking at Canica, smiling at her red fur and pointy ears, the way her tongue hangs out. She's too cute. She's puppy number one. It was dad who brought her home, that's what ma keeps saying, like it's his fault. We know. He *did*, we say in response. She peed all over his truck, she says. We remember, we say. Then she tells us in a worried way to let her do all the talking. No se metan, okay?

After dinner, brother and I walk La Aspiradora again. Brother says, you know, they say if you take a dog's eye boogers and put them in the corners of your own eyes, you'll see ghosts. Forever. Like all dogs do. And then he asks, grinning, wanna try? I don't answer right away. I just look down at her, the Vacuum, the Heartbreaker, eating daisies casually, like she hasn't ruined everything. Doesn't look like she's seeing any ghosts now.

Why do dogs see ghosts, anyway? I ask.
He shrugs.
Canica's too pure, too sweet to be seeing ghosts.
Yeah, well, that's what they say.
Is that why she's never scared of ghosts? 'Cause she sees them all the time?
Yup.
You're a liar.
If you don't believe me, ask ma.
He wasn't lying.

Dad comes home and ma puts on her cheerful voice, helps him out of his jacket. She puts herself between him and us, then breaks the news. We all hold our breath. But he doesn't scream or whip out his belt like brother said he would. Instead, he lets out one of his long-drawn-out sighs then sits down on the couch. Canica goes to him, looking up at him with her sweet crusty little eyes, tail wagging, and he pets her. Ma sits down on the couch too. I sit by the Christmas tree, admiring it. The colored lights are on, and all the ornaments we made at school, on there too, looking pretty. Dad flips to channel 66, one we get only because of our stolen cable box. A trailer comes on. In it: pills, syringes, pupils dilating, a shaking fridge, a TV on wheels rolling through a neighborhood. You guys seen this one? he asks.

No, we say.

Starts in eight minutes, he says.

Brother turns off the Christmas tree, makes popcorn. I lie down on the floor next to the couch and Canica joins me. After giving her a few of my popcorn, she keeps staring at me. I stare into her little eyes, the boogers streaking away from them, and remember what brother said. I scratch one off as the movie begins: An infomercial plays, a man yells and takes his mother's TV. I press Canica's eye booger into the corner of my own eye. Music plays: violins, like the world's ending. And everything's dark except for the screen, glowing. It's our first Christmas without a big party. Just me, brother, ma, dad, and Canica. I pet her, make my Christmas wish, kiss her right between her eyes and whisper Merry Christmas. With one hand on Canica's head, I stare at the screen. I wait to see them.

I wait.

I wait.

[Three months after their first weekly session.]

Therapist: Go on.

Christian: As a kid, I'd have this recurring dream. [Pause.] I'm in my bed, awake, waiting for someone. A woman.

Therapist: Not your mother?

Christian: No. Someone I don't know. A woman who comes at night through the window. At the time, I was still sharing a room with Julio. But he's never there, in the dream. And this woman, when she does finally come, she climbs into bed with me, kisses my ear, sucks on it. And she has these hands, rough but also delicate, that move like spiders over my body. She flips me over onto my stomach, spreads my legs with her own. She's sniffing my hair, grinding her head into mine. She takes off my shirt, my underwear. Then takes off her own. Shirt, then underwear. And it's like I'm not there anymore. My body's there, but it's not really me. It's like a doll. And I just watch as she plays with it, me. She pulls my arms back behind me and presses into my back with her knee. And I can't explain it, but it's like she wants to grow something out of me. Like my body is hiding a seed and in order for the seed to grow, she has to break me open, split me in two. That's all she's doing, just helping it along. It looks painful but I'm not feeling it, because I'm not there, in my body.

Therapist: I'm thinking about what you shared last week, about being raped as a child.

Christian: Yeah.

Therapist: I know you've only allowed yourself to look at it all these past few months. It's a lot to reckon with after so long. I can only imagine how deeply it must have affected you. All parts of you. Your sense of yourself.

Christian: I guess so.

Therapist: Why do you think, in this dream, it's a woman who's violating you?

Christian: I don't know. But it's weird, I never thought of it as a nightmare, really. Not compared to some of the other dreams I've had. Seeing her working on me, it was like when I'd watch nature documentaries, and the predator catches its prey. Like, this is just what happens.

Therapist: The rape, and this dream too, it was around the time you first tried to kill yourself?

Christian: Yeah. I never put it all together, though. Just always felt like a monster. I couldn't really see myself as anything else.

Therapist: Made it easier to ignore. To protect yourself. Where were your parents, your mom, when it happened?

Christian: I don't remember. I know we've been talking about this, but I just don't remember. And I don't feel any anger toward any of them. Not toward my father, and definitely not toward Julio or ma.

Therapist: I'm not saying you should *only* feel anger, but you were just a little boy. There were a lot of signs, weren't there? Something being wrong.

Christian: I know what you're saying, but I wasn't around for Julio or ma either.

Therapist: You were just a child.

Christian: Look, I know what you're saying. [Pause.] But I'm not denying or repressing it, the anger. 'Cause I was so angry for so long. And now I just don't feel it. I don't know if I'm done. But it's just gone.

Therapist: How much of this have you shared with your mother and brother?

Christian: Not much. None of the sexual stuff. Even the thing with my parents' friend, making me suck her breast. It's just too weird, you know? I've told Julio about my suicide attempt. And obviously, they both know about the fight with my father.

Therapist: What did Julio say when you told him?

Christian: He just said he was sorry he wasn't there. He cried. I just told him I'm okay now, and that he *was* there. Enough of the time. I survived, didn't I? We hugged and just kept talking. I don't remember about what, but it was like this pressure—I didn't even know it had been there, the whole time, forever—it was gone.

Therapist: Has he shared anything with you like that? Times he was struggling?

Christian: Not as much, I don't think. [He pauses, stares down at his shoes, laces untied.] Once, not long before I left Stockton, he told me he was having these panic attacks, how it freaked him out, he didn't know what to do with himself. He'd be driving on the freeway and start having these thoughts, of turning into oncoming traffic. He called a suicide hotline. It helped, I guess. I mean, it helped and it didn't. It relieved some of the pressure, but the panic attacks, they still happened for a while after that.

Therapist: Why was he having those panic attacks, do you think?

Christian: I don't know. He never talked about it… [Pause.] I never asked.

Therapist: I know he's a couple years older, but your father never hit him the way he did you?

Christian: I mean I don't know for sure, but I don't think so.

Therapist: And you don't think that what happened to you could've happened to him too?

Christian: [He sighs.] I mean, I really don't think so. It's hard to imagine… Like, I really, really don't think so. [His leg starts twitching, his breathing becomes erratic, his eyes bouncing across the room, avoiding hers.] I mean he just wasn't alone in the way I was. I can't explain it. I was just set apart from everyone. And I don't know why. I never did. I mean, now when I think about, it doesn't make any sense. It just, for that to happen to Julio, I can't, I can't— [He pauses, covers his mouth. His whole body begins to shake. He cries. Cries long enough that she rises and sits on the couch beside him. She lays an arm on his shoulder until the crying subsides.]

Therapist: [She returns to her seat, across from him.] I'm not suggesting he was hurt in the way you were. But when it's never talked about...this is what silence does. It separates us from each other, closes us off.

Christian: What the fuck is wrong with me, I never even considered that? [He starts crying again, slow steady crying.] Never thought about him. Brother. He was a kid too. He was a kid too. Who the fuck was looking after him?

Therapist: You were. You two were always together, no?

Christian: I mean, we were for the most part, and then we weren't. And then I didn't know what the fuck was going on with him. Or him with me. It was like we couldn't fucking see each other. Couldn't look at him and not think about all that shit growing up: my dad, ma, my curse, all the crazy fucked-up shit we saw running around, no one looking after us.

Therapist: And does that still feel true to you now?

Christian: No. God, no.

Therapist: Well, I think you know what I gotta say about all that, then.

Christian: [He hugs the pillow on his lap. Neither speaks for a few minutes.] Fuck, man, can't I just *live*?

Therapist: [She laughs softly.] Oh, you for sure know what I say to that.

Christian: I know. I know.

2022. Stockton. It's mid-October now and I'm at a flea market with ma. We're about the only two people still wearing face masks. From now until Christmas, it's the worst time to come. The best, ma insists. It's festive. She won't tell me why we're here. She says it's a surprise, a good one. She says it with a teasing smile, knowing I don't like them. Surprises. Never have. I tell her I doubt I'll like this one.

You'll see, she says.

She gives me a side hug, tries to bump me into a garbage bin. She laughs. I tell her she's crazy. She spots a stall with plants, gardening equipment, and steers us over to it. She picks out and inspects a pot with ruda, a few tiny cacti, one of which, I think, looks more like a stone than a plant.

Are these for your classroom? I ask.

No todas, she says, the corners of her eyes wrinkling.

I can tell she wants me to ask again, to beg, playfully, to be let in on her secret. She won't tell me but wants me to ask so she can say, be patient, all will be revealed in time. I don't play along, I pretend to sulk. Fine, I say, taking the box of all the little plants she's just bought. She feigns woundedness at my sulking, calls me malo. We laugh. She loops her arm through mine and we keep walking.

We buy a couple of churros and champurrado. We make our way over to another stall with more plants, flowers. The old man who runs it greets ma like they're old friends. I can't place his accent, but it sounds African.

Amiga, he says, ¿cómo estás?

Bien, bien, ma says, she laughs. How are you doing? How's your wife?

I don't remember ma being so friendly when we were kids; of course, I think a part of that was how uncomfortable she felt with English, but even then, when we'd go to stores where they spoke Spanish, she wasn't like this, so friendly. Whether my father was there or not, with strangers, she was never warm. And now here she is, laughing, sharing inside jokes, introducing me as her son. The man goes into his van and comes back with a brown paper bag.

Everything you asked for, he says, smiling.

Ma pays him. He tucks the money into a fanny pack, grasps ma's hand with both of his, buena suerte, he smiles.

Gracias, she says.

On the drive back, I ask ma if she's finally gonna tell me what this is all about. She tells me to look in the bag.

What for?

You'll know.

The sack is packed with all kinds of flowers, purple, white, an orange almost gold, satin blue, and a deep deep red, dahlia, poinsettias, an orange sunflower, milkweed, sage, beardtongue. I pull out a small pot. A rose-tinted orchid.

Not that, she says.

I know, I know, I'm looking. I feel a pack of cigarettes. I pull them out.

What the hell, I say.

They're not for me, she says. She takes one hand off the wheel. Rummages into her jacket pocket with the other. Pulls out a lighter. Hands it to me.

They're not for me, pero dame, give me one anyway.

Are you serious?

It'll be fun.

Ma, you had cancer.

Not in my lungs, she says. I swear they're not for me. But why not? I'll have one. My second one ever. I ever tell you about the first time I smoked?

No.

I stole one of my father's cigarettes. Marlboro. I had seen the brand in magazines, on billboards. I wanted to try one, so one night, I take it, the one I've been saving, and sneak out with one of my sisters to smoke it. We thought he was sleeping. Maybe he was. But the window was open or something. I don't know. I don't remember. Anyway, I only had a couple of puffs before he was there, standing behind us. Madre santísima, he beat our behinds so bad, I never smoked again.

Until now.

Until now. She grins. At a red light, she takes the cigarette from my hand, puts it in her mouth. Leans over, wanting *me* to light her up.

No, I say.

Do it, or it's bad luck.

No.

Si no lo haces, me va a dar cáncer otra vez.

Jesus Christ, okay, okay. I light it. She takes a drag, puts her window down, and blows out.

Ahhhhh, she says. She takes one more drag off it then stubs it out in the cupholder. They're for you, by the way.

What? I don't want them.

Well, she says, you won't be smoking them. I will. Oh, relax, don't look at me like that. You're my son, don't be so serious. I'll smoke just one and throw away the rest.

You've already had one.

That one was just for practice.

For fun, more like it.

That's right. Don't be so serious. You're too young.

Not that young.

Mírame, twice your age and half—

As serious.

What good comes from being so serious all the time? Eh? ¿Dime? She bares her teeth at me, makes a mischievous sound.

I can't help but smile when she acts like this. I tell her working with kids all day has turned her into one.

¿Y qué tiene?

I put my hands up. Fine, fine. You win. You win.

The light turns green. She takes off, laughing.

Only when we're back home does she tell me what it's all for. She's been talking with one of her sisters who still lives in Mexico. My tía put her in contact with a curandera, a very well-respected one. People come from all over to see her. Tu tía has been working with the curandera, she says. On what? I ask. She says I don't have to worry, it's mostly already done. Most of the cleansing done, from a distance, by the woman in Mexico. I realize then why she asked me, a few weeks ago, for a recent photo, one that included my whole body.

Only the final step remains, she says.

Final step? I ask.

Yeah, and you'll be cleansed.

I follow her into the kitchen, she grabs a pot and pours all the petals out into it. She fills it with water and puts it to boil. She tells me I'm to shower like normal, but when I'm done, I should pour it, she points at the pot, over my head.

But it's boiling hot!

She takes the pot off the burner. Her eyes narrow, no empieces. It'll have cooled by then. Okay? Just make sure you pour it over your whole body, and don't towel off after, just put your clothes on directly. Then I'll come with the cigarette, easy.

Sounds uncomfortable.

Just do it, okay?

Fine, I say.

I shower like normal. Remember that first ritual, the man hammering his fist into my back. Every blow knocking the air out of me. For hours, it felt like. Betrayed by everyone. By ma. Had never felt so alone. In the end, it didn't solve anything. The curse remained. Along with everything else, and all of it going unspoken. I turn the water off, open the sliding door, and grab the pot off the counter, where ma left it. Dip a finger into the water to check the temperature. Still warm. I raise it over my head and let it wash over me. It's cooler than I expected. Wakes me the fuck up. My body all goose bumps and quick shallow breaths. Lay the pot at my feet and am shivering. There are a few petals still stuck to the bottom. I scoop them out, rub them over my neck, behind my ears, in my armpits, my thighs, and between every one of my toes. I close my eyes, take a deep breath out. And out again. Start to feel lightheaded. Dizzy. I brace against the wall and smile. Maybe it's working. I do as ma told. Put my clothes on without drying off. Everything sticking to me like damp leaves.

When I come out, ma is there, waiting for me.

Ya casi, she says. She lights a cigarette. Mutters to herself. Lays her palm flat on her chest and takes a long drag from it. Blows it out over me. She stands to my right and does it all again, and then at my back, and one last time to my left. She puts out the cigarette.

Done, she says.

There are still petals in my hair and I'm dripping all over the carpet.

Well, how do you feel? she asks. She opens her arms.

I open mine too. I feel good, really good, I say. We embrace. And it's true. Has been for a while.

She presses her cheek against mine. Cachetón, she says.

Cachetona, I reply.

For a long moment, we hold each other. Neither wanting to break the embrace. Until I do. I pull away. I'm afraid to ask, but I think of my therapist, what she said about silence. I ask, why did you all let that man beat me?

She tilts her head to the side. Her eyes narrow. You mean your father?

No, the curandero. That day after I cut my hand.

That man never hit you.

What do you mean? Of course he did.

No, she says, shaking her head. We agreed, if you were going to be hit, it would be your father to do it. He told your father what to do. Instructed him as to where and how, with what force to hit you. She pinches the used cigarette off the counter.

What?

It was your father.

Are you sure?

Of course I'm sure. She brings the cigarette near her chest. Rubs it until it starts to tear in her fingers. She sets it back down. I was there too, wasn't I? I saw it with my own eyes.

2022. Stockton. The sixth house, the one the three of us live in now. I shower, stand before the steamed-up mirror, clear it with my hand. I look at myself.

Brush blue eye shadow onto my lids. Then lipstick, the one ma helped me pick. *There* I am. A little more *there* now than before.

Back in my room, my closet, I touch the dress, electric blue and fuchsia, plunging neckline. Next time, I think. Next time. Tonight, I settle on my leather jacket, black jeans, and boots. I check the bedroom mirror, make sure I look presentable.

I smile. And smiling, I'm there a little more. Every day, more and more.

I tell ma I'll see her later.

Le dices que le recuerde a su mamá, okay?

I will, I will. I say.

Okay, cuídate, te quiero mucho.

Yo también.

I get in Selena's little blue Prius. We head to Paradise, the only queer option around here.

Dude, she says, check this out.

She hands me her phone. A meme, from Instagram. A man wearing a costume pretends he's getting fucked by an alien. Drunk. On all fours on the grass. He keeps saying, ay, no mames, no mames. Funny, I say. You should send it to my mom.

How is she, by the way?

She's good, she told me to tell you to tell your mom—

I know, I know. Mom's looking forward to it. We'll all be there.

Yeah, thanks. She's like a little kid about this party, it's funny. The big five-oh.

What are you gonna get her?

I don't know, any suggestions?

Dude, she's your mom.

It's still early for Paradise, not much of a crowd. We sit at one of the tables out back, on the patio, so I can smoke one from the pack. I offer Selena one, but she shakes her head.

Five o'clock. What do you think of her? Selena asks, slurring a little. She tilts her head in the direction of a woman with short black curly hair, big gold hoop earrings and a septum piercing, her eyes severe, like she's expecting a fight. Selena's eyes glassy, she's smiling, licking her front teeth, buzzed, as always, after just the one beer.

Not really my type.

God, not for you. *For me.*

She looks like you, no, except for the curly hair.

She rolls her eyes. No, she does not.

Maybe you're not even bi, you're just vain.

I'm gonna fucking hit you if you keep playing.

I'm just fucking with you. Chill.

Entonces, dude, what you think?

Yeah, she's really hot, you want me to go ask for you? She's looking over here, by the way.

All right. I'll go. You mind?

I shoo her away.

I'm just finishing my cigarette when I notice him at the table just across, sitting alone. He's tall, taller than I am, and downcast, brooding, nursing a beer. Maybe he got bad news. I look over at Selena, she's smiling, teeth shining under the purple patio light. The other girl can't take her eyes off Selena, that smile. Good for her. I hope her mom comes around.

Fuck it. I go over to where he's sitting. Open my pack, offer him one. He's off in his own world and doesn't even see me there, in front of him. It's cute, I think. It'll be cute for another twenty seconds, tops.

You mind if I sit? I ask, lighting a second cigarette. He looks up. His face still holding something dark, but when our eyes meet, it starts to brighten, to open.

He nods. I sit, look up at the moon, full, intermittently covered by clouds. The hit of nicotine making me sit up straight. Like my whole body, all my senses, are suddenly at attention.

I look at him and take another pull from the cigarette. I look up, and there are clouds again, covering the moon. I add my smoke to it. I smile at him. And the thrill of his gaze, his face, lit up now. He's awake. Lips full, eyebrows thick and inviting, I want to run a finger over them. As he smiles, a softness. To remain composed, I tell myself it's just the nicotine.

I'm sorry, he says. Just work. Work on my mind.

Well, please, I say. Tell me. What's up?

I got promoted. His eyes darken again, he looks down into the mouth of his bottle, empty now. If he wasn't so hot, this routine of his wouldn't work.

A promotion's good, isn't it?

I only got promoted because they fired my friend. I think, he says, I think I know why they fired her too.

I see. And are you gonna ask her?

Yeah, of course. I already have, but she won't say.

So what're you gonna do?

I don't know. After a pause, he says, just be more honest. Direct with her, I guess.

Makes sense. I put out my cigarette. On the other bench, Selena is still talking with her new friend. They're leaning against each other, the friend running a finger up and down Selena's forearm.

I'm sorry, he says. I'm being an asshole. I'm gonna go for another beer. What do you drink?

Just water, I say. But I'm good. I extend my hand, I'm Christian, by the way.

Yeah, sorry, Rodrigo. We shake hands. His hand is warm. And the feel of it, rough and delicate. My lips tingle. I tell myself, it's just the cigarette. The same ones ma gave me. Guess they are good luck. You sure you don't want anything else? he asks. Then gets up.

I nod.

Don't go anywhere, all right?

After he goes in, Selena, her new friend, and the friend's friends join me at my table. They leave the seat beside me empty, for Rodrigo.

We all introduce ourselves.

When Rodrigo comes back, he's surprised to see all these new people. He composes himself, smiles. Sits down.

Again, introductions. I'm sorry, Rodrigo says to me, we just kept going on about me, what do you do?

He's a writer, Selena says quickly, knowing I'll deflect. He's writing a novel.

Oh, no way, what's it about?

About growing up here, I guess.

Oh my God, his novel is *so* good.

She's my oldest friend, don't listen to her.

A novel, huh. How's it coming?

I'm almost done, actually.

Don't be so humble, Selena says. She says more than she ought to.

Just remember that she's drunk. And none of that is really worth talking about.

Well, congrats anyways, salud, Rodrigo says.

I lift an invisible glass and tip it back.

We sit there and talk for another hour, just the two of us, knees touching, the girls absorbed in their own conversation. He tells me about his family, about school. We figure our paths must've crossed, in elementary, in high school. Before he leaves, he asks for my number and I give it to him.

Selena waits until he disappears back into the bar, then sends up a howl. Your turn.

No way.

Oh, go on.

I do a very soft one. *Aaaouh.*

You were never as good at that as I was.

One-drink McGee is still too keyed up to drive, so we go inside, a large crowd has formed. We make our way to the middle. We dance. Lose ourselves in it. Dance to all the hits. Dance and sweat and laugh.

At some point, I come back to myself and look around at all the other people there—dancing. And everyone, just straight-up fucking beautiful.

2022. Leaving the sixth house. Pa, last week was ma's birthday. Like the old days, everyone was there. You would've loved it. First time the house was so cramped since your funeral. Your wake.

I'm driving now down El Dorado. Been doing these drives all week. Been going back to all the places I remember. Taking photographs of all of it. Gateway, Victory Park, Stagg, the other four high schools I went to. And to every one of the houses we lived in: where I was raped; the one after, where you put a basketball hoop on the tree; the big one that was lost to the housing crisis; the one after, where we had our fight; the house after that too, where I stayed in my bedroom, trapped myself, ashamed of all that I had done to you, to our family. Still unable to look at all that had happened.

I want you to know that I'm still asking ma about you. Though it's hard to get more than snatches, she mostly refuses to talk about the past. Especially if I ask about her. More willing if it's you I'm asking about. Like you both living out of a car when you first came to Stockton. That first month, staying near McKinley Park. An older Mexican couple noticing you and letting you all come in, to shower, prepare meals for brother, who was just over a year old then. But even as she shared that, her voice cracked, makes it hard to insist.

Did ma hang around there? Or did she wait in the car while you worked? I'm remembering photographs that I've seen, you at construction sites, working; the film, the clothes, was ma the one who took those pictures? Or did she have to stay around McKinley with brother?

On El Dorado I keep going south, driving down until I'm all the way out of Stockton. Make it to French Camp, factories, shipping facilities, manufacturing all along the left side of the road, and on my right, farmland for miles. Where I was born, where your first job was. The job you moved to Stockton for, job that earned you that first check with which you moved ma and brother into an apartment. That job only lasted about a year, then the company shuttered. You were out of work for the first time since you were fourteen. Ma's told me about how you used to steal: clothes, food, et cetera. Why didn't you ever think to share this? Learning all of this secondhand, sometimes I get mad at you, then myself. This is all I know about that time when you were stealing: By then a couple cousins had also moved to Stockton, and they were also out of a job. Ma was pregnant with me and I've heard the stories of you both looking between couch cushions for the odd nickel, penny, and dime, counting it all out so that ma could have enough money for her and brother to take the bus for medical appointments while you went out looking for jobs. What happened to the car? This fucking city, you can't do shit without a ride.

Ma told me a cousin called you late one night, drunk, with two of his own cousins, asked if you wanted to go with them to the mall (to steal), and you said sure. You all got caught coming out of the store, guns drawn while they were still shuffling their way into someone's borrowed car. You got stuck in county for six months for that. Stealing a leather jacket. During one of ma's visits to the jail, eight months pregnant with me, ICE shows up to county, and her and brother get deported. She had to scramble, fought her way back in just a month so that I could be born here.

She refuses to go into detail about all that went on, still don't know if it was this time or the first, when she crossed with brother, that he started crying, and the group that ma was crossing with wanted her to smother brother so that they wouldn't get caught as they hid from nearby Border Patrol. When she told me this much—her voice breaking all through her telling—she wouldn't look me in the eye. I hugged her and asked for more, but all she said was to never ask her again. About any of it.

I drive down the gravel road. I pull over, get out of the car. Go up to the chain-link fence. Matec, that's what the company was called, right? Some of the equipment is still here. Feels a bit like a time capsule, rusted-over pipes, old bulldozers, tractors, tires as tall as I am, and dirt roads all around the property.

Ma told me about your Puerto Rican cellmate. He was slightly older than you and took you under his wing, showed you how to navigate the system, look up your case, prepare for it, wrote down trial dates, translated things for you since everything was in English. Breakfast at 6:00 a.m., and lucky if they let you shower twice in the same week. I wonder if you would've shared about this time in your life if you knew what brother got around to doing as a teenager. Maybe it wouldn't have changed anything, but somehow I doubt that. You told ma all of this, had to, why couldn't you tell your sons?

Ma told us about your speculation, your paranoia, that your cellmate was only really helping because he knew you were going to get out before him. And he wanted you, once out, to claim his belongings, to reach out to his family, and take his things to them. Wanted you two to stay in touch. Why was that impossible? Shame? Fear? She told me how sorry you were about getting caught, leaving her alone to handle everything. That you cried, asking for forgiveness. Why couldn't we ever cry in front of one another?

How did ma make ends meet during that time? I know, I know that's unfair to be asking you. But all I can do is guess because none of us can ever really share. What did you do, how did you handle your guilt? Did you make a pact? Bury the past with hard work? Was that the only option you saw growing up?

Don't know why exactly, but I feel a kind of guilt in knowing that ma did manage to get back before I was born. And you stole diapers and baby food for a couple more months after I was born. Until you got a steady job, and then you did everything in your power never to be without one ever again. Always working overtime, weekends, when the fuck did you rest? You got promotion after promotion, by the time you became a foremen and learned enough English to get by, you were able to move us out of Gateway. Not renting anymore. I don't know how much you can know, but that alone has changed my and Julio's lives. And then you moved from one company to the next, bigger and bigger raises, bigger and bigger houses, then you became a supervisor, a salary then, then the housing market crashed, and we lost that house, went back to renting, and work slowed down, I remember what you said then, after the layoffs began, only the best will keep their jobs, you said you weren't worried. I don't know if that's true, or how much you really believed that, but still, you kept working, Gateway always behind us, not ahead of us. That I and brother never had to worry about having a roof over our heads, that was because of you, ma says as much too. And still, sometime after all of that, I did what I did. And then you left.

Here's the latest I've learned, and part of why I'm here, looking at this old workplace. You've worked in some capacity since you were eight. The first job you had along with two of your siblings, a brother and sister, nine and eleven respectively, herding cattle across a highway, every day for months. Sometimes it hailed, sometimes there was thunder, really scared the sheep, the cows, and when there were rainstorms, the way back would flood, and you'd all have to wait it out, under a tree, sometimes until nightfall, but sometimes you still found it fun.

Things I'll never know about you: the first time you cried, how you felt seeing your mom for the first time after all those years she was away, what was that like, what was your relationship with your father like. And after you left home and hugged your mom goodbye, were you scared about that possibly being the last time you'd ever see her? What was driving you: fear, excitement, hope?

Getting back in the car, I follow the road for another mile, and then I make a right. This is the most prominent, most important road in the small unincorporated town of French Camp. First, there's the county hospital, and behind it is county jail, and between them on the other side of the road there's a cemetery. A little triangle of sorrow: hospital, jail, cemetery. What French Camp is known for, that triangle. And all its farms, of course, its migrant farmworker residents. As I drive by, a herd of cows crosses the street. Nobody with them. They go slow. A few cars behind me, someone is honking. I put my car in Park. The cows don't seem to mind the honking. They keep their pace. I look around for a broken fence but don't spot one.

A cow brushes against the hood of my car, we share a glance, it has these wonderful gleaming eyes, it sticks its tongue out, licks the air. I photograph it. One of them up ahead has a bell, it clinks and clinks, draws the attention of all the rest of them; at the sound, the one I'm sharing a look with turns too. They all follow that cow as it keeps moving farther and farther along to the other side of the road. The leading cow wanders into the cemetery. The honking starts up again. I pull onto the shoulder. I get out of the car and I light another cig. I watch the last of the stragglers trickle in through the front gate. The clink of the cowbell gets farther, fainter. A cow moos and I think of following them in there but instead I take another drag, I close my eyes, and I listen for the bell.

It's gone.

When I open my eyes again, the cows are gone. I watch the warm orange yolk of the sun as it sets, sinking down behind the cemetery.

It's dark now. I get back in the car, turn the headlights on. I roll the windows down.

I make my way back home.

2022. Halloween. On the weekends, brother paints. It was only last year that he started again. During the week, he's too busy: between teaching, prepping, grading, lifting, sometimes cooking. But on weekends, all of that recedes.

In the garage, huge tarps cover the concrete floor. And his canvas, as tall as he is, is propped up on a couple of two-by-fours, the back leaning against the garage door. He's working on it now. Crouched, paintbrush in hand. Slow, methodical strokes. Working on some silhouette, I can't see exactly, standing right behind. Soon I'll have to go and start on dinner, but for now, I'm here, watching.

The music bumping. Kendrick Lamar, *To Pimp a Butterfly*. Brother's always been one to insist on the importance of listening to an album front to back. It's the only way, brother says, to see the artist's vision; a track can give you a feel for it, but it takes an album, a full listening, to really understand it. By vision, brother means: a philosophy, an aesthetic, a wish for the world. And a sense, too, of the life that fed it. The only way not just to see, brother says, but to feel it, that vision.

I'm watching him paint, the way his body moves, as part of the artistic vision that gets expressed, laid onto the canvas.

His hands gentle and calm, like waves lapping along the edge of the canvas. He could be a surgeon, I think, with how delicate and precise he moves the brush.

I don't know why he ever stopped painting. He was always so serious about it. Art on his mind since he was a kid, always getting in trouble for drawing on his desks at school. Graduated to tagging every corner in Stockton. It was around the time I started writing seriously that he stopped. I never asked him why. I was too absorbed in my own little world—world of pain—isolating myself, not seeing anyone else, not brother, not ma.

I wonder if he stopped painting because he had to get serious about school, jobs, life as an adult. Maybe he didn't know, as I didn't and am only learning now, all the ways an artist can appeal for institutional help. Or maybe it was something else entirely. In any case, I want to know. About everything. Same goes for ma.

I keep watching him work, making his brushstrokes, one color and then another. Blue. Gray. Brown. White. Blue. Green. Gray. Brown. Yellow. Green. Blue. Brown. White. Red. Yellow. He takes a few steps back and considers his progress.

Back before he stopped painting, I asked him how he knew when he was done. That's easy, he said. When the feeling I had when I started isn't in me anymore. When it's all there, he'd pointed to the canvas—he'd been working on one, high on mushrooms, when I asked—and all that's left of it, in me, is the memory. And maybe the memory's still painful, he'd continued, but once you get it out of you, the feeling itself, it can't hurt you. Not in any way that's new.

In the painting he's working on now, a boy is lying on a bed. The light—the only light—seems to come from somewhere outside the painting's frame. A bedroom door, I suppose, only slightly ajar. A spear of light cuts across the boy's mouth and cheek. He's lying on top of the bed, not in it, and with all his clothes still on. Even his shoes. Staring wide-eyed, terrified, at nothing at all. His eyes are so wide, they look as if they're being pried open. A waking nightmare.

The boy's hair looks wet. And not just his hair, his clothes too. He's soaked through. And now looking more closely, everything's wet, actually. The bed, the floor, everything. And under the bed, a dark supine figure in silhouette, shaped just like the boy. The way the silhouette is laid, coffin-like. And the longer I look, the more it seems like the source of all the painting's gravity.

You okay? brother asks. He points with the brush at my hand. I'd been making a fist.

Yeah, I say, releasing it.

He hands me a soda. What you think?

It's good. Really fucking good. I feel my throat tighten. I cough. Take a sip of the soda. Have you titled it yet?

Yeah, it's called *After My Brother's Drowning.*

What? I ask.

From that night, when you—

Yeah, but why's it called that?

What do you mean why?

You were the one that drowned.

Me? No dude. No fucking way. But you best believe, I fucking wished it was me. I felt, he pauses. We're both looking at the painting. He resumes, I know, I should've been looking out for you. He pauses.

I wasn't. And I'm sorry.

I'm looking at the face of the boy in the painting. I'm not sure why but I can't recognize it as brother's. I want to tell him he's wrong, that he's remembering wrong, but the longer I look at his painting, the terror in the boy's eyes, the harder that becomes.

I'm your big brother and that day, he croaks, I failed. A lot of days, actually. I let you down.

We were both just kids, I tell him. I stare at the figure underneath the bed. That shouldn't have been your job. Still, though—you did, didn't you? You saved me. So many times. And that night too. Right?

No, I mean I tried, I got you out of the pool, but it was this firefighter.

I swear I don't remember.

Yeah, well, you were fucking unconscious for like three minutes. And in and out for a long time after. Anyway, I never apologized. I'm sorry.

Don't be. What you did... I trail off, still looking at the shadow figure under the bed.

What you did, it was everything, I mean it meant everything. Like my whole life. I turn from the painting to face him. You changed it.

He's crying. I put my arms around him. Brother doesn't like hugs, but he takes this one. Gives it back and then some.

When we finally release each other, I tell him, I don't even like soda.

He laughs, I know, he says. I know. But that's all I got out here.

We both take another step back and look at the painting.

Is it done? I ask.

Basically, he says.

You know how proud of you I am? My better half. Way stronger than me. And confident, and always having to be the grown-up. And look at this fucking painting. I love you.

I love you too, dude. So fucking proud of you too.

We stand in the silence for a while. I'm sighing, trying to collect myself, and he's drinking his soda, looking at the painting, smiling.

Guess I gotta get dinner going.

Yeah, I know, he says. He smiles wider. Let me know when it's ready.

He takes his brush up again and steps toward the painting.

2022. Halloween. Later that night. Every Thursday and Sunday I cook. Nothing special about my cooking. But I've been wanting to make some pozole for a while. My favorite dish. Growing up, ma would always make it on my birthday. I don't stray from her recipe. I try to replicate, but my interpretation isn't so good. Something about her technique eludes me. Even though the steps are pretty simple, actually. You chop an onion, peel some cloves of garlic, throw them in a pot with beef or chicken bouillon, then you add the pigs' feet and neck bone, bring it all to a boil. You hold off on the hominy until the end and just let it simmer for a while, a couple hours. While it's simmering, I slice the cabbage, radishes, limes, take out the oregano, the Tapatío, then I wait, most all of what I do is wait.

And while waiting, I prepare a small bowl, take it to the altar next to the kitchen table, and place it there, for pa. There's a photo of him in the center, he's smiling, leaning against a palm tree at a park. Around the photograph, there's bowls of sunflower seeds, salt, oranges, candles, pan de muerto, cempasúchil, chrysanthemums, a sugar skull that brother painted, a pitcher of water, a tall can of Modelo. I go into my pocket and tuck the last of the cigarettes there behind his photo. He quit when I was still a kid, no reason for that now. It's all ready for him, to be here with us. It's Halloween now, he'll come tomorrow, but still, when I look at his photo, close my eyes, I say a prayer for him. Ma and pa, I imagine, grew up with this tradition too, but after they immigrated to the US, they stopped. This is only the second year we're doing this. And it seems strange to me now, to think of all the family, brothers and sisters, parents that ma has lost, that pa is the only one here. Something else I'll have to ask her about. I light a candle and open the front door. I go back to the kitchen.

When dinner's ready, I let them know. Ma and brother set the table, make a place for dad as well. Then we sit down and eat. At the table, ma asks brother how the painting's coming along. It's almost done, he says. Ma doesn't understand why he won't let her see the paintings until they're finished, and why that apparently doesn't apply to me. Sometimes she gets a bit frustrated by it, can only really see it as a personal slight. Still, she relents.

When we were kids, thirteen, fifteen, I remember ma got a call from one of her sisters. They talked about her son, fourteen at the time. And because he was an only child and my aunt an anxious person, he was sheltered in ways we weren't. Apparently, he'd just started masturbating, and that had sent him into an existential spiral. He thought there was something wrong with him because of the white stuff that kept coming out. Thought he was dying. Sought comfort in religion.

After weeks, he'd finally caved, told his mother and father all about it, how scared he was. Ma told us the story and then asked us both, directly, if we masturbated. We must've denied it. Though what I actually remember is just standing there awkwardly, not saying anything. Not wanting to lie but refusing to admit it. I remember ma asking over and over, wanting us to know that we could tell her. We wouldn't. Refused even to acknowledge the question. Met with our stone silence, ma cried right there in front of us. And we didn't apologize, didn't soften, just stood there sullen, ashamed.

I've been masturbating since fourth grade, I say.

What? ma says. She laughs nervously.

Dude, I'm eating, brother says. He points at his bowl with both hands.

Do you remember when you asked us if we masturbated?

Oh yeah. Brother smiles, he takes another bite of his food, she did do that, huh?

¿Qué? she says. I never asked that.

Yeah, you did, I say, and we didn't say anything.

You made dad talk to us about it, brother says. That was so awkward.

No me acuerdo, ¿pero qué tiene? We all have bodies, and those bodies have needs.

We know, brother says.

Y yo soy su mamá, ¿por qué no me pueden hablar de lo que sea?

Some things just shouldn't be brought up, brother says.

¿Y por qué no? We're a family, aren't we?

Yeah, that's right, I say.

Brother side-eyes me. Yeah, but we're not white.

That has nothing to do with anything, ma says.

Yeah, it does, brother says.

It shouldn't, though, I say.

Really? brother says. Therapy's rotted your brain.

Maybe, I say. But some things are better when they've rotted, like cheese. And brains. You should try it.

He shakes his head, that stuff is just—

It's just nothing, says ma. We're your goddamn family. Nothing is off-limits.

I raise an eyebrow at him.

Fine. Fine. Fine. Brother throws up his arms. It's weird, though. And gross.

You can talk about shit and farts, but this is gross? ma says.

Shit and farts are funny.

Ay, Dios mío, ¿por qué son tan necios? She looks up at the ceiling, her hands spread as if in prayer, ilumínalo Dios.

You know, I say, smiling, one time, back when we still shared a room, I don't remember what I was looking for, but I was over on Julio's side of the room, looking in his drawers, under his bed, and stuck between his mattress and the wall, I found a DVD. *Girls Gone Wild.*

Oh my God, brother puts his spoon down, covers his face with his hands.

Hijo cochino, ma says.

Tell him, ma, un pinche cochino.

Ma snorts, makes little oinking sounds.

I laugh and ma laughs too. We laugh long enough that brother starts to laugh as well.

Wait, how old were you when this happened? ma asks.

I don't know, I don't remember. Middle school, maybe. Or maybe I was still in elementary, and brother was in middle school? Hmmm, who knows.

God, brother throws up his arms, pinche tattletale.

Why shouldn't he be? ma asks. Tú, cochino. Under my roof, no way.

I oink and we all laugh again.

It's been over an hour now since we finished eating. We're still at the table, just laughing, enjoying each other's company. Part of me feels guilty for what I'm about to do. For what I'm about to say. But for things to be good, I need to talk about it, all of it. To start to talk about it, anyway. However much I feel like an asshole for bringing it up now. There's no good time. Never was. I don't know what we'll be after, but we're already a family, and I know nothing I say, nothing any of us says, will ever change that.

Ma, Julio, I say. My voice slightly cracking. I reach for their hands. They reach for mine. Their eyes soften. I hold on to them for a while. Then I squeeze and release, draw my hands back across the table. I want to look away, feel the urge to run, but instead I keep my eyes on them. And pressing my hands together, like a prayer, I begin.

ACKNOWLEDGMENTS

Want to start off by saying that everyone mentioned here has made my life better. This book exists in part because of the kindness, the love, and the generosity that they showed me. Each in their own way altering my life, changing my perspective, becoming the reasons why this whole journey has been worth it. I have so many thanks I want to give, will continue to give whenever we're in person, and I hope they can see this book as another form of thanks I wish to give them all in return for the support they have given me.

To my brother, I'm still here because of you. In a way I know you know, and in other ways it still has been hard to fully express, but still, you've saved my life; it's not something you should ever have had to do but you have. Thank you. Thank you for being the best brother I could ever ask for, for talking shit, hanging out, challenging me, and reading everything I've ever wanted to share. You've always been my first reader, but even before that, the first artist I ever knew. The person who taught me that art is meant to be shared, and that so much of the joy that exists in the afterlife of an artwork exists in communion. Before I had a heart I saw yours. You're curious and playful, and I see so many of the things I value, both as a writer and as a person more generally, directly influenced by you. I'm so proud and happy to call you my brother. And I hope that this final version still had a few things that surprised you!

Ma, siempre me dices que tan orgullosa estás de mí, and I just want to say I am. I don't say it enough, but I am so proud de todo lo que has hecho, without your love and support this book would've been impossible. En escribiendo este libro, me acordé tanto de nuestras conversaciones que tuvimos antes de que me fui a Berkeley. En cómo tú también cambiaste. En una de esas maneras, tú a veces espontáneamente empezabas a break into verse. Siempre me sorprendía de cómo te venían las palabras, como algo divino. La inspiración como algo divertido. No sé si en parte lo hacías porque mirabas cuanto gusto me daba, cuanto me hacía reír. Pero en haciendo eso, creando poemas en un instante, tú fuiste la primera poeta que conocí, y más que te pueda decir, tú me hiciste pensar que tal vez yo también tendría ese don con las palabras. Por esa y tantas otras razones, gracias. Te quiero mucho.

Christie, this book is better, my life is better because of you, your thoughtfulness, sensitivity, and questions that go beyond the page. Your wonderful soul has meant everything. Our conversations have challenged me and have been a steady reminder to keep doing the kind of work I set out to do when I first began writing, to be open and curious, and to try to understand. With love, thank you for all your notes, your meticulous line edits on every page, conceiving of the title when I wanted to change it, and for your joy and all your genius. When your novel's out, everyone will know what I already do, you're undeniable.

Cecy, thank you for your kindness and generosity, for all the lovely meals and baked goods you prepare, for becoming family.

Pa, agradezco todo lo que has hecho por nuestra familia, te quiero mucho, y gracias por soportar la creación de este libro.

Also, special thanks to mi tío Beto, for teaching me a little of his knowledge about sobadas, and to both my immediate and extended family for their stories, generosity, hospitality, and for the culture.

A huge thank-you to all the professors who've helped me out along the way, for going above and beyond, for their advice, their letters, their stories, a kindness I never expected from any adult growing up. Their generosity and their words I'll carry with me always. Thank you so much to Vikram Chandra, Marisa Silver, Matthew Salesses, Lysley Tenorio, and Sarah Shun-lien Bynum, and for a belief in my work I didn't know I needed but that I carry with me always now, special thanks to Michelle Latiolais (you wrote to me once that it was clear I wasn't afraid to write anything, thank you for all your wisdom), Lucinda Roy (when I told you I was leaving the program, you told me I was going to have a wonderful career, remains to be seen but I appreciated the kind words!), Lyn Hejinian (I remember when I asked for a letter of rec, she smiled and told me to just remember when I was in her shoes, I promise I'll never forget, and also, for her correspondence, and sharing about her experience in the south, and articulating that thing as "theatrical eyes," may she rest in peace), Raymond Lifchez (he was incredibly kind, generous with his praise, the first professor I had who reflected the personal, as the most special, he also loved to talk shit, which I admired, may he rest in peace).

Huge thanks to my cohort, roommates, and friends at Irvine, Blacksburg, Berkeley, and abroad. And thank you for giving me a sense of community, for the beer, the shit talking, their notes, and for helping me stay sane more than they probably knew, thank you, Derek Moseley, Daniela Chavez, Lee Eisen, Maggie Love, Michael Malpass, William Eng, Sarah Beth Ryther, Zainab Hussein, Korey Bell, Kathryn Campo Bowen, Christina Nguyen, Mirri Glasson-Darling, Daniel Kennedy, Camila Quintana, Micaela Zaragoza-Soto, Franky Spectre, and Marcus Ong Kah Ho.

I've met quite a few assholes through the health care system, but luckily I also met some wonderfully kind and helpful therapists, a social worker, and psychiatrist. For my own privacy, I won't say their names, but I'm incredibly thankful. They're often on my mind, and I wish them and their families all the best.

I'm indebted to Laura Cogan and Oscar Villalon and the rest of the *Zyzzyva* staff, for publishing my first story. I didn't know at the time how much that one publication would lead to, but even beyond all of that, it felt validating, and it encouraged me to finish a draft of my novel.

I have a lot of gratitude for Evan Hansen-Bundy, my first editor at Algonquin, who worked with me for about a year before a book deal was in place to make my story better. He understood my vision, helped make it greater, offered a path to double the size of A Losing Game (and so much more), for instance, which was so much fun, and his extensive line edits pushed me to honor the task I set for myself. I'm also thankful for his help in introducing me to my agent.

Huge thanks to Mina Hamedi, my agent, for all the care, attention, and help she's given to my writing and to making this dream of mine real. Your support means the world, and it's been an honor.

Also huge thanks to Jovanna Brinck and Nadxieli Nieto for their thoughtful edits, careful reading, their support both with the manuscript and beyond, and for helping make the transition feel as painless as possible.

Many thanks to the rest of the Algonquin team, Stacy Schuck, Allison Merchant, Brunson Hoole, Eliani Torres, Dana J. Lupo, Lisa Marty, Melissa Mathlin, Steve Godwin, Katrina Tiktinsky, and Kara Brammer.

Also thank you to Andrew Tonkovich for publishing a couple of my stories in the *Santa Monica Review*; to Al Encinias, Jose and Susana Encinias, for the wild stories and the scholarship; to all the wonderful people at Community of Writers, the Carolyn Moore Writing Residency, for providing time and space, and extra-special thanks to everyone at Tin House, I had never been around so many queer people at once, let alone queer writers also, and it truly meant the world to me, it fucked me up in the best possible way to know that places like that can exist. Also, huge thanks to the Henfield, without it I wouldn't have been able to dedicate as much time to finishing the novel!

And lastly, my deepest gratitude to (Rage Against the Machine for the epigraph, my first musical love) any and all who read and blurb this book!